In a bi▸ ▏le

by

Mike Sleater

Other titles

On the road with Doris.

Acknowledgements

Whilst this book has characters that may be based on real people the personalities and their actions portrayed in the book are fictional. The events are fictional and the real club that the location is based on has never had committee members that can ever be compared to those in this plot. It should be obvious from the chaotic nature of the plot that none of the characters in this book could be real ... could they?

A number of my pals have agreed to allow me to use their names and some of their traits may peep through from fact to fiction. They, being true friends, are happy to allow me to use their names, for 'The Craic'. I suspect that if I make a few quid on this book, they will want some commission, or they'll probably sue.

These pals have helped me to construct much of the dialogue, just by paying attention to the nature of our day to day conversations. They are a really funny bunch of codgers and for their friendship and their input, thanks lads.

Thanks also to Dave Wilson who was kind enough to help me with information on self publishing. He is a successful author who specialises in more serious murder mysteries, available from Amazon in Kindle and paperback.

Thanks also to Erin Bradley for designing the cover, top job Erin.

I passed the manuscript to my niece Sarah Hooper who devised and writes the popular Mount Pleasant TV sitcom and she suggested I try my hand at turning the story into a TV plot. Thanks for your help Sarah, I have just completed it and I am trying to get it placed.

Last, but by no means least, a big thank you to Anne, my patient wife, who did much of the proof reading. It was much needed as I am a slow and careless typist and smell chicking siftware ain't perfec.

- In a bit of a hole -

In a bit of a hole

CHAPTER 1

- Club for sale –

Alan and Mike sauntered into the gentleman's lounge of the North Saleston Golf Club and made their way to the bar. Two barmaids were deep in conversation, both clutching a mug of coffee. There were a few barflies dotted around the U shaped bar, some chatting, others waiting for their companions to arrive. Two women sat in the mixed lounge, nursing cups of tea, waiting for their buttered scones, and their plastered husbands. They looked a bit fed up. Their husbands were in the gent's lounge, still loudly discussing their bad luck which accounted for their equally bad scores.

It had all started quietly enough but as additional players came in they added to the numbers, and the volume, which was rising in direct proportion, becoming louder with each passing pint.

The room was buzzing with a variety of voices, now on a variety of subjects, football, the economy, sex, television programmes, politics and sex (sex cropped up a lot but was always brief in content); all competing with the "wanna-be pros" who were reluctant to talk about anything else but their morning round.

Alan, a local builder, tapped on the bar with the edge of his account card and said loudly, "Come on you two. Get some bloody work done instead of gassin'. There's some thirsty punters over here."

Jayne and Larraine looked round at Alan, smirked and returned to their conversation.

He turned to his companion, "Usual Mike?"

"No, I'll have a lime an' Soda for now, please mate," replied Mike who was trying to cut down on his intake of beer, without a great deal of success. Strong will power was not his forte, much like the rest of his pals.

"Lime an' Soda y' puff? Why don't you have a proper drink? Jayne, get this tart a lime an' soda will you and I'll have a bitter, with a lemonade top."

"Oh, you mean a shandy?" said Mike with a smirk.

Alan pulled a sour face, "It's just that the bitter's a bit bitter these days."

"Too strong you mean. That lemonade top makes it weaker as well you know."

"Well I'll just have to have an extra two pints won't I?" he snapped. "Anyway, it's a bloody sight stronger than your crappy lime and soda, mate. You used to be able to drink once."

"Well, I can't now, not since someone pointed out that it was probably the drink that gave me the dizzy spells."

"Hmphh... " Alan grunted.

"It's true," said Mike, "the more I drink the dizzier I get; and when I found out it was the drink that caused the headaches in the morning, well.....," he left the rest unspoken.

Alan looked round the bar, ignoring the sarcastic Mike, and then turned full circle to take stock of the lounge. Half the tables were occupied by club members, attired in various modes of dress, some dull, some bright, some old some new, but unmistakably, all golfers.

"Where the bloody 'ell have them two got to," he grumbled.

"Oh Jack'll be a bit yet, he's probably washing his balls," said Mike.

"Hmph, it would be simpler if he did that in the shower. Anyway, why does it always take him so long to put his kit away?"

"Chattin' mate, he likes to keep up with all the gossip."

Alan was still weighing up the people in the lounge. "Just a nosey sod if you ask me," he said quietly.

"Well he likes to get tidy as well. Not like us scruffy sods."

A dapper, smartly dressed man entered the bar and joined the bickering pair.

"Calling me again eh?" said the smiling Jack. "And if I wasn't a nosey sod, as you so rudely put it, you wouldn't know that the subs and booze are both going up," said Jack, "and I also found out that there's someone about to put in a bid to buy the club."

"Yer jokin'," said Alan, "they promised they weren't goin' to touch the subs."

"Well, the club is broke and there needs to be big changes to survive. If we don't get some revenue in sharpish, we'll go bust," said Jack picking up his shandy. "Cheers." He raised his glass to Alan.

"What about John?" said Jack. "He's out there having a smoke. You'd better get him his usual or he'll sulk."

"Jayne, you'd better add John's usual to that lot, an' one for yourself," said Alan, completing his round.

They were interrupted by Jimmy, a car salesman at the main Ford dealer at the south side of Manchester city limits, who had sidled round the bar where he had left another group laughing loudly at his latest joke. Jimmy was the club joke teller, always a new one up his sleeve. He always maintained that it was a required talent in the car sales business.

"Have you heard the one about the two old codgers in the brothel?"

"Go on then," said Alan. "Hang on, here's John, you'd better wait for him."

Jimmy waited for John to saunter to the bar and slowly pour his bottle of Pils into a tall glass filled with ice.

"Can't you pour those bloody things a bit faster," complained Jimmy, "I'm waiting to tell this bloody joke and you're being an awkward sod. I'll bet you've heard it."

"Look dear boy," said John, without the slightest indication of rushing his task, "your joke will be all the better with this little pinch of suspense."

The drink was poured, John took a swig; they all watched him and waited. John raised a quizzical eyebrow. "Well, go on then."

Jimmy began.

"Two old codgers, having consumed a fair bit of beer, are coming to the conclusion that they are close to their last days and ponder on the wisdom of having a last night on the town. After a few more drinks, they decide to go for it and they end up at the local brothel.

The madam takes one look at the two doddering old geezers and whispers to her manager, 'Go up to the first two bedrooms and put an inflated doll in each bed. I'm not wasting two of my girls on these two old bastards. They're that drunk, they won't know the difference.'

The manager does as he is told and the two old men stagger upstairs to take care of their business. Later, as they are walking home, the first man says, 'You know, I think my girl was dead!'

'Dead?' says his pal, 'Why do you say that?'

'Well, she never moved or made a sound all the time I was giving her one.'

His friend says, 'Well it could be worse. I think mine was a witch.'

'A witch ??... Why the hell would you say that?'

Well, I was making love to her, trying to get her going by kissing her on the neck, etcetera and I gave her a bit of a bite.'
'Did it work?'
'Not too sure about that. She just farted and flew out the window... Took my bloody teeth with her.'"

A burst of laughter makes Jimmy grin widely.

"I hope our quick look in at the new lap dancing club in the village, Pole Cats, last week didn't remind you of that joke," said Mike.
Jimmy looked sharply at Mike and snapped, "Er, when were you in there?"
Mike stroked his chin dramatically and looked at the ceiling.
"Let me see now," he said slowly, as if trying to remember. "We were looking for a late drink, me and Al. One night in the week it was."

Jimmy scowled and started to push his way past Mike who stood firmly in his way.

"Just a mo. You should know when it was. It was the night we saw you scootin' up the stairs with ol' Juicy, remember?"

Mike paused with a wicked grin spreading across his face. "I mean, it looked like you. Mind you, it was a bit dark like. Maybe it was someone who looked a bit like you, eh?"

Jimmy's audience looks closely at his reddening face.

Jimmy pushes harder, trying to pass Mike. He stutters, "Not me mate. Never been in the place."

Mike's grin grew even wider and he steps back to let the glowering Jimmy pass.

"Only jokin' Jimmy," he said. "As I said, it was dark."

A fresh burst of laughter made Jimmy grin sheepishly. "Smart arse," he muttered to Mike as he started past him.

Mike just carried on grinning.

"Have you heard anything about the fees going up?" said Jack to Jimmy.

"Doubt it old chum, somebody is winding you up." Jimmy points at Mike and scowls, "A bit like he does."

"The club's full of stirring bastards," said Alan. "Who told you about the subs Jack?"

"Pete Harris."

"Pete?" said Mike, "He'd wind up a Buddhist Monk on Prozac. He's done it on purpose; he knew Jack would tell us."

"Why would a Buddhist Monk take Prozac?" said the puzzled Jimmy, brows deeply furrowed. "I thought they were cool dudes anyway. Y'know, inner calm, peaceful karma an' all that stuff."

"Not if they were members here they wouldn't be," said Mike, grinning.

"Or had to listen to you Muppets," said Alan, joining in the wind up.

"Or his crap jokes," said John, pointing at Jimmy.

Mike leaned against the bar and spoke in a patient tone to Jimmy, "It's what's known as a subtle joke, right," he said.

"I know you lads in the motor trade won't be familiar with subtle but that's a perfect example of one. Let me explain. In an endeavour to demonstrate the lengths that Harris would go to in order to wind someone up I had to choose a person who would be hard to wind up, see. And, in case a Buddhist Monk was too easy for Harris to wind up I added an extra soupcon of a difficulty factor, Prozac, a drug used to calm down those who find life a bit tense. People who need calming down, in fact. Thus, the calmest monk known to man would be even calmer under the influence of the most famous calming drug in the world.

My point is that Pete could even overcome this combination and incite this almost comatose man into a frenzied axe murdering rage, just 'cause he can."

Jimmy stared blankly at Mike. "You're really weird."

Mike stared back. "How is it you always circulate around the clubhouse telling crap jokes when you are totally bereft of a sense of humour?"

Jimmy continued staring, blinked a couple of times and then stalked off in a huff to join another group by the captain's table.

He could be heard starting his new joke again. "Have you heard the one .....?"

Mike broke the silence that Jimmy had left behind at the bar. "Come on Jayne, we're bloody parched here, let's have another drink. Get off yer bum an' get us regulars a bit of service.

"Cheeky sod," said the smiling barmaid, "Usual?"

"Yep, but I'll have a bottle of Becks this time please."

"Do you want a glass with this bottle?" asked Jayne as she began to put the beers on the bar.

"Nope, tastes better from the bottle," replied Mike, "and besides, I like to wind up the President."

"Well you've succeeded there anyway," said Alan. "He gets apoplectic when he sees you doing that. He says you're a slob."

"Well," said Mike with a smile, "he's a snob. Funny that, isn't it? One letter in it, y'see."

"What d'yer mean one letter?"

"Snob, slob. What would you rather be? Slob? Snob?"

"Oh, see what y'mean. Slob for me. Wouldn't like to be one of them snob fellers. You'd have to play with him," replied Alan, nodding over to the captain's table. "Anyway, never mind that slob, snob stuff. What about the rat piss?" he added, ignoring the dubious lesson in etymology.

Mike picked up his drink, turned to walk to the table, looked pointedly at Alan's beer and said, "You can carry your own beer mate, I'm not a bloody butler."

"No, no, the rats in the cellar," said Alan following him. "They piss all over the place and I'll bet there's loads of it on them bottles. You'll come down with some horrible disease one day."

Mike stopped in his tracks, turned and rolled his eyes towards the ceiling. "If there's rat piss on the bottle top, don't you think that a bit might get right up under the cap, close to the lip of the bottle. Y'know, capillary action, if you know what that is. When you pour it into the glass, don't you think that there is the likelihood that the beer touches the lip of the bottle? And what about the glass touching the neck of the bottle? Some of these germs are quite athletic y'know. For instance, did you know that a flea can jump 70 times his own height? That's like us jumping a five storey building. I'll bet one of those rat piss bugs you're going on about could easy manage a bit of a jump from a bottle neck to a glass."

Jack and John followed the laughing pair over to the table.

Five minutes later they noticed the entrance of another of their usual group, Dermot O'Carroll, followed closely by Derek Smith and Peter Billington. Dermot ordered a round of drinks for his group. They collected their drinks and joined the seated group.

"Did I hear that right in the locker room?" asked Derek "You know, about the subs going up."

"Nothing has actually been decided yet," he said.

Peter was a committee member, a Membership Committee member, which was not that important since it was easy to become a member these days. He was a fair source of information on the machinations of the club's officers and kept the lads abreast of as much information as he was allowed to be privy to. "Well if it gets any dearer here I'm leaving," he added.

"Why would it get any dearer for you?" said Alan. "You aren't that fast at spending it anyway. Just slow down a bit more at getting to the bar and you wouldn't see the difference."

"I get my share in you cheeky bastard," retorted Peter angrily.

"What was that other snippet about someone putting an offer in for the club?" asked Mike.

"Oh yeah," said Jack, "I'd forgotten about that with all the talk about rat piss and fleas. There's an offer for the club on the table apparently."

"Off who?" asked Mike.

"Don't know. Nobody's saying. All the committee must have been sworn to secrecy."

They all looked at Peter.

"Don't look at me, I'd tell you if I knew anything," he said indignantly. "They tell me nowt. They even stopped talking when I went into one meeting."

"You're on the bloody committee," said Jack. "A bona fide member, representing the good of the club members. You should have pulled them up on it."

"Oh, I tried that. I asked them if they were hiding something. They just look blank, laughed it off and said I'd imagined it."

"Well how do we know it's not just bullshit?" said Alan. "It's probably just another wind up by Harris."

"Well, I suppose we don't know it's not a wind up, but the rumour is a strong one.

It doesn't come from Harris, it was Tony Drummond and he's a trustee. He would have to be involved and he's not the type to spread rumours for the fun of it."

Vinny McConville, the last of the group, joined the table,

"Hello lads," said Vinny, "how's it going?"

"Hi Vinny," they all chorused.

"Were just talking about the fees," said Jack, "and how they are going to be increased."

"Some of us were," said Alan. "He was talking about fleas," pointing at Mike.

"Fleas?" said Vinny, brow extremely furrowed.

"And rats," said Peter.

"Don't ask," said Mike.

"Fair enough," said Vinny, none the wiser. "Fees, not fleas."

"Or rats," said Alan.

"Or rats. OK. Fees it is," said Vinny. "Yeah, I heard something about that a few minutes ago in the locker room."

"I was just telling the lads about another bit of news involving an offer to buy the club," said Jack.

"What?" said Vinny, "who'd want to buy this place, it's skint?"

"Mmm. I wonder if it's as skint as they are saying," said Mike slowly. "And, like I said before, what does it mean to us anyway?"

"I'm not sure really," said Jack, "Probably nothing, but bad if anything. Anyway the bid has to be put before the members and voted on."

"Well that's it then," said Derek. "The members won't like having a club where the privileged few can take preference on all things golf, getting the best starting times, their own parking spots and putting up the fees whenever they like."

"You mean a bit like it is now?" said Peter. "All the committee elite grab the best times, get free golf, car parking spots and preferential treatment at the bar."

Jack interrupted, "Look, you've got to realise we're broke and if this offer isn't accepted we could turn up one day and find it has been changed into a big car park for the Metro extension."

"Hang on," said Mike, "who says we're skint?"

"The annual accounts seemed a bit disastrous when they were released at the last EGM, didn't they?" said Jack.

"I know," said Mike, "but who puts the accounts together?"

"What do you mean?" said Jack. "The treasurer does, of course."

"Yes, yes," said Mike, "I know he prepares them, but is it possible he's being fed with bad information? I mean we were pretty well off two or three years ago and with all this dosh we got for the electricity pylon and the Metro we should be even better off. Where's all that money gone?"

"Well, I know we've spent quite a bit," said Jack, "but you're right, it does seem a bit of a swing in our fortunes. What's you actual point?"

"Well if we were not skint and we wouldn't be considering any kind of offer, would we?"

"No, but we are."

Alan broke the brief silence, "Y'know, vested interests seem to be raising their ugly heads here. Is that what you are getting at?"

"Yep," said Mike. "That's exactly what I'm getting at."

Derek joined in, "And it would be a lot easier to cook the books if the treasurer was in on it, eh Maybe we should do some asking around. What d'yer think?" He looked over at Jack, "Jack, you've got the most clout. Can you do a bit more digging?"

"OK," said Jack, "I'll have another word with Tony."

"Right," said Alan, stopping the discussion by banging his empty glass on the table, "enough of this crap. I still think it's a wind up but, just in case, we'll do a bit more diggin'. In the meantime, whose shout is it? I got the last one."

"Where the bloody hell has Peter gone anyway?" said Derek "He should be able to help get to the bottom of this lot, shouldn't he?"

"Crafty sod has gone to the fruit machine again," said Dermot. "It's uncanny how he times his disappearances when it's his round."

"Well we can wait the bugger out. In fact, just order the round and tell Jayne that he'll pay when he gets back." said Alan. "He can get them out of his winnings, eh?"

"I doubt it," said Jack. "He doesn't win that often. Anyway, I'm off, I've a bit of digging to do."

CHAPTER 2

-New members -

The black BMW 735 slipped smoothly down the tree-lined drive towards the imposing, white Victorian house. Waiting on the putting green, Jack and Alan watched it as it swung carefully over the gaudily striped bump at the entrance to the car park that warned the visually impaired about the presence of the 'sleeping policeman'.

"Look at that," said Alan scornfully. "Did y'see the way that berk went over that bit of a bump?"

"He's just looking after his suspension," said Dermot as he joined the pair on the putting green. "Those bloody bumps can knacker the springs and shockers, y'know."

"Bollocks," said Alan. "Technically, it's not a bump. There's not enough tarmac in it to make a bump." He paused, mid rant. "The bloody paint's thicker than the tarmac."

"Yeah, well some car owners like to treat their cars better than they treat their wives," said Dermot, smiling at Alan's comments.

"Alan's right y'know," said Jack. "Thinking about it, modern suspension systems have been developed over the years to take the strain of bigger bumps than that. Blokes like him don't seem to have grasped this fact and they waste that much time negotiating these perceived exhaust wreckers that they cause untold fury to the drivers of the following cars who have to slam on their brakes to avoid a collision."

"Not to mention additional fuel consumption getting speed back up," agreed Dermot.

"And the wrecked bumpers of the cars who aren't quick enough on the brakes," said Jack. "Not to mention the cost of the recovery vehicles."

"For Christ's sake," wailed Alan, "You're gettin' worse you two. I was only sayin' that he was going too slow. You two have just turned it into a soddin' motorway pile-up."

Mike joined them as Alan finished his grumble.

What's up, chaps?"

"Oh, it's these two," said Alan returning to his putting.

"We were actually agreeing with him, for a change," said Dermot. "We were just commenting on the Captain's caution over the speed bump."

"Speed bump?" laughed Mike. "Call that a bloody speed bump?"

"The club committee actually commissioned those gaudy obstacles in an attempt to protect our members from the more cavalier drivers who like to make a bit of an announcement on their arrival," said Jack. "Squealing tyres are pretty effective at getting posers noticed; they think it's more macho than the toot on the horn."

"Yes, but the House Chairman was a bit naive when he listened to O'Malley from the estate. 'Oi've a bit of d' black shtuff over from d' mothorway conthract' was a bit of a giveaway, no?" laughed Alan. "Like I said, there's more paint than tarmac."

"Well he works on the motorway, doesn't he?" said Mike.

"No he doesn't. He's a bloody plasterer. He **did** work on the M62, but that was, forty years ago, as a navvy. Anyway, why would **he** have a bit of tarmac over? Like I said, he's a bloody plasterer."

"In truth," said Jack, thoughtfully, "a toot on the horn is frowned upon at most golf clubs. It tends to create a bit of havoc with the nerves of the more timid players."

He looked over at the tee where four players were warming up before adding, "Sudden noises during the agonised backswing of a seriously infected victim of the Golf Bug have been known to cause considerable damage to both man and property."

"I suppose you're right," said Dermot. "Lots of things can happen when the intense concentration of a retired accounts clerk is shattered by the sound of a carelessly honked horn."

"Bloody 'ell Dermot," said Alan, "you sound like Mike."

Mike gave Alan a sly look. "Dints in the bodywork of parked cars are not really life threatening events but heart stopping shocks from the interruption of concentration, or the rage brought on seeing one's ball disappear into the bushes can be fatal," he said

"What about the direct body-strike possibility," said Jack, not recognising the opening he was leaving. "A wildly sliced golf ball is a pretty lethal projectile."

"Yep," said Mike, now ready to go into his best smart-arsery.

"No matter what the golf pundits may say about a slice not getting real distance on account of the poor dissipation of power at the point of impact and the effect of sidespin and backspin, it will still reach speeds varying from a modest seventy or eighty miles an hour to a more deadly one hundred and eighty miles an hour. It doesn't take a mathematical genius to imagine what a ball, roughly one and eleven sixteenths of an inch diameter or, to be more European, about forty three millimetres, will do on contact with any part of the human anatomy at any of those speeds."

He paused and looked at the open mouthed trio before continuing, "Did you know; only slightly more than four hundred years ago the equivalent of our atomic scientists were experimenting with projectiles of similar dimensions at similar speeds with world domination as the spur to their efforts."

"Oh, I can't stand any more of this shit," said Alan. "Don't you ever stop yappin'? You're a retired draughtsman not a fuckin' doctor of nuclear physics."

"Just tryin' to educate you dunces," said the smiling Mike, smugness fast setting in.

"Do you remember that Cosworth that wrecked the lady captain's Fiesta?" said Jack, laughing at the memory. "That was the final straw on the matter of slowing down flashy car drivers."

"Yeah, I remember that," said Alan. He also started laughing at the memory. "He didn't stop there though, did he? It was like he was tryin' a fast hand brake turn. Crashin' into the Fiesta and bouncin' off it; finished up just about there." He pointed to a spot between Dermot's legs. "There was some nifty footwork called for to avoid the bloody thing. Ripped dirty great furrows in the putting green and, considerin' the average age of the players, it was a soddin' miracle that there were no fatalities."

"Anyway, the committee decided that tyre squealing could spoil a chap's start to the round and it would have to be thwarted," said Jack

"He should have been thrown out really," said Dermot.

"Who? Gareth Jarvis?" said Jack scornfully. "The captain's son? Get real. That's what dad's are for. Getting you out of the mire."

"He'd only picked the car up an hour earlier," said the smiling Alan.

"Had to impress his 'Friday evening crowd' pals usually posin' around the putting green, showing us old farts how to flick their lob shots as high as they could; up into the air, right onto the green."

"Yeah," said Mike, "they used to gather on the practice green after work on Fridays, entertaining themselves with their keepy-uppy ball juggling skills, yappin' about missed putts and shit luck in un-raked bunkers. That particular Friday added considerably to their tall stories, even though most of them were in the snooker room. "

"Yeah, well Gareth and his dad were conspicuous by their absence for some time after, until the fuss had died down. If I remember right, he got away with a month's ban, the jammy sod."

"That's outrageous," grumped Dermot. "Old Harry Rodgers got a six month ban for less than that."

"Well that's a matter of opinion really," said Jack. "He pissed out of the window in snooker room, letting it drizzle down the dining room window. The lady captain was not too impressed."

"Nor was the visiting lady captain," added Alan. "She was just finishing her ice cream when she spotted it."

"Poor old Harry, he had a weak bladder," said Mike, "and he said he couldn't make it down to the bog in time. It was that or he'd have pissed down the stairs."

"Well, that was his story," said Alan. "Mind you, he was eighty four. You'd have thought they'd have given him the benefit of the doubt."

The black BMW saloon that started this convoluted conversation arrived at a much more sedate pace as it made its way smoothly to the spot in the car park reserved for the captain. It was driven by the current incumbent, Simon Partridge, a retired civil servant, who had plenty of time to spare enabling him to deal with the demands of his new office.

He was a captain.

As he thought, a proper, old style Captain.

In fact he was. Full of snobbery and out dated traditions, he was a blast from the worst of the past.

Some of the more gaudily dressed members waved at him as he manoeuvred the car into his parking spot, marked with a sign, 'The Captain'.

Normally staid, conservatively attired solicitors, bank managers, civil servants and even policemen seemed to change their sense of taste completely when they join the golfing fraternity. Bright colours replaced the pinstripes and gaudy designs were spread across generous stomachs and many even more generous posteriors had trousers stretched across them, very close to bursting point and revealing some curious designs on underpants visible through the light material that seems to be the norm in golf trousers.

Many shirts and sweaters were decorated with the shape of a golfer in various poses and in varying sizes. It was as though golfers had to advertise to the world that they played golf, mistakenly believing that their playing strip endows them with enhanced 'street cred'. They could not see the conceptual similarity between their dress code and that of the fat bellied football fans bursting out of their replica Manchester United shirt bearing the legend, 'RONALDO', underscored by the digit 7.

Such attire was banned at golf clubs, seen a ridiculous and gaudy, worn by people with no taste or breeding.

Stepping out into the sunlight Partridge was greeted with the stock salutation uttered by his subjects, some sycophantic, some sarcastic, some automated but all the same.

"Evenin' Mr Captain."

"Evenin' Mr Captain."

"Evenin' Mr Captain."

"Hello Skip."

He glared after the offending rebel.

"Mister Captain, to you!!" he bellowed at the young lad, "I'm not a bloody kangaroo."

The mortified new member stuttered his apologies and slunk off thinking that his future with the club was now decidedly shaky. He was to have two weeks of sleepless nights and suffering a loss of appetite that was to lose him half a stone. He almost lost his job as the gnawing fear of expulsion affected his concentration. It was only the cheery wave from this pillar of the club a fortnight later that finally convinced the poor lad that he would survive the incident providing he worked hard at ingratiating himself to the hierarchy. He was a captain in the making.

Partridge was a dapper man; modelling his appearance on the slicker of the fifties Hollywood stars.

During the day he was always neatly dressed in a blazer and a white shirt with a Paisley cravat. Making his way up to the clubhouse entrance he met Charles Blezzard, the club secretary.

"Hello Charles, old boy," he cheerily sang, pleased with the world in general and looking forward to the evening's task of interviewing the latest batch of proposed new members.

"Good evening, Mr Captain," replied Charles, not so cheerily. He was not really looking forward to the evening like Partridge was. Charles's wife, Janice, was playing up again, taking the piss out of his efforts to join the ranks of the "pricks in the striped blazers."

Jack and his three pals collected their trolleys and made their way to the first tee. They were going out for a few holes before they had a few drinks at the bar.

They caught sight of the captain and the secretary chatting at the front entrance and Mike said, "What are those two Muppets up to now?"

"Membership meeting tonight," replied Jack. "Interviewing likely candidates."

"Why on earth would anyone want to be a captain," asked Mike, "if they had to wear that daft blazer?"

The blazer was a gaudy striped affair similar to the style that thousands of children who attended private schools were delighted to put on communal bonfires at the end of their schooldays. Narrow maroon, black and beige vertical stripes, almost Victorian.

"He should have a straw boater with that jacket," said Mike, "That'd complete the outfit. Actually, he'd be better with the straw boater. It'd cover up the rug."

"He's got three, y'know," said Jack.

"What, blazers or boaters?" said Mike.

"No, wigs. All different lengths. He thinks that people don't know about his tonsorial cover up and he changes his rugs to give the impression of sometimes needing a haircut."

"Your jokin'," said Dermot.

"Yep, it's true," said Mike. "I've been to his barber. That young doris in Sweeny Bob's in the village. She didn't know until I told her.

They all have a look in the shop now, walking past the chair, tryin' to see the join.

They even take photos of it on the sly. Every time he comes in, the shop suddenly fills up. Bob's delighted, even told young Tracey to give him a discount."

"And that stupid cravat he wears," said Alan. "Where on earth would you be able to buy a Paisley cravat?"

"Don't know," said Jack, "it's a mystery to everyone. They were last seen over fifteen to twenty years ago and I thought they were extinct."

Partridge, his wig and his "stupid blazer" pushed through the hall doorway heading for the meeting, followed by his envious companion who gazed longingly at the striped object of his desire and ambition. The sight of it reminded him of his wife's parting barb as he left the house.

"How can you even consider wearing one of those stupid jackets?" she had said contemptuously. "Like a walking bloody deck chair."

"Look, I'm tired of telling you. It's a very old tradition and they date back over eighty years," he had blustered, "They are respected all over the north of England."

"Bollocks," she scoffed, "They are laughed at all over the country and his kids think he's one of the cast of the Old time Music Hall." He had grimaced again at the coarseness of his Janice's tongue. She was like a whore's apprentice sometimes when she got mad and she always got mad when the subject of the golf club was brought up. He often thought that it was fortunate that the Black and White Minstrel Show had been disbanded or the piss taking would definitely have taken a racist turn.

"What am I going to do with her when I get the captaincy," he had thought. "I can't have her sat with me at the club dinner. She's an embarrassment. Slurps her soup, smacks her lips when she's chewing, belches between courses and, worst of all, insists on telling filthy jokes after her fifth pint."

He had met her when they were both young graduates, freshly out of university with the world at their feet. Members of the local sports club, he rugby, she tennis. Drinking pints and farting in mixed company of rugby players had a certain daring attraction to certain impressionable berks and he, being one, had taken a bit of a shine to her at first sight.

Very pretty and friendly, she seemed very confident and sure of herself.

He tried to date her for months without success and had almost given up hope when she had agreed to go out with him the week that all the lads had gone on the club men only tour. His patience was rewarded (or was it punished) when he consummated their date with his first ever taste of carnal pleasure with the opposite sex.

It took him a bit by surprise, really. He had taken her to the club for her usual six pints and, as it was a bit quiet with the lads being away, she had suggested they go for a walk down to the pub instead. "A bit more lively," she had said, bored shitless with the nervous young Charles. No sooner had they got to the far end of the pitch, away from the prying eyes in the clubhouse, than he was locked in the clutches of what appeared to be a skilful all in wrestler with a tongue that could reach clear to his tonsils. He wasn't aware of her reputation as the club dick-park and that he was the only one who hadn't had a parking spot.

Well, he got a parking spot that night all right.

The following weeks were a blur. Pregnancy test; engagement; job at the local secondary modern; wedding bells. He didn't really know what had hit him and still didn't to this day. The world was no longer at his feet but was now perched firmly on his shoulders with talons firmly attached.

Two daughters followed, now old enough to be as bad as Janice was in her earlier life. To be fair, she was still as bad. She had passed on all her vices to the girls and they had all ganged together to give him twenty years of pure hell.

His current life was now bearable and the less he saw of the 'Witches of Eastwick' in his living room the better he liked it. The two girls had married early, as careless as their mother, providing another four miniatures of the original, which he was now left behind with. She did have her good points. She never actually suggested that he shouldn't go to his meetings so he was able to attend every one, avoiding three generations of his eventual nemesis. This was also a good point in his favour with those who were in charge of choosing captains, impressed as they were about the amount of time he gave to his duties.

Janice still loved shagging and was very good at it, seemingly unable to get enough. Charles didn't care, having lost all interest in gymnastics long ago and he was happy knowing that her talents also made some of the club members happy. All assignations and a list of her participating partners were noted for future use. Blackmail was not just a means to financial gain.

"Just six to see tonight, I believe," said Partridge.

"That's right, just the six."

"Do you know any of them?" asked the captain, giving himself an appreciative gaze as he caught his reflection in the hall mirror, adding, "I could do with a haircut, its getting a bit untidy."

"You mean apart from the two that the treasurer has prop...?"

"Shhhh ... you prick!" hissed Partridge fiercely, between tightly clenched dentures.

"No," replied Charles, hastily, "not one."

"Who's down on duty with us?"

"Mr Ex and Peter Billington," said Charles, now recovered from his gaffe. "They're here already. Snape and Best said they might sit in as well."

"Yes, I saw Billington's car. I do hope he's not been at the brandy."

"Well, you know the signs as well as I do. So keep your eye on him."

"No," said Partridge, pausing in his stride, "you keep an eye on him. He's your pal and you introduced him. Can't understand how he got on the committee anyway, the bloody drunkard."

"He was voted on by the members, remember," grunted Charles, bad humouredly. "And he's not my pal. Gordon asked me to second him and I could hardly refuse the President, could I?"

"All right! All right!" retorted the captain, "I know, but you must admit he's becoming a bit of a nuisance."

"True, he seems to have joined up with that bunch of reprobates that block the end of the bar every night. More to the point, he seems to be happy to keep them abreast of what's been happening at the meetings. I've heard policy decisions repeated to me from all sorts of nosy herberts, only days after we've discussed it in council," said Charles.

"Well, we'll have to keep the treasurer's candidates under wraps. The least that Billington knows about them, the better," mused the skipper, scratching the side of his wig and tipping it slightly over to one side. "Have you fully briefed them?"

"All in hand," said Charles uneasily, "all in hand."

"Well, it better had be," said the captain. "It wouldn't do to be seen to be doing favours for the treasurer. Smacks of Jobs for the boys and all that, eh?"

"Now that you mention it," said Charles, "why are we creeping round him anyway. It's not as though we haven't done this sort of thing before. Why all the secrecy?"

"Not sure really," said Partridge thoughtfully. "He just asked to keep it under our hats. As you say, it's been done before, loads of times. In fact, if I remember rightly, that's how you got in."

"Trust you to remember that," said Charles under his breath. Charles was never allowed to forget it. Partridge was another one on his list, a list which he intended to put to full use when the time was ripe. "I'll show those smug bastards what's what when I get my pay-out," he said to himself. "And that waspish nymphomaniac of mine can carry on shagging the whole of the North Saleston membership if she wants 'cos I'll be off to Thailand with my cut, after publishing my memoirs that is." He followed Partridge to the meeting mentally hugging himself as he thought of the pleasures to come, as listed in the travel brochures stashed in his locker.

The captain bounded up the stairs eager to get on with the meeting. He entered the committee room to face his "cabinet".

The captaincy was the pinnacle of his golfing career, his personal triumph over mediocrity, the zenith of his miserable boring life.

To have made it to the position of Chief Librarian of the University Library seemed, to most of his golfing cronies, to be an achievement in itself and he was considered to be a successful man with a salary that made him, and his very large wife, "comfortable."

However, he knew better. Long service and arse-licking had got him to the top of his particular pile. In addition, filling dead men's shoes was his forte, giving him an extra boost in his rise to the top.

Librarians are not renowned for their ambition so that those who possess it, even a little, don't have much competition on the ladder.

Not to the top anyway. Salaries in the higher rungs of the public sector bureaucracy are generous, as are the pensions - maybe to compensate for the crushing boredom.

This particular term of the captaincy of the golf club was earned in a similar way. Lots of time on the various committees interfering with the wishes of the members, arse-licking those who chose captains (themselves past captains), playing in all the mixed frolics, more arse licking and being a general nuisance around the clubhouse.

Since a golf club captain doesn't need to have any rudimentary skill at the game of golf, his lack of prowess proved to be no barrier to his ambition. Even a handicap of twenty seven could only be maintained by imaginative accounting procedures that would have qualified him as treasurer. His cheating was legendary and known throughout the immediate local golf clubs. His nickname was Pele, given to him by a not too respectful playing partner after observing him carrying out a rather tricky ball juggling feat. (Or should it be feet?)

On me 'ead," he shouted over from the other side of the fairway, in an attempt to add a little humour to an embarrassing situation. The captain, having no sense of humour, ignored the jibe and played out the hole, knocking off the single shot he regularly did at every hole as well as ignoring the penalty.

There have never been as many children in Brazil named after their famous "Black Pearl" as have been christened so in English golf clubs. Reporting the incident proved to be totally fruitless as blind eyes were possessed by all the committee members when faced with such monumental problems. It was said that Horatio Nelson was on the committee of his local club.

"Good evening everyone," said Partridge brightly, addressing the assembled members of the membership committee. He nodded at each in turn, "Harold, Arthur, Jonny and,....where's Peter, I thought he was turning out?"

"He's in the bar, on the fruit machine," said Jonny Best.

"As usual," grunted Arthur Snape sourly. He's either on that bloody machine or hanging out with those reprobates at the bar, telling everyone what goes on in here."

"In fairness, he was first here and the meeting was supposed to start early," said Harold Jarvis. "And those reprobates, as you call them, represent some twenty percent of our bar takings."

"Well we were supposed to be discussing some of our financial issues after this, I believe," said Snape. "And we don't want Peter present while we do that, do we?"

"Well there are some developments on that score," said Charles. "I only had time to phone the captain to tell him that item would have to wait for a few days, didn't I Simon?"

The Captain nodded his acknowledgement.

"Thanks for that," said Jonny. "I have something on tonight and I'll have to get off in a bit to see to it."

"Get off for a bit, you mean" thought Charles, knowing exactly what the "something on" was. "You weren't actually down for that meeting so you can get off at any time, if you wish," he said to Best, looking meaningfully at Arthur.

The Greens Chairman, Jonny Best, never seemed to stay long at the committee meetings these days. He always said he was getting off early in order to catch the green keeper, Chris Jones, who he suspected being up to no good. Best wouldn't specify exactly what this "no good" was but since the rest of the committee knew what Best was up to in 'Pole Cats' anyway, it didn't really matter. He did actually have some suspicions about Jones though and vowed to follow him one night when he wasn't up to his own "no good".

The door opened and Peter Billington walked in clutching a very large brandy. "Arrived have we," he said pointedly, looking at Partridge and Blezzard.

"Oh, hi, good evening Peter," said Blezzard quickly. "Sorry about the mix up. Let's get on with it, eh?"

CHAPTER 3

-Three Hundred Grand-

"Yes, yes," said Dave Jordan, a bit impatiently.

The smartly dressed young man who was sat beside him in the parked Porsche paused at the implied accusation in Dave's tone that he was being over-picky with his line of argument.

Dave gripped his partner's arm gently and with great patience he reassured him of the simplicity of the plan. "Don't worry Jerry, it's in the bag. That pair of old fools at The Hall are already in our control, they're desperate."

"But, Dave, we haven't got much time and the cat could be out of that bag you've just referred to," insisted Jerry. "And if the cat does get out, it's going to be covered in crap."

"Look, once we're in as members it's going to be easier to manipulate the old codgers, hide the cat a bit deeper, and get the deal done." Dave grinned wolfishly at his companion's uncertain face. "Then the dosh is ours. We'll both be rich." He paused and added slyly, It's the big one you've been waiting for and the cat will still be safely tucked in the bag when we bury it under the new Metro station foundations."

"I hope your right, Dave," Jerry sighed, "I don't fancy a handful of shitty cat."

"Oh come on, let's get on with it," said Dave, opening his door and sliding elegantly out of his seat. Jerry opened his door struggled out of the low slung car as best as he could, not quite achieving elegant. He never mastered the art of looking cool when alighting from a sports car, not like Dave. They both made their way to the clubhouse of the North Saleston, Golf and Country Club, formed in 1902, one with a confident stride, one following with the hunch of a condemned man.

The nickname of the clubhouse, The Hall, was a deliberate attempt to imply a connection to the glories of times past. When the "Gentlemen" of the area were only invited to join the elite and actual applications were not tolerated.

Those who had the effrontery to apply for membership were certainly not fit to be considered.

Whilst the building was indeed old, it was actually not a hall; it was a gatehouse, one of many at the extremity of the historic estate of the family who had owned it since the civil war.

Times had changed, however, and, although there are still the traditionalists who yearn for the past, any applications are now accepted as long as the fee is paid. Money talks and the louder it speaks the faster the route to gaining membership to any club. Even "Royal" North Saleston.

There still exists a healthy queue jumping procedure within the club hierarchy and all new members are briefed soon after they are initiated into the club. "Old pals act" charters are soon made known and new committees are formed very much mirroring the round tables of the past. Akin to the membership of the Masons, Rosicrucians, Knights Templar, and the more modern Mafia. Foot soldiers (ordinary members) can, if approved, rise in the ranks to become committee members, chairmen of sub committees and finally captains and presidents. The status quo seemed to be set to last forever.

The clubhouse itself however, whilst looking an imposing building, had many defects and was not all it seemed to be. Its facade hid a multitude of lethal faults that had only been concealed from the appropriate authorities by the fact that the senior officers of those authorities were also North Saleston committee members. Structural faults abounded and the state of the roof was legendary, as was that of the cellar. The maze of wires below the feet of the unsuspecting members were hung from the gas and water pipes in the most dangerous manner, defying anyone to touch any part of the monstrous, malevolent looking tangle. When adding state of the ancient gas fired boiler and the tinder dryness in the joists that was almost a bonus to anyone with predilection for arson, it was clear that the whole place should have been condemned years ago.

On top of all that, the biological contents of a kitchen that could provide the laboratories of the world with enough raw materials to be considered an international power in germ warfare, was only waiting for the right moment to poison any gathering cocky enough to think that the French chef could manage a steak tartare.

Even without the intervention of any of the aforementioned disasters, the structure was unlikely to survive long enough to support itself or the aforementioned status quo for very much longer.

"Go and get the drinks in Jerry," said Dave as he stopped at the imposing, twin pillared front entrance overlooking the eighteenth green. He looked down the fairway and, keen to observe the "No Smoking" rule of the day, he pulled out a large cigar from the monogrammed leather case that had been drawn smoothly from his inside breast pocket. Its bulk made the kind of bulge in his jacket that had caused minor background panic at some of the more formal functions he had managed to gate crash.

He sat down on the wooden bench on the patio and rested his elbows on the trestle table in front of him. He spotted four players in the distance as he puffed contentedly on his cigar. The players were endeavouring, in turn, to reach the final green with their wildly flailing weapons, each failing miserably. The players were all in their seventies and past their best. A best that would still have left them a long way short of their desired objective, the green, in the required number of strokes. The most optimistic of the quartet was the one under a very bushy bush. The other three were watching him very carefully, especially his feet.

Dave was joined by another smoker, not cigar but cigarette.

"Great game this," he mused out loud to his new companion, taking a couple of puffs. "Those boys are just demonstrating how the unlimited heights of optimism can be changed to the bottomless depths of despair in the beat of a butterfly's wing. Or, in their case, the swing of a golf club."

His new friend followed Dave's gaze out to the subject of this burst of unwarranted philosophy, not sure how he should respond, or indeed, if response was required. He decided that sober men shouldn't come out with such crap and refrained from any response in case he had to listen to any more.

They sat in an uneasy silence and watched the distant figures making their way towards the last green seemingly intent on avoiding the fairway.

They occasionally stopped in attempts to propel their balls forwards whilst simultaneously trying the keep their remote controlled trolleys under some semblance of any kind of control.

The trolleys stopped and started at will, sometimes in a backward direction, sometimes in a mad pirouette but generally heading approximately in the same direction as the players. John Eastham, Dave's reluctant companion, started to chuckle as he recognised the players.

Dave finally tired of this little diversion and, after stubbing out his half-smoked cigar, he followed Jerry into the clubhouse without further comment, not wishing to bear witness to any more of the antics of the battling septuagenarians or to acknowledge the rather rude bastard on the bench who seemed to find his philosophical observation on life funny.

Two hours later Dave and Jerry climbed back into the Porsche, confirmed as members of the club, backs still tingling from the welcoming slaps, hands almost numb from the handshakes from most of the excited committee members. Jordan's magical and immediate understanding of their plight and his smooth, if vague, promises of possible financial solutions had left all but a few in high spirits, soon to be converted into higher spirits before the bar closed.

"See," said Dave, "just as I said, putty in our hands."

"It was those two duffers who laid the groundwork though," said Jerry.

"Yes," replied Dave, "but who supplied the spade, eh?"

He laughed as he started the car. "Let's go and do a bit more gardening."

"Well, they got in OK, didn't they?" said Arthur Snape, the club treasurer after the membership meeting.

Arthur Snape was sat in his office having a whiskey with Charles Blezzard and the mood was happy. It was the second tot; a large one.

"Easy peasy," said Charles, who couldn't stop grinning. "That arrogant dick head Partridge lapped it all up like the gullible bastard he is. He can see his name in lights now. The saviour of North Saleston. He thinks his photo will go to the top of the line up of club captains. Probably even want a full portrait over the mantelpiece."

"The only photo he'll get is on the front page of the local news when they arrest him.

If the plan gets out he'll be seen as the main mover when I've finished with the accounts," laughed the treasurer.

"Don't forget the minutes of all the meetings," grinned Charles, "He thinks that his name on all these initiatives will make him a legend, 'Leaving a Legacy' so he thinks."

"Famous for generations."

"Infamous." They both laughed.

"The next step is to get him and a few others behind Jordan and it has to be done without it ever being referenced back to us."

"We can easily manipulate the captain through Janice," said Charles. "I'll give her a bit of cock an' bull about a buyout, rumour of course, and infer there's a few quid in it if it goes through."

"Isn't she doing a bit with the greens chairman as well?" asked Snape. "Aren't you bothered or jealous?"

"She's doing a bit with everyone, I think. Lost count and I'm not really bothered at all, certainly not jealous."

Snape shook his head slowly, "Well, whatever we do, it'll take a bit of work and we have to move fast." He sat back and, as he did so, stretched his legs under the desk, kicking over the waste bin with a loud clatter.

They both jumped, startled by the noise.

"Clumsy sod," laughed Charles as he bent forward to start shovelling the contents back into the bin. Arthur, also laughing, bent forward to help. Neither noticed the appearance of Jonny Best at the part open door. He paused in the gap, puzzled at the antics of the two men, groping for something under the desk and laughing like a pair of naughty kids. He decided not to enter, staying hidden instead, ready to find out what the two club officers were doing with their arses in the air under a desk, laughing.

"It is going to take a bit of political in fighting but, with a bit of cunning, we can swing this," said Arthur. "We stand to make a great deal of money out of this, so stay alert. Don't let anyone into the plot. Just me, you, Dave & Jerry."

"Listen," said Charles, "I'm keener than you know to pull this off and Torquemada, the head of the Spanish Inquisition himself, couldn't get information out of me on this. Bloody hell, if they only knew that we were a hundred grand in the black and not two hundred grand in the red."

"Christ, keep your voice down," growled Arthur as he sat up. "Someone might overhear and I don't want to share my few bob out of these accounts, not to mention Dave and Jerry's very generous donations to my pension fund."

"Knock, knock," said the greens chairman from the door.

Arthur swivelled around to the door and Charles's head smacked into the underside of the desk. They looked at each other, panic in their eyes, Charles rubbing the fast swelling lump on the back of his head.

"Who the bloody hell's that?" said Charles.

"Torquemada," said Jonny appearing from behind the door.

The two conspirators glared at the smiling Best as he leaned on the open door. "You should keep the door shut if you want to talk about fiddling the members' funds. I'll bet old Torquemada never had such an easy confession."

"How much have you heard?" growled Arthur.

"Oh, enough." Jonny paused, just long enough to get their attention. "Three hundred grand enough."

The three looked at each other, in turn.

"I think that's about one fifty grand each for you two, eh?" John added. "That'll do nicely for me as well. Should just about buy a nice big gag, or should I say, Jag. Har, har, har."

CHAPTER 4

- A butterfly's wing -

This was Saturday, competition day, a day when the serious stuff took place. Players took Saturdays seriously and serious players took their game really seriously. They practiced their putting, chipped their chips, drove their three-hundred yard drives into the nets that were three yards away and performed the type of warm up exercises that were seen more often at athletic meetings.

All this activity generally made no difference to the majority of the participants, many failing to reach the brook some sixty or so yards from the tee. Others denied themselves any such warm up antics or practice, implying that theirs was a natural talent.

After the battle with the game was ended, the member's lounge would start to fill up with players looking for a drink or bar snacks or both. Soon the place would be buzzing with conversation, mostly about the day's round; who was leading, who was slow, how bad the luck was and other such topics that usually started the flow of social discourse that would change with the consumption of alcohol.

As the afternoon progressed the makeup of the occupants morphed into a different demographic profile. Made up of older members, less keen on the higher mechanics of the game and certainly less keen on attempting to master any of these mechanics should inclement weather be making conditions tricky.

Any such adverse weather would see this breed of golfer at the bar much earlier in the afternoon which would, in turn, see them in the bar longer, ultimately resulting in a noisier gathering. On rainy days, as the afternoon progressed this section of the bar would naturally attract a variety of like minded players who were more intent on having a laugh than having a game of golf in the mud.

This was such a day and Mike, Alan, and Dermot were in full flow, taking the Mickey out of Derek and the latest escapade of his unruly trolley.

"You had to be there," said Alan to John, who was already at the bar when they had come in. "We had just finished out the hole at the second when Derek noticed his trolley was missing.

He looked in the usual place which is forty yards back down the fairway but it was nowhere to be seen.

"Where the bloody hell's me trolley," says he. No sign of it was to be seen. However, there were only two places it could be and knowing Derek's luck we looked in the worst place first."

"Not the brook?" laughed John.

"Well done Sherlock, the very spot," said Mike.

"It's a bit steep right next to the third tee," said John, anticipating the resulting resting place of the trolley.

"Well that bank down into the brook is steep anyway," said Alan.

"And deep," said Derek.

"We had to form a chain. Three of us," said Alan. "Me, Mike and Derek."

"Bloody hell, I wish I'd have seen that," said John. "What were you doing Dermott?"

"I couldn't help 'em," said Dermot, laughing as he recalled the sight in his mind's eye. "I was dying for a pee and all that laughing made it worse. I just had to have a pee. I didn't even have time to get me bloody phone otherwise I'd have got the whole thing on video. Could have had a million hits on You Book, or Face Tube, or whatever it's called."

"I don't think that that woman walking her dog on the footpath was too happy with your peeing though," said Mike.

"Look," said Dermott, "when you gotta go, you gotta go."

"Well she didn't quite see it that way." Mike turned to John. "If your wife was out walking the dog," he said solemnly, "and she was accosted by some lunatic with his dick hangin' out, laughing like a crazy bastard, what would you expect her to do?"

"Call the police," said John, guessing the back end to the story from the buzz in the clubhouse about the police on the course.

"Right on," said Mike. "That's exactly what she did do. Took a lot of explaining, that did."

"If I'd have had time to get me phone, I'd have been able to give 'em some proof, wouldn't I?"

"If you'd have had time to get your bloody phone, you wouldn't have been having a piss, would you?" said Alan.

"Anyway," said Derek, "if you had managed to calm her down a bit quicker you might have got her to send the dog into the stream to fetch my cap. I got soaked when I lost me footin'."

"Another quick end to a round, eh?" said John.

"Yeah," said Derek. "It's usually 'cause we are gettin' wet from the top down, not from the bottom up."

John went out for a smoke with Alan and promised himself a few laughs recounting the story to a few of the lads at the other end of the bar as he spotted his own playing partners coming in. At least it would explain the appearance of the police on the course. There were bound to be questions asked by the committee members.

As the afternoon wore on the clubhouse got busier. Members old and new mingled in the gent's lounge, swapping stories and tales of woe until the football started. The local derby between the two Manchester giants was being shown and there was a definite division of loyalties in the room. Supporters of the two teams began taunting the opposing camp, praising their own team, insulting the opposition and placing bets as to the outcome.

The captain arrived in with his playing partners, Jordan, Vaughan and Snape and he pushed his way to the bar, taking advantage of his right to get served immediately no matter how many were clamouring for attention. He ordered his drinks and sauntered over to his table, taking his position on his throne, "The Captain's Chair".

The chair was impressive and expensive, high backed, velvet upholstery, ornately carved arms, all topped off with the club's coat of arms and motto positioned at the back of the occupant's head. A photograph of the current captain was hung on the wall at the back of the chair, like a passport really. The face of the occupant of the chair must match the face in the photo, or there would be trouble. Nobody else is allowed to sit in that chair.

The captain's playing partners followed, all settling themselves down to wait for the drinks to be brought over by Jayne.

Mike watched the performance and said, "Look at that bunch of tossers. He's just pushed everyone out of the way, ordered his drinks and made Jayne ferry them over to his table."

"That's what captains can do, it's their right, their due," Said Derek.

"What, like in medieval times, y'mean. His DROIT DU SEIGNEUR?" asked Mike

"What the bloody hell are you talking about?" said Alan "What's draw de sinyure when its at home?"

"Well in days of yore when the local baron found out that the local famer's son was going to marry the wench from the pie shop, his DROIT DU SEIGNEUR, or his Lord's Right, meant that the said lord could have it away with the said lass from the pie shop on the first night."

"Yer jokin'," said Alan. "What, conjugals, you mean? Before the farmer's son can have a go?"

"Yep, full Monty," said Mike. "That's unless the farmer's son got there before him, when he was courting, like."

"Bloody hell, that lord would've been busy round here, wouldn't he?"

"Don't be such a smart arse, Mike," said Jack, who had just joined them and overheard Mike's smartarsery. "It's just a courtesy that's afforded the captain. Although, I agree, some do take liberties, like Partridge."

"I suppose I should know better than to be distracted by such trivia when there are more important things to think about," said Mike. "Like, who are those two guys with Partridge and Snape, for instance. I saw the shorter one arriving in a bloody Bentley before we went out."

"He was the one who I was telling you about," said John. "I saw them come for their interview in a Porsche. He was the one philosophising about you boys when you were battling for the usual two quid."

"The butterfly's wing shit?"

"Yep," said John, smiling at the memory.

"That's David Jordan, chairman of JD Developments," said Jack. "I've been looking up his details as well as asking around and it appears he is a bit of a player in the property game around the north of England. He's made a few quid here and there, a lot around Liverpool apparently. Tales of back-handers, flash holidays for councillors, one chairman of one of the planning departments seems to have acquired a share of a holiday home in Fuengirola."

"Well he came in a Bentley today," said Derek.

"A bloody Bentley?" said Dermot. "I didn't notice a Bentley in the car park."

"I think that a Bentley would be a bit conspicuous in our car park," said Jack. "It's also a bit of a temptation to some of the scrubbers who pass by the main gate. No, he was dropped off by a chauffeur. He looked a bit of a tough cookie as well. If he says it's Christmas, I suggest you start singing carols."

"Unloaded his clubs an' all; even put his trolley together." said Mike.

Jack sniffed. "He stood there and watched him do it too."

"Oh, come on," said Alan. "You're just jealous. You'd love to be able to do that."

"No I wouldn't," said Jack. "Well, not unless it was you doing the donkey work."

"No need for that," said Alan in mock hurt tones.

"More to the point, could he be the party interested in buying the club?" said Mike. "It seems a bit coincidental, club in difficulties, rumours about buy out, new members, captains table with Snape, loads of dosh, developer!!"

"Hmm, quite a list," said Jack. "Have you been watching Tales of Sherlock again?"

"Who's the other guy?" asked Dermot.

"He works for Jordan," said Jack. "He's the FD at JD."

"FD at JD?" said Alan. "What's the bloody hell is the FD and furthermore, what's the JD?"

"FD, Financial Director," said Jack, rolling his eyes. "JD, JD Developments."

Alan furrowed his brows for a moment. "Shouldn't that be JDD then?" he said with a smug look on his face.

"No the JD stands ...." Jack stopped. "You're just trying to wind me up. Look, if you don't want to know the latest news, just say so. I'll be happy to go and talk to someone sensible."

"Take no notice Jack," said Mike. "Give us the latest, we're all ears."

Derek grabbed four Kit Kat bars, sugar needed to help old chaps complete eighteen holes on their Sunday round; passing a fiver over the counter to Tom Jackson, the assistant professional.

As Tom opened the till to give Derek his change, Mark Norton, the professional, emerged from his office and said, "Where's the three sets of Ping irons that I brought in yesterday?"

"Over there in the rack," said Tom, rooting in the till for the correct coins.

"Well, stick them in the back as quick as you like will you," said Mark sharply.

"Hang on old chap," said Derek, "I think he's serving me at the minute. What happened to customer comes first?"

"Yeah, right," replied Mark. "Well when you've finished with the sweeties, shift the clubs. I don't want them there when the Ping rep comes this afternoon and he'll be here soon.

Mark went back into the office and Tom raised his eyebrows with a jerk of his head towards the disappearing pro.

"Grumpy get," said Derek, "I'll start buying my sweeties at the supermarket if he's not careful."

"Christ, we'll not be able to survive," was the sarcastic reply to Derek's threat.

"I guess that sweeties aren't good enough since he started to get better deals off his suppliers, are they." said Derek, indicating the well stocked racks.

"Those prices are too good to be true. If he's hiding Pings from the Ping rep, he must be getting them from somewhere dodgy," he thought. Although he wasn't that bothered really, he felt a bit of moaning was expected and he didn't like to disappoint. And as an ex-copper, he also liked to do a bit of nosing around, keep his hand in.

"Look, take no notice of him, he's been a bit grumpy lately," said Tom. "I don't know why 'cause his sales have been bloody good for the last few months. His sales figures should make him a happy camper not the miserable, nervous wreck he is now."

"Well he'd better buck his ideas up when I come in for my sweeties, that's all I can say," mumbled Derek as he left the shop.

Tom moved the clubs as ordered, just in the nick of time, because as he came out of the storeroom the shop bell announced the arrival of the Ping representative.

"Hi Tom, Is Mark in?" asked the rep.

"Hi Paul, I'll get him, he's in the office." Tom looked in the office window. "Actually, he's on the 'phone.

"OK, I'll have a bit of a browse."

The rep wandered around the shop making a mental note of the stock on show paying particular attention to the Ping corner.

Mark came out of the office after Tom signalled the arrival of the rep, casting a black look at his assistant.

"Hi Paul, come into the office," said Mark, turning his attention to the rep. "Tom get us a coffee from the kitchen will you?" he added sweetly.

"I can make a coffee here," said Tom.

"Nah, that's instant, we'll have a bit of the good stuff off Curtice, eh?"

Tom, not happy at being sent on such an errand, went off sulkily to see Curtice, the French chef, in the clubhouse kitchen. He knew that Mark was up to something with the Ping rep but couldn't get anything on them. "It's nothin' to do with me I suppose but there's something odd about hiding those clubs," he thought. "Might be knocked off, even."

Derek manoeuvred his remote controlled trolley carefully down the path holding on to the handle in case it did one of its unnerving changes of direction. He always maintained that this was 'the bloody faulty bloody remote bloody control device' causing his problems but the lads knew differently.

"That grumpy pro's a bit sharp these days," said Derek, bringing the trolley to a sharp, skidding stop next to the three players waiting by the first tee.

"Yer a bit late," said Alan, ignoring Derek's attempt at an excuse, ball already on a peg ready to be teed off.

"I had to get some Kit Kats," retorted Derek. "You'd do some moanin' if you had nothin' to go with your coffee."

"Kit Kats?" said Dermot, "Where's the pies?"

"I had a bit to do this morning and I was a bit late, OK."

"Stop moanin' and let's get off before this next lot," said Mike. "They'll be up our backsides soon enough without them harassing us here."

They all quickly teed off in turn with varying results, none of which were too impressive, all in different directions.

Tom watched them trailing after their balls with their trolleys weaving down the fairway as he ferried the coffee to the pro's office.

"Too late to give them old tossers any lessons," he thought. "They're all past lessons now. Past a lot of things I suppose. They look as though they could do with a few lessons with those bloody trolleys too."

As he got to the shop door it flew open before he got to the handle and the Ping rep, stormed out muttering angrily "I know what you're up to, y' tricky sod ...," brushing roughly past Tom, almost launching the tray full of coffees, and stomping off into the car park.

"What the hell's up with him?" asked Tom as he put the tray with coffee pot and cups on Mark's desk.

"Nothin'," said Mark. "But we're going to have to do some stock taking over the next few days. So don't make any dates 'cause you'll be working late."

That news didn't really bother Tom. He didn't have a girl friend anyway, so dates were not an issue. The golf club was his only life and the more time he was there the better he liked it.

Anyway, he had found the key to Mark's desk earlier and popped down to the local do-it-yourself shop to get a copy made. He had already made his mind up to have bit of a root around the following day while Mark was out doing his rounds.

CHAPTER 5

-Noisy flies in the honey-

"This is definitely a day for the Bentley and the chauffeur," thought Dave as the gleaming black saloon swept into the club car park on Monday afternoon. "Show these Muppets that I've got the clout to carry off the rescue mission that they think I'm going to provide."

The meeting was set for two o'clock; he was meeting Jerry at the bar. The Bentley pulled up next to the Captain's parking spot and Brian, the chauffeur, got out and opened the passenger door.

"Just station yourself here Brian," said Dave, "and see if anyone's got the balls to ask you to move.

"Right O boss," said Brian. "Wot if they do ask me to move it?"

"That's OK, move it," said Dave grinning. "We'll see if they ask you the next time we come."

Dave got out and sauntered along the path to the clubhouse. He met a flustered looking Jerry who was waiting at the entrance.

"You look a bit bothered," said Dave. "What's up?"

"There's been bit of a cock up," said Jerry. "A wasp in the honey, so to speak."

"A what?"

"Y'know," said Jerry, reddening. "A wasp in the wossname, soup; or jam, honey, whatever."

"Are you talking about flies and ointment, by any chance?"

"Flies? Oh, yeah, that's it, fly." Jerry took a deep breath and tried again. "There's another greedy bastard looking to be cut in on the deal. Snape and Blezzard let someone sneak up on them when they were gloating about their cut, counting their pies before they hatched. A guy called Best. He's green, apparently. Whatever that means."

"Green?"

"Well that's what they called him, green chairman."

"Not that bloody green if he was able to get himself involved with an earn as big as this one," growled Dave. "We'll have to get him frightened, won't we? I'm not feeding any more of these bastards any more of my money."

"Look Dave," said Jerry, pulling his boss into the hallway, "I can't help being a bit nervous about this deal. There's too many crooks getting involved with this soup."

"I think you mean cooks, and broth."

"Cooks ... crooks ...., what's the difference? I know what it means and it means trouble," said Jerry, clearly panicking. "It means we could finish in that soup or broth, and anyway, whatever it is that we're cooking could just turn out to be porridge, a large dose."

"Oh stop whining Jerry," snapped Jordan. He went quiet for a minute. It seemed longer and Jerry looked a little apprehensive.

"Right, where are the dopey sods that let the cat out of the bag?" said Dave. "I'm going to let them know what's what. And, if they can't sort this greens feller out, I'll have to sort them all out."

"There's that soddin' shitty cat again," groaned Jerry.

" Will you stop with that effin' cat," barked Dave as he pushed his way past Jerry making his way along the hallway and up the stairs leading to the offices and the committee room, Jerry following glumly in his wake. They burst into the Secretary's office where Blezzard and Snape sat facing each other over a desk, both turning as the door reached the extent of its hinges with a bang.

"What the bloody hell's going on," yelled Dave, "and who's this green bastard that's shoving his snout into the trough? Have we been invaded by fuckin' Martians?"

"Calm down," said Snape, "we can sort him out 'cause he's as bent as we are. It's just a matter of how much."

"If you'd have kept your mouth shut," yelled Jerry over Dave's shoulder, where he was concealed from view, "we wouldn't be looking at how much. We'd already sorted out how much. You two are getting enough to sort him out. What with the fiddling of the club books as well as our bung, you're quids in."

"I never saw your lips move then," said Snape, smiling at the visible Jordan coolly, pretending not to see the invisible Jerry. "And let's not forget how cheap this deal is going to be for you. Since it's our skills that have been able to put the club in this desperate plight, you should not forget our importance. The club would not even talk to you if they weren't so desperate. Now they'll settle for any quick fix."

"It's not just the money," said Dave, "it's the bloody legality of it all. My mate Jerry is right to be worried.

If this goes tits up we'll all be in the dock before we can blink."

"It's not only us who'll be upset at your Martian," said Jerry, "what about the other investors. They don't like any changes in their agreements." He looked at Dave meaningfully. "Do they?"

"Correct," Dave said. "We'd better get this Martian up and have a word with him."

"What're they talking about, Martian?" asked Charles.

"Never mind the Martian," said Snape, "what's this about 'other investors'? "

"I think Jerry is not too familiar with committee procedure," said Dave with a smile, "I thought it amusing to pretend we thought that the greens chairman that you refer to as 'greens' is a Martian. Y'know, green. You can forget about the other investors, they're our problem, not yours."

"Martian, green, very droll. Anyway, this is all getting a bit loud," said Charles, moving forward. He dragged Vaughan and Jordan inside and closed the door. "These walls have ears."

"And some of them have lips," said Snape. "Green lips for starters, although I'm not over worried about the Greens Chairman. He just wants a bit of dosh. It's the bar staff I'm concerned with. They do have a propensity to gossip and this would make a juicy morsel for any one of them."

Arthur Snape didn't know it, but his caution had kicked in a bit late. Larry, the bar manager was passing the bottom of the stairs just as Dave had made his rather dramatic entrance and he managed to catch some of the louder exchanges. He was currently putting his own linking words into the gaps that he couldn't make out. This has always been the modus operandi of the practiced gossip. Making up a few keywords to add into a story, no matter how inaccurate, was the mark of a premier division gossip. He went downstairs mentally concocting the revised scripting of his expanded interpretation.

He had just made it behind the bar before Blezzard arrived into the lounge and Blezzard, spotting John Best talking to Brian Fordham at one of the tables, wandered casually over to him.

"Can you excuse us for a minute please Brian?" asked Charles sitting down.

"Certainly Charles," replied Brian, who then stood up, picked up his pint and went to the bar, close enough to try to earwig what was being said. He failed to pick up a single word as Charles whispered to Best. It appeared to Fordham that there was a little tension in the muttering that passed between the two and decided to make it his business to find out what was going on. Best and Blezzard suddenly stood up and Best spluttered, "Right, we'll see about that, won't we?"

The two whisperers left the lounge and headed upstairs. Fordham went to the bar where Larry was busy polishing his favourite glass. "What was all that about, I wonder?" asked Fordham.

Larry adopted the typical barman's stance, one towel over his shoulder, the other wiping the inside of the glass and said, "There was a bit of an argument going on upstairs with Snape, Blezzard and those two new guys. Y'know, the one with the Porsche and the Bentley."

"Christ, they're a bit new to be rowing with the treasurer already aren't they?" said Fordham. "They can't be moaning about the subs, surely, not if one's got a Bentley."

"Well....." said Larry moving closer to Fordham, the way I heard it ....."

Jonny Best entered the secretary's office and was faced with the grim faces of Jordan, Snape and Vaughan. Blezzard, the grimmest face, followed him into the office and shut the door.

"Are you lot involved in a bit of goal post adjustments?" said Best. "'Cause y'see this **Best** is not going to be fobbed off with any **second best** arrangements that you might be trying on."

"If you don't keep you voice down," said Dave, with a bit of menace, "there won't be any **best** at all, if you get my drift."

"I hope that's not a threat," said Best. "I do have a bit of a tale to tell the rest of the members and, as yet, I've got no actual connection to the contents of your sordid plans. I can still report you all to the Captain and the police and anyone else who might be interested. You'll all be in the mire and some of you could do time. All of you will never play golf again.

You won't even get onto a driving range. So," he paused and

looked around at each one in turn, "don't start issuing threats or try to downgrade the amount of the cut I've already agreed with these two bozos." He nodded towards Blezzard and Snape.

"Hang on," said Blezzard, "we didn't actually agree to any amounts. I said we'd put the matter to these lads for their consideration."

"Look, you two were set to make £150K each and that sounds like a nice round sum. It'd allow me to relax a bit, y'know," said Best with a smile on his face. "I've been totting up the potential value of any likely construction deals that would benefit from the development around this location. Motorway at the end of the road, new metro station less than two hundred yards away from the clubhouse, a lump of land that could fit a fair sized hotel within ten minutes from the airport, surrounding farmland that would be sure to be reclassified from green belt, park and ride, etc. . . . . . . Need I go on?"

It was now very quiet in the room. Nervous glances were exchanged between the original conspirators and Snape broke the silence.

"OK Jonny, you're right. There is a lot of advantages for selling the club to the right people. But there's also a hell of an investment in place already."

He paused, as though he was coming to some kind of decision. "In the light of this new development Charles and I will share our little windfall with you, so we will all get around £100K. How's that?"

"You can fuck off with your £100K," snapped Best, "we agreed that we'd all get that £150K and I'm not settling for a penny less."

"Well I'll tell you what, you prick," growled Jordan, "there's some foundations already being dug a mile or so away and you might get a chance to have a close look at the bottom of them the way you are going on."

He jumped up suddenly and swept out of the office followed closely by Arthur Snape.

"Jesus, Jonny," said Blezzard, "negotiation was never your strong point, was it?"

"I'm telling you Charles, if I don't get what's coming to me, I'll spill the beans. Not only that, I want something in writing before tomorrow night or I'll be singing like a bloody canary."

Jerry stood up and made for the door. He turned as he got there and said, "Don't worry, I'll have a quiet word with Dave. He's just wound up like a chicken on a hot tar roof at the minute. You have to understand that the investors I alluded to before are a little strict on their terms and conditions."

"That's your look out," said Best. "I know that there's got to be a big earn in this and £450K is small potatoes."

"Leave it with me," said Jerry, tapping the side of his nose like a conspiratorial barrow boy. "A shrug is as good as a smack on the nose with a shovel," he added. "I'll be in touch before tomorrow night." He turned and left the room.

Jonny and Charles looked at each other, open mouthed.

"Chickens? Hot tar roof? Smack on the nose with a shovel?" muttered Jonny, as he left the office scratching his head. "How does he get a job?"

He made his way back downstairs and rejoined Brian who sat waiting at the table with a couple of fresh pints, ready to quiz his pal.

"I've just seen that new guy, Jordan," said Dermot as he joined Mike and Alan at the bar. "He was in a bit of a hurry and he got to the Bentley before his driver spotted him. Gave the door a right kick."

"What?" said Alan, "kicked his Bentley?"

"Yep, and the big gadget who got out of the car was built like Lennox Lewis. I thought he was going to deck Jordan but he just opened the back door for him and closed it, nice and quiet like."

"He must be paying him well."

Larry had sidled over from the other side of the bar after Fordham had resumed his seat and said, "You've just missed a right good row." He picked up a glass and started to polish it with a grubby looking towel.

Mike dug Alan in the ribs and said, "See that! That's why I drink out of the bottle. There's no way that glass isn't collecting a host of bacteria off that towel. We've got a dishwasher that's supposed to clean glasses and dry them. Why is he doing that?" He looked at Larry, "Why are you doing that?"

"What?"

"Rubbing germs into that glass."

"Y'what?"

"That glass was perfectly clean when it came out of the dishwasher, why are you dirtying it?"

Larry looked at the glass then looked at Mike, "Is he always like this?" he said to Dermot.

"Just tell us about the row," said Alan, "and take no notice of him. He's still trying to excuse his slobby habit of drinking out of the bottle."

"I just can't tell a story without polishing a glass," said Larry looking at the glass. "It's a kind of mental crutch."

"Look, forget the bloody crutch and the dirty glass. Just tell the bloody story," said Dermot, throwing his eyes at the ceiling. "This gets more and more like the Muppets corner. And don't make up the bits you didn't hear like you usually do."

"How d'yer mean, make it up. If I can't make it up I might as well put the bloody glass down."

Tom, the assistant pro, walked in and interrupted the beginning of the story, ordering a pint of orange and lemonade. Larry poured Tom's drink and placed it on the bar.

"I'll get that," said Alan, impatient to hear the gossip. Derek joined them, delaying the eager Larry even further. Larry poured Derek's lager and took Alan's card to till in the order. He returned the card to Alan and took a breath, ready to spill the beans.

"Can I have some ice, please?" asked Tom. There was a collective groan as Larry paused and went to the ice bucket.

He started to spoon ice cubes into the orange liquid and began to unload his fractured rumour. He tried to stay to the facts but some made up bits managed to filter in the storyline. "Fiddling bastards, dodgy accounts, investors, assets, stock," and other non specific phrases littered a vague account of the argument and Derek said, "He's better when he makes things up. Why are we listening to this crap?"

Larry tried harder to impress them. "Jonny Best was up there as well, he'll be able to back up what I'm saying."

They all peered over the bar into the lounge and spotted Best and Fordham deep in conversation.

"Besty won't tell you anything if he's involved," said Alan. "He's a right tricky bastard. I'm sure he's up to something with Mark. Him and his mate, Fordham."

"Maybe that's what the row was about," Larry said. "Maybe someone has found out about his tricky bastardry."

"Shit, you never give up do you? Making up stories, that's all you're doing. Why don't you get the full story before you start and then we could have a proper gossip?"

"Well," said Tom, "actually I can tell you that Jonny Best is up to something with Mark. There is definitely something going on with Mark's stock." He paused, taking a swig of his orange. "And the Ping rep seemed a bit miffed about something to do with a discrepancy in sales against stock levels."

"What's that got to do with the treasurer and secretary?" said Derek.

"Dunno," said Tom sheepishly, "just thought it seemed to fit in with what you were saying. He backed away and slunk into the lounge to watch the television.

"Strange lad," said Alan.

"Oh, leave him alone," said Mike. "He's only a kid. He might just have something there though. It wouldn't be a good thing if Mark was fiddling with stock here since he supplies the other local clubs. It could form the basis for a right juicy scandal and you know what our lot are like for huffin' and puffin' about scandals."

Larry and the old codgers looked through into the lounge at Fordham and Best, the latter having just returned from his meeting looking decidedly flushed. The two were engrossed in a close head to head conversation.

Brian got up and ordered another round for himself and Best, noticing the five pairs of eyes staring over towards him. He looked behind him in case they were looking at something past him that he had missed. When he looked back, the eyes were on the other sides of their owner's heads and Larry's one pair of eyes was in front of him, just below a pair of quizzical eyebrows. He shrugged and thought, "Must have imagined that."

He ordered up two pints of lager and, after checking for the eyes at the other end of the bar, he ferried the lager over to their table and sat down.

"Another one? Bloody hell, I'm gettin' a bit pissed," said Best. He smiled to himself. "I think I might just nip down to see Juicy Lucy before I go home."

"You're getting to be a bit of a regular down there, aren't you?"

"Well, what would you rather do? Don't tell me, you'd sooner go home and watch the telly with your missus. Anyway, you should talk, you do a bit down there as well. I know all about you."

"All right, all right," said Brian looking around furtively. "Keep your bloody voice down." He gave his pal a conspiratorial nudge in the side and said, "I don't go as much as you though, do I? Must cost you a bomb."

"Don't you worry about me old pal. I can look after myself where money's concerned.

"Look Jonny, I'm more bothered about you gettin' dragged up to the office. You're not in any bother are you?"

"Bother, humph, bother," he smirked crookedly, the lager just beginning to get the better of him. "Listen mate, I know somethin' that'll make me a good few quid. Might even leave my moanin' doris and move in with Lucy."

"Move in with a lap dancer? Are you losing your mind? She's a hooker and they're very high maintenance, hookers. You'd need a good few quid to keep a hooker happy."

"She's not a hooker, she's an exotic dancer," replied Jonny in a bit of a huff.

"Yeah . . . . Whatever." Brian paused. "Still high maintenance. You'd have to have to know something special to get the kind of money you'll need for Juicy. I think you're having me on."

Fordham was purposely being a bit dismissive of Best's tale and he knew that by goading him he would not be able to resist spilling the beans in order to prove that his claim to a fortune was a solid one. Keeping such a secret is hard, especially after five pints of premium lager.

"Well that's what you think," retorted Best in a hoarse whisper, leaning closely towards his friend so as not to be overheard. "I know that the club's not skint, I know that there's a plan to sell it to a private developer and I know who's behind it all and, how much they stand to make if it goes through." He dropped his voice another notch. "One hundred and fifty grand each. I found out, see, and I've demanded the same or I'll blow the whistle."

Brian sat back in amazement. He looked around, at the bar, at the door, out the window, back at Jonny. All in all, a significant pause, before he exclaimed, "Bollocks!"

He took a swig of his lager, wishing it was a brandy.

"That's not possible. It's not possible to get a sale like that through without the members finding out."

"Well I found out, didn't I, and the deed is nearly done," said Jonny, unable to keep the smug smile off his face.

Another bout of silence lasted just long enough for Brian to gather his senses, his face brightening.

"I don't suppose you could get a slice of the pie for your old mate, could you?"

"Oh, don't worry, I'll give you a few quid out of my slice," said Jonny. "Five grand will go down nicely, wouldn't it? You can treat your missus to a cruise or somethin'. Anyway I'm off to see Lucy. Don't forget, mum's the word."

Best tried to tap the side of his nose with his index finger, missing on the first two attempts but succeeding on the third and fourth.

He got to his feet unsteadily and made his way past the bar, shouting "G'nite, suckers," to the Larry and Jayne, finally waving to the four old farts at the other end of the bar who had been staring intently at the little meeting in the lounge.

Mark Norton saw Best from the shop window, staggering toward the car park, and he waylaid him at the end of the path.

"Oy, I want a word with you, matey. We're going to have to cut back on our orders," he said.

"Cut back?" replied Best, "What do you mean, cut back?"

"I've had the Ping rep in today and he gave me a bit of a grilling. He's not too happy about my orders drying up when he's hearing so much on the grapevine about my sales being so good. He thinks I must be getting stock from somewhere else, and since he's the only one I should be gettin' it from, he smells a rat. It's only a matter of time before he puts two and two together."

"Well that's your problem mate," said Jonny. "Can't you do something about his stuff?"

"Like what?"

"I don't know. I'm not a soddin' shopkeeper, you are. That's why I got you the deal. Remember?"

"I suppose I'll have to sell some of his stuff at a loss," said Mark. "But you'll have to take some of the hit as well."

"Bugger off, I'm taking no hits," said Jonny sharply. "You can do what you want about your Ping rep, mate, but I've just ordered another container from Mr Wu last week."

"Well, you'll have to cancel it," said Mark.

"Sod off. It's at sea now and I don't think they are able to turn a fuckin' big container ship around just to drop one big box back on the dock. And not only that but I dread to think what Wu, our dodgy looking Chinese import agent, might say if I asked him. That strange tattoo on his neck does tend to throb a bit when he gets excited. Anyway, I'm off for a bit of fun now, can't stop here talkin' about shit."

He brushed past Mark and headed for his car. Just as he opened his door a hand grabbed his arm. Best thought it was Mark and said, without looking round, "Look, I told you to bugger off, didn't I?"

"Don't you tell me to bugger off," said a totally different voice than Mark's. It wasn't Mark; it was Chris Jones, the head greenkeeper.

"I want a word with you," said Chris. "What's all this snooping about you're doin'? Stickin' your nose into my shit.""

"Oh, it's you. Like I said, you can bugger off as well, see. Cause I'm off home, see, and I haven't got time to talk about grass now."

"Grass?" Jones stepped back, his eyed widening. "Wot'jer mean, grass?"

"Greens, made of grass, what else would I want to talk to you about?"

"I don't want to talk about grass; I want to know why you've got it in for me. I've heard you're trying to catch me out at somethin'."

"Well you are a bit of a tricky bugger and I know you're up to something, and I'll catch you at it, don't you worry. Now sod off out of my way, I'm off."

"You just get on with your grubby visits to the knockin; shop and leave me alone," growled Jones, "'an' I know all about you giving that Blezzard doris too much attention as well. And that lady captain, Jennie Milbank. I'll fix you up good if you don't keep your nose out of my shit."

"Watch your mouth you cheeky bastard or I'll stick you in one of your shit bunkers, upside down."

Best got into the car, started it and screeched off out of the car park. He went that fast that his exhaust scraped loudly over the sleeping policeman at the gate, the only car to have done so since it was first laid.

Jones waving angrily after Best , shouted at the car, "I'll stick **you** in a bunker, dick 'ed." As he stood shaking his fist and shouting angrily at the disappearing tail lights, he heard a bin clattering at the kitchen door. Curtice looked over and nodded.

"I'll do for him one day," said the fuming Jones to Curtice.

"You weel 'ave to stand een line," said the French chef, laughing. "Zere's a few 'oo would be een front off you." He turned and went back into the kitchen.

Mark had slammed the door to the shop as he thought about his stock problem. He was now considering telling Tom about the scam but he was not sure how much information he should share with him. The stock fiddling was getting harder to hide and Mark had to shift all the gear single handed.

"I'll swing for that bastard," he said out loud as he made for the office.

Tom emerged from the stock room and said, "Who?"

Mark spun round. "What are you doing in there?" he said sharply.

"I was just tidying up," said Tom. "Ready for your stock-take, like you said. Swing for who? Who's getting up your nose?"

"Oh, it's that bloody green's chairman," said Mark, going in to the office. "He's going to screw up a very good business if he's not careful."

"How?"

"I'll tell you tomorrow, but it is serious. Might just close us down, put us both out on the street. But I'll stop him, one way or another. You can get off home, I'll see you in the morning."

John had arrived for an "early doors" drink a little later than usual. He insisted on buying a drink for the four gossipers, who were still at the bar. He was the only one in the group that was not retired.

Over the past few years he had adopted this crazy old bunch, finding their company much more entertaining than the most of the regular members.

Their grumpy anarchical attitude suited his own outlook on the general fabric of life, well golf club life anyway.. Likewise he had been adopted by the old farts for similar reasons, one of which being his eagerness to get a round in.

"We were just going, but it'd be rude not to join you," said Dermot. "You're a bit late aren't you?"

"Got held up on the M6," replied John. "Anyway, what's been happening to keep you lot here so late?"

"Oh, just a few rumours; and some aggro upstairs. Wild accusations of twisting stock and fiddling accounts," said Mike. "Larry heard it all, apparently."

"No," said Dermot, "he heard a row, some phrases, probably some misguided suppositions about our losses; and he knitted the rest together into a sort of barman's scoop. He should have been a reporter for the Sun."

"So the reason you're all still here is .....?" asked John with a knowing smile

"Well it all sounded as though it might have been about right when he told us exactly what he overheard and then young Tom came in. He kind of added a bit to the mix with a rumour of his own concerning Mark and Best."

"And possible stock fiddling," added Alan.

"And a row upstairs between Besty and the treasurer," added Mike.

"And," said Derek, not wanting to be left out, "Fordham seems to be in cahoots with him."

"Cahoots? Cahoots?" John laughed. "Where are we, in Dodge City?"

Jayne brought John's swipe card back after tilling his round.

"I think that these lads have got the wrong end of the stick here. John Best was arguing about the club accounts, not the pro's accounts," she said.

They all turned as one towards her.

"Club accounts?" they chorused.

"Oh thanks John," pocketing her tip.

"Club accounts?" they repeated the chorus.

"Well I was just leaving the snooker room after having a quiet chat with Vinny when I saw one of the new members go barging into Snape's office. Y'know, that little feller with the Bentley."

"Quiet chat with Vinny?"

"In the snooker room?"

Jayne blushed and then bridled, quick to deny the implied accusation she said, "I went in for a sneaky fag, you cheeky sods. There was no one about and it saved me from going outside. Vinny had arranged to meet a pal for a game and we were just having a chat. No hanky panky, get it? Anyway, if you lot are going to start dodgy rumours about me and Vinny I'm not going to tell you what I heard." With that she flounced to the other end of the bar.

"You'll get nowt off her now," laughed John. "Winding her up like that."

"Oh, don't worry," said Alan. "She's dying to tell us. If we don't find out today, we will tomorrow."

"Has Jack found anything more about the actual accounts?" asked John. "This ruckus could be connected to our suspicions about their accuracy, no?"

"They're definitely up to something up there and you can guarantee it's not going to benefit us," said Alan. "I'll phone Jack and get him to pull his finger out."

CHAPTER 6

-Green mist in the copse-

Jonny Best dragged his clubs out of the boot and then he unloaded his trolley. He assembled it and strapped his bag in place. He then made his way down to the third tee, very slowly, having decided to play a few holes before he went home to face the music.

Being a bit the worse for wear as he left the golf club the night before was due to that nosey Brian.

"I should have kept my trap shut really," he thought. "Cost me five grand that piss up."

However, in some compensation, he was happy that the golf club lager had given him enough courage to visit Pole Cats and partake of the lovely Juicy's charms.

His lager infused rebellious mood had been further enhanced with a bit more "hero" sauce as he waited for his turn with Lucy.

The stuff they served in Pole Cats was a bit dearer than the club's lager and a bit stronger. The combination of lager, cheap whisky and his sexual exertions had finally sent him into a deep sleep that the athletic lap dancer could not wake him from.

She solved the problem by locking him in the room and went home, leaving a message for Tarquin, her transvestite pimp. Tarquin could handle the drunk when he arrived in the morning.

The pimp was quick to eject the hung-over Jonny out into the back entry of the brothel threatening to charge bed and breakfast rates the next time it happened.

"...... and I can assure you our B&B rates are a lot dearer than your usual ten minute shag with Lucy." were his parting words to the very dizzy Best as he shoved him into the street.

It was still very early and, like his current mood, a bit on the gloomy side. His courage having disappeared overnight left him searching for an excuse to explain his absence from the matrimonial bed last night. A few holes of golf might help to clear his head.

Although it was past dawn the light was not too good and he sliced his first shot into the copse on the right of the fairway.

"Bugger," he thought. "That was a good ProV that was." He made his way towards the copse with a worried look on his face.

He knew that this particular copse was a bit on the thick side and the chances of getting his expensive ball back were a bit slim.

He pushed his way past the first of the smaller trees and started to root about with his 9 iron. There was no sign of the ball but, as he looked further into the gloom he notices a small sliver of light.

"What the bloody hell is that?" he breathed. He peered towards the light and slowly made his way forward, his golf club held in front of him like a sword. He could make out the dim shadow of a shed that was very hard to see, pretty well camouflaged with branches and bracken, some of which had fallen away from one of the walls. This was where the light was coming from, a chink in the boards.

He moved closer for a better look. He was able to get his fingers into the small crack and force the weak timber slat to one side, improving his view of the inside of the shed.

"Bloody hell," breathed Jonny, "will you look at that."

He could feel the warm air from the heaters at each end of the shed and, in the light of the spot lamps shining from the roof beams he could make out the numerous, verdant rows of very healthy cannabis plants.

"Got the bastard," he thought as he pulled more slats aside enabling him to get his head inside the shed.

"I knew he was up to something and this looks big. Our Mr Jones must be on a tidy earn. Well, he wanted a word with me last night so now I'm ready to have to have a nice chat with him," he thought, mentally calculating how much he should sting him for.

Best went to the door and saw it was fastened with a sturdy padlock. The hasp wasn't so sturdy though and he managed to prise it off with the handle of his club. He pulled open the door and went into the shed to get a closer look. He examined the plants more closely, feeling the soft leaves between his fingers and then sniffing them.

The hum of the fans deadened the sounds of the stealthy footsteps behind him

Curtice opened up the back door of the kitchen ready for the early delivery of his supplies. Tom was already there getting one of the golf carts from the buggy storage enclosure. They both jumped as the door slammed open, both looking as though they shouldn't be there.

"Bon jour Tom," he said hurriedly.

"Sorry eef I frighten you only I am a beet late an' I zink I 'eard ze van with ze supplies."

"Hi Curt," replied Tom. "Yeah, well I'm a bit early as well. I was supposed to be giving a lesson at 8:00 but, no show. Now I'll be at it all day stocktaking for Mark." He paused, raised his eyebrows and added, "Bacon butty would be good."

"Ten meenutes, OK?" replied the chef.

"Perfect," said Tom. He backed the buggy out and shouted over his shoulder, "See you in ten."

He drove the buggy round to the front of the pro shop and parked it up. The shop lights were on and the door was already open. "Bloody hell, he's early," he thought.

Pushing his way into the shop he saw Mark disappearing into the stockroom. "Morning Mark," he shouted.

"Who's that?" was the muffled answer from the stockroom.

"It's me, Tom."

Mark's head appeared, looking a bit sheepish. "You're early," said Mark's head."What's up?"

"You're the second one complaining about me being early. What are you looking so jumpy about?"

"I thought you might have been someone else. Anyway, you can go and get some bacon butties now you're here."

Brian Fordham had been awake most of the night thinking of what he had heard from the drunken Jonny. He tossed and turned throughout the night, earning an earful of abuse from Jill, his wife. She was already up, disturbed by Brian's mumbling and his spinning round in the bed like a pig on a spit.

Brian got up out from under the covers, scratched himself thoroughly, donned his dressing gown and made his way downstairs to the kitchen. The smell of toast and coffee perked him up and he went over to Jill and gave her a peck on the cheek, grabbing a piece of toast in one movement.

"What was wrong with you last night?" she said grumpily. "I didn't get any kip with you spinning, coughing, muttering and farting."

"It's that bloody lager," said Brian, spluttering crumbs of toast as he spoke, trying to decide on how much he should tell her. "It always makes me fart."

"Who were you with?"

"I was having a good old chinwag with Jonny, as a matter of fact and he was telling me about something that might be worth a few quid."

"To him or to you?"

Brian was thinking fast. He mustn't tell her too much or she'll have it all over the women's section. She always liked to think that she knew what was what at the club and if she found out about the buyout she'd have the scoop of all scoops and the money wouldn't matter. She wouldn't be able to help herself. There'd be no brown envelope for anyone if the word got out.

He knew she would love to sell Besty down the river, or grass him up, or whatever the damn term was, to put him behind bars. Jill had always said he was a barrow boy and would have a bad ending; and she had heard the rumours about his visits to the lap dancing bar as well as tinkering with that slut, Janice Blezzard.

She didn't like Brian associating with Best in case some of that tinkering rubbed of on him."

"To him and to us," said Brian. "We'll both make a few quid."

Jill's ears pricked up."How much?"

"Enough for that cruise you keep looking at every Sunday morning."

"What cruise?" said Jill, just a bit too hurriedly.

"Oh I've seen you with the travel supplement every Sunday, drooling over that Caribbean Cruises page."

"That much? A cruise worth? It'll be over two thousand each you know. Is it worth that much?"

"Maybe," said Brian. "Maybe."

"A Caribbean Cruise, eh? Wait 'til I tell that bunch of snobby sods down there. They'll be as jealous as buggery."

"I knew it," he thought. "Her big mouth will drop us all in the shit."

"Listen," he growled. "Just you keep your trap shut at the club until I get my hands on the dosh or there won't be any cruise."

"What do we have to do to get all that much money?" she asked.

"You have to do nothing, except keep quiet about it. I'll do what has to be done and I'm not telling you what it is 'til we're on the boat."

Jill went to the fridge and opened the door. "Do you want some bacon on that toast?" she said with a large grin on her face.

"Bloody hell, she's positively purring," he thought. "I might just have a few beers later on and then go down to the 'Pole Cats Bar'. I've not been down there for a bit – might be some new blood."

"I'll be late tonight, love," he said casually. "I've got a couple of meetings to organise."

"Meetings?"

"Oh yes, I need to nail Besty down and it'll take a bit of doing."

"A bit of doings at Pole Cats' sounds good to me," he said to himself.

Himself said, "You can't afford 'Pole Cats'."

"Oh, I can now," he said to himself, aloud.

"You can what now?" said Jill, putting the bacon toasty in front of her husband.

Brian looked up, smiling and said, "I can now? Oh, yes . . . . I can now get my hands on a few quid and we can now have that voyage up the Nile that you've always fancied."

"Ees zere any news about Best?" asked Curtice. He had just brought a full English breakfast to one of the early morning players and was returning to the kitchen when he passed Larry at the bottom of the main stairs.

"How do you mean, news?" said Larry. "Why should there be news?"

"Ee's been meesseen seence last night," said Curtice. "an' ees wife, she 'as been on sree times an' zee police has also phone. Zey 'ave got two uniform neekneeks out zere askin' questions, makeen' ze members nerveeous."

"Neekneeks? What the hell's a neekneek?" said the puzzled Larry.

"Neekneek, eets what John calls ze police weez ze uniform. Ee weel neek you eef you do naughty theengs."

"Neek?"

"Oui, neek. Like I am goin' to neek you for speedin'. Arrest an' lock you up een ze neek."

"Oh, nick. Right, two uniformed officers, right." Larry shook his head in wonder.

"Pidgin English and slang; very hard to get the hang of," he thought. "That bloody crew at the corner of the bar do it on purpose."

He was quiet for a few more seconds. "Well Besty was a bit pissed when he left last night. Have they been to see Juicy?"

"Oo would 'ave zee balls to tell Beryl Best zat her 'ubby has been ze top customair down ze 'Pole Cats'," Curtice paused, and added with a grin, "Zee Best customair, if you'd excuse ze pun."

"But that's the first place they should look. Anyway, what the bloody hell do you know about puns?"

Larry went over to the phone and picked up the receiver. "Frenchmen. Puns. Bleedin' hell. What next?" he thought. "I'll phone the fuzz and tell 'em," he said out loud.

Curtice followed him and said, "You're sure you kanow what you doeen'? Geteen eenvolved wiz zis affair could end een ze tears eef you get eet wrong. Ee'z only meessin, not dead."

"Dead, that's a bit severe . . . . Dead, eh? Yeah, you're probably right; it's Besty we're talking about. Why would he be dead? He'll just have been out shaggin' and daren't go home now he's sober." He put the phone down and started to tidy up the bar

"I saw eem las' night when I was putteen' out ze beens. Ee was arguween weeth Mark an' hafter weez Chrees Jones. Zey was very hangry." said Curtice. "Meestair Best went out ze gate very queek and Mark, 'e stamp off een ze, 'ow you say, 'uff. Chrees was hangry too, waveen' an' shouteen' at eez car."

Curtice went back to the kitchen without further comment. He couldn't help thinking of the previous night in the car park.

There was a quiet knock on the secretary's door.

"Come in," barked a harassed voice, soon to be more harassed.

"Hello Charles, can I have a word?" said Fordham as he pushed the door closed behind him.

"I'm a bit busy at the minute, can it wait?"

"Not really," said Brian as he pulled up a chair. Charles was not happy with this body language. It didn't auger well.

"Well," he said apprehensively, fearing bad news. "What can I do for you?"

"I had a long chat with Jonny Best last night and he shared some very disturbing news."

"News?"

"Well, it was news to me," said Brian. "It's not news to you, obviously. I believe he has accused you and others of cheating the club members out of a considerable amount of money. Not only that, you are selling the club down the river to that Jordan Developments guy."

"What? . . . It's a damn lie," blustered Charles.

"Well why is he getting a large brown envelope off you lot then? There's no point in denying it, he's given me all the technicalities and the more you waste my time denying it the less time you will have to convince me not to report you, to the club and the cops."

"Ooohh noo..!" groaned Charles, cradling his head in his hands. "Not you as well. It's getting like a bloody Whitehall farce this lot."

"Look Charles, lets keep this simple, eh? I know that there's a load of money at stake here and to be fair Jonny has already offered me some of his brown envelope. A good pal, see, wants to share his good fortune with his best mate."

"Oh, well that's OK then. What do you want here then if Best is sharing with you." His face brightened a bit, just a bit.

"Ah well that's just the thing, y'see, it's not OK. The tight bastard only offered me £5,000."

"Five grand? That's a lot of money, isn't it?" said Charles a bit too brightly, hoping that Best had kept the true figures low so he didn't have to give too much of his share to Fordham.

"Mmmm... There's the problem, y'see. Yesterday, I'll agree, it was a lot of money, but today . . ."

Brian sucked his teeth dramatically. "Y'see Jonny made the mistake of telling me how much he was getting. He was a bit pissed, you understand, and, y'know what he's like, he couldn't help boasting about how he caught you clever buggers out. Fiddling the club members, eh? Your friends and your colleagues. Bad lads, you are. I can see it now. Court, judge, jury, chains, jail, Big Harry's bitch."

Blezzard's heart sank. He had a brief vision of the meeting he would have to call with Snape, Jordan, Vaughan and that gobby sod, Best. They'll kill him, then they'll kill Best, then they'll kill Fordham."

He immediately thought of the other mystery investors that Vaughan had mentioned,

"And if our lot don't kill us, they probably will," he thought. "Whoever they are, they didn't sound a very attractive bunch."

"I'm going to have to talk to the others about this," he said, pulling himself together. "I'm sure we can give you a bit more than five thousand," he said hopefully.

"Well you better talk to them quickly 'cause if I'm going to have to report you I'll have to do it tomorrow."

"Why tomorrow?"

"Well if I don't report you by then, the timing will show I knew about it. There were witnesses to Besty's confession last night."

"Witnesses?" wailed Charles.

"Don't worry, they couldn't have overheard what we were actually saying but they'll have known it was important and they may put two and two together. I could be implicated in your plot whether I get paid or not. So, tomorrow afternoon should be enough time to get the mafia together and organise that 'bit more' than five grand. One hundred and forty five grand more, in fact. Just like your cut. No less. Get it?"

"Blezzard slumped back into his chair. "A hundred and fifty?" He groaned and slumped even further. "Yes, I get it."

"Good, I'll wait for your call."

"Do you know where that big-mouthed bum is?" asked Charles.

"Why would I know? He'll probably be at home, tucked up with Beryl. Making plans for spending his loot, thinking he only needs to give me five grand probably. Well I've saved him five grand, haven't I?"

"He's not at home. He's missing, didn't get home last night. The cops are out looking for him."

"Missing? Well he was a bit pissed when he left," said Brian. "In fact, I seem to remember saying he was thinking of getting down to see Juicy Lucy, his favourite hooker at 'Pole Cats'."

"You'd better try and locate him and I'll get hold of the others. I'll get back to you later today."

Fordham left the office as Blezzard picked up the phone. He was smiling. Smiling a very wide smile.

"We've got a problem," said Charles into the receiver, the earpiece already some inches from his ear, in anticipation of the storm that was sure to follow.

"Fordham, the house chairman, has managed to get the full story out of Best,"

"What? Why the hell would he spill the beans to the house chairman?" growled Jordan.

"Well Fordham is Best's golfing buddy, best pal in fact."

"And what sort of problem would that cause?" Jordan was unnervingly calm. "Is he going share with his buddy or to report it to the cops?"

"No, he's not going to the police – yet. He wants the same share, one hundred and fifty thousand – or else."

The earpiece now needed more airspace between it and Charles' ear as the mention of money stirred up a verbal cyclone. He listened to the tirade of abuse that seemed to go on for minutes, marvelling on the ability of the ranter to rage on at such rapidity and volume for so long without the need to draw breath. He also noted that the quantity of the words used to express Jordan's displeasure could have been halved by just removing one verb, sometimes in the form of an adjective, past and present. "It seems that coitus is very much a part of Jordan's make up," mused Charles as he waited for a break in the verbal assault.

"I know," said Charles, finally able to detect a slight pause, "but he is demanding a decision today or he's going to spill the beans tomorrow, to the club first and then to the police. I said we would meet this afternoon."

"Find that bastard Best," yelled Jordan. "And get his greedy pal there as well. We'll be there at two o'clock, me and Jerry. Make sure they're there." He paused slightly, mid rant and said slowly, "So we can explain the real facts of life to them."

"We don't know where he is," moaned Charles. "And I've got a bad feeling about it. The police have been called in 'cause he's been missing since last night." He paused, suddenly having a horrible thought. "You don't know anything about his disappearance, do you?"

"How the fuck do I know where he is?" screamed Jordan, "He's your fucking Martian, not mine."

"OK, OK, keep your hair on. We'll find him and we'll all be here at two o'clock."

Charles hung up, waited a few minutes, then picked up the receiver and dialled another number.

"Arthur," said Charles, not sure whether he would get the same reception he got from Jordan to the news, "It's me Charles. I'm afraid another problem has cropped up, similar to that raised by Best."

"Best's blabbed to someone else, hasn't he?"

"How do you know that?" said Charles. "I've only just told Jordan, and that was immediately after the person he blabbed to left here."

"I just feared he might, you know what he's like after he's had a couple of pints. But I must admit, I thought that Jordan's threat would keep him quiet."

"Well it seems I've added insult to injury as far as Jordan is concerned. I've just insinuated that he might know about Best's disappearance and he flew even further off the handle than he already was, if that's possible."

"Whose disappearance?"

"Best's. He's been missing since last night. He left here pissed and was seen driving off in a bit of a hurry. No one's seen him since."

"Bloody hell," breathed Snape into the phone. "You don't think ....?"

"Nah, he's just missing. Probably run into a ditch somewhere, hopefully."

"Well, it would solve the problem of his share, I guess," said Snape. We'd be able to give it to Fordham, eh?"

"Hang on old chap, murder or any kind of death isn't on our agenda, accidental, self inflicted or otherwise. You can't use murder as a convenient fiscal solution. That's what the bloody Mafia is famous for and we can't start knocking off every member who finds out about this." Charles paused. "They're famous for that as well, come to think of it."

"You're right," mused Snape, looking distractedly out of the window. "I suppose if Best starts yapping to that floozy at the knocking shop, half of the members will be battering down our door looking for their cut. We'd have to stand them in a line and use a bloody Gatling gun to get shut of them. Have you checked out whether he's at 'Pole Cats'?"

"He shags there, he doesn't live there," said Charles, getting really stressed, "just like all the other buggers who should know better. I can't believe the number of our members that go there. Don't they think they're not going to get found out? Talk about crapping and doorsteps. Kevin Basset lives two doors down from the front entrance, for Christ's sake. His missus passes it every day to get to the supermarket . .   how she's not spotted him . . . She must be soddin' blind."

"I think you'll find she is, Charles. That'd explain the Labrador and the white stick, maybe?"

"Jesus, you're a cruel bastard, Arthur. It's not a blind dog and the stick is a walking stick. She's just stupid."

"Whatever; just try your best to find Best ... and get him here this afternoon. We'll have to get that Jordan to pay up and shut up quickly or we'll have to ditch the plan and "find" the mistake in the accounts."

"What? Give up. Bollocks, I've got plans matey, life-changing plans and I'm not giving them up that easy," said Charles, thinking of his new life in Thailand. "I'll get him here and you can forget about giving up the plan."

CHAPTER 7

- Snotty breaks the rules -

"Help, murder, murder...!!!"

A dishevelled looking figure came running through the front door into the corridor followed by a small terrier. He was dressed in a combat jacket belted at the waist and he had a red beret perched on his head like a refugee from a Dad's Army Parachute Regiment.

The dog was dressed in a collar.

The dishevelled figure burst into the gent's lounge looking wildly around, trying to catch his breath, which was some ten yards in front of him. The dog was barking loudly and the few members that were in the bar stood and stared open mouthed at this blatant breach of the club dress code and the rules concerning dogs, barking or non-barking.

The spell was broken by the President, Gordon Major, who had called in for a lunchtime tipple, dressed in his usual striped blazer.

"I say, Smithson, what's the meaning of this? Get that bloody dog out of here and take your hat off inside the clubhouse. You know the rules."

Smithson finally caught up with his breath and repeated his earlier speech. "Help, murder, murder, bloody bugger.....!"

"Yes, yes," said Major, "that's all very well. But, I mean to say, a bloody barking dog? It's not done, old boy."

"Snotty, he found the body," said an indignant Keith Smithson, ignoring the President's protests about the club's dress code. "The body that look's very much like the Greens Chairman, Best. Jonny Best, greens. I'm not too sure, you understand, but it looked very much like Best's shape to me, and his arm."

"His arm?"

"Yes, his arm. In that copse beside the third fairway." He looked over at Jayne, "Give me a drink, anything. A drink, quick!" he gasped. "In that copse beside the third fairway. Give me a drink," he repeated, "c'mon. Quick."

Jayne rushed over to the optics and put a double measure of brandy into a goblet as they all stood staring at the shabby, beret clad harbinger of death, accompanied by his yapping dog.

Keith grabbed the glass with a shaking hand and gulped it down in one.

He smacked his lips loudly and then put the glass on the floor in front of Snotty who began to lick at the drops with gusto, chasing the goblet around the floor in order to get every last dreg.

Gordon Major was appalled.

"Can you believe that," he spluttered, disgusted by the dog licking the glass and Smithson's disrespectful failure to remove the offending beret. He was just about to start on the combat jacket when a shocked Jayne interrupted.

"Murder." she wailed. "I can't believe it, a murder on the course. We'd better call the police."

"Never mind the blasted murder, he's still got his hat on," shouted Major, "and that dog's getting pissed."

"What's going on down here?" said Charles bursting in to the lounge. "And what's that bloody dog doing in the clubhouse barking his nuts off?" He looked closer at Snotty. "Is he drinking?" Charles was as dumbfounded as the President.

"Yes, he is," yelled the now apoplectic President. "What are you going to do about it?"

"Me? I'm not a bloody sheriff. I'm a secretary. I take minutes of meetings, write letters, open the post and all that."

"Well, it's not stopped you interfering before. You're always writing to members telling them they've broken some bloody bye law or something."

"Well you're a President, a Major by name. You could arrest the bugger."

"What, arrest him for wearing a beret?" said Harold Jarvis, Major's drinking buddy. "Seems a bit harsh."

"Stop it you two. Jonny Best's body's been found out on the course," said Jayne quickly. "Snotty found it."

"Jesus," said Charles. "Hang on, how did Snotty know it was Jonny and, how did he manage to tell you? He's hardly Lassie. I know Lassie seemed to be able to make some of his pleas for help understandable. Skippy was good as well. But Snotty?"

"I was with him you stupid twat," shouted Smithson, now fully caught up with his breath and getting angry at this turn of events. "I saw him dig up this bloody arm and try to drag it off, but it was attached to something."

Keith's demeanour changed from anger to horror.

"It turned out to be the rest of his body. Before I could stop him Snotty scratched away more of the soil and suddenly Best's bloody face was looking up at me. And I can assure you I wasn't swearing when I said bloody. It was bloody, very bloody."

"There were two coppers in here asking about Best this morning." said Larry. "They said he'd been missing all night. Where are they now?"

"Probably still in the back with the sausage butties they'd asked for," said Jayne.

"Go and get 'em, now." said Charles.

Jayne rushed through to the kitchen searching for the two constables and Charles rushed upstairs to tell Arthur Snape.

"I've never seen anything like it, a white face covered in blood wearing a very surprised look, and an arm sticking up in the air where my poor little dog tried to dig it out," said Smithson pointing at Snotty. "Poor little bugger was well disappointed. He probably thought he had found the best bone ever. I won't be able to sleep tonight, nor will he."

"Here," said Larry, "have another drink."

He had poured another brandy, a single. Keith Smithson took the glass, this time with a steadier hand, and said, "This is a single. A bloody single, after what I've been through?"

Larry took the glass back and put another shot in it. Keith accepted the new measure with a faint smile on his lips, sank it in one and put the glass on the floor again in front of the waiting Snotty.

Two uniformed constables rushed into the room, Constable Pete O'Hara already talking on his radio. "..... dog found a body, thinks it's Best." he paused, listening to the muffled, crackly voice responding.

"No sir, not the dog, the owner of the dog. The dog owner seems to think it's Best," he said slowly and patiently, raising his eyebrows skywards. "Yes sir, right away."

He looked around at the occupants of the room and then down at the dog who was still licking around the brandy goblet enthusiastically, wagging its little tail as he chased it around the floor.

"Is that dog drinking?" he asked.

Then, looking up at the blazered president he shook his head and said, "What kind of golf club is this? I've not even seen dogs in any golf club I've ever been in. And drinking?"

He grabbed his colleague by the arm. "Come on Trev, we've just been ordered to secure the area." He turned to Keith and said, "Where's this body then?"

"What're you looking at me for, I'm not going out there again," said Keith. "I'm going to have nightmares for weeks as it is."

"I'll take them," said Frank Dobson, who had, until that moment, been stunned into inactivity. He was one of the elders of the club and he thought he had seen everything until then.

"Come on, follow me."

Frank and the two constables trooped out of the door of the lounge, along the corridor and out the front door, just missing Brian Fordham taking the stairs up to the offices two at a time. He knocked on Snape's door and heard a, 'Wait a minute, I'm on the phone,' shouted, so he walked over to the snooker room where he was met by smiling Jayne, tucking her blouse into her belt as she headed back downstairs. Inside he found Vinny just setting up the balls for a game of snooker.

"Fancy a game Brian?" asked Vinny.

"No thanks, I'm waiting to see Arthur Snape"

"Heard about your pal, have you?" asked Vinny.

"He won't be far," replied Brian. "Probably got a lock-in with Lucy," he added with a wink.

"Lock-in? Don't think you're up to date, mate. He's brown bread."

"Brown bread?"

"Brown bread, dead," said Vinny, forgetting that many of the golf club hierarchy were unfamiliar with rhyming slang.

"Dead? You're joking."

"Well I'm not sure we're on the same wavelength on what constitutes a joke Brian. But I have just heard that Besty is DEAD. Murdered."

Brian sat down, stunned.

"When?"

"Apparently Smithson's dog has just dug him up."

"Snotty? Dug up a body. He's not much bigger than a cat. How would he dig up a bleedin' body?"

Vinny looked up from the table where he was about to break off the recently racked balls. He regarded Brian with a baleful stare.

"Are you doing this on purpose or are you really that dim? The dog discovered the body. He didn't actually dig him up and drag him back to the club."

"Bloody hell, bloody hell," groaned Brian sinking his head into his hands.

Vinny shrugged and started to practice, breaking up the reds with a crash.

Snape had just got through to his old pal Denis Cope, Captain of neighbouring Ashington, a nine-hole course with attitude (pretending to be a proper full sized course by manipulating the tee positions). He was also the Assistant Commissioner of the County.

"AC, old chap. How's it going?"

"Don't you start with the AC/DC shit," said Cope. "The whole force is at it. It's not going to help my application for commissioner if everyone is seen to be equating my initials to some seventies heavy metal rock band is it?"

"All right, sorry about that," said Arthur. "I've just this minute heard that a body's been found on the course and it appears to be Jonny Best, our greens chairman."

He looked over at Charles, hoping that the bloody fool had given him accurate information. He knew he had to act fast to try to defer some of the inevitable investigation away from their gigantic fraudulent land grab.

"Who? Best, not that bugger who's been having it off with the Chinese imports?" asked Denis.

"Yep, that's the feller," said Snape. "Or *was* the feller." He lowered his voice to almost a whisper. "I'd like to try to make sure that any investigation into his demise is made aware of his tricky dealings with the pro here, and that Chinese mob from Leeds."

"Well I can certainly sow some seeds, but the boys on the front line will be asking lots of questions as you would expect in a murder enquiry."

"I know that, but I have got something brewing here that's worth a few quid and, you know me Denis, I am good at gratitude. So do your best, eh."

"I'll see what I can do," said Denis. "Problem is there's something that's not right about that Mr Wu and he's attracted interest from our spooks. They won't want their water muddying with efficient murder investigating." Cope paused, "In fact, I know just who to assign this job to. Leave it with me."

Arthur put the receiver down and turned to Charles. "I hope you're right about this. If you are it means that the extra payoff that Jordan is fretting about is now out of the way."

"Never mind about that. What did you mean about Best and the Chinese mob from Leeds?" asked Charles.

"Oh, I've been on to that for ages," laughed Arthur, "Silly bugger thought he could fool me but I knew it would come in useful."

"Knew about what?"

"He's been importing hooky copies of clubs and all sorts golf gear from China and selling them all over the North West through Mark Norton. The guy he's dealing with, though, looks a right villain. Chinese, but big and mean looking. Got a strange tattoo too."

"What? Tutu? He's got a tutu?"

"No, a tattoo, you moron. Ink in skin, with needles, saying 'I love mum', worn by sailors and convicts ......"

"Moron? Don't you call me a moron," bristled Charles. "And why didn't you report him?"

"Oh, calm down. I had no proof and I had to be sure. It's a serious accusation to make about a fellow member of a gentleman's club," said Arthur with a frowning disapproving look on his face. He was beginning to enjoy this, seeing a number of ways out of what first appeared to be a tricky situation. He was intending to nail Best with the facts and get himself a nice rake-off. He was glad he had waited now.

"Go and shout that dimwit Fordham in," he said.

Just as Charles made for the door, it burst open and Jordan barged in looking as serious as when he had left the previous day.

"I've just seen two coppers rushing out onto the course and I can hear sirens everywhere," he said.

Vaughan came in right behind him, "What's going on? The car park is filling up with squad cars and vans. There's police all over the place."

"You go and get Fordham," said Arthur to Charles. "We need him in here fast."

When Charles left the room he said, "Best is dead, murdered."

"What, dead as in not alive?"

"Definitely not alive. Fordham can have his share now, so you don't need to get to your other investors for more payoff money, do you?" smiled Arthur.

"You're a bit late there, old chap," said Jordan, darkly. "I've already told them about Best and Fordham and I can tell you, they were not very happy. I can't promise you that Fordham will be in the mix much longer if he doesn't behave. Or maybe he'll be in the mixer."

Arthur swallowed and said "It seems that your associates might have been a bit too hasty. The last thing we want is the police all over the place. However, I've got a good connection in the force and I think I've given them a good lead as to who may be responsible for Best's death, whoever it really was. If any more bodies turn up though, then that motive will no longer stack up and any further enquiries could unearth some embarrassing facts."

"Just a minute," said Jerry Vaughan, "Don't you insinuate we're to blame. We had nothing to do with Best's death. We're not the 'Costa Brava' sending fishes and horses's heads to anyone that doesn't agree with us."

"Costa Brava?"

"Yes, those Brazilians that practice Umberto and who rub out all their opponents when they break the Umberto."

"You mean Cosa Nostra, Sicilians and omerta, you berk. Didn't you read The Godfather?"

"No, but I saw the film and I know what I heard," said Jerry, sulking.

"Shut it Jerry," said Dave, "I'll handle this. Our associates haven't got any horses to spare but, they can be a bit naughty. However, now that the deed is done, whoever did it, let's move on. Let's clear up the rest of the deal before the feds start on us. Where's this Fordham?"

"Where's me trolley," wailed Derek.

"Bloody hell, Derek," laughed Alan, "we're going to have to lash you to that thing."

They all looked around. Only three trolleys could be seen. On the left was water, but that would mean the trolley would have had to cross the fairway and one of them would have noticed that.

"It must have headed for freedom, into the copse," said Mike. "Come on, we're heading that way 'cos your ball's gone in there as well."

The four of them trudged off down the fairway following the three trolleys. They got to the copse and started to root about in the undergrowth.

"It can't have gone that far in," said Derek.

"No, but your ball can," said Dermot. "I assume you are putting as much importance to the ball as the trolley."

"It's a new ball," said Derek, huffily.

"Here's your trolley," shouted Mike.

"Right, just the ball to find now," said a relieved Derek.

They tramped around thrashing at the undergrowth and Dermot spotted a shape that he was not expecting.

"Is that a shed over there?" he said to Alan.

Mike came over and joined them. "A shed? When did that get put up then?" They moved closer. "That shouldn't be there," said Alan.

They looked at each other as they heard more thrashing to their left, followed by the figure of Derek emerging backwards into the clearing.

"Looks like I've lost it, but looking on the bright side I've just found three more," he said with a smile. "Got me trolley as well." He stopped as his three pals looked back towards the shed. "What are you lot looking at?"

"That shed," said Alan. "It's new. Well, it's not a new shed but, it's not been there very long and it looks a though someone has gone to a lot of trouble to camouflage it as well."

"How often do you get in here then?" Mike asked, turning to go, fast losing interest in the joys of the woods. "How d'yer know it hasn't been there for years?"

"'Cause I've been in here loads of times with my slice. Not this deep, you understand, but deep enough to have noticed a shape that big," said Alan. "I'm going to have a closer look."

He moved forward, followed by Dermot.

Derek followed Mike back to the fairway, happy with his haul of balls and his recovered trolley.

"Bloody hell!!! .... Fuck, fuck ..., a body. Call the police."

The shout came from where Dermot and Alan had delved further into the trees, where they had been intent on inspecting the shed.

Mike and Derek turned back into the trees. They followed the cursing and swearing of their two pals, now much quieter, and burst into a small clearing next to the shed to see them staring at the ground in front of them. They saw at an arm raised in a silent salute and they joined in the open-mouthed silent screams of their two pals.

"Is that a dead body or someone who's just fainted?" said Derek, finally breaking the shocked silence. He was furthest away from the object of their attention and hadn't really focussed fully on it.

"Fainted?" said Mike, looking at Derek as though he was a half-wit. "He's half buried. Blood all over the place and half buried. If he's just fainted, how's he got half buried? "

"I ain't no expert mate, but that looks like a dead body to me," said Alan, who had been staring at it a bit longer than the others. "Not only that, it's Jonny Best.

"Jonny Best? It can't be," said Derek. "We saw him going home last night, looked a bit pissed, but otherwise, right as rain. It seemed like only hours ago."

"He must have got a bit lost to finish up here," said Mike.

"And he must have banged his head, look at all that blood," said Dermot.

"Well, he must have known what was going to happen," said Alan, a bit sarcastically really, "'cause he buried himself as well."

"Didn't make a very good job of it, did he," said Mike.

"S'murder, isn't it?" said Dermot quietly, bringing them all back to serious.

"Well done Sherlock." It was the sarcastic Alan again.

They suddenly heard voices and the cracking of twigs and branches behind them.

"Fuck me, I hope that's not the killer coming back," whispered Mike.

"Killers, there's more than one of them," said Alan. "Quick get yourselves a weapon." Mike and Alan were already armed with a golf club each so Derek and Dermot got behind them. They backed slowly away from the noisy intruders, the first of who suddenly appeared into view.

"Frank, thank fuck, it's Frank," whispered Mike, recognising the old comps chairman.

Alan looked at Mike. "Wait a minute; he could be one of the killers." They all retreated another step. "We need the cops," he added. "And me mobile's in me bag, on me trolley."

Frank's two companions loomed into view just as Dermot took a step too far. "Aaarggh," yelled the stumbling Dermot.

That step too far resulted in his tripping over the raised hand of the recently deceased Best. The outstretched hand appeared to grab Dermot by the leg. That vision accompanied by his terrified scream threw them all into further panic and they dispersed in a frenzied dash in opposite directions trying to escape from the zombie that had suddenly come back to life.

It was later pointed out to the two constables by their apoplectic DI that this burst of frenetic activity completely ruined what had previously been a fairly tidy crime scene A scene, until then, spoiled only by the obvious signs of the dog's discovery of the body.

CHAPTER 8

- Keystone Kops –

"Where is it?" asked the Detective Inspector.

"Out in the bushes, over there Guv," said the sergeant.

They were standing in the car park at the rear of the club. There were already six squad cars, three paddy wagons and an unmarked coroner's ambulance lined up together with three other saloon cars that DI Hedly had recognised immediately. DS Clowes's Mini was there in prime position and he recognised the black Saab belonging to the pathologist parked next to it. The other one belonged to DC Ghosh.

"Where's Alco?"

"If you mean DC Hollis," said DS Clowes, "I'd be guessing that he wouldn't be too happy with the Alco Hollis tag or the inferred meaning of the nickname."

"Right, right. But where is he?"

"Not here yet Guv."

"And why not?"

"He was at a funeral yesterday, if you remember," said Clowes. "His grandmother, if you remember, Very cut up about it, if you remember."

"Oh yeah, I remember now." Hedly paused. "That was in the afternoon. This is the next morning and there's a murdered body out there that needs attending to. You know, questions and stuff. The stuff we have to do, like find out what happened to him and bring his killer or killers to justice."

"I hope that's not sarcasm that's creeping in there sir," said Clowes. "The speech, I mean. Only I don't think Hollis will respond too well to that sort of attitude, given the circumstances."

"Oh, yeah, and what response should there be? I'll tell you shall I. 'Yes sir', is what he'll say. Followed by, 'Right away Guv', if he knows what's good for him."

"If he's had the kind of skin-full that he usually has at weddings, funerals and suchlike, he will not respond well to sarcasm or, for that matter, reasoned argument," said DS Clowes, "You remember the last time you tried to pull rank."

"Wait a minute; I do, now that you mention it. It was, let me see, his grandmother's funeral. Yes, that's it, his grandmother. She's not risen from the dead and died again, has she?"

"I think that probably counts as sarcasm as well, sir." She paused for a heartbeat and said, "Look sir, I don't want to bring this up seeing as how you're a senior policeman an' all, but how many grandmothers do you think most people have?"

"Oh, yeah, I see what you mean." said Hedly sheepishly. "Two."

"Gooood ... And what if you are part of a broken home and your mother and father marry again? What if you get adopted? What if ....?"

"Right, right. I get it."

"Given that Hollis qualifies on at least two of those counts I respectfully suggest that you do not mention grandmothers dying and being resurrected. He might take that as extreme sarcasm and then react like he did last time."

"OK, right . . . where's that body?" said Hedly quickly.

"This way sir."

They walked off towards the copse where they could see a number of uniformed officers rooting half heartedly in the bushes. The copse was ringed by bright yellow and black striped tape fluttering in the soft breeze, secured at intervals by obliging branches. There was also a path marked out in the same tape leading from the car park to the copse held in place by iron rods driven into the fairway.

They made their way along the designated route and were greeted by Constable Trev Partington, guarding the entrance to the copse. He saluted as the two detectives marched past. They ignored him and went into the crime scene.

"Hello doc," said Hedly, "what's the score. a) The how and b) the when, is what I'm after, followed sharply by c) by the who and d) the where is c) now?" He punctuated his points by dramatically counting them off on his fingers.

The pathologist, Doctor Geraldine Maxwell, looked up from her stooped position, where she had been examining Jonny's remains.

"Score? What's the score?" she said, casting the smartarse DI a withering look.

"Well I suppose its one nil to the bad bastard with the blunt instrument. Or, in your world it's, a) bang on head, b) can't say yet without further tests, but not long ago and, as far c) and d) goes, you lot will have to work that bit out yourselves. That's the bit that you're supposed to do."

Dr Maxwell was a slim, grey haired, bespectacled woman in her fifties, clad in a white plastic SOCO suit. She was not a fan of the Inspector and was the first to spread the word about the circumstances surrounding his promotion.

It seems that it was the whim of a hung-over Commissioner just after his leaving do. He was about to throw this particular candidate's application in the bin when he looked at the initials on the page more closely. He started laughing at the part acronym that formed on the paper. It screamed at him, Detective Inspector Kenneth Hedly.

"This is too good to miss," he said over the phone to his wife. "DI K Head, it's got to be done."

"I've heard all about Hedly off Geraldine," replied his wife. "She says he's useless and he already thinks he's George Gently, that copper on the telly. He'll be unbearable if he's made up to DI."

"I know but it's a perfect present to leave to the force for making me go so early and giving me that crappy clock."

It was done, and before the letter had dropped on Hedly's desk his nickname was all around the North West police fraternity. Geraldine was the first to hear about the appointment from the ex-commissioner's wife and the rest is history.

Before Hedly could think of a rejoinder he was interrupted by a dishevelled figure stumbling into the clearing coughing and spluttering over a half smoked cigarette. The man took a big pull on the stub before flicking the smouldering remains into the hole from which the body had just been removed.

Hedly looked at the crumpled figure and barked, "That's a bloody crime scene Hollis. You've just contaminated it you incompetent moron."

Hollis looked up and glared at Hedly. He took a step towards the Inspector, but before he could reply, the Inspector quickly added, "How did the funeral go?"

Hollis stopped in his tracks. "Okay, as it happens. We were all gutted but we managed to get through the service and once we'd got some booze going, we cheered up a bit."

"Oh good," said Hedly, "And how's your granddad, how's he taking it?"

"Granddad?" Hollis glared at Hedly. "I told you last week, you unfeeling bastard. He was holding the ladder when granny was fixing the loose roof tiles. Remember, the ladder slipped, she fell."

"Oops!" said Clowes, nudging Hedly.

"Well, I'm sorry about that," said Hedly, thinking the nudge was one of encouragement. "Did he get the blame, or something?"

"Blame? She fell on him. We're burying him tomorrow. I told you already, granny yesterday, granddad tomorrow. How the fuck did you make inspector with Alzheimer's?"

"'Scuse me sir," said Annie, grabbing Hollis's arm and dragging him over towards the body that was now laid out beside the makeshift grave, already in an open body bag.

"Just concentrate on the job," she said quietly. "Take no notice of him, he's a moron and the only way we will get shut of him is to get him promoted or demoted."

"That bloody hole looks a better alternative," growled Hollis, now calming down.

"We'd better get the uniforms busy on this and get some statements off the members. Those two Muppets out there have totally wasted the scene so the cigarette you dumped in there won't have the slightest affect on any findings that the CSI team collect. I've already alerted them but they won't find any forensic that hasn't been contaminated before the fag end arrived. C'mon, let's get on with it."

They both turned round and began to make their way out of the copse. Hedly blocked their way and said, "Better get the uniforms to round up the members in the clubhouse. We can get statements off them for starters. Hollis, you can also organise a door to door on the neighbours to see if they heard anything, eh?"

"Door to door?" Hollis asked.

"Yes, door to door. Y'know, procedure. Just follow the procedure. Get plenty uniforms knocking on doors. I'll get the crime scene investigating team down here and we'll go over it with a fine tooth comb."

"Right Guv," said Annie smartly. "We'll get on with it now. C'mon Al, let's do it." Her staged enthusiasm was lost on Hedly but Al Hollis was a smarter beast and he smiled, replying with mock enthusiasm, "Right sarge, let's **do** it."

"Door to Door," said an exasperated Al when they were out of earshot. "Door to fuckin' door. The nearest door, apart from the clubhouse door, is about half a mile away. What the bloody hell does he think they'll have heard? And then the next two nearest doors are on the farmers cottages over by the river bend. Door to Door, they don't just call him dickhead because of his initials, do they?"

There was a bit of a hubbub at the bar as the news of the murder spread. Mike, Alan, Derek and Dermot had already stowed their trolleys away, changed their clothes and made their way into the clubhouse. The number of members that were in there was growing fast and they listened, enthralled, to the various accounts of the discovery of the body and the part each of the discoverers had played. In order to prolong the supply of free drinks, they all played on the trauma of the resulting shock created by the blundering police constables who had been led into the crime scene by the now equally shocked old Frank. Keith Smithson was still there, now the worse for wear with a surfeit of brandy inside him. Snotty was curled up under Keith's chair, snoring in time, and tune, to his master's lead.

Brian Fordham came into the lounge, bumping into the gaudily clad, dreadlocked figure of the Social Secretary, Winston Djemba.

"Yo Briaan," said Winston as he craned his neck to look along the buzzing bar. "Bit of a full 'ouse for a Toosday, innit?"

"You'd better ask that lot of vultures mate," said the glum Brian, as he pushed roughly past Winston, ordered a pint and retreated to the other end of the bar clutching his lager, studying the glass intently. He remembered how he and Jonny had persuaded Winston to put his name forward for council and how they had both reminded the shocked members of the current council that they would be skating on thin ice if he wasn't voted in. "Race relations and all that."

Once he was voted on, he was seconded to Brian's House Committee. "Social Secretary? We'll be having bloody beach parties and reggae nights before you can blink," said Charles Blezzard when he found out.

The memory made him smile but then the thought of his pal, so cruelly murdered, made him sink back into his black mood.

"What am I bothered about?" he said to himself, suddenly brightening up. "I'll be loaded next week. I'll have a drink on him while me and Jill are sailing up the Nile." He took a long pull on his pint. "If he hadn't spilled the beans last night I'd have been mourning as well as poor. Well done Jonny boy."

Winston sidled up to the bar next to the president and tried to catch Larry's eye.

"Can't you find something more appropriate to wear when you're in the club, old boy?" sneered Major, looking down at the lime green trousers and black sandals worn by the social secretary..

Winston could see the enquirer in the mirror behind the bar so he didn't need to turn towards him. His handsome, dreadlocked head towered above the older president and his yellow golf shirt stood out against the striped club blazer. He was used to such attitudes wherever he went and he was not fazed by the likes of Gordon Major.

"D'y meean like Tony, de John Daley fan?" he replied pointing at Tony Burton, a short fat golfer who had just entered the lounge, dressed in a bright orange shirt that topped a psychedelic pair of trousers whose colours were brighter and louder and more vividly fluorescent than any of the brightest on display in the lounge. "Or d'y tink I should get me one of deze stripey jac*kets*?" he added, pointing at the comical president's blazer and stressing the 'kets'.

"Hmmpph . . " The president turned away and rejoined his group, tut-tutting to them about the club going to the dogs.

"Greetings," said Winston finally getting Larry's attention. "Pint of dat lager, innit. What's all de fuss? Place is crawlin' wid de Babylon an' de bar full of cacklin' vultures."

"Babylon?"

"D' Polees, de fuzz, de cops."

"An' vultures?" said Larry, pulling the lager.

"Well, dat's what Briaan jus' call dis lot."

"Oh, he's a bit upset about Jonny."

"Well, we all gets upset 'bout Jonny. What he done now?"

"Done breathing. Dead."

"Wot? Dead?"

"Yep, dead, murdered."

"Well, dat explains d'vultures."

Snotty found the body earlier."

"Wot, de dog foun' de body?"

"Yep. He nearly ate his arm off. He's asleep over there now," said Larry, nodding in the direction of the slumbering dog under the chair of his slumbering master. "A bit pissed actually, so's his owner."

"Pissed?" Winston's eyes followed Larry's nod. "I ain't not been tole about de relaxin' of de annymaals in de bar' byelaws."

"Everybody's a comedian today," said Larry as he turned to attend to another punter.

Mike had phoned Jack and John who both said they were on their way, not wishing to miss all the excitement.

The pro, Mark, had just come in and was ordering a drink. Normally a teetotaller, he broke his habit and ordered a double brandy. He nodded to the dark haired member standing at the bar toying with a large whiskey, recognising him as one of the recently joined newcomers.

"Blimey," said Jayne, "You don't normally have a drink and it's not as though he was a bosom buddy."

"Oh, we were closer than you think," said Mark absently into his drink.

"Who, you and Jonny Best?" said the ex Captain, Harold Jarvis, who had earlier been sat with the President but now at the bar with the rest of the gathered members.

Mark looked up, realising he shouldn't have said that. Well, not like that anyway. "Oh, we weren't that close, you know, but he was a good customer and paid promptly. Not like some," he said meaningfully.

"Hhrumph," hhrumphed the ex Captain, trying to ignore the pointed innuendo. "Well, I didn't think he would be classed as a good anything actually." He paused as he took a sip from his G&T. "Don't want to speak ill of the dead but....."

"You will anyway," sneered Mark. The thought of containers and tattooed Chinese triads was taking over his natural deference to members such as the ex Captain, aware of the damage he could inflict on his career. He gulped down his brandy and kicked away an attentive Snotty who had suddenly revived at the mention of 'double brandy'. He was not a dog to miss a trick where brandy was concerned.

"When did you start allowing dogs in here?" growled Mark before barging past Jarvis and the rest of the members congregated around the main players in the discovery of the dead body. The dark haired new member watches him as he stumbled into the hall, almost knocking the incoming Sergeant Clowes into the notice board mounted on an easel, bearing the results of the monthly raffle.

"Oy, you," barked DC Hollis. "Watch where you're going. You nearly had this defenceless young lady over then."

Mark pulled himself together. "Sorry, I'm very sorry. I've just had a bit of a shock that's all. A very good friend of mine has just been murdered. It's a bit of a shock." He put his hand out to Annie, "No hard feelings, eh."

"A good friend, was he?" asked Annie, ignoring Mark's outstretched hand and reaching into her pocket.

"Well, yes he was," replied the puzzled Mark, miffed at her failure to take the proffered hand. "Not that it's any business of yours." His mood was darkening again and this cheeky doris who had rebuffed his friendly gesture was not making it any lighter.

"Well, that's where you're wrong, old bean," said Annie, holding up her warrant card. "It's very much our business. Where are you off to?"

Mark took a sharp step back, finally knocking over the notice board. "Er, I was on my way to the shop. I'm the club professional and I have work I have to get to this afternoon."

"Righty Ho," said Annie. "Just make sure you don't go sloping off. We need to get an interview room set up here and when we do we'll want a word; especially with the victim's friends."

"And enemies," added Hollis.

Mark bolted for the door, leaving the notice board where he had knocked it.

"He's up to something," said Hollis. "He's one we want to know about."

"Right, let's find who's in charge around here." Annie and Al made their way into the bar. Al caught sight of Dave and Jerry hurrying down the stairs and assumed they were a couple of members or even council members. He made a mental note of their faces.

CHAPTER 9

- Alibis and Wakes -

"Ay up, here's trouble," said Derek, recognising the strangers. He didn't know them, but he knew *them*. He knew the type. He knew the type because he had been in the force, many years ago. Made sergeant and that was enough. So he recognised their entrance.

He moved slyly to the back of the group, not wishing to be the first to help. He knew that the first helpful witness in a case such as this would finish up as the acting go-between. "Who's in charge around here? Who's that? Where's this? How do we get that? Can you organise a cup of tea?"

"Who's in charge around here?" asked Hollis.

Before he got an answer to his question, Charles Blezzard rushed in. Having finished his meeting about the Fordham issue, he had been attracted by the racket made by the falling notice board and he had rushed downstairs to investigate.

"What's all that noise about?" he barked.

A real bark answered his bark. Snotty was getting a bit aggressive with the booze.

"Is that bloody dog still here, and why is our notice board all over the hallway? And who the bloody hell are you," he frowned at Annie, "and are you signed in? Guests have to be signed in. There's coppers all over the place and we could get prosecuted if you're not signed in."

Annie's warrant card was still in her hand and she shoved it under Charles's nose.

"We **are** the coppers," she said, smiling. "Who are you?"

"He's in charge," chorused the group at the bar.

"Goody, we'll go somewhere quiet and have a chat then, eh?"

Clowes followed the secretary upstairs to his office and Hollis started giving instructions to O'Hara and Partington, the two blundering constables whose footprints were all over the murder scene.

He outlined the procedure for taking down the particulars of anyone, who was still breathing, who may be wandering around outside for future questioning.

"When I say anyone breathing, I don't mean any dogs, OK?" The two sheepish constables left to find breathing witnesses and Hollis followed Annie and the secretary.

"Bloody hell, this is a bit busy for a Tuesday afternoon," said John Eastham as he walked in. "There must have been a murder, or something."

"How the hell did you know that already?" asked the president. "They've only just found the body an hour ago."

"Jungle drums mate. They say that a Mr Best has been found dead... ," John put a theatrical hand to his ear, as if to listen more clearly, mouthing silent words, making the president wait for the finish, ".... by the side of the third fairway, in a shallow grave. Something about waving goodbye . . . .?"

"Stop it, you twat," said Mike laughing. "What're you having?"

"Jungle drums.....?" Gordon Major was amazed. "I can't hear any bongos. How the hell does he do that?" he asked Frank.

"Come on Gordon," said Frank. "Haven't you got a mobile phone?"

"Ohhh . . . Yes, I see. Never thought of that. No one ever phone's me, y'see."

"Have you given anyone your number?"

"Number? How do you mean?"

"What's your mobile number?"

"I don't know. I didn't know it had a number. Where do I find that, then?"

"Have another glass of wine, eh?" said Frank with a heavy sigh.

"You had better get Jack a G&T as well, I saw his car pull in as I came in the front door." said John to Mike. "What's all this about then?"

"I think we'd better wait for Jack," said Alan, "or we'll have to go through the story twice."

"I'm surprised they haven't got a copper on the front gate," said John. "You'd think it was just like any other day if you just came along for a few holes."

"Well, actually, the detectives only just got here half an hour ago," said Dermot.

"They've only just put the yellow tape up and a guard on the body. The rest of the Keystone mob came haring in and shot round the back like scalded cats. The cops are all over the copse, so to speak, beside the third fairway."

"Har har," laughed John, sarcastically. "Cops by the copse. That's a good 'un. By the third, eh?"

"That's where they found him."

"Yeah, I think that the two detectives who have just gone upstairs with Charles are supposed to be organising them all," said Derek. "And by the way, I think we'll need a bunch of taxis when we go. Y'know, leave cars behind. Bobbies all over the place; nick-nick, geddit?"

"What's been going on?" said a breathless Jack, rushing in to the bar. "There are police all over the place, loads of them. Buggered me off when I tried to park in my usual spot at the back."

"C'mon, let's sit down and we'll bring you up to date," said Alan.

They all collected their drinks and went over to their usual seats by the window to fill the two newcomers in on all the gory details. Tom, the young assistant pro walked over carrying an orange juice as they dragged over extra chairs and arranged themselves around two tables. "Can I join you, lads?" he asked.

"Sure, grab a chair," said John.

"Besty, eh," said John, "who'd have thought it?"

"Lots of people might have thought it," said Mike, "but do it?"

"Well he was always going on about following that green keeper, Jones." said Jack. "I wonder if he finally caught him at something."

"Chris Jones?" said Alan, "Nah. Chris knew Best was always talking about him but he wasn't in the least bit bothered. He said Best was only using that excuse to cover for his visits to the hooker's shop."

"How do you know that?"

"Actually, Winston told me," said Dermot, butting in.

"He's a big buddy of Chris. Seen them together a few times down the Stoat when I've been to watch the footy. Winston said that Besty was trying to catch Jones out at something, wouldn't say what.

But, the last time I saw them in the Stoat I overheard Winston telling Jones to watch out for Jonny, 'keep a low profile, keep your head down', he said. They suddenly changed the subject when they noticed me."

"Strange partnership, though," said Mike. "Chris and Winston Djemba, I mean."

"I suppose Winston goes in there so he can wear his loud shorts and flip-flops without the stares he gets in here. Have you seen his bright green strides?" Dermot nodded towards Winston at the bar. Then, as one, they all spotted Tony Burton and started laughing.

"Yes, but Winston gets stares in the Stoat as well, it get's bloody cold in October an' he's dressed for the Caribbean sun. Must be that dope he's always smoking," said Mike.

"Well it's not allowed in here," said Jack.

"Pot's not allowed anywhere," said John, deliberately misunderstanding to what Jack was referring.

"The shorts and flip-flops, I meant," said Jack, rising to the bait. "I'm not aware of the rules that cover pot."

"I saw Jonny having a row with Chris last night," said Tom.

"When, last night," said Mike, "He was in here last night."

"He was just getting in to his car when Chris grabbed him and they were growling at each other for a minute or so before Jonny jumped into his car and gave it plenty of revs out of the car park. Chris was wavin' his fist after him."

"Well then, there's a bit more on Jones, eh?" said Dermot.

"Can I have your attention please, gentlemen," said Charles from the door of the gent's lounge. "Will you please make yourselves available to the investigating officers and give them full cooperation with their enquiries. We may be here for a while so I've asked Curtice to make sure that none of you go hungry."

"Oh, that's a bit of a shame," said John. "I'll have to go and phone the wife. It looks like her dodgy lasagne might have to go to the dog again. He'll eat anything."

"Bloody hell," said Alan, "does that mean we'll miss 'Strictly Come Dancing'?"

There was a smattering of laughter at Alan's sarcasm. Jayne came over to collect some empties and said, "Don't worry; we normally watch it later when you lot have buggered off.

So you won't miss it. You'll catch it all here while you are waiting to be grilled." she smiled to herself, knowing it wasn't on.

Jayne ignored the groans and started to carry the empties over to the bar. She suddenly turned back to the table. "Don't forget what me and Larry heard, the arguments upstairs I mean."

"Yes, you'd better tell the fuzz all about that," said Jack. "The real version, mind, not the embellished stuff. That might be important. Wouldn't put it past them bastards upstairs to murder poor old Besty."

"Christ, that's two more suspects," said Mike. "You'll have half the club in the clink if you go on like this. And what's all this 'poor ole Besty' bit? He was the perfect victim a minute ago, just waiting to be murdered."

"Just a minute Tom," said Mike, "didn't you say that you thought that Besty was up to something with Mark yesterday?"

"No. I thought that there might be, but I was only guessing. Mark said that he had bought a bit of stuff of him six months ago and he had just asked if he could get more. Cheap refurbished lake balls or something, for the juniors, I think."

"Yeah, but you said something about the Ping rep and stock levels the other day," said Mike.

"I know. But when I asked him about that he just mumbled something about trying to show Paul Groves that he had shifted the last delivery already. He'd just asked me to hide three sets of Ping clubs in the back before Paul had arrived."

"More rumours," said Jack. "All rumours if you ask me. More suspects. Where's it all going to end?"

"Jack, have you found any more information about the accounts?" asked Mike.

"Apart from a brief call to Tony Drummond, no. Although he's just as puzzled as we are about the results. He did say that he had the auditor in to have a butchers but he gave them a clean bill of health."

"Auditor?" said John.

"Harvey Jackson," replied Jack, "works for Prentices."

"Prentices, eh?" said John thoughtfully, rattling the almost melted ice cubes in his empty glass, signalling the need for a refill.

"Right," said DC Hollis, who suddenly appeared at the table.

"Can we have a chat with the four who found him first?"

"Well, to be accurate, it was Keith Smithson over there who found him first," said Dermot, pointing at the fed up Keith and the equally fed up Snotty. "To be even more accurate, it was his dog that dug Besty out. You might need to get yourself a dog whisperer if you want his evidence."

"Is that so?" said Hollis, "The dog, eh? I know just the man for that," he added as he saw Hedly come in to the room.

Annie's phone rang.

She said, "You sort Hedly out and I'll have a chat with this lot when I've got this call."

"Er, phones aren't allowed in the lounge," said John with a sly grin.

Annie stood up and said, "Don't worry; I'm not letting you nosey herberts listen in to police business anyway."

She went to the other side of the room and Hollis walked over to intercept the inspector who was giving the lounge the once-over. "Right sir, we are just about to interview the guy who found the body."

"Who found it?"

"That guy there, with the dog."

"OK," said Hedly, "where are we setting up?"

"Through there in the mixed lounge."

"Mixed? Mixed with what?" said Hedly, obviously puzzled. "I hope this isn't a racist thing."

"Oooh, I'm not sure about that," said Hollis, peering from side to side as though looking for some sign of racism. "Shall I ask around?"

"Yes, but be discreet. One wrong word or phrase and we could find it backfiring. OK, send him in."

"What about the dog?" said Hollis.

"What about him?"

"Do you want him in as well?"

"The dog?"

"He's a material witness sir."

"He is a fucking dog," said the inspector. "Dogs can't give evidence. They break down under cross examination. They also lick their arses in the witness box, distracting the jury."

"I think you'll find, sir," said a Hollis, adopting a patient, condescending, attitude, "that the dog will have to be examined for forensic reasons; hairs, saliva, elimination, etc."

Realising he had fallen into one of Hollis's piss-taking traps and that his outburst of witty, scathing sarcasm had been wasted, he grunted, "Send the dog in with the finder. What's his name?"

"Snotty," said Hollis whilst simultaneously thinking 'gotcha'.

"Snotty?"

"Yessir, Snotty."

It was now dawning on Hedly that Hollis was winning this bout of deliberate verbal misunderstanding and that he should retreat and hopefully get him back another day, or another way.

"All right, send Mr Snotty in to the interview room." He saw the thin triumphant smile on Hollis's face and added, "Tell him to bring the dog as well."

Annie got to the doorway of the lounge and watched Hollis leading Snotty and his owner into the mixed lounge. She beckoned to him and he acknowledged her signal, indicating he would be with her momentarily.

"Where's Hedly, he should be interfering by now?" she said when Hollis joined her.

"He's in there, grilling the guy who found the body," said Hollis, smiling. "He's got the dog as well. That should keep him quiet for a bit."

"Dog?"

"I'll tell you later," said Hollis, laughing. "What next?"

"I've just had a call from pathology," said Annie. "It was this morning and he hadn't been long in the ground. An hour to one and a half hours, she reckons."

"Blimey," said Hollis, "that dog must have thought it was its birthday."

"And they can't have missed the killer by long, eh?"

"Somebody must have seen something. There is some cover but there's also open ground near the car park."

"I've just had a chat with that club secretary," said Annie. "He's very edgy and he's hiding something. I also met the treasurer, a guy called Snape.

He's a bit of a smooth bastard. Cagey, also got something on his mind. What about you? Have you spoken to anyone yet?"

"I was just about to get busy with that tableful of old farts over there," he said, nodding in the direction of the regulars, huddled in deep discussion. "Four of them were the bunch that O'Hara and Partington blundered into."

"OK, let's have a chat with them first."

"One at a time?"

"Nah, we're only starting here and we need to get some background as fast as possible. Hopefully the first finder and his dog will keep Dickhead quiet for a while like you said."

"Now then boys," said Annie, approaching the now crowded table with a friendly smile. "Who were the crew that blundered into the crime scene?"

"Hang on, young lady," bristled Dermot, "it wasn't a bloody crime scene when we were blundering about. It was a lost trolley scene."

"And a lost ProV scene," said Mike. "Very important are lost Pro Vs."

"Provees? What's a provee when it's at home?"

"Three and a half quid each is what it is, Titleist ProV balls. Golf balls," said Dermot. "And Derek doesn't take too kindly to losing them, either."

"You mean that you pay three and a half quid for one golf ball?" asked Hollis.

"Oh, he doesn't pay for them," said Mike," he finds them, but they're three and a half quid's worth when they're new. That's the point."

The two detectives looked at each other. "Were going to have trouble with these," said Hollis. "They must have gone to the same piss taking school I eventually ended up in."

"And they've been at it longer, had more practice," added Annie.

"OK, let's start again, shall we?" she said addressing the waiting group. "Which of you gentlemen actually discovered the body this afternoon?"

Mike was the first to respond to this enquiry by saying, "Me, him, him and him," whilst pointing at the other three finders in turn.

"Good," replied Annie, sweetly. "Can we all go somewhere and have a quiet chat then?"

The four of them rose as one and headed for the door. Alan led them towards the lounge door and said, "Dining room's good, there's never anyone in there. Don't know why they bothered decorating the bloody place."

They met Curtice as they reached the door. "Hi Kermit, "said Dermot, "Is the dining room empty?"

"Curtees, not Kermeet," said the chef. "Why ees eet you call me Kermeet?" he looked hurt.

"'Cause you're a frog," said the smiling Dermot. "Y'know, French, frog, Kermit the frog, Muppets, etc."

"*Je ne suis pas sûr que j'aime vous m'appeler une grenouille,*" grumped Curtice.

"What?"

"I theenk I no like eet when you call me ze frog," translated the glum Frenchman, "eet ees no respec'ful."

"Look Curt, it's really a term of endearment. We are having a bit of international fun," said the smiling Dermot. "Y'know, cross channel friendly rivalry. You lot call us 'Rosbifs' and we don't moan about it, do we?"

"Can we get on?" said Hollis, "We are trying to solve a bloody murder here."

"Oops, sorry Curt, we're in a bit of a rush here, I'll speak to you later, explain it a bit better. Anyway, I think the lads over there might want to order a snack as well."

They all passed by the slightly mollified chef and headed for the dining room across the corridor. Curtice went into the lounge and looked around for anyone who wanted to take advantage of the club's generosity by ordering one of his specials. He spied Tom waving and went over to the table. Tom, he felt, was his friend.

"Sausage, eggs, beans and chips with tea bread and butter would hit the spot, Kermy," said John in reply to the invitation to free grub. His wife was in the habit of attempting foreign recipes with a minimum of fat content and, whilst the dog seemed to like it, vegetable lasagne didn't quite float his boat. Any chance of good English repast was always grabbed with gusto, with loads of tomato ketchup. "Oh, maybe you should forget the tea. I think I'll stick with the beer."

"Stop weeth ze Kermeet," said Curt. "Ze name ees Curtees."

"Oh stop being a French tart," said John. "If you want to be part of our gang, you'll have to accept to have the Michel taken. We all have to accept it. Thin skins not allowed."

"Michel?"

"Yes. Michael, Mickey, takin' the piss, bit of a gentle laugh at the expense of a friend."

"Jus' ze boys at ze bar, eh?"

"That's the ticket."

"I 'ope you don' zink zat ze French are no good at anyzink."

"On the contrary old boy," said John, warming to the task. "You frogs are great, especially at cheffing. What about the omelette? That's French. Known all over the world, the French omelette is."

"Hokay," said Curtice, reluctantly. "Jus' so ze rest of ze club don't start wiz eet."

Tom ordered the same as John but Jack declined, not trusting Curtice with his delicate digestive system, ordering an omelette, with some toast.

"See," said John. "Omelette. French. Just up your street so you better make it a good one, eh? We don't want Jack giving you a bad review now, do we? Now off you pop and get our grub."

The four old reprobates who found the late Jonny Best sat facing the two detectives at a table in the dining room. They waited for the opening questions.

"Right," said Annie," let's introduce ourselves first. My name is detective sergeant Clowes and this is detective constable Hollis."

"OK," said Mike, "I'm Mike Sleater, This is Alan Brunton, Derek Smith and Dermot O'Carroll."

"Can we start with whereabouts first Mr Sleater?"

"Please call me Mike," said Mike.

"Annie," she replied. "That's Al," she added, pointing at Hollis whilst also waiting for the inevitable. Listening to their earlier dialogue she thought it might be better to get it over with. Especially before they found out about Hedly's full title.

"Annie?" Mike looked at the rest of the lads. "Clowes?"

"I know, I know. I thought it better to get it out in the open early. Ann is my name but as soon as I got to detective, I was rechristened. I'm stuck with it."

"Nice one," said Dermot grinning from ear to ear. "I like your style. They say confession is good for the soul."

"Well if you think that one is funny, said Hollis. "You should know that our guvnor is not just know as 'dickhead' 'cause he is one but 'cause his initials are DI K Hedly. Detective Inspector Ken Hedly. Geddit?"

"Priceless," said Derek. "What about you. Have you got one?"

"Right, funny confessions over," said Annie, interrupting before it got out of hand. "And I'll bet the confession we're after will be a lot harder to get than ours, so let's get on. Whereabouts, seven to nine o'clock this morning please. We'll start with you if that's OK Mike."

"Sure. Up at seven; watched news on telly while I had brekky; 'til about half eight. Got a shave; dressed and walked to the shop for a paper, which I read for the next hour. Is that OK?"

"Wasn't the Sun then?" she said, lifting her head and smiling.

"I thought you said 'fun over'," said Mike, returning the smile. "Verification?"

"If the wife and paper shop man are OK as alibis, I've got two."

Al Hollis took notes as they all took turns in relating their early morning habits, which rarely varied and could have referred to their movements on any day in the previous six months and, apart from this current blip of excitement, the next six months.

"I know I shouldn't say this," said Annie, leaning conspiratorially towards the quartet when all their movements had been listed, "but I have a nose for this sort of stuff and I'm pretty sure that you lot will feature pretty low on the suspect's list. But, I do want you to think very carefully about Mr Best's movements over the last few days as well as anything you may think of that may point us to whoever had so much against him that they did him in. I mean anything, the slightest row or argument he may have had, whether you heard it or heard about it."

"Suspect's list?" said Derek. "That's a bit rich. You're just trying to scare us, trying to make us blurt out something that we might think will get us even further down the list, eh?

"You were in the job, weren't you?" said Annie, looking more closely at Derek.

"Yes I was, and I got out when it started to get me looking too closely at my friends.

Fastest way to having no friends that, being a copper. Except those in the job, that is, and they weren't the friends I wanted. Your instinct about our involvement in this is quite correct so the reward of lower ranking suspect qualification isn't going to get you any more than you were going to get anyway."

"Thought so. Well you're right, Derek, you know the script. We need to gather information fast, so please help us to do that, will you?"

"OK. His biggest and noisiest arguments happened over the last few days," said Derek. "The committee row was overheard by Larry, the car park rows with Chris Jones and Mark Norton, overheard by Curtice and young Tom and there was a row with Percy Milbank over his wife that was witnessed by half the club. A list was quickly formulated, the others eager to add their two pennyworth. Names of the protagonists in each incident were added as well as approximate timelines.

"Bloody hell," said Hollis later, when the codgers had left them alone. "He was a murder waiting to happen."

"We'll those lads certainly gave us a few things to go on didn't they? Who's first on the list?"

Hollis flicked the pages on his notebook back and forward before he started, "The committee members, who he seemed to be having some arguments with, and that new member, Jordan, who he also seems to have had some angry words with. Then there was the row with the greenkeeper that was witnessed in the car park the night before he was topped."

"Who was it who saw that?" asked Annie.

"The assistant professional told the lads about it this afternoon. He said the chef heard it as well."

"You can get the young assistant pro in next, he was at the table when we collected our canaries and he may still be there. I'll go and have a go at the treasurer and the secretary." She looked at her watch, "I'll see you in the bar when I get finished, should be about ten minutes" She stood up to go and said, "Hopefully Dickhead is still grilling the dog. If he shows his face you'll need to update him on time of death and what we've found out off the four musketeers."

"Why not change the emphasis of their input a bit and insinuate that the lads know more than they pretended?" said Al Hollis with a sly grin on his face. "I'll bet that he insists on having another go at them. Y'know, get one over on us two."

"Right," said Annie, "I'll have a bit of that. It should keep him busy for a bit. Whoever sees him first then."

They left the dining room and went their separate ways.

"Hello Tom," said Hollis, "can I have a word?"

"What about my grub?" wailed Tom. "It'll be here any minute." Tom was uneasy about his free meal going astray, especially with the return of the four body finders. They were always pinching chips; sometimes bread as well, to make chip butties.

"It'll only take a minute," said Hollis. "We can ask your mate Kermit to keep it on a pan for you, don't worry."

Tom stood up and followed Hollis to the dining room. He groaned when he saw Curtice, with a pile of food on a tray, heading to the now crowded table. He had just come through the door at the other end of the bar. "Look, he's bringing my meal,"

Hollis was unimpressed and said, "Look, kid, this is a murder investigation and I've had nothing to eat since breakfast. So come on. Let's get this over with. The sooner we do, the sooner you eat."

Tom reluctantly followed Hollis out after taking another look at the chef bearing his steaming dinner.

"I believe that you witnessed an argument between Best and Chris Jones, the greenkeeper. Is that right?" asked Al after settling the young man down.

"Yes, Jones was shouting something about Jonny following him about, trying to catch him out at something, and that he should stick to shagging his lap dancing friend and leave him alone."

"Lap dancer?"

"Yes, it was a well known secret. He was spending a lot of time and money at 'Pole Cats', on Lucy. I think they call her Juicy."

"Did you see anyone else around?"

"Yeah, the chef was out at the bins, I heard the lids banging. He must have heard the racket as well."

"Right Tom, thanks for that. By the way, where were you this morning?"

"I was supposed to meet Jonny Best for a lesson so I came down at about eight, well ten past actually, but he wasn't there. I thought he might have gone off in a huff so I was expecting a bollocking off him. Anyway, I suppose he won't be giving me a bollocking now, eh?"

"What did you do then?"

"I went to get the spare golf buggy out from the back of the clubhouse, near the kitchen. I saw Curtice there and he said he would do me a bacon butty. I moved the buggy to the shop front and saw the light on so I went to say good morning to Mark."

"What time was that?"

"Could only have been about fifteen, or maybe, twenty past."

"How long had Mark been there?"

"Don't know, he didn't say. Actually, he seemed a bit jumpy but I thought it was because he was surprised to see me there so early."

"Why would he be jumpy?"

"Dunno," said Tom sullenly.

"Look Tom," said Al with a serious look on his face, "if you know anything, you should tell us now. It will come out later and if you don't tell us you may be in big trouble."

Tom looked at him; then he looked down at the table.

"Tom......"

"Well, there's a big Chinese bloke that has suddenly appeared the other day and said he was looking for Jonny Best."

"And....?"

"Um, when I told Mark about him he barged into his office and I heard him yelling at someone over the phone."

"Then... ?"

"He yelled something about keeping that bloody thug away from the club."

"What did he look like, this Chinaman?" asked Al.

"He was a big bugger, with a tattoo up the side of his neck, a dragon."

Hollis picked up his phone and, as he punched in Ghosh's number, he said, "Thanks for that, you can go and get your egg and chips now."

"If there's any left," said Tom sulkily as he made his way back to the bar.

"Get down to "Pole Cats" and question that lap dancer and anyone else who may have come into contact with the victim," barked Hollis into the phone as he made the connection to the rookie.

"Y'mean that knockin' shop in the village?" replied Ali.

"That's the one. And look out for yourself. We don't want you catching anything dangerous in there."

Hollis went out into the hall and met Annie as she came down the stairs with Jayne. He waited until Jayne went to the bar.

"Looks like we've got another suspect Annie."

"Who?"

"Jimmy Wu. He may be the connection with the Chinese imported fake gear that Snape was talking about?"

"Wu, eh? We know him, don't we? We'd better have to have a look for our Mr Wu, eh?"

"Righty ho." Hollis paused. "Oh, and I've sent Ali down to 'Pole Cats'. Do we need reinforcements for Jimmy Wu, he's supposed to be a dangerous man," said Hollis.

"Nah, he didn't do it, but he'll tell us what the connection is if we look as though we are going to pin the killing on him. We can't do anything about the fake goods anyway. That's down to the club really. I'll just go and see if that guy Snape is in before we go. I got a bit waylaid before. See you at the car."

Annie went to the stairs and Al left to get the car. The dark haired stranger watched them go before finishing his whiskey and following them.

DC Ghosh rapped his knuckles hard on the front door of "Pole Cats", the new house of repute that was the talk of the locality. There was some movement from behind the door that sounded a bit like furniture being rearranged. It sounded to Ghosh like there was someone putting a desk against the back of the door; a heavy desk.

The policemen knocked again, this time with a closed fist.

"Come on, Tarquin, open up. It's me, Ali Ghosh."

A square flap in the door slid back to reveal a pair of bushy eyebrows that could have made a large cat think twice about tackling them. Below these angry brows was a pair of narrow eyes, closely spaced and showing a minimum of pupil, pupils that were not accustomed to bright light.

"Oh it's you is it," said one of the eyebrows, Ali was not sure which one. "What are you doing here at this time? It's a bit early for you."

"Just open the door," said Ali with a sigh.

The flap slammed shut with a bang accompanied by more scraping of table legs behind the door which then opened slowly to reveal the very large figure of Tarquin, the pimp and minder. Tarquin didn't really have the brains to hold down two jobs but neither was he aware that he had two jobs.

"Bloody 'ell Ali, I thought it were the cops. I thought it was a bloody raid; banging on the bloody door at this time of the day."

"I am the bloody cops you cheeky sod. An' what d'yer mean, this time of the day? It's four in the bloody afternoon. And I'm here on official business, so less of your lip, eh?"

"Official business? Like what?" The eyebrows were now very close, almost touching.

"Like murder, matey."

"Murder?" The eyebrows shot in the opposite direction, then upwards.

"Who's been murdered?"

"Jonny Best, Lucy's best customer."

Tarquin's surprised face took on a puzzled demeanour and the eyebrows resumed their ritual courtship dance. He scratched his head and then, his face brightening, he remembered his earlier meeting with Best.

"Blimey, I saw him this morning; slung him out at about seven, seven thirty."

"Seven bloody thirty? Was he here all night?" asked Ali. "Must have cost him a fortune."

"Nah, he passed out last night after Lucy had fleeced him. She couldn't wake him so she locked him in her room and went home. She left me a note to dump him out the back door when I got in, which I did."

"Are you sure you didn't give him a clip to send him on his way?"

"Best? A clip? That was hardly necessary. It's Best we're talking about. He's a bit loud when he's pissed but he's never been any trouble here."

*"**Was** a bit loud and someone **did** give him a clip, a hard one, with a shovel even, or something similar. Where's Juicy?"*

"She won't be her 'till after seven. She's got a job y'know."

"What, another job besides this one?" He took out his notebook. "Well, we'll have to have a word then. Where's she work?"

"Pass. I can't help you there mate. You'll have to wait 'til tonight."

"That'll please the boss. He might come barging down here to harass you so you better be prepared. Get your paperwork in order or he might shut you down."

"Thanks for the tip Ali. I'll phone the gaffer and get him to prepare the girls. Dress 'em up a bit."

"Dress?"

"I believe that if they cover their chuffs, they can't shut us down. Anyway, I suppose that's his worry. See you in the week, eh?"

"Oh, I think I'll give it a miss for a week or two. At least until the chuffs are back on show, anyway."

"Hi, it's me again," said Annie after entering Arthur Snape's office on his "Come in" reply to her knock.

"I'm following up on some information that's just been passed to me about your dealings with Mr Best."

"I don't know where you've got your information from," replied Snape, not without a little bluster, "but I can assure you that, apart from the normal business of running this golf club, I have had no 'dealings' with Best."

"Well witnesses have overheard you having the kind of argument with the deceased that would indicate more passion than running a golf club," said Annie, without showing any emotion, merely a stating a fact.

Snape stood up. "Look, the only row I've had with Best recently was to do with his association with Mark Norton, our professional."

"What sort of association?"

"It has just come to my attention that there may have been some dealings between them, allegedly involving counterfeit golf equipment from China. When I broached the subject, he flew of the handle and said some things about the way that the committee was running the club.

He was making all sorts of wild accusations in an attempt to deflect my questions. He left here shouting and bawling all sorts of threats at me."

"When was this," asked Annie, busy scribbling as she listened.

"It was on Monday."

"Who else was involved on the row?" asked Annie, without looking up from her notepad.

"It was a bit embarrassing, actually," said Snape, "We were just trying to negotiate with someone who could save us from some belt tightening measures; a substantial increase in fees that would have made our members very unhappy."

"Well, we don't want that, do we?" smiled Annie, looking up from her notebook. "Who, exactly?"

"Members. All of them. They don't like paying their subs anyway."

"No, not members. Who was at your embarrassing meeting?"

"Oh, yes, meeting. David Jordan, Jerry Vaughan and Charles Blezzard, our secretary, who you've already met. Dave and Jerry are new members and Dave has some ideas for improving our financial state."

Annie scribbled away for a few minutes and then said, "Just for the record, where were you between seven and nine this morning?"

"Mmm, let me see, I left the house at about seven twenty and went into town. I parked up at about half eight-ish and went to see a client on Market St."

"Client being?"

"Actually, possible client would be more accurate. I had a meeting with Jerry Vaughan."

"One of the new members you mentioned?"

"Well, yes. He's the Financial Director at JD Developments."

"Time of meeting?"

"Nine Thirty."

"Early then, were you?"

"Just making sure, y'know. I don't like being late."

"You boys like to keep your parking tickets I suppose?"

"Sure. I'll dig it out. It'll be in my receipts somewhere."

"Took you a bit of time to get to town, didn't it?"

"Well, you know, traffic. Then parking can be a bitch, can't it?"

"Can't it just?" agreed Annie. "Where can I find Blezzard now?"

"He should be in his office down the hall. Shall I ask him to come in here?" said Snape.

"No, that's OK; I'll nip down there now. Can you arrange a full list of these people who you have just referred to? I'll need their contact details too."

"No problem. I'll get Charles to do it before you leave."

Annie shook hands with Snape and went looking for Blezzard. He was not in his office so she made her way to the stairs, heading down to the gent's lounge, bumping into Jayne as she passed the snooker room.

"Hello," said Annie, "You work downstairs, behind the bar don't you?"

"Yes," said Jayne, straightening her skirt. "I was just checking the snooker room for empties."

"Has anyone been to see you yet?"

"How do you mean," said Jayne with a start. "I was only collecting empties."

"I mean policemen," said Annie, putting two and two together.

"Oh...... police, no," said Jayne, "but I should be here 'til seven."

"Erm ..... I'm sorry," said Annie, "but I'm afraid you'll be here until we say you can go. Murder enquiries are a bit of a bugger if you are seen as either a suspect or a material witness."

"Oh, it's like that is it?" Jayne paused, "A suspect?"

"Or a material witness."

"What if I'm not either?"

"We have to decide on that one, I'm afraid so you'll have to wait 'til we get to you."

"Bang goes my date, then. I was hoping to slope off early." Jayne looked very glum and Annie felt a bit sorry for her.

"Look, I'll try to get to you as soon as possible, maybe before six, eh?" she said, smiling at Jayne as they both made their way down the stairs. Hollis was waiting there for Annie.

"See, we didn't eat all your chips after all, did we?" said Derek to Tom, who was just wiping the last of his egg yolk up with his bread, being careful not to miss the tiny smear of ketchup next to it.

"I'm grateful," said Tom, smacking his lips. "I was starving and, I must say, I thought it was a goner when I saw it passing me at the bar."

"That was John's and we told Kermit to hold yours for ten minutes, knowing you wouldn't be long."

"I'm glad it's over," said Tom. "I wouldn't know anything anyway. Nobody ever tells me anything around here."

"Oh, it won't be over. They've just started, gathering up information, sifting the facts; comparing versions of events."

"You mean I'll have to see them again?"

"'Course you will," said Derek. "Why? You've got nothing to hide, have you?" The **'have you'** was stressed, dramatically, by Derek and it brought their little conversation to the attention of Mike and Dermot.

"What's up, Tom," said Dermot. "You're not holding back are you? Are you and that Mark up to no good in that shop?"

"I'm up to nothing," said a startled looking Tom, misinterpreting Dermot's banter. "I only missed out the argument with Mark because I didn't want Mark to get in bother."

"What argument?"

"I told them about the row with Jones but I missed out Mark's argument with Best," continued Tom, now panicking.

"When was that?" asked Derek, "and why the hell didn't you tell the old bill?"

Tom looked at Derek and after a moment's pause he said, "Mark was angry and he said that Best could get the shop closed and put us both out of a job."

"How?" Alan had joined in and John and Jack were now starting to pay attention too.

Tom put his head in his hands and said, "Oh, I don't know. All I know is that Mark grabbed Jonny as he was going to his car and they had a blazing row about something. Besty wrenched his arm from Mark's fist and went to his car." Tom looked up, scanning the faces of his inquisitors. "That's when Jones grabbed Best and started shouting his mouth off, like I said."

"What's that got to do with the shop closing?" said Jack. "And what were they arguing about?"

"I don't know," moaned Tom, head back in his hands. "Mark said he would let me know something this week." He gave a big sigh. "I think he might be letting me go. I'll not get another job like this one,"

"Oh, pull yourself together," said Derek."Just tell the cops what you heard. If Mark did it they'll have to get another pro. If he didn't do it he'll never know you grassed him up, he'll think it was the Frenchman, or Jones, whenever he turns up. Anyway, you'll have to tell the cops."

"I will, I will," said Tom, "but not now. She said I could go home so I'm off home. See you tomorrow." He got up and headed for the door.

"Is he still with the dog?" asked Annie.

"Out walking with him, apparently, visiting the path they took, checking out how they could come across such a well hidden body so easily," replied Al.

They were at the bar comparing notes and they had ordered a soft drink each. They were also aware of the attention they were drawing from the table occupied by the old farts who found the body, attention now magnified by that of other interested members. The table was full of bottles and half empty pint glasses of various shapes and sizes. They were getting a bit noisy and Annie said, "I don't know how those lads got here but I hope they're not thinking of going home in a car, other than as a passenger."

"I've just had a quiet word and it seems they had already got the picture," said Hollis. "I said it was the boys in uniform they would need to look out for, not us. We want them on our side for now, don't we?"

Annie didn't bother to answer that. "How long ago did the dog whisperer go out?"

"About ten minutes ago. I had filled him in on the latest information from the pathologist but he didn't seem to hear. He thought that the guy who found him was acting very strangely and seems to have 'A Hunch' about him and his dog. He'll probably calm down when he realises that Smithson would hardly bop our victim on the bonce, bury him and then come rushing in to announce where his body was, giving him no time to cover his own tracks."

"Doesn't matter," said Annie. "It gives us more time to get some real work done."

"Oh no, you spoke too soon." Hollis spotted Hedly walking past the widow, alone. "He's on his way in."

Hedly strode into the lounge and confronted Clowes and Hollis. "Taking a break are we?" He looked at the drinks on the bar. "Hope there's no vodka in there Al," he said, making sure to leave out the 'co' bit that formed Hollis's nickname.

Hollis ignored him and took a long swig from his orange juice. He put the half empty glass down, smacked his lips and said, "Did Snotty recreate the crime then sir?"

"There are too many bodies wearing blue uniforms out there now, stamping around looking for forensic stuff. They completely distracted the dog. All he could do was run around between them, with a stick in his mouth, wagging his tail."

"No arms then?" smiled Hollis.

"Look, Hollis, Smithson's hiding something and that dog is going to give him away." He looked at the drinks on the bar and paused, hoping one of them would offer him a drink so that he could join them. The offer never came so he continued, "Anyway, I've sent him home and told him to stay close. I haven't finished with him yet. What have you two been up to?"

"We've spoken to the four guys that were in the copse when our two bright plods went to secure the scene," said Annie. "They have given us some stuff about the greenkeeper and the young assistant pro. Al spoke to the young assistant pro and he gave a full account of a blazing argument between Best and the Jones, the greenkeeper in the car park last night at about eight."

"He said that the chef heard it all as well," said Al, "so I'm going to get hold of him in a minute and see how his version ties in."

"The guys also told us about a wild shouting match upstairs with Best at it again, bawling the club secretary out," said Annie. "I managed to catch the treasurer who was also involved. He admitted that there were three other members in the room at the time."

Hollis took over. "We kind of think that these four guys who wrecked the crime **scene** were holding something back as well. They were a bit evasive about their relationship with Best and the ex-cop sort of cut in now and again, insinuating that we were going a bit too far with our questions."

"Yeah, they could have gone in that copse to tidy up the scene, not knowing that the body had already been discovered." said Hedly, clutching at the false straw that Hollis had held out to him.

He was getting confused and it showed.

His eyes were darting between Annie and Al, in an agitated fashion and the signs were recognised by his two subordinates. "I'll get to them tomorrow and I'll get to the bottom of their involvement, ex cop or not."

Annie closed her notebook and said, "It's all a bit confused at this point and we were just about to get through the rest of the people who were witness to the victim's movements and then prepare a report for an update in the morning. I've also sent DC Ghosh to 'Pole Cats' to interview his mistress."

"Mistress?"

"Well, she's a lap dancer and a hooker actually and he seems to be a bit of a regular customer. We need to find out when he was there last and if there is anything more we should know about her."

Hedly looked at her in silent thanks.

Annie added, "If all that's OK with you, guv?"

"Good idea Annie, well done. In the meantime I'll get back and report to the A/C. He told me I should get back to him every day when he assigned me the case this morning."

"Cope assigned it?" said Annie.

"Yeah, I thought that was a bit odd as well as it would normally be the chief constable. Anyway, I'd better get off. See you in the morning." He turned and walked out of the lounge without a backward glance.

"Right, he's gone," said Annie. "You have a word with Jane, the barmaid, and I'll see if I can get hold of that manager. You can also get to the chef before he goes home."

"OK, see you back here later."

There was a knock on Snape's door. "Come in," he said, recognising the soft apologetic tapping. It was Charles, wearing a very worried countenance.

"They must have done it," said Charles. "I knew it was getting out of hand. That bastard Jordan said he would get him and he did."

"Pull yourself together, man," said Arthur, standing up and closing the door behind Charles after checking the corridor. "They haven't got that kind of background and I've been checking up on these so-called other investors and they are not what Jordan led us to believe."

"What, you mean not gangsters or Mafia?"

"Nope. They're employment agents. Local boys made good and rolling in un-invested profits."

"Made good, bloody hell they must have made it bloody good. There's a lot of cash required for this deal and peddling a few bodies won't amass enough to buy a cub-hut never mind a golf club," said the nervous Charles.

"You don't know much about business do you," sneered Arthur. "These boys peddle bodies, as you put it, all over the world. Over the years they've turned over millions and have made margins big enough to have made Al Capone jealous. I think he'd have got in on the act if the labour agency game had been around in his time; much more profitable than skimming off the unions."

"Why do they need to invest it anywhere else then? asked Charles.

"Times have changed and margins are smaller, the big spending oil and gas companies have got wise to it and they've sliced margins to the bone," explained Arthur. "The deal we're setting up is an opportunity that comes along once in a lifetime and the pickings are so big that Fordham was right when he said our payout is peanuts. Mark my words; we will get more than we agreed on before this is finished."

"What about Best's share?" said Charles.

"Well, he's not going to need it is he? Look, it doesn't matter about his share. What I'm trying to demonstrate is that there was no need for Jordan to have Best killed, he had no real motive, no matter what he tried to make us think."

"Why does he rant and rave so much, then?"

"'Cause he was just trying to scare us; keeping the price down. I'm sure that he stands to make a significantly higher cut than we do," said Arthur, elbows on his desk, fingers steepled.

Charles had stopped shaking and the colour was returning to his face. He sat back in his chair, now much more relaxed than when he came in.

"Jordan's on his way so you may as well stick around," said Arthur. "Oh, by the way, have the police been to see you yet.

"No, I went off before they got to me. I wanted a drink at home, away from all this madness. To calm my nerves and, I wanted to be the first to tell that slapper of a wife of mine that Best was dead."

"Oh yes, I forgot about Janice. How did she take it?"

"Didn't bat an eyelid," said the disappointed Charles. "She must be getting it somewhere else as well. I'd have thought she'd cut down to one at a time by now."

"I think you would be advised to let the police know you were aware that they were at it, and that you didn't give a toss," said Arthur.

"Why the hell should I?"

"Because, old chap," said Arthur patiently, "if they think you cared about it you would be a prime suspect, wouldn't you?"

"You're right. Bloody hell, I hadn't thought of that."

"Milbank won't be so lucky though," said Arthur after a few seconds. "He's been very uptight about his Jenny's antics with Best over the last month or so. I believe Percy threatened him at the last Barbecue."

"Maybe that's why Janice went elsewhere if he was at it with Jenny as well. She wouldn't be happy sharing with a lady golfer, she hates the golf club," said Charles.

"Go and find out if those two detectives are due back, or better still, try and contact them and apologise for sneaking off. Tell them you are available for questioning any time."

"Why?"

"We don't want the police tramping all over the place and digging around our affairs looking for motives. Not club motives anyway. Just a bit of hanky panky generated motives would suit us better. Even better still, hooky Chinese golf gear motives."

"OK, I'm on it," said the now perkier Charles, plans for Thailand back on the cooker.

The usual golf club barflies were now gathered in their usual spot at the bar discussing the day's events when Jimmy joined the group.

"Have you heard the one about the Liverpudlian lass at the welfare office?"

"No Jimmy, we haven't but, we're going to aren't we?" said Mike. And, I hope it's not racist, you know we don't approve of racist."

"Look, it's only a bloody joke," said Jimmy.

"Do you always have start your jokes like that?" asked Mike.

"Like What?"

"Well you always seem to have to say 'It's only a joke' before you start."

"That's because you awkward bastards start dissecting it, generally after I've told it; but it seems now you're doing it before I start."

"You could make it your catch phrase," said John. "y'know, like that feller who used to say, 'It's the way I tell 'em'. Yours could be 'Look, it's only a joke'."

"Take no notice Jim, we could do with a laugh with all this lot going on," said Dermot. "By the way, Liverpudlians are a race, y'know."

Jimmy, looked quizzically at Dermot, ignored him and, now feeling under a bit of pressure from this small audience, he began.

"A Liverpool girl goes to the welfare office to register for child benefit.

'How many children?' asks the welfare officer.

'Ten,' replies the Liverpool girl.

'Ten?' says the welfare worker. 'What are their names?'

'Nathan, Nathan, Nathan, Nathan, Nathan, Nathan, Nathan, Nathan, Nathan and Nathan.'

'Doesn't that get confusing?'

'Naah...' says the Liverpool girl, 'It's great because if they are out playing in the street I just have to shout 'Nathan yer dinner's ready!' or 'Nathan go to bed now!' and they all do it.'

'What if you want to speak to one individually?' says the curious

Welfare worker.

'That's easy,' says the Liverpool girl, 'I just use their surnames.'"

The guffaws rang around the room attracting disapproving stares from the president who was at the bar, getting his round. He tut-tutted and went to join his cronies who had gathered to keep abreast of this sensational turn of events. "They've no respect for the dead," he said.

"Now that is racist," said Mike. "That's another racist joke. How come you can't find any politically correct jokes to tell?"

"Liverpudlians are not a race," said the exasperated Jimmy, "despite what that bugger says."

"According to one very famous comedian they are," said Dermot. "In fact he said that they are largely made up of Irishmen who could swim, but who couldn't afford the bus fare to Manchester."

"You lot are all the bloody same," replied Jimmy. "You think you're funnier than the jokes."

"You should be able to handle barrackers by now," said John. "You're a comedian and you should learn to handle such riposte, replying with some quick wit and repartee thus making any loud mouthed barracker shrink in embarrassed shame, causing him to skulk from the audience with slumped shoulders, head bowed. You should go to the QW&R College."

"QW&R College?"

"Quick Wit and Repartee," said John.

"Fuck off John," said the even more exasperated Jimmy.

"Oh, you've already enrolled," exclaimed John, brightly. "That's it. Now you've got it. Quick wit and repartee, just the ticket."

"You're all weird," was Jimmy's farewell comment as he went to spread the new joke around.

Winston joined the laughing group at the bar.

He touched Jack's arm and motioned him to one side. "I don' s'pose you seen da greenkeepa', 'ave ya?" he asked, quietly.

"Chris Jones, you mean?" said Jack.

"Yas."

"No, I've not seen him for a couple of days," said Jack. He raised his voice over the laughter and said "Anyone seen Chris Jones today?"

There was a general murmuring of 'no' and, 'not for a couple of days' as well as a, "lazy bastard is probably at the Stoat, skiving'.

"The cops were looking for him earlier," said Larry from behind the bar. "They need to question him."

"Question 'im?" said Winston. "Wod about?"

"Best's murder, what d'you think?"

"Best, murdarred?" Winston feigned surprise.

"Bloody hell Winston, where have you been today?" said Jack. "They found him this morning, buried in the copse by the third fairway."

"Wot? Buried in da copse?"

"Yes, the one on the right of the third. Didn't you notice all the police cars in the car park?" asked Jack.

"Polees in da car park?"

"Stop it," said John.

"Stop it? Stop wot?"

"Yes, stop it. You're repeating every bloody sentence. It's driving me mad." said John.

"Drivin' you mad? Oops, sorry." Winston pulled himself together. He was already in shock at the news about Best and the missing Jones but pretended he didn't know, hoping to get some more information about Jones. "Well, dere was a polees maan at da front enteraans but he was jus' havin' a fag next to his nicknick. I tought he might be on da motorway duty and skivin' off. I was goin' ta tell you boys to mak' sure he gone befo' you go."

"You've obviously parked in the front car park. The rest of the cavalry are around the back," said Larry.

"Yeah, we're all getting taxis or phoning wives. We've been here since half one and getting more ratted by the minute," said Mike.

"Anyway, what do you want with Jones?" asked Jack. "You're on the social committee aren't you? Or are you after Best's job already?"

"Wait a minnit, innit. I didn'ta even know he dead."

"Yeah, leave him alone," said John. "He couldn't be after Jonny's job. He'd need to know something about grass, wouldn't he?"

"I think he might know SOMETHING about GRASS," said Mike stressing the 'grass'.

"Yes, but you'd need to know a bit about the fairway grass to get the, now vacant, Greens job, wouldn't you Winston?"

Winston blushed, but they could not discern the change in the West Indian's colour. "Da greens chairman's job ain't in my scene man, I be sure bout dat."

"But... I mean.... after his job, eh?" said Mike, sensing a wind up.

"I ain't after him bloody dam job," said Winston through gritted teeth. "I wan' ta see Chris 'bout sometin' else."

"Like what?" asked John.

"None o' yo, dam business," snapped the now miffed Winston.

"ooooOoooooo," chorused the choir at the bar, now all listening to the fun.

"Look, you're going to have to tell the police when they come to grill you," said Dermot. "So you might as well come clean now."

The angry Winston, not spotting the wind up, turned and made for the door.

"Y'know, I think that he must have been doing a bit of dealing with our Chris," said John. "Either supplying or being supplied."

"I think you've upset him Mike," said Jack.

"Oh, he'll get over it. He's OK our Winston," replied Mike. "Very laid back, normally. I think John's right, by the way. He looked a bit anxious then, more about the missing Chris than the dead Best, I think."

"I don't know how they can be having such a good time over there," said the president. "You'd think that they were at a wedding not a funeral." He was sat on the far side of the lounge with Harold Jarvis, Charles Blezzard, Arthur Snape, Brian Fordham and Frank Dobson.

"But, it's not a funeral yet," said Charles, "and don't forget who's actually dead. There's not too many who'll turn up at his funeral." He looked around the room and over at the noisy bar. "Not as many as are here, I'll bet."

"In actual fact, it's more like a wake," said Frank Dobson. "There's three of those lads who have strong Irish connections and, in times like this, they'd have a wake."

"A wake?" said Jarvis. "What's a wake?"

"It's a kind of tradition that religious types follow, very popular in Ireland. It's a gathering of friends and relatives who will watch over the soul of the deceased and generally turns into a bit of a party, involving lots of drink. The early part of the proceeding, whilst they are still sober anyway, involves sad, sentimental stories about the departed's life with a few mournful songs accompanied by a fiddle or a harp. Then, once they have passed one or two a jugs of whisky around, the fiddler will be joined by a harmonica and maybe a banjo, and/or an accordion and a drummer. The singing gets much more animated, the party gets more crowded and then the dancing starts. The noise attracting more passersby and now you have a proper party. The coffin, which will start at the centre of the parlour, often needs to be moved out of the way for the dancers."

"Dancing?" gasped the awe struck president. "With a coffin in the house?"

"Oh yes, they like a bit of the diddly-diddly dancing at a wake," laughed Frank. "I once heard of a wake where the coffin, still open of course, had to be stood up in the corner with the occupant looking out on the proceedings. One of the nephews was seen talking to the corpse, his ex uncle, for half an hour, only stopping when another sympathetic uncle pointed out who he was talking to, and the fact he was actually dead. 'Bejasus' said the nephew, 'Y'd never tell. Sure, oi only saw him last week an' he didn't look as grand as dat' he said, pointing at the solemn looking stiff."

Everyone but Snape laughed at the story. "Well we don't want that sod, Best, standing in the corner at this wake," he said, staring into his malt whisky, with a pensive look on his face. He suddenly looked up at his companions and said, "Neither do we want any bloody diddly-diddly dancers."

The mood quickly changed to an uncomfortable silence, Arthur's nasty comments neutralising Frank's humorous description of strange Irish parties and, in addition, nobody wanted to be accused of showing disrespect to a fallen colleague. Snape suddenly finished his whisky in one gulp, rose from his chair and said to Charles, "Come on Charles we need to do a bit more work before that meeting."

"What meeting?" asked Charles.

"The 'Saving the Club' meeting, you fool," said Arthur, stomping off, grim faced.

Charles followed Arthur meekly, not reacting to the insult. He would have his say upstairs in the office.

"Bloody hell," said Frank. "That was a bit strong."

"I agree," said Fordham. "Just because he is a bloody fool it's a bit strong to call him one to his face, eh?"

Brian Fordham was a bit nervous because he knew he would be at that 'Saving the Club' meeting and he wanted assurances about getting his money out of the process. He had thought that maybe Snape and Blezzard had done away with his pal but, thought it prudent to have a plan up his sleeve in case it was them - and he had one. He waited at the table for ten minutes, excused himself from the remaining company and followed his co-conspirators up to Snape's office. He passed DS Clowes and DC Hollis as he left the lounge, nodding to them as he passed.

Annie went straight to the bar and said, "Where's the bar manager? Larry, isn't it?"

Jayne stood up from her crouched position at the dishwasher, in which she was busy stacking glasses. "Oh, it's you two again," she said. "Yes its Larry, Larry Ball. He should be in his flat upstairs but if not, he could be anywhere."

"I'll go and have a look," said Annie. "You see if you can find the chef."

Five minutes later she returned to the bar where Hollis and Jayne were laughing at some shared joke.

"No reply at his flat," she said, interrupting the moment. "Tell him I need to speak to him." She handed a card to Jayne. "He can get me on this number."

"Ok. I'll tell him. Can I go then?"

"Oh, yes. Sorry I forgot about your date. Have a good night and we'll see you tomorrow."

The two detectives left the lounge.

"You were supposed to find the chef. What happened?"

"I got chatting to that barmaid and she was telling me about that row upstairs. She seems to think that it was a bit more serious than Snape makes out. She also confirmed that there were loud accusations from Best about the club's accounts as well. Anyway, she said that the chef had sloped off and wouldn't be back for an hour or so."

"And the joke you were sharing?"

"She was trying to explain about the snooker room rumours being untrue."

"Snooker room?"

"Don't ask, she was doing a load of rambling about crafty fags and someone called Vinny. Didn't make a lot of sense really."

"OK, let's ring HQ and see if that dope Hedly is still there. If he is, He'll be out of our way and we can crack on here."

"Where's Stansky and Hutch?" asked Larry, as he came back into the bar carrying two crates of bottled beer.

"You've just missed them," said Jayne. "That Clowes woman wants you to ring her." She handed the card to Larry. "As soon as possible, she said," added Jayne with a sniff.

"You don't like her, do you?" said Larry.

"Not bothered really."

"Have you spoken to them yet?"

"No, I haven't," said Jayne, adding another sniff. "She was supposed to get to me before six o'clock. But she's just buggered off making me wait to give you this message and now I'm late for my date."

"Why haven't you gone home if you're late?"

"'Cause she said we all had to wait. Cow."

"Look, they've gone, so sod off home." Larry looked at the card. "So you haven't spoken to them, eh?"

"No, I already told you."

"Hmmm . . . . . . OK, see you tomorrow."

Jayne grabbed her bag and her tips and headed for the door.

"Thanks Larry. I'll see you tomorrow."

Larry stood at the sink, staring at the card for four or five minutes. He remembered the argument that he had overheard upstairs the previous day between Best and the two council members.

"Better get that information to the police before Jayne does," he thought. "It was me that heard it and she'll just get the facts wrong, like she managed to do yesterday."

His train of thought was interrupted by a cheery "Evenin' all," from Sarah, the next barmaid on the rota, arriving for the last shift of the day.

Larry looked up as the members at the bar all reply in turn with various ribald comments.

"Hello Sarah," Looks like you might get a busy night tonight."

"You said it'd be quiet," said Sarah grumpily. "A good night to learn the ropes, you said."

"Well we've had a bit of a murder here today and everyone wants a front row seat."

"A bit of a murder? You mean the victim's just a bit dead?"

"Don't start with the sarky comments," snaps Larry. "Just get busy at that end of the bar. I'll get this lot, they're barmy and you don't need barmy on your first night."

Larry responds to JOHN'S ice and glass rattle, forgetting his intention to contact Annie.

CHAPTER 10

- Hanky Panky -

"I've just been rooting about in the files," said Charles, "and guess what I've found?"

"Look Charles," said Arthur with a sigh, "I'm not into guessing games at the best of times. The grandkids daren't ask me to join in their Christmas after-dinner charades games any more 'cause I'm such a miserable bastard about guessing games. So, can you please refrain from asking such a question again? Now, what have you found?"

"Well, they're not wrong there, are they?"

"Who?"

"Your grandkids."

"What have you found?" growled Arthur through clenched teeth.

"Well ... It appears that the clubhouse is actually a listed building."

"So?"

"So, the plans that the consortium have outlined to me would entail knocking this place down."

"So?"

"So, the listed building tag will prevent them knocking down the clubhouse, 'cause you know what the 'listed' mob are like. They always dig their heels in about knocking down the country's heritage."

"Charles, old boy," said Arthur adopting an obvious patronising tone, "don't you think that our benefactors have thought of that?"

"Maybe not. For some reason, it seems not to have been added to the land registry record. Well, not the copy that Jerry Vaughan had in his paperwork, anyway."

"Listen, they'll have a way of greasing the palms of the powers that be and if that doesn't work, they'll just knock it down and say, oops!"

"Ok, I see what you're saying. But if we were to tip the local newshounds off, our "buyers" will be hard pressed to say they didn't know. Not only that, they'll have to get past all the tree huggers that are sure to gather wherever there's any chance of saving anything from a crested newt to a stately home."

"Stately home? That's a bit rich. It's hardly a stately home. It's a bloody old lodge, servant's quarters, even."

"Don't matter to a tree hugger, matey."

"How's that going to help us, anyway?"

" might be able to up the ante if we play our cards right. A bit of friendly persuasion plus a threat to tip off the media could be a good lever."

"Are you nuts," said Arthur. "Do you want to finish up on a slab in the mortuary beside Jonny Best?"

"We can document everything and lodge it away safely. The police will get the lot if anything happens to us. It would be our insurance policy, eh?"

"Y'know, you might be right there Charles," said Arthur thoughtfully, steepling his fingers under his chin.

He then swivelled his chair round to look out of the window. "There might be a plan in there somewhere. Let's mull it over and see what we can come up with." He turned back towards Charles. "Don't mention this to anyone else. Especially not to Fordham."

"You're the chef aren't you?" asked Annie.

"Oui."

"We need a word... ," Annie hesitated. "I don't suppose we could get a sandwich first could we?"

"Sure," said Curtice. "I can get you someseen. What weel you like?"

"Bacon for me please," said Annie.

"Bacon? At this time of the day?" said Al.

"Bacon's good at any time of the day," laughed Annie. "Anyway, when did you become the cuisine critic?"

"Yeah, I suppose you've got a point there," said Al. "Sausage and bacon ok?" he added, turning to Curtice..

"Oui ," said the chef, "no problem."

"An' brown sauce," chorused the two detectives.

Curtice went to the kitchen leaving Al and Annie to move tables and chairs into some semblance of order. They had set up a whiteboard turned away from prying eyes, facing the rear wall and the room was set out with four interview stations.

"Right, let's get a list of who we want to talk to," said Annie.

"What time's Hedly due?" asked Al.

"Any time now, I guess. Hopefully after we have scoffed our butties, eh?"

Ok, let's look at the list."

They went round to the other side of the whiteboard and started to compile their list. Annie made a table with three headings and started to add some names.

Members	Connected	Outside Connect
Mark Norton		Jimmy Wu
Chris Jones		

"There's these two for starters," she said as Curtice returned with a tray with two plates and a pot of tea, complete with mugs. She indicated the left side of the table. Then she added Jimmy Wu's name to the right side.

"Nice one Curtice," said Annie. "Now why not sit down and we can start with you."

"Pourquoi? Why me? I know nozzeen about ze death of Meestiar Best," Said Curtice, making a mental note of the names on the board.

"Yes, but you know about him, no? When did you see him last, for instance."

"Las' night I see heem. He argue weeth Mark an' Chrees an' zen he drive away very queek. Vite."

Curtice related the events of the previous evening's altercations in the car park, including Chris's threats to 'do Best in'.

"So, he threatened to do him in did he?" said Al.

"Oui, zat is what 'e say to me. When I was puttin' ze beens out."

"Beans? Beans? Why do you put beans out? You're not after the golden Goose are you?" asked Al with a grin. "Har, har. Like Jacques an' the beanstalk, pronouncing 'Jacques' as 'Jakuse'. "You've got more chance with the lottery."

"I think he means 'bins' not beans," said Annie.

"Oui, beens, weeth ze trash in."

"Oh, right," said Al, still tickled with his own joke, "and what about Mark. Did he threaten to do Best in, as well?"

Curtice looked blankly at Al and shrugged his shoulders, still trying to work out where the goose came in.

"Is there anyone else who was angry at Mr Best?" asked Annie, pulling the plate with her bacon sandwich off the tray.

"Oui, zere was Meestair Meelbank an' Meestair Blezzar'. Zey haf ze problem weez ze wiffeez."

"Wiffeez?"

"Oui, married wiffeez."

Al looked at Annie for help.

"Oh, wives. I get it," said Al, his face brightening. "Having problems with Best and their wives? You mean hanky panky?"

"'Anky? Panky? Je ne se quoi, zis 'anky panky. Larry say zat Percy Milbank, ze lady capain's 'usban', 'e make a row wiz Meestair Best at ze last candle leet deennair. Zey were in ze car park, Best an' Jenny Milbank. Percy, 'e saw zem return, wiz red faces."

"And?"

"Well, Larry say zat Percy say, 'Watch your back, Best, I'm goeen' to do for you'."

"Hanky panky," said Al. "There you are, I told you."

"Zat ees 'anky panky? I sought zat was a sret."

"Sret?"

"Oui. Like eef you say, 'I punch you up ze srote eef you don' watch eet."

"No, No, that's a threat. Th, th, threat," said Al.

"Ok,ok," said Annie, "stop it. We'll ask someone who knows about a bit more about hanky panky and threats. Anyone else?"

"Oui, 'e 'as a shouteen row weez Meestair Snape and Meestair Blezzard as well."

"When?"

"Las' night."

"Bloody hell, we'll have to get a bigger whiteboard," said Annie. "What about you?"

"Moi? I no 'ave any row weez 'eem."

"Where were you this morning at eight?" persisted Annie.

"'Ere, een ze keetchen. I see Tom getten ze golf cart an' 'e ask me for ze bakkon sandweetch. We 'ad both jus' arrive for ze work."

"Where's Tom now?" asked Annie, adding two names to the list, Blezzard and Milbank.

"Een ze shop, as always. At zis time, 'e will be zere."

"Ok, all that lines up with what Tom told us earlier, except he didn't say Mark was also rowing with Best," said Al.

"Yeah, I think we'll have to speak to Tom again," Said Annie. "Can you nip over and get him for us please. We can start attacking these butties before Dickhead gets back," said Al, ripping the top of the brown sauce sachet and opening his sandwich in one fluent movement.

He was just about to take the first bite when Larry appeared behind the bar carrying another crate of beer bottles which he dumped on the floor in front of the cold shelf.

Al looked at his sandwich longingly before returning it to the plate.

"Just the man," he said.

Larry turned towards the detectives. "Oh hello, what can I get you?"

"Some answers will do for now," said Annie, still chewing her first bite. "We hear that Best seems to have had a few arguments in the past day or so."

"Year or so, y'mean. He was always having a row with someone."

"What about you?" asked Hollis.

"I try not to get into arguments with members, especially committee members. Not good for the job prospects, y'see."

Annie took over. "And where would you happen to have been at eight this morning?"

"I happen to have been in the cellar humpin' a bloody delivery of beer as that lazy bastard of a drayman watched me. I'm sure that the effort of talking to you to verify that won't tax him too much."

"Your barmaid, Jayne, said that Best was having a row with the secretary and the treasurer yesterday," said Annie.

"Yes, he was, and he was accusing them of all sorts of fiddling. I overheard bits of it when I was on my way to the bar. I told Jayne but I also told her to keep it to herself. Staff shouldn't be gossiping about that sort of thing."

"Bloody hell, it must have been some row if you could hear all the way up there from here," said Hollis.

"It was when I was passing the bottom of the stairs. I could hear it there. And they were having a good old rant, voices raised, angry."

"What about?" asked Annie.

"Well I thought they mentioned club accounts, but couldn't be sure."

"Why would they argue so loudly about that?"

"Fiddling was one of the accusations that Jonny was bawling about, or it sounded like fiddling. And I suppose that with the club going bust it might even be true." Larry paused before continuing. "Having said that, I suppose that's the sort of accusation someone like Besty might make in the circumstances, eh?"

Larry had decided that his embellishment of the events he had previously recounted to the customers at the bar was probably a bit over the top and would not go down too well if proven a bit embroidered.

Annie finished her notes about the argument and looked up, "What about this guy Milbank?" she asked, changing tack.

"Milbank? What about him," said Larry.

"We're told that Best was up to no good with his missus."

"Oh yeah, she's one of many."

"He threatened Best?"

"Well yes, he did but threatening and doing are two different things. I don't think Milbank's got the bottle, just a bit of beer talking."

"OK, thanks for that," said Annie. "We'll talk again later."

Larry gets up and heads back behind the bar.

Annie closed her notebook and said to Hollis, "We'd better have a word with the Milbanks anyway, eh?"

"I'll have a word with the old farts shall I?" said Hollis, nodding over to where the said old farts were gathered in rowdy conversation. "About Milbank, I mean."

"Ask about the club finances as well, just in case there's something in the reason for the row in the office. I'll try and locate the Milbanks."

Hollis made for the other end of the bar and Annie headed for the office to get the necessary contact details of all the characters that were being added to the suspect's list.

The banter at the noisy end of the bar was hushed as Hollis approached the group of members who seemed to be a permanent fixture, always the same group in the same spot.

"Now then lads," said Hollis as he approached them. "I've just got a few more questions if you don't mind." He pulls out his notebook and licks his pencil.

"Ask away," said Derek.

"It's come to our attention that the club is in some financial difficulty. Is that true?"

"Rock bottom, mate," said Jack. "There are some moves afoot to save it but if we can't convince the bank we can pay the outstanding interest charges, I'm told that they are going to pull the plug."

"And the accounts; are they kosher?"

"How do you mean, kosher?" asked Jack. "Kosher as in cooking or as in fiddling?"

"What's the difference?" asks Hollis.

"Well cooking is done for the benefit of the members, tax, VAT and such," said Jack. "Fiddling is at the expense of the members. Skimming off the top, say. Benefitting only the skimmers."

"Or the bottom," added Mike.

"In that case, both, but mainly the fiddlin' one."

"Why do you ask that?" said Mike, who was the original disbeliever as to the veracity of said accounts.

"Well your barman seems to have overheard Mr Best accusing your treasurer of a bit of said cooking; a bit of the fiddling as well, apparently."

"See, I told you," said Mike turning to his pals.

"It's Larry we're talking about here," said Jack, "Larry the nosiest gossiper south of Hadrian's Wall. We've already dismissed his interpretation of the so called 'Snapegate' tapes so why should we believe they are accurate now?"

"Well I hadn't dismissed them," said Mike. "I think they're at it. Snape, Blezzard and the two new members, Jordan and his mate."

"What would the new guys have to do with the accounts?" said Jack, "They've just joined; they had no input to accounts."

"I know, but they're up to something," said Mike, frowning.

"What about Percy and Jenny Milbank?" asked Hollis, totally bemused by the answers he had just got from his first question.

"Percy?" chorused the lads.

"Milbanks?" queried Jack. "The Milbanks have nothing to do with the accounts. She's the lady captain and he's just her husband. Bit of a knob really."

"I'm told Mr Best was having it away with the lady captain," said Hollis with a sly wink.

"Well there is a rumour but not really confirmed," said Jack with a frown. "We shouldn't really be judging people on rumours, should we?"

"Mmm, don't know about that Jack," said Mike. "Bit more than a rumour old boy."

"Yes," said Alan. "The last candle lit dinner, remember. Coming in from the fire escape. Besty and Jenny, red in the face. Both of them."

"And they hadn't been for a jog, like she said when Percy had asked where they'd been, had they?" laughed Alan. "And there's one or two that would have given the sarcastic bitch a clip for that attitude," he added.

"What was the outcome?" asked the detective.

"Well Percy threatened to give him a smack if he didn't leave Jenny alone," said Mike. "But Percy's not that tough, big enough but not tough. No one took him seriously, especially Jenny."

"Now that you mention it, I did hear Percy grunting something about a 'dark night' when he shuffled away," said Alan.

"Thanks lads, that'll do for now." Hollis snapped his notebook shut. "See you later," he said as he walked off in search of his sergeant.

CHAPTER 11

- Percy's picked up -

Jenny Milbank opened her front door in answer to the chimes of 'The Bells of St Mary's' emanating from her electronic doorbell at the same time as the rat-a-tat-tat of the knocker.

"Where's the bloody fire?" she growled at the face of DC Ali Ghosh who had been ordered to interview a possible hostile witness.

"Bloody 'ell," he thought, "they were right. She's a proper nowty sod."

"Good morning Mrs Milbank," he said politely, flashing his warrant card, "My name is detective constable Ali Ghosh and I am here to ask you some questions about the murder of Mr Jonny Best. I believe you know him."

Jenny paled and her hand quickly covered her mouth, her eyes widening. She slumped against the door frame.

"Murdered? Jonny?" she gasped. "No, he can't be."

"I'm sorry, it's true. He was discovered this morning with a big dent in his skull."

"You had better come in," she said, standing to one side to let him in. She struggled to gather her wits about her as she led him into the lounge.

"What happened?"

"According to my training, I think process is for me to ask the questions and you, as well as other suspects, are supposed to answer them. When we have enough truthful answers we should be in a position to tell you and whoever else should ask 'what happened', what happened."

"Eh?"

"Where were you this morning, between eight and ten pm?"

"What?"

"This morning, where were you, eight to ten pm. I believe that's a fairly simple question. What will you do when we get to the difficult questions?"

"No, I mean, what's it got to do with me? I didn't murder him. Why should I?"

"I dunno. Jealousy?" Ali was already struggling a bit with this situation.

His appointment to detective status was really quota driven by the new government directives for the appointment of detectives. He was the brightest of the ethnic group that the directive was aimed at. So here he was in the lounge of the Lady Captain of the local golf club insinuating that she had murdered another member. He was a bit overwhelmed.

"Jealous? Jealous of what?"

"Well maybe you found out that he was married."

"I've known him for fifteen years, I know his wife, also for fifteen years." She was beginning to get a bit tense. "I know he is married and why should that make me jealous?"

"Well, maybe you found out that he is a regular at the local knocking shop. That would make you jealous, no?"

Jenny's patience was beginning to suffer. "I don't give a shit if he had ten wives and owned the local fucking knocking shop. Ask his wife if she is jealous, not me."

"But you were having a bit of hanky panky with him. Don't you care?"

"No, I don't care about that. He's dead. I care about that."

"Well your husband seemed to care. He said that he was going to beat him up if he didn't stay away from you. Mentioned a 'dark night' I believe. It was dark last night."

"It's dark every bloody night," said a puzzled Jenny. "And anyway, he's all mouth and trousers. He wouldn't have the guts to stand up to Best or, for that matter, knock him on the head."

Ali had enough of this and decided to change tack. "That's for us to say. Where is Mr Milbank now?" he said sharply.

"He's out. Playing golf as it happens."

"Hah, that's where you're wrong. He can't be. The golf club has been closed. It's a crime scene."

It was now Jenny's turn to have had enough. Enough of this dimwittery. She grabbed the incumbent dimwit by the arm and dragged him out into the hall towards the front door.

"There's more than one golf course in the north of England you moron. Go and find one, he'll be there." She opened the door and pushed him out, slamming it behind him.

Percy Milbank was not in a happy place.

Some three hours previously he had been met at the eighteenth green of the prestigious Morton Hall Golf and Country Club as he was shaking hands with his companions at the end of their game. Two burly constables were waiting at the side of the green with the course manager and even though Percy had actually noticed them pointing in his direction he just assumed that it was one of the other of his playing partners that they were there to meet.

"Mr Milbank?" said one.

Percy looked at his playing partner and then at the constable.

"Well, yes," he said. "What's the problem?"

"My name is Constable Norton and we need you to accompany us to Manchester in connection to a serious crime."

"A serious crime? What sort of crime?" blurted his partner, George Burlington, the captain of Morton Hall.

Constable Norton looked at Burlington coldly and said, "If you are not his legal advisor sir, I suggest you should say goodbye to Mr Milbank. He is coming with us now." He turned to Percy and said, "Shall we go, sir?"

A stunned Percy said, "What about my clubs? My clothes, shoes and other stuff?"

"Don't worry Percy, we'll look after them," said Burlington as he watched Brian being hustled into the back of the squad car. Looking at the remaining two playing players in the fourball he added, "Well what about that, eh? Milbank in the clink. Wait 'til I tell I tell Mary, she always said he was a bit odd."

Percy was now in the interview room at the police headquarters faced by a grim looking Hedly and a bored looking Annie Clowes. It was getting late and Annie wanted to go home.

"Where were you when Best was murdered?" asked Annie after switching on the recorder and stating time, date and the names of those present at the interview.

"Best, murdered?" said the dizzy Milbank, head spinning with the shock of his detention and the subsequent trip to the police headquarters. His captors had kept a sullen silence on the way from Preston, as they had been instructed to. "We don't want to give him a clue as to our suspicions and the fact we know he threatened the victim," said the inspector.

"Oh, don't come the innocent with us, mate," said Hedly. "You know well that he was murdered and we just want to know where you were."

"When?"

"This morning. Where were you?"

"Best? Dead, eh?" Milbank seemed to brighten up, probably giving the wrong signals to the inspector.

"Yes, where were you?" he asked.

"When? When are you talking about?"

"This morning, as if you didn't know," said Hedly, sarcastically.

Milbank thought for a moment. "You mean this morning as in after midnight, this morning," he paused, "or, do you mean this morning as in just before midday, this morning?"

"This morning as in between seven and nine o'clock this morning," said Hedly.

"Well that's easy," replied Percy, "I was on my way to Preston. Game of golf, y'know. Your Pinky and Perky will vouch for that. Met me on the eighteenth and showed me up, arresting me."

"Yes, but they didn't actually arrest you sir," said Annie. "And that was at five o'clock." She paused and added, "If we allow even five hours for your round you must have started at twelve. It doesn't take four hours to get to Morton Hall, does it?"

"That's true, but I had to go to the club to get my stuff and then I had to get petrol. Oh, and there was a hold up over the Eccles interchange. That took another three quarters of an hour."

"What time at the club?"

"Which club?"

"Your club," said Annie, "and stop being a smartarse. It's not helping y'know."

Milbank glowered at her and said, "I suppose it was about seven thirty or so."

"Did you see anyone?"

"No, it was a bit early."

"How long were you there?"

"About fifteen minutes I suppose."

"Still a long time, getting to Preston I mean."

"Well, there was going to be a spot of Brunch on the cards but as I was a bit late, I had to make do with a bacon sandwich."

"Looks like we'll have to let him go," said Annie.

"Why? He was at the club at the right time and there's a bit of a large hole in his alibi," said Hedly.

"Yes, but it's a bit too easy, isn't it? I think if I was him I'd be inclined to miss out the fact that he had to pick up his gear. If he hadn't seen anyone he would think that no one had seen him. He clearly didn't know what time the murder had been committed and he certainly was surprised at the news. And, as his wife said, he's not got the bottle. She wasn't the only one who thought he lacked the bottle, the barman and the lads that found the body thought so as well."

"Well I think he's our man," said Hedly. "But, you're right about having to let him go." He paused for a moment then added, "Get Ghosh to keep an eye on him."

"Ghosh? Keep an eye on him? Are you sure?" said Annie. "He's a bit green isn't he?"

"Green? Are you colour blind Clowes? He's brown." said Hedly with a smirk.

"I think, sir," sighed Annie, "you should take greater care about some of your witty remarks."

"Mmmm ...," mmmed Hedly, "I suppose you're right. Might not be too PC for a DI."

"Or even PC for a DC," said Annie, smiling inwardly. "Which is where you'll be if one of our more PC colleagues overhears such a remark."

"OK, OK. I get it. Just get someone on his tail and also follow up on that alibi. I don't believe him, see."

"Yessir," said Annie, punching Hollis's number into her phone as she turned to go.

CHAPTER 12

- Winston's quest -

Hedly's phone rang for the sixth time. He was at the gym where he was trying to arrange a game with one of the more influential members of the squash club. He thought that such liaisons were the reason for his rise in the ranks, being totally unaware of the real reason for his last promotion. He was also unaware of the flurry of disappearing feet whenever he showed up at the club. He answered the phone when he recognised the number on the display. It was his boss, Chief Inspector Nelson. The phone emitted a tirade of muffled electronic yells dotted with expletives that couldn't quite be heard exactly but were unmistakably rude, even at a distance.

"Cannabis? In the shed?" he groaned, immediately aware he was in for a bollocking. He listened to another blast, holding the phone a little further from his ear. He wasn't having any difficulty in hearing the Chief Inspector very clearly.

"Don't worry sir; I'll get to the bottom of this immediately. I can't imagine why they didn't look in there immediately."

Another blast assailed his ear which was now beginning to redden, as was his face.

"MI5? Nobody told me about any MI5."

Another blast. "Yessir, I know sir, I know... I'll see to it sir."

Another blast scorched his ear. "Good idea, sir. I'll see to that too. Splendid ruse, sir."

He winced even more animatedly at an further barrage. "Yessir, straightway sir," he said, disconnecting the call and headed for his car, his face now reaching a more puce hue.

"Have you managed to reach him yet?" asked Hollis. He was stood with Annie at the front of the golf clubhouse.

"No, I had to call Nelson."

"Nelson? Why did you do that? Dickhead will go bananas."

"Listen Al, Hedly will try to blame us as it is and, if I know him, he'll try to pin this cock up on us as well. I had to move this up the line and he was not answering his phone. So I had to do it."

"Drugs, eh? This puts a new light on things, doesn't it?"

"Yes, it does," said Annie thoughtfully. "I think you can call Ghosh off of his tailing of Milbank for now and get him back before Hedly gets here." She was interrupted by a squealing of brakes around the corner in the car park. "Too late, sounds like him now. Go and phone Ali, I'll deal with Hedly."

"Why didn't you phone me?" fumed Hedly as he stormed over to Annie. "I've just had an almighty bollocking off Nelson. Why did you phone him?"

"Whoa, Whoa, boss," said Annie, "Hold your horses. You didn't or wouldn't answer any of my calls or Al's calls. We tried you more than once, y'know."

"Well, ok, I was busy. But why Nelson?"

"Drugs, boss. Drugs. You should know the score. It's always high priority and, not only that, we left the shed unchecked. A scene of crime, body right next to it. Questions about why will bounce all over the force. I had to get it out as soon as possible 'cause it's still only twenty four hours later. Better than thirty six or forty eight, eh?"

"Yes, but Nelson," he sulked. "You should have checked it," he added accusingly.

"Oh no you don't," snapped Annie. "You're in charge, the directing officer. You directed us to do interviews and house to house. Remember. You should have directed the rest of the plodders to open that shed and have a look in, shouldn't you?"

"You didn't say that to Nelson, did you?"

"No I didn't. That's your job. Let's get on and solve it before we do any more damage."

"Well you'd better look out for an MI5 spook while you're at it," said Hedly.

"MI5? What on earth are they stickin' their noses in for?" said Annie. "It's a murder not a royal assassination."

"I believe it's that Chinaman. He might be an MSS operative."

"MSS? Who are they," said Annie.

"The Chinese Ministry of State Security, very tough and ruthless boys, apparently."

"Who, Mr Wu? A Chinese intelligence agent," laughed Annie. "They're wasting their time there. He's not that bright. And before you say he could be acting, he's not."

Hedly turned and headed for the shed. "Let's have a look then."

They walked over to the copse and they were joined by Hollis as they entered the clearing. The two uniformed constables let them past and they went into the entrance through a doorway that boasted a splintered door hanging from one hinge. They were met by the sight of rows and rows of healthy plants ready for harvest. Lights hung from the rafters connected by wires strung between them.

"Bloody hell," said Hedly, "It's a soddin' Tardis. It didn't look this big from the outside."

"A cunning arrangement of branches and fir trees were arranged to disguise this section here," said Hollis pointing to the far end of the shed, which was really the size of a low barn. From the outside it looks like a small shed. Even that part was camouflaged."

"It must have been that Jones, the green keeper. He's our man now. Best must have surprised him in the shed and paid the price."

"I've put an 'all points' out on him, He didn't turn up for work yesterday or today. He's not at home and his passport is missing. Looks like he's done a runner."

"Looks like Milbank's off the hook, eh? Call that tail off."

"Already done sir."

"Who did you use, by the way?"

"Ghosh." She paused, noting Hedly's surprised look. "The brown one, remember."

"Right, ok. And while you're at it I want this whole section of woodland taped off and it needs to be guarded closely. I don't want anyone coming back here to harvest this lot. It must be worth a bundle. And don't put this in any of your reports yet."

"Why not sir?"

"'Cause the chief said so. Not until we're sure about the connection otherwise we'll have the drug squad all over the place as well as the bloody feds. In any case, if Jones did it and there is no mention of the drugs he may think that we're not on to him. He might even try to get back to retrieve his stash."

"Would he be that dumb?"

"Bet on it. If he was dumb enough to bury Best next to the haul of cannabis, he's dumb enough to try to get it back. We'll be here waiting for him, won't we? Tell the rest of the squad, keep mum about the drugs."

"Good as done, sir."

"You won't believe this one Mike," said Larry. "That shed in the clearing, where Best was found."

"What about it?" said Mike after a swig of his beer.

"Full of drugs," said Larry out of the corner of his mouth.

"Drugs?"

"Cannabis."

"Cannabis? Bloody hell, how much?"

"I don't know," said Larry, "they didn't have a price list."

"Oh very funny," said Mike.

They were joined by Derek and Alan who were trying to avoid Jimmy. He was trying to remember his latest joke.

"Have you heard about the cannabis?" said Mike to Alan.

"What cannabis"

"I've got one about cannabis," interrupted Jimmy. "A druggy walks into an appliance store and asks the owner, 'How much for that TV set in the window?'

The owner looks at the TV set, then looks at the stoner, and says, 'I don't sell stuff to potheads.'

So the druggie tells the owner that he'll quit smoking pot and will come back the next week to buy the TV.

A week later, the druggie comes back and says, 'I quit smoking pot. Now, how much for that TV set in the window?'

And the store owner says, 'I told you I don't sell to potheads!'

So the druggie leaves again. He comes back a week later and says, 'How much for that TV?'

The owner says, 'I'm not going to tell you again, I don't sell to potheads!'

The giggling druggie looks back at the owner and says, 'How can you tell I'm a pothead?'

The owner looks back and says, 'Because that's a microwave.'"

They all broke in to laughter and Jimmy walked on, happy with the fact that he had not had any sarcastic remarks from this very hard to please audience.

Mike ordered a round and took up with the news about the cannabis once more. "Larry here, says that the cops have found cannabis in that shed where Best was found."

"Dope? Bloody hell, that's serious," said Derek. "The place will be full of drug squad cops now, you watch."

"Maybe the committee have been at it. That'd explain some of their potty ideas," said Alan. "Potty, Geddit?"

"Never mind pot. Has anyone got further with finding out about why we're skint?" asked Mike. "We're that skint they can't afford sand in the bloody bunkers and the greens haven't been mown for the past few days."

"Well hang on a bit. The Greens Chairman's a bit indisposed at the minute. Dead, in fact, so you can't have a go at him," said Alan.

"He doesn't mow the bloody greens, the green keeper is supposed to organise that. Every day as a matter of fact," said Derek, "and I happen to know he's been missing since yesterday morning.

"Bloody hell," said Alan. "Greens chairman dead an' the greenkeeper missing. We're all doomed."

"The course is," said Derek. "The green staff won't know what to do without Jones. And I'll bet he knows something about the weed in the shed as well."

"He's going to be the prime suspect now, eh?" said Mike.

"You've been watchin' too much telly, mate. Prime suspect....," scoffed Derek.

"Y'know," said Alan, "that might just explain why Jones was looking for Besty yesterday and why they were meetin' regularly down at the Stoat. Remember, Dermot was telling us the other day."

"What was I telling you?" said Dermot entering the bar in time to overhear the last sentence. "And whose round was it, I'll have a Guinness."

"We were talking about Chris Jones. He's not been seen since yesterday."

"And?"

"Besty was murdered yesterday."

"And?"

"Well, they found a shed full of cannabis this morning, next to where they found him," said Mike.

"This morning? Cannabis? Like maybe it had just been delivered?" Dermot started laughing and they all joined in. "With the Milk?" he added, still laughing, now much louder.

"How the hell did they miss that?" said Mike after they had all pulled themselves together. "How come they didn't find that yesterday?"

"They obviously didn't look very hard," said Derek. "Whatever happened to searching the area for forensic evidence? Like the murder weapon, for instance."

"I seem to remember something about the forensic aspect of the scene being knackered by some clumsy bastards holding a barn dance," laughed Alan.

They all started laughing again.

Mike turned back to Dermot, "We were thinking that Chris was the cannabis farmer and if Besty had caught him at it he may have earned himself a biff on the bonce, eh?"

"What makes you think it was Chris Jones's stash?" asked Dermot.

"Well If I remember rightly you were telling us about him and Winston," said Mike. "And he acted very jumpy when we ribbed him about it yesterday, didn't he? We all know that Winston likes a puff and you said he had been seen down there regular like in Jonesy's company."

"Winston? Likes a pouf?" said Jack who had now joined them. "There's nothin' poufy about Winston. I'll have a G&T by the way," he added as he saw Dermot's Guinness arrive. "Straight as a die, is old Winston, even if he does wear odd clobber."

"No, no, Jack. Not puff as in poufter, puff, as in cigarette puff. As in smokin' cannabis puff," said Mike. "Look, if there's dope involved and Jonesy's missing, the cops will be after him. Dead cert."

"Hey, there's Winston now, coming down the path," said Derek. "We can ask him."

"You ask him," said Jack. "He's generally a friendly sort of soul, but I'm not sure he'll take it that well if you are insinuating that he's involved in dealing in drugs. He's a big chap and looks as though he might possess a mean left hook."

"Oh don't be a wimp," said Alan. "He likes you and you are more diplomatic than us. Go on. Go and ask him."

"No!"

"Stop it Brunty," said Mike.

"What?" said Alan, smiling slyly.

"You know what I'm talking about. Stop winding Jack up."

"I think you lot should stop gossiping and leave drugs and murders to the police," said Jack. "I think you, as members, should be more interested in what I've managed to find out about the sale of our club."

They all turned and gave Jack their full attention.

Winston entered the lounge looking around as he made his way to the bar. He ordered a rum and coke and handed his card to Larry.

"Yo' seen dat Chris Jones t'day?" he asked.

"Nope. Nor yesterday. Seems to have done a runner after Besty was found."

"A runner? Bloody 'ell," said Winston, "you don' tink dat de Babylon tink he done dat killin', do you?"

"Well....., they found a load of drugs in the shed next to the body. What do *you* think?"

"Drugs?"

"Cannabis plants. Rows and rows of 'em. Ripe and ready for pickin'."

Winston's face dropped. He took a deep slug of his drink, wiped his mouth on his sleeve, attracting a disapproving stare from the president, and said, "Well wot dey say 'bout dat?"

"Well, it's him isn't it? He must have whacked Besty when he found him out. We all know that Besty was keepin' an eye on him an' he must have caught Jonesy at it. Why else would he scram if he didn't do it?"

Winston's face fell further and he gulped down the rest of his drink, looked at the president and pointedly wiped his mouth again, this time with an added flurry. He gave him a low bow, turned on his heel and strode out of the lounge.

CHAPTER 13

- Double your money -

"Come in," called Snape in answer to the sharp knock on his door. "Oh, it's you, Fordham. What do you want?"

"A word about our deal for a start," said Fordham closing the door behind him. "It appears that there is a listed tag on our clubhouse."

"So?"

"So, if our investor mates find out about it, they may pull out, eh?"

"And who will tell them, and why would they?"

"Well, I seem to remember at our last meeting, that you were a bit reluctant to include me in your little plan. I think you'll find that this news and my knowledge about it is a little reminder that you should."

"Look, Brian, we have already said that you are in and there is no reason why you should feel the need to threaten the situation."

"Good, I'm glad that's settled. Now what is happening about Jonny's share?"

"Jonny's share? He's dead. Why would he want a share now?"

"Y'see, the way I see it," said Brian slowly, "his share should pass to his partner." He grinned and pointed to his chest, "Namely me."

Snape's face froze. "Brian, you seem to have developed a bit of a greedy streak in the last couple of days. You also seem to have missed the possible reason for your partner's demise."

"Reason?"

"Do you think it might even be possible that Jonny met his end because maybe he got a bit greedy?" said Snape, adding a bit of menace to his voice.

"Now who's threatening?" Brian's face clouded. "If you think that I haven't covered my tracks and put an exit plan into place, you underestimate me and if anything happens to me you'll all be up to your armpits in shit," his voice raising to a shout over the last few words.

"Now, now, Brian," said Snape, "Keep your voice down. We've already had too many rows up here recently and the walls have ears.

We don't want the police to overhear any of this, do we? They're all over the place at the minute, so keep it down."

"Bollocks to them, you just make sure that I get what's coming to me or they'll find out everything soon enough without having to listen at keyholes. *Geddit*?"

With that Brian stormed out of the office slamming the door behind him, almost knocking Curtice back down the stairs.

"What the bloody hell are you doing, skulking outside doors, you nosey frog?" growled Brian.

"Pardonnez-moi, monsieur," said the indignant Frenchman, "I jus' bring ze san'wich for m'sieur Snap. **You** bump eento **me**."

The sandwich in question lay forlornly on the stairs, one slice of bread on the top step, butter down, and the remaining slices and the scattered filling of prawns with Parma ham draped over four of the top treads. There was also a generous helping of lettuce, tomato and cucumber arranged around the prime ingredients as if designed deliberately

"Well....." blurted Brian, "just watch it. Just ...." He looked at the remnants of the sandwich, then at Curtice. "I've got a mixed league dinner here later; just make sure that you've got everything ready for it. And you'd better get that lot cleared up. I can't stand around here all bloody day teaching you your job."

He brushed past the open mouthed Curtice and ran down the stairs.

"Bluddee committee membairs," cursed Curtice as he stormed back into the kitchen with the remains of his wrecked sandwich. "Zey sink zey own ze place."

"What's up Curt?" said Jayne as she followed Curtice into the kitchen.

"Zat bluddee Brian Fordham. Ee jus' knock ze plate out of my 'ans. All ovair ze stairs. Ee was shouteen' an' swaireen' at m'sieur Snap."

"Blimey, not another one rowing in that office. What was it this time?"

"Ee say ee kanow everyzeen an' heef anyseen 'appen to eem, ee weel put zem all up to ze armpeets in ze sheet. An' zen he say ee want what eez comeen to eem, hor helse."

"Cor," said Jayne. "I wonder what he means, 'I know everything'?"

"Ee don't kanow evryseen. Ee don't kanow 'ow to come down ze stairs for a start. An' ee don't kanow 'ow to say sorree eezair," said Curtice, buttering another slice of bread. He then proceeded to arrange the ingredients that he had gathered from the stairs back onto the bread and arranged the lettuce cucumber and tomato neatly around the repaired sandwich. "Zere we are. Good as new. Comme neuf."

The still fuming Curtice picked up the plate and said, "Zat 'ouse sharman, 'ee should kanow betair zan to mak ze chef hangry. 'Eel be sorree." He then made his way out of the kitchen and up the stairs to Snape's office bearing his rearranged offering.

Jayne made her way back into the bar and walked over to the gathering at the noisy end.

"Same again, please Jayne," said Derek.

Jayne busied herself gathering the necessary drinks that made up the order and collected Derek's swipe card before going to the till. When she returned the card and collected her tip she watched Fordham standing by his car as though he was thinking about something.

"He's just nearly knocked poor old Curtice down the stairs," she said to Derek.

"Who?"

"Him, that Brian Fordham, Jonny Best's pal."

"Bit rude, eh?"

Jayne leaned closer to Derek and said in a quiet voice, "I've just heard about another row up there. It's getting to be a regular occurrence, isn't it?"

As one, the rest of the group all turned towards Jayne.

"Bloody hell," she laughed, "Have you all got some kind of a special aerial for picking up gossip?"

"Yep," said Alan. "Always tuned in to the Gossiper's Channel. Set to pick up the juiciest first and then the closest to us the second. What row?"

"Well, Curt didn't hear it all but he was nearly knocked down the stairs by Brian Fordham. Curt heard Fordham yelling at Snape. Said something about knowing everything and threatening to drop them all in the mire if anything happened to him and if he didn't get what was coming to him.

He then barged out of the office and ran straight into Curt.

He called poor old Curt a nosey frog. That wasn't a very nice thing to say, was it?"

"But he is a nosey frog," said Mike.

"Even so, you shouldn't say it to him," replied Jayne with a pout. "He was really mad, y'know. It was a good job that he wasn't near them knives of his, that's all I say."

"Anything else," asked Derek.

"No, that's it," said Jayne, turning to attend to another member who had been trying to attract her attention for some minutes. Clearing his throat and uttering polite 'excuse me's weren't working but the dropping of coins onto the bar signalled a possible tip. A heavy clunk could mean a quid.

"I wonder what that was all about?" said Alan.

"Yeah, what does 'knowing everything' mean?" added Derek.

"More to the point," said Mike, "what did he mean by 'if anything happened to him'?"

"He's Jonny's pal and I'll bet he knew what he was up to," said Alan. "Maybe what Jonny was up to got him killed, eh?"

"If Fordham's not careful, he'll be next on the slab, annoying our Kermit," said John.

"Maybe we should tell the dibble," said Mike.

"Dibble?" said Jack. "What the bloody hell is a dibble?"

"Dibble, cops, police. Didn't you ever watch Top Cat on TV?" laughed Alan. "We all thought it was a gas calling the cops, dibble."

"Why?" insisted Jack. Why on earth would that be a laugh?"

"Because Officer Dibble was the blundering copper that Top Cat always got the better of."

Jack was now looking a bit uncertain. He could feel a wind-up coming on but he persisted, "And who would Top Cat be?"

"Stop it, Alan," said John.

"What?" said Alan innocently.

"You know, just stop it," said John. He turned to Jack. "Jack, it was a cartoon series and the main character was an alley cat called Top Cat. Juvenile youths, like this lot here, thought it amusing to taunt our boys in blue with the name of the inept policeman who used to chase the feral alley cats without any success."

"Spoilsport," laughed Alan.

"Why is it that all of our serious conversations seem to regress into meaningless trivia?" sighed Derek.

CHAPTER 14

- Venetian Dogs -

"He wants Best's share as well," said Snape into the phone.

"Who does?" asked the phone.

"Fordham. He's just been in here demanding to be included, after I'd already told him we might get him something. But now that Best is no longer a partner, he wants his share."

"Well, he can fuck off," said the phone angrily. "You tell him he's going to end up like Best if he's not careful."

"He said that he's got some insurance against that. Maybe we should take things a bit carefully before threatening him with death."

"Now look, matey," said the angry phone, "If you think I'm going to let some greedy bastard like Fordham take the piss out of me you've got another think coming. I'll sort him out in my way, leave it to me." The phone went silent and Snape shuddered.

"Hello, is that DI Hedly?" said a voice on the phone clamped to Hedly's ear.

"Yes, speaking."

"I have some information that might be connected to the death of Jonny Best," said the voice.

"What would that be?"

"I don't want to tell you over the phone,"

"Well, who's speaking?"

"Look, I can't talk now; I'm in the club hallway on the payphone and it's not a good place. I don't want to be overheard. Meet me at the club in the morning and I'll tell you all I know."

"I don't know who you are. How will I know you?"

"I'll know you. Nine o'clock in the men's lounge, it'll be empty at that time and we will be able to talk there."

"Who is this?" said Hedly impatiently.

"Nine o'clock." The line went dead.

Hedly dialled the club number. It rang for a few minutes and a female voice said, "Saleston."

"Who was just on that phone?" said Hedly sharply.

"Y'what?" answered the voice.

"On that phone. Who just made a call from that phone?"

"Look matey, this is a private members club and we don't give information about our member's phone habits or any other habits to any dick head who asks, see. So bog off." With that the line went dead.

"How did she know it was me?" said Hedly to himself, thinking that the girl was referring to his nickname. "When I find out who she was she's going to be in bother; talking to me like that."

He dialled Annie's number and when she answered he said, "Annie, I've just had a mysterious phone call from the clubhouse and someone has arranged to meet me in the morning with some info relating to Best's killing."

"You've arranged to meet *'someone'* at the clubhouse tomorrow," she stressed the word, someone, a bit sarcastically, thought Hedly. "Who?"

"He didn't give his name."

"How will you know who to talk to? Especially if there's more than one bloke there."

"**Sergeant** Clowes," said Hedly, stressing the sergeant, "You are going to go down to that clubhouse and you are going to find out who it was, aren't you?"

"Yessir. What time was it when he called?"

"About ten minutes ago, so he'll probably still be there if you get your bum into gear."

"On our way, sir."

Annie looked at Al and said, "Another trip to the Muppet show, I'm afraid."

"What now?"

"I'll explain on the way," she said grabbing her bag.

"I think that Fordham might be up to something," said Charles Blezzard.

"He's up to something all right. Up to trying to get Best's share as well as his own," said Snape.

"What?"

"He was in here earlier. He brought up the listed buildings matter and said that we should keep it from the buyers. 'Would be a shame if they found out,' he said. The bastard was hinting he might pass the information on if he wasn't included."

"But we'd already agreed to include him. He was getting Best's share."

"Ah, well that's where he moved the goalposts. He wants his share and Best's share. If we don't agree I think he means to tell the buyers and the cops."

"That explains the phone call," said Blezzard.

"What phone call?"

"I was just on my way up here ten minutes ago and I overheard him on the phone in the hall. He was making a call and I'm pretty sure it's to the police, I didn't actually hear who he asked for but it was about information affecting Best's murder. He's arranged to meet whoever he was talking to here tomorrow. In the gent's lounge at nine."

"Shit!" said Snape. "We'll have to assure him that he's in on the deal and that we'll try our best on the other share. Go and find him and tell him."

A very happy Brian was engaged in the boring details of the mixed league events and competitions throughout the season. He was finding it difficult to concentrate as his mind was elsewhere. His table companions were recollecting various games, close victories, missed putts and mixed opinions about the worthiness of the final winners of the league. At best they were probably lucky or at worst, they had cheated.

Before he went in for the dinner he had just had a quiet conversation with Charles Blezzard and he had been assured that he would be getting his hands on at least one hundred and fifty thousand smackers. Maybe three hundred thousand. Cruise city here we come. Next year he would be showing these boring bastards the photographs. He would tell Jill later. She would be over the moon as she had been hinting about cruises for years, driving him mad. He had also managed to convince Charles that he was meeting Hedly, the police inspector, merely to throw in some red herrings to keep him away from the club's finances. It was nice to see that the bastard was so nervous.

Him and his arrogant buddy, Snape.

His cup was running over and as Curtice passed his table, collecting the plates after completing the three course meal, he remembered the altercation at the top of the stairs.

In an attempt to make up for his angry outburst at the Frenchman he decided to compliment him on the quality of the pretty average steak that had challenged his suspect dentures, followed by the oversweet chocolate pudding. The gristly steak had been personally chosen by Curtice as revenge for the insults thrown at him by the angry House Chairman, as had the extra portion of castor sugar in his pudding.

"*Fuede meude servey parfait por les dodges, er, hote chiens du Venice,*" said an uncertain Brian, battling with his schoolboy French in an attempt to ingratiate himself with Curtice.

Unfortunately "Food fit to be served to the high Doges of Venice" does not translate to "*Fuede meude servey parfait por les dodges, er, hote chiens du Venice.*"

"*Quoi? Il a dit merde..*" yelped the astounded chef.

"He's just called my Chocolate by death, shit. Shit only fit to be served to the dodgy dogs of Venice," thought Curtice, in proper French; nothing like the crap French that the House chairman was attempting.

The incandescent chef stormed back into his kitchen so that he could throw a proper tantrum. He picked up a handy cleaver and began to attack the rib of beef destined for the Captain's table at his dinner to the committee.

The slap on the back from the House Chairman, who had followed the chef into the kitchen sensing the miffed reaction to his compliment, was badly timed really. The sharp end of the cleaver just missed Fordham's head as the mad chef swung it towards him but the handle caught him a glancing blow on his temple, knocking him to the ground.

The rage turned to horror and, as he realised what he had done, the mortified chef fled out the kitchen, barging into Tom who was looking for a bit of a snack after working late on the stock taking.

The horrified chef crumpled before the assistant pro, wailing, "Ze bastard say ze food eez sheet. I 'eet eem wiz ze kanife, almos' keel 'eem."

Tom grabbed him, "A knife? Hit him with a knife? Hit who with a knife? Calm down. What's happened?"

"Eet's zat bastard, Ford'am. Eet's ze secon' time zat 'ee's 'ad a go at me." He shuddered and pulled himself upright, glowered back at the kitchen and said, "I weel keel eem nex' time."

"You calm down and finish up in the dining room or you'll get the sack for skiving, not murder. Let's see if I can calm him down, make sure he's ok and see if we can clear this up."

In the meantime Fordham sat stunned, staring at the cleaver that had narrowly missed him. He slowly put his hand to the fast growing lump on his head. "Bollocks to this, I'm going to get a cop. He bloody near killed me then."

"It seems to me that there are a few people here that would like to have given Besty a knock on the head," said Derek.

"Who've you got in mind?" asked Alan.

"Well there's Janice Blezzard for a start."

"Janice? Why would she want to kill him? Wasn't she doing a bit with him?" said Mike.

"Yes, I know," said Derek. "But I didn't mean her, I meant Charles. He wouldn't be too happy about it, would he?"

"Charles didn't give a toss who was having it off with Janice," said Dermot. "Well known fact. He wouldn't have killed him for that but I suppose he might have other reasons."

"Well, what about Milbank?"

"Ah, well that's a different case. He'd want to give him a clout but he's not got the necessary,"

"He might have got someone else to do it," said Derek.

"What? Like a hit man?" said Mike. "Like Mack 'the Shovel'."

"Don't you mean Mack the Knife, like the song?" said Jack.

"He was hit with a shovel," said Mike, "Why would Mack the Knife use a shovel?"

"Isn't a shovel the same as a spade?" asked Dermot, entering into the spirit of the daft discussion.

"Yes, but calling him Mack the Spade would lead one open to accusations of racism. Wouldn't it?"

"Are you at it again, you two," laughed John.

Tom came rushing into the bar and, spotting the lads, he asked, "Has anyone seen Brian Fordham?"

"He's in the dining room with the mixed league mob," said Jayne, overhearing Tom's question.

"No he's not, I've just looked in there and I could only see Jill."

"Have you looked in the kitchen?" she asked, "I saw him following Curt in there about ten or fifteen minutes ago."

"No, I looked in there first. I just saw Curt and he said that he had just had a bit of a barney with Fordham. Apparently the house chairman had criticised his cooking in some way and I think he may have been clouted."

"Clouted? Blimey, I've heard of complaining to the chef about the grub, but I didn't think you were allowed to clout 'em," said Alan.

"No, Curtice clouted Fordham, with a knife or a cleaver," said Tom.

"Er, I think the technical term for clouting someone with a knife, is stabbing," said Derek. "i.e. stabbed."

"An' with a cleaver, chopped," added Alan.

"Whatever," said Tom irritably, "I can't find him now, clouted, stabbed or chopped."

"Where's Curtice now," asked Alan.

"I just saw him serving coffee to Jill Fordham and he looked his usual self, as though nothing had happened," said Jayne.

"Well, where the bloody hell is Fordham?" said Mike. "We'd better go and find him or Kermit's for the chop. Oops, I mean sack. C'mon, split up, find him and then calm him down. And whatever you do, don't tell anyone else about the argument, especially the clouting with the cleaver bit."

"Have you seen Brian?" said Jill Fordham. She had gone into the bar and waited for Jayne to finish serving.

"No," said Jayne, "I thought he was in there with you."

Jill, a bit fed up with waiting to get Jayne's attention, leaned forward and put one elbow on the bar. She put the point of the index finger of her other hand under her chin and rolled her eyes up to the ceiling as if in thought. After a short pause she said, "If he was in there with me I would hardly be stood here wasting my breath asking you where he was, would I?"

"Oh, I don't know," said Jayne sweetly, "It wouldn't be the first time that he had been ignored as though he wasn't there. He can be quite invisible can our Mr Fordham, often ignored by some people. At least that's what he told me."

Jill glared at Jayne and then looked along the bar to see Jack come in through the other door. She went round the bar to meet him. "You haven't seen Brian on your travels have you?"

"Erm, no Jill, we.... erm, I mean, I haven't."

Mike barged in through the same door and blurted, "He's not upstai..., Oh, hello Jill. Can I have a round over here please Jayne?"

Alan piled in after Mike. "Not in the locker roo.... er, hi Jill."

"I'm looking for Brian," said Jill to Alan, "Have you seen him?"

"Um, not since I saw him go into the dining room earlier. It looked as though he'd come from upstairs. He looked rather pleased with himself now that I think of it."

"I thought he was out here getting a round in for the table," said Jill.

Brian? Getting a round in for the table?" laughed Dermot as he walked in. "was he holding the kitty?"

"Kitty?" said the puzzled Jill.

"Well the only time he seems to get a round in is when he's holding a kitty. Usually gets himself a scotch on it and slugs it down before he gets back to the table," said Dermot laughing. "You've found him then?"

"How did you know I was looking for him? You weren't here when I asked."

Before Dermot could answer Annie and Al, the two detectives, entered the lounge.

"Hello," said Annie, "Perhaps one of you could help me. If someone were to make a call from down here, which phone would they use?"

"It depends," said Mike. "If it was a member, they'd use the phone in the hall. It's a payphone. Staff or committee members would use that one behind the bar or the private phones in the offices. Why?"

"Is the one in the hall used often?" asked Annie, ignoring Mike's question.

"Not really, most people have mobiles now and if they were making a call from their own phones they would make one from down the hall or outside," said Jack.

"Why's that?" asked Hollis.

"Against the rules to make calls in any of the club lounges."

"Was anyone seen making a call in the last hour?"

There was a collective shrug.

"Brian was on the payphone about then," said Jayne. "I was trying to make a call and I heard his voice on the line so I hung up."

"Did you hear what he was saying?" asked Al.

"No. He would know someone had picked up this handset and I was the only one here so I put the phone down, rapid like."

"Where is he?" asked Annie.

They all looked at her, then at each other.

Jill was first to break the silence. "He's been missing for the last twenty or thirty minutes. We were in the dining room when he suddenly jumped up and went out. I thought he had gone to the gents and when he didn't come back I thought he had just got waylaid by another member and was gassing about his latest exploits on the course, as men are prone to do. You'd think it was unarmed combat the way they go on."

"Have you had a good look around?" asked Annie.

Derek, the last of the clandestine search party, burst in behind the detectives and, not recognising them from behind, he said, "He's not outside and his car had gone."

"Who's not outside Derek," asked Annie, turning to face the breathless ex copper.

"Oh, it's you," said the sheepish Derek, realising he had probably dropped a clanger. "Er, we were looking for Brian Fordham."

"Why?" chorused Annie and Jill.

Derek looked at his pals and sighed.

"I suppose we had better tell you about his argument with Kermit."

"Kermit?" said Annie.

"Kermit?" said Jill.

"Oh, I mean Curtice, the club chef. It appears that Brian insulted his cooking and they had a bit of a row. Seems Kermit, I mean Curtice, had a bit of a swing at Brian."

"And?"

"Well," Derek shrugged his shoulders, "Brian appears to have done a runner. Car gone, Brian gone."

"And this Kermit," said Annie looking at Hollis, "Where can we find him?"

"You had better do a runner Curtice," said Tom. "We can't find Fordham anywhere and the police have turned up. He must have phoned them."

"Ho, sheet!" groaned Curtice, "Hi weel loose my job, for sure. Ze bastard weel sack me an' ze gendarmes weel put me een ze Bastille."

"Just disappear for a day or two," said Tom. "We don't know why he's missing but his car's gone as well. He might have gone to the A and E to get his head seen to. He'll calm down when he sees that it's not serious."

"Hay an' he? Is zat like ze hay hay?"

"No. The AA is for cars, cylinder heads. A and E is in hospitals, for human heads, in Fordham's case, dick heads."

Tom grabbed Curtice's arm and dragged him out the back door. "Come on, let's do one."

They both headed for Curtice's small Citroen intent on getting out of the line of fire.

Annie and Al barged into the dining room "Right, where's that chef then? We want a word."

"Excuse me," blustered the Lady Captain, leaping from her chair an instant before the Gent's Captain, Simon Partridge.

"I'll handle this," said Partridge, dismissing Jennie Milbank's effort to take control of the situation. "This is a private function for members only. If you wish to organise a function for *non* members," he said, stressing the non, "you will have to make an appointment with the Hon Secretary, Mr Blezzard." He looked around, displaying his smug contempt for the rude intruders. "Now, if you will excuse us, I am about to make the prize presentations."

"I am Detective Sergeant Clowes," replied Annie, "and this is DC Hollis. We are here in connection with the murder of one of your members as well as a possible assault on one of your committee members. I'm afraid your presentation will have to wait until we have a word with your chef as well as anybody who witnessed the assault or who has any information pertinent to that assault. Now, where's the chef?"

Partridge sat down with a bump, the room was silent.

"Well?" barked Hollis, "Where is he?"

There was a general hubbub as the seated diners looked at each other and then at the two dumfounded captains before Mary Agnew, the Lady President, said offhandedly, "Well, he was here a few minutes ago.

I suggest you look in the kitchen, where you would normally find people like chefs."

Mary was a well known snob and women's rights activist. She still fought a fight that had long been won and even the women members were tired of her strident views on the battle of the sexes. She would have made a perfect man and, had she been accorded that status, she would certainly have banned all women from any golf club she had been a member of.

"We've just come from there," said Annie, "and failing to find him there we headed for the place where we thought we would find people who should know where their *servants* were. Seems we picked the wrong room, or the wrong people, eh?" She looked around the room at the shocked assembly. "I would appreciate your not leaving here until we find the missing chef. We would also like to hear from those people who saw him last."

The two detectives then turned and left the silenced room.

"We can't keep them here for long, they'll kick off in about five minutes, huffing and puffing about their rights and claiming close relationships with the chief constable or the prime minister or some such big wig," said Annie. "Let's bugger off and get an APB out for the two of them before that lot start."

They exited the building and climbed into Annie's car. As they headed out of the car park Annie had to swerve to avoid the car that has pulled in of the road, swinging a bit too far over as it did.

"Bloody hell, that was close," said Annie. "Shall we go back and bag that bugger?"

"I thought you wanted to get away," said Hollis. "It was only Milbank anyway. We can still give him a bollocking when we speak to him next."

"OK, let's go and get a beer somewhere. I'm fed up with this bunch of weirdoes."

Milbank went to the back of the club to park his car intending to slip in unannounced to see if he could catch his wife at it. He switched of his engine and noticed a shadow in the trees at the far end of the car park.

He walked over slowly and saw a figure leaning into the boot of a car hidden in the bushes.

Recognising the registration as Brian Fordham's he crept up closer. "Hi Brian," he said cheerily as he got up to the car, slapping the House Chairman on the back. "What are you up to? 'Ere, you're not Brian........"

"We're going to have to tell them who told us about Kermit and the knife/cleaver incident y'know," said Derek. "Tom is bound to spill the beans as soon as he is asked about tonight."

"Why should they ask him, he wasn't here when the cops arrived so they won't connect him to our reason for looking for Brian?"

"Where is Tom, anyway?" asked Dermot.

"If he's got any sense he's buggered off," said Mike. "What made him think that he could have straightened it out between Fordham and Kermit anyway?"

"Well we can't cover up too much," said Derek. "If we are asked direct questions we'll have to tell them who told us about the row, otherwise we will be perverting the course ... etc. Can be a bit naughty that one."

"Perverting," said Mike, "Like paedophiling, y'mean?"

"Don't start," said John. "Jayne, more beer, here, now," he shouted over the bar.

"Where are you and Hollis?" said Hedly into his phone.

"In the pub," said Annie, "We're just having a quiet drink before closing time, just made it."

"Well you'd better get back to the club and let them lot out. They're going ballistic."

"What, you mean they're still there?" laughed Annie, "I thought that arrogant bunch at the dinner would have buggered off as soon as we left."

"Not so," said Hedly. "I'm on my way now as well."

"You sir? Why would you need to go?"

"Because there's a man missing in the vicinity of a murder scene, that's why."

"Who? You mean that Fordham?"

"Yes."

"He can't be far away. He was seen by over thirty or forty people only ten minutes before he actually disappeared.

And not only that, he had an argument with that French chef before leaving in a huff. In fact they're both missing."

"Chef? No one mentioned the chef."

"I've just mentioned the chef..... Hasn't Fordham been found yet?"

"You're supposed to be the bloody copper, why should anyone else have found him? His missus is going spare, getting a bit hysterical, in fact."

"Look sir, technically they're not actually missing yet. They need to have been gone for twenty four hours. That Fordham may well have gone to that knocking shop, say. Because he can't be found by his wife doesn't mean he's actually 'missing' as in 'missing'."

"You look," said Hedly through his now clenched teeth, "just get down there and tell those people that they can go home and then organise a search for this Fordham. I'll see you in thirty minutes."

CHAPTER 15

-Pole Cats and a hole in two-

"Have we tried 'Pole Cats'?" said Derek.

"I'll go," said Alan, a bit too quickly really.

"No, I'll go."

"Me, I'll do it."

"No, me. Let me."

There was a chorus of voices now rising in pitch, all eager to volunteer to check out 'Pole Cats'. Just then Jill Fordham returned from the payphone where she had unsuccessfully tried to reach Brian at home. She pushed past the baying bunch of volunteers and reached Derek at the front of the mob.

"What the bloody hell's going on?" she yelled at him above the din.

"I'm trying to organise a search party and when I asked who would check out 'Pole Cats', this started."

"Pole Cats? What or who is Pole Cats?"

"Er, don't you know?"

"If I knew, I wouldn't be asking," she said.

"Well," Derek hesitated, aware that he was treading on dangerous ground. "It's a kind of dance studio." It was the best that he could do, on the spur of the moment that is. Given a bit more time he thought he would have done better, but it's doubtful.

"Dance studio? Why would you want to check a dance studio?"

"Um ..... Some of the lads thought it would be a nice surprise for the ladies," said Mike butting in smartly. "Y'know, for the next candlelit dinner function, like. Surprise you all with their dancing prowess....."

Jill looked at Mike, blinked a couple of time and then looked at Derek. Derek gulped and looked at the ceiling.

"Y'know, you old buggers are bloody barmy. I've never heard such bollocks in all my life."

She started to walk back to the dining room then hesitated before turning back. "Just a minute," she said, eyes narrowed and lips pursed, "Pole Cats. Pole Cats. That would be a great name for that knocking shop in the village."

"Knocking shop?" said Derek, eyebrows raised in mock surprise, "In the village?"

"Bloody **bastarding** lap **fucking** dancing knocking **bloody** shop," spat Jill venomously, accentuation every expletive. "The one with no sign on the door, just a picture of a pouting prostitute pretending to have her hair done. That's the one, isn't it?"

"Oh there," said Derek weakly. "I thought that was a hairdressers; never paid much attention really. I don't think they mean there do they Mike? ..... Mike?"

Mike had turned his back and hunched his shoulders as though sheltering from a storm. The storm that was sure to come.

"You bastards. My Brian wouldn't be seen dead in there. Not like you old has-beens. I'll bet you lot are always in there, all going short, ogling the naked prostitutes. I'll bet you pay for a shag as well."

Dermot turned around, face clouding fast and growled, "Oy, don't you start calling us old farts has-beens. None of us have even been inside that dump. We're just having a laugh. Not like your darling' Brian and Jonny Best. I believe Best was their best customer, followed closely by his pal, Brian Fordham, your Brian."

"He did a bit with Janice Blezzard the club bike as well, according Keith Smithson, our duck chaser. He's seen them at it when he was taking Snotty for a walk," added Mike, equally miffed at Jill's accusation about frequenting 'Pole Cats'."

"What? Janice Blezzard. That's worse than that knocking shop. I don't believe you," said Jill.

"Please yourself, love. But if you want to make sure you have looked everywhere, I'd send someone down to that hairdressers," said Mike. "And have a word with the Lady Captain as well. There's a rumour that she's been spreading her favours about during her term."

"The bastard! Bastard!" she started to sob. "He was going to take me on a cruise," she added through her tears. Then, pulling herself together, her tears turned to anger again. "The lousy bastard said he had a lot of money coming his way. Those bitches must have been paying him." The anger was building "I'll kill him when I find him; I'll kill him twice over. Where's that whoreing Lady Captain? She should get a job at that whore house." With that she stormed out of the bar.

"Oops," said Derek, "We appear to have dropped Brian in the shit."

"Never mind," said Alan, "You've probably saved Kermit's skin. By the time Jill gets through with him, he'll have forgotten his bust up in the kitchen. And, if he's managed to do any stabbin' or choppin', she might give him a big tip."

"Well," said Hedly as he joined the two detectives. "Have you found him?"

"Who? The chef or the House Chairman?"

"Fordham."

"Well, the one that Mrs Fordham's kicking off about is the House Chairman, her husband, and he is still missing, for starters. And the other one we'll find when we actually start looking for him."

"Why can't you look for both of them?"

"We've only got the word five minutes ago and there's only two of us. Give us a chance guv."

"I've brought reinforcements," said Hedly. O'Hara and Partington, the two constables who were guarding the scene of the murder, sauntered into the bar and stood behind Hedly. They didn't look best pleased but they probably hadn't got round to calculating the overtime yet. When they did, they'd be happier and it was warmer inside as well. "Ghosh is on his way. I've asked him to call into Pole Cats on his way. I believe he's a regular."

"Who, Ali," said Al. "I thought they weren't supposed to fornicate."

"Not Ali, Fordham," said Hedly. "Anyway, 'course they fornicate. If they didn't, how come there's so many of them?"

"Sir, you're at it again," said Annie. "And how did you know that Fordham was a regular?"

"Ghosh was there earlier asking about Best and was smart enough to get a list off the doorman," said the chastened Hedly. He promised himself to try to stop with the inappropriate comments as they were clearly not impressing the sergeant.

"He did well there, didn't he? Not normal for that sort to be helpful, is it?" said Annie.

"Whatever. He's going to have a look anyway, so let's get ourselves organised, shall we. We've got work to do."

"That was a bit exciting last night, wasn't it," said Alan as he swished his club back and forward in an effort to un-stiffen his stiff muscles. It was a useless exercise and never worked. Alan and his pals always believed themselves too good at the game to need to warm up properly and would generally turn up at the tee five minutes before tee off time, have fag, a bit of a swish and then drive off. Generally into the stream some seventy yards from the tee, or the trees, a similar distance at about thirty degrees to the left.

"Have they found Fordham yet?" asked Dermot.

"Dunno," said Mike. "They all seem to have disappeared themselves. Not seen them this morning anyway so they must be covering the stations and airports," he added laughing.

"It was a bit queer what Jill was saying about his promising a cruise, eh," said Dermot. "He's not that flush usually, especially spending his hard earned down at Pole Cats. Where would he be getting cruise money?"

"You're right there," said Derek, "Where indeed? Remember the other night before Jonny disappeared. They were deep in conversation that night about something and Besty was a bit cocky as well if I recall, called us suckers. That smacks of *'I'm a smart bastard and I've got loads of money. You bums haven't'.*"

"Could they have both been involved with that cannabis they found?" said Alan.

"That tête à tête was the day that Besty was rowing with Snape and Blezzard," said Mike. "I wonder if that involved club affairs or drug affairs."

"What, you mean Snape knew about the drugs?" said Derek. "Nah, not Snape, he's too smart for that."

"Not if it means selling the club," said Dermot. "He may have seen it as a last resort."

"I think you're barking up the wrong tree," said Derek. "We know that Snape and Blezzard are up to something with those two new guys and I think that there is more than meets the eye about their involvement. Let's see what else Jack finds out."

"Are we playing golf, or what?" said Alan before taking aim.

They spent the next half hour attacking the course, carefully rearranging its layout with subtle removal of parts of the fairway.

After donating a few balls to the invisible ball monster that had to be fed from time to time, they found themselves on the third tee, ready to pass the recent crime scene.

"Try and stay out of there lads," said Mike pointing at the copse after triumphantly hitting his ball straight down the fairway. "All that tape wrapped 'round the trees means that you can't go in to find any balls that may stray in there, don'cha know." This little gem of information was meant as added pressure on his opponents as such a taunt generally resulted in the exact opposite.

Derek put his ball on the tee and surveyed the fairway ahead of him, failing his attempt to ignore the yellow tape that denoted the area he was meant to avoid. His wild swing achieved the result that Mike had engineered. The ball arced toward the copse just as the unkempt figure of Keith Smithson burst from the trees in flurry of branches followed by his barking dog, Snotty.

"**Help, help, murder**..." yelled the frantic Smithson, accompanied by the barking Snotty. Smithson was waving wildly and pointing towards the trees where he had just appeared from.

"It's Keith," said Mike. "He's the one that found Best."

"Looks like he's found him again," said Derek. "Come on, let's go and help him, he must have cracked up, eh?"

"Sod off," said Dermot, "You go an' help him. I'm still having nightmares about it. That dead body grabbed me by the leg, I'll never forget that. You should be helping me not him."

Derek, Mike and Alan hurried towards the trees where Smithson was bent grasping his knees, gasping with the effort of yelling. The dog was still barking.

"Calm down old chap. You must try to forget about it," said Derek, taking charge.

"Another one.... In the same bloody hole as the last one," said Keith.

"Another what?"

"Body. Another body."

"What? Who?" said Mike.

"I don't know. I didn't stop to have a close look. Snotty did it again."

"Well, where's the police guard?" said Mike. "Aren't they supposed to be guarding this place?

It's a crime scene and there's a shed-full of cannabis here as well."

"I think they're all looking for Fordham if you remember," said Derek. "Let's hope we haven't found him first."

They started forward into the trees when Derek held out his arms stopping their progress. "Wait a minute, the last time this happened we got a bollocking for tramping all over the crime scene. Let's not do that again, eh?"

"What?" said Alan. "Bugger off, we'll be careful. We have to have a look."

"One of us will have a look, just to confirm what Keith has said. You call the clubhouse and get them to call the incompetent bastards that left this place unguarded."

"When were you promoted to Chief Constable?" said Mike, miffed that he couldn't see the body. He wanted to have a look at the cannabis stash as well. "You just want to find your ball, don't you?" he added.

Alan started laughing and they all joined in, nervously at first, but grew in volume as they saw the funny side.

Dermot and Keith, having heard the laughter, mistook it for a sort of all clear and decided to venture further into the trees. Keith thought that the laughter signalled that what they had found was not a body after all and that he must have been mistaken. Snotty carried on barking. Their noisy progress into the trees, along with the barking, encouraged the others towards the clearing, thoughts of securing a clean crime scene and alerting the authorities forgotten.

Winston was a worried man. He had borrowed a substantial amount of money from Garfield Bassong, a cheerful but deadly drugs baron from Wythenshawe, in order to finance the growing of the cannabis with Jones. They all stood to make a lot of money.

Winston had tried to explain the situation VIS A VIS the murder and the discovery of the cannabis to Garfield, without any real success. ""You get yo' black ass down dere and get dat stuff or yo is dead," was the terse reply to his pleading of shit karma.

He did as he was bid and got his darkish bum down to the shed in an attempt to harvest enough of the stash to placate the grumpy drugs baron.

His intention was to sneak in under darkness, hoping that the shed wasn't guarded, but when he got to the club there was a bit of a commotion around the car park. He got closer and he witnessed the panic caused by the missing Fordham. He watched as all the police gathered by their cars and then saw them disburse in all directions.

He waited for a couple of hours and when they didn't return he set about his task. He had surmised, correctly, that the guards would be missing until the following morning and was able to collect a significant quantity of ganja in sacks and stack them into his unmarked van hidden at the back of the car park. He was still in the shed, collecting his last sack, when he heard the commotion outside the shed, generated by the shell shocked Keith and his rowdy dog. By the time he had tied up the sack he heard the approaching golfers and, not wishing to be discovered, he hastened away from the shed in a different direction to that which he had arrived. Straight into the shallow pit where Snotty had only just discovered his second body, the body of Brian Fordham, lying face up, staring accusingly at Winston.

Just as the laughing group and the barking dog emerged into the clearing, the horrified Winston was rising, pretty quickly, from the pit.

The night before he had taken the precaution of being less conspicuous than usual by donning a black jumpsuit as well as disguising his generous dreadlocks with a large ski mask. The mask featured two eye holes and a single slash at the mouth; the slash allowing him to breathe more freely. It was a very black ski mask and his extremely wide eyeballs were very white, so were his teeth, now bared ready to emit the scream of terror that was waiting to enunciate the fear that had just been generated by the open-eyed body of the ex house chairman.

The scream was the cause of another crime scene being contaminated, initially by the dog, which had immediately stopped barking and ran for its life, spraying a stream of dog shit behind it, worthy of that of a much larger dog.

Keith and the golfers managed to surpass their previously successful destruction of a crime scene, completely obliterating any possible forensic evidence when they all tried to run in different directions, all away from the apparition in front of them;

all screaming louder than the terrified Winston; all trying to stop themselves from adding to the produce of the dog's incontinence.

Hedly surveyed the scene, holding a handkerchief to his face in an effort to block out the smell. Clowes and Hollis joined him, followed by Ghosh. The two constables were stationed at the entrance to the clearing, once again guarding a crime scene, albeit the same one.

"Where's Maxwell?" asked Annie.

"On her way," said Hedly. "I told her she'd need a mask. No point in getting scene of crime techies here, the place is wrecked again. Does this bloody murderer bury 'em and then hold a bloody war dance? Shat all over the place this time." He blew his nose. "Look out for a Red Indian with shit on his shoes and we've got our man."

"I think you're at it again, sir," said Annie.

"What?"

"Racist comments, sir."

"Racist?"

"I know sir, it's a bit harsh and we wouldn't report you sir, but...." she looked around theatrically, "the trees..."

"The trees?" Hedly looked at the nearest offending tree. "What about the trees?"

"Have ears, sir."

"Right, I get it," he sighed. His shoulders slumped at his failure to avoid this terrible racist trend in his character.

"How the hell did he get another one in here? It's only a bit of a hole." He looked accusingly at Annie. "Isn't it supposed to be a guarded crime scene?"

"Well, if you remember sir," said Annie, adopting a bit of a patient tone. "We had a hysterical woman looking for her two timing, missing, cheating bastard of a husband, just to mention one or two of the attributes she gave him, last night."

"So?"

"So we were short handed, sir. You took O'Hara and Partridge of the observation to try and find him. Ghosh as well, if I recall correctly."

"Still a bit audacious, isn't it? I wonder if he was watching us."

"Quite possibly sir. He may even have been in the clubhouse, heard your instruction regarding the observation detail."

Hedly didn't like the way these details were being presented and looked decidedly glum. He would have to work hard on the reports to avoid taking the total blame for this mess. He looked around and caught sight of a dark shape in the bushes. "What's that over there?"

Hollis followed his gaze and, spotting the shape, he walked over to inspect it.

"It's a sack, sir," he said.

"Of what?" said Hedly, "and don't say shit," he added threateningly.

Hollis cut the twine with his pocket knife and opened the sack. The contents spilled out onto the floor.

"Looks like cannabis, sir," said Hollis.

A look of horror crossed the face of the Inspector. "Please don't tell me someone has had it away with some of that cannabis."

He turned and looked at the shed. The door was open. They looked at each other and they all made a dash to the partly open door. Hollis was first to it and he threw it fully open. They trooped in and stared at a completely harvested floor. All that was left was a pile of boxes and some empty sacks pushed up to the end of the large shed.

"Jesus, someone's had it away with the whole crop. It was worth thousands," said Hollis.

Hedly was speechless. He looked at the empty floor with a gradually growing sense of dread. He was done for. No amount of report fiddling would get him out of this.

"Look sir," said Annie, "forget about the cannabis. The chief doesn't need to know it's missing. What he doesn't know won't hurt. We can hide its disappearance until we have solved the lot. We have to concentrate on the murders."

He looked at Annie, a puzzled look on his face. Like a poodle that can't find the ball under the settee.

"He said to keep the cannabis out of our reports and to keep it under our hats, remember? Now, c'mon sir," she stressed. "We **have** to get going on the murders. Forget the grass for now."

He shook himself like the poodle he was just compared to. "You're right Annie. The murders. What have we got?"

"Well, we've got two dead bodies for a start," said Al with a nasty grin. "That's what started it all; the first one."

"Ok, ok. Who found the second one?" asked Hedly.

Annie screwed her face up and sucked her breath in through pursed lips, "Well, that's it you see. It was the same crowd who found the first one."

"Crowd? How did a crowd find it? Was it them bleedin' Indians that turned the ground into shit?"

"Sir, stop it," said Annie with a frown. "It was the dog, Snotty and his owner, Smithson, who found it first. They were here in the copse, the dog was looking for balls again."

"Looking for balls? There's a fucking big ring of yellow tape that says 'No Entry', 'Crime Scene', 'Don't Come In Here', wrapped around the whole bleeding bunch of trees. Can't he read?"

"He's a dog sir. Pretty smartish, able to drink brandy an' all, but just a dog," said the smiling Hollis.

"Not the dog you imbecile," snapped Hedly, forgetting who he was talking to. "Smithson, the bloody dog owner. Can't he read?"

Annie stepped between them before Hollis could react to the 'imbecile' bit and said calmly, "The dog went in first sir and wouldn't come out, y'see. Smithson had to go in to get him and there he was, in the hole, scraping away at the ground."

"Him or the dog?"

"Him or the dog what, sir?"

"Scraping away at the ground."

She sighed, looked to the heavens and said, "The dog sir. The dog was in the hole, scraping away at the earth that was covering the body, sir." She brightened up a bit and added, "He's done quite a bit actually, uncovered the top half of the body as well as the face."

"Oh goody, perhaps we can get him a part time job as a gravedigger. I'll have a word with old 'Digger Graves', the local undertaker, shall I?"

"Er, that's that sarcasm stuff again, is it sir?" said Annie quietly.

"Ok, ok," sighed Hedly. "Carry on. Where does the 'crowd' bit come in?" he continued, fighting to compose himself.

"I don't think you're going to like this bit either, sir. Perhaps you should take a deep breath."

Hedly glowered at her, still fighting his temper. "Go on. Tell me."

"It was the same four that trampled all over the ground when they found Best."

"Give me a drink of something Larry," said Keith, "I've just found another one."

"Another what?"

"Body, that's what."

"Body, dead body?"

"Course its bloody dead. Whoever head of a live body?"

"Who is it? Or should I ask, was it?"

"Am I gettin' a bloody drink, or what?"

"I'm not sure," said Larry. "This body findin' lark isn't on the 'approved expenses' list an' it's costin' us a bit too much recently. I'll have to have a word with the House Chairman."

"I can't wait 'til they elect a new House Chairman," said Keith.

"Eh?"

"House Chairman. That's who was in the hole. That's who Snotty uncovered."

"Bloody 'ell," breathed Larry. He turned to the back of the bar and pushed the brandy optic twice with the glass, "Here. Have a double," he said, handing the glass to Keith. He picked up another glass and returned to the optics. "In fact, I'll have a large one meself. Bollocks to the 'body finding' tab."

"Can you sort Snotty out as well?" asked Keith. "He's had a hell of a shock when Fordham's ghost jumped out of the grave."

"Y'what? Ghost?"

"Well ghost or demon. I'm not sure what the fuck it was. We all did a sharp exit when we saw it, him faster than the rest of us. You should have seen the trail of shit he laid. It was phenomenal."

"What...... like, he shat himself? I didn't know ghosts needed to shit. I mean they don't eat anything, do they?"

"Not the ghost, y'fool. Snotty. He shat himself."

Larry looked at the dog, who was looking up at the bar. "Oh right, the dog." It seemed to Larry that there was a kind of hopeful look on Snotty's face.

"You had to see it to believe it. Mind you, the rest of us were close to beating him. Frightening, it was. Frightening."

Keith took a gulp of brandy, shaking his head at the memory.
"Rest of us?"

"What?"

"You said, 'rest of us'."

"Oh yeah, this lot." Keith indicated the four pale looking members as they entered the gent's lounge, grim-faced and silent.

"Give us all some of that brandy," demanded Alan as he reached the bar.

"What, like on the 'dead body' tab you mean?"

Alan looked at Larry then back at the rest of the troop then back at Larry. "Er... yep that'd be it. The 'dead body' tab would be ok." He looked back at the lads and shrugged his shoulders as Larry went to the optics.

"And don't forget Snotty," said Keith.

"Don't you mean shitty?" said Dermot. "It's a good job I was wearing my waterproofs. They were covered in it. I've had to chuck 'em in the bin."

"They might be waterproof but they're not shitproofs are they?" said Mike. "I can still smell it."

"Ah well, I'm not actually sure that was the dog," said Dermot. "It was a bit of a shock y'know. I was just heading for the bog to check it out."

"What were you lot doing in there anyway?" said Larry. "I would have thought finding Best would have cured you. Especially after that Hedly copper had given you such a hard time over the crime scene. Messin' it up and all."

"Well he can't blame us this time," said Derek, "Not after the mess he made," he added, pointing at the sullen terrier, who was still waiting for his drink. "We all saw it. It was 'orrible."

Alan had a gulp of his brandy. "It was big an' black," he said, staring into space. "And it had a great big black head with two big staring eyes."

"Big an' white an' bloodshot," added Mike. "Don't forget the bloodshot."

"Yeah... an' bloodshot."

"An' don't forget the big red mouth with the pointy teeth," said Mike.

"Yeah.... pointy teeth."

"Blimey," said Larry, mouth open, enthralled by the tale of horrible monster. "You'd better have another."

He commenced pouring another six shots of brandy while Snotty made short work of the dregs in the, now empty, glasses littering the floor.

"They've found Fordham," said Charles Blezzard. "Those bastards have done him in, haven't they?"

"What? You mean he's dead?" said Snape.

"Yes, dead as mutton. Those bastards mean business and we're next."

"Which bastards?" said Snape.

"The bastards that did for Best," said Charles. "The bastards that are supposed to be sorting us a nice retirement. Well, we weren't supposed to be getting a permanent retirement, were we?"

"Oh pull yourself together man," said Snape. "They didn't kill those two greedy bastards even though it looks a bit suspicious."

"How do you know?"

"I've already spoke to them this morning and they had already agreed to pay Fordham his double share."

"What!"

"Yes and it wasn't hard to get it. They agreed very easily, even said that we were to get a bit extra as it wouldn't be fair that he should benefit more than we did."

"Well they would agree to it if they knew he wasn't going to collect, wouldn't they."

"They don't know. I hadn't told them because I didn't know myself until two minutes ago."

"If they did it then they do know," said Blezzard. "Are you blind?"

"Blind?" Snape bristled, unhappy at Blezzard's insult. He paused for a couple of seconds and then said quietly, "There is that possibility, but I have arranged to meet them in an hour. Maybe you should be there to see their reaction when I tell them. They said they would be bringing fifty percent of our payout. That means there would be no turning back."

"Fifty percent? Bloody hell, that's seventy five grand each," said Blezzard, his voice barely a whisper.

"One hundred and twenty five. Our bonus was included."

Visions of sun kissed Thai beaches and willowy Thai girls pushed away all his fears of being fed to the fishes.

"Where?"

"There, in my office at eleven."

"Right, I'll be here, waiting for you."

"I'll be there in fifteen minutes," said Snape before hanging up.

Three large brief cases lay open on Dave Jordan's expansive mahogany desk. Each case contained one hundred and twenty five neat bundles of fifty pound notes, each bundle banded together in one thousand pound blocks.

Dave and his FD, Jerry Vaughan, stood staring at the brief cases and each thought their thoughts. Dave calculating the diverse factors in the project he was putting together and the resulting massive profit whilst Jerry was struggling to comprehend the complexity of the double and treble dealing that his boss was perpetrating.

"I know," said Dave patiently, responding to Jerry's observation on the quantities in each case.

Jerry had reminded Dave that he had agreed to pay Fordham double because of his demands.

"I know what I said, but when the greedy bastard sees that lot, he'll be happy enough to agree to our revised proposal. Especially if we threaten to put it back in the car. The other two will see to the rest. You know what they say about a bird in the hand, eh?"

"Gathers no moss?" suggested Jerry, looking hopefully at Dave.

"What?"

"Flock together? Lay their eggs in one basket?"

"Bloody hell Jerry, you're shit at proverbs aren't you? A bird in the hand is worth two in the bush."

"Two birds in the bush. But surely two is better than one?"

"Yes, but you haven't caught the two in the bush, have you?" said Dave testily, his patience wearing a bit thin. "You've got one in your hand so don't be greedy hoping to catch the two in the bush. Geddit?"

Jerry saw the signs and said, "Oh, yeah, I see. Not caught yet. Right."

"OK," said Dave relaxing, "let's get this lot in the car.

We're meeting the two stool pigeons at eleven and we don't want to be late. Let's get this done."

"Is that the two in the bush?"

"What?"

"Is it the one in the hand or the two in the bush?"

"Jerry, I hope you're trying to be humorous. If you are, stop it. If you are serious, you're fired," said Dave threateningly.

Jerry thought for a moment. "Humorous, of course."

"Right, what have we got?" said Hedly. "Who are the possible suspects?"

"We've got a few for Best, sir. If Fordham was done by the same perpetrator we'll have to give it another coat of looking at."

"Who's on the list?"

Annie went over to the whiteboard that was covered with a sheet which she flipped over. A list of names was revealed.

Motive	Connections	Notes
Mark Norton	Jimmy Wu	Imported forgeries?
Chris Jones		Cannabis
Percy Milbank	Jenny	Threats re Jenny
Blezzard/Snape	Janice?	
Jordan/Vaughan	Takeover?	
Jill Fordham		Would need partner.

Various notes were scribbled beside each name and Annie began to go through them.

"Mark Norton was seen arguing with Best on the night before his killing. That was probably about his fake golf gear."

"Is that where Jimmy Wu comes in?" asked Hedly.

"Yes, but he wouldn't have done Best in. He didn't need to. As far as we know, all he was waiting for was the next shipment."

"What about his other activities?"

"How d'yer mean?"

"Well you said he might be MSS or somethin'"

"Nah, this isn't spook territory. It's a bloody golf club."

Annie continued, "Chris Jones was also arguing with Best and that's more interesting. I know we haven't actually factored the drugs into our reports but if Best was involved with Jones or had discovered his activities, then that could indicate a motive for Jones to do him in."

"Any sign of Jones yet?"

"No sir, we're still waiting for news from airports and ferries. We think he may have skipped the country."

"What about Interpol, have we contacted them?"

"Yessir, but we've not a lot to go on really."

"What about this Milbank?"

"Well, we've had him in once but couldn't get anything really. We are going to have another go at him though because rumour has it that his wife was at it with Fordham at some stage, as well as Best."

"Blimey, she must be a bit of a goer, eh?" said Hollis.

Annie and Hedly looked at Hollis, both frowning.

"Well, she must ...."

"Get on with it," said Hedly turning back to the board.

"Milbank was seen coming in to the club car park last night, so he was in the vicinity."

"Who saw him?"

"Er, we did. We were on our way home, well, to the pub."

"Pub?"

"Yes sir. We had just been here in response to Fordham's wife kicking off about his being missing, if you remember. All we got was a load of lip from the arrogant bitch that was presenting some bloody golf prize. There was nothing we could do. No Fordham. No Kermit."

Kermit?"

"I mean Curtice, the chef."

"Kermit? Where does that come from?"

"Well, he's French sir. Y'know, frog."

"Frog?"

"Kermit, the frog. Muppet show?"

"Isn't that racist?" said a smug looking Hedly.

"Probably sir. You'll have to take that up with the members, sir. That's what they call him," she paused, "and he seems to answer to it."

"Go on," said the disappointed Hedly.

"Well we have now found out that the French chef had been arguing with Fordham last night and had allegedly hit him with a cooking utensil, possibly a knife or a chopper. So he's now in the frame as well."

"Do we know what killed Fordham yet?"

"No, but there's no evidence of blood in the kitchen or in the vicinity of the scene of the argument. That would tend to rule out a knife or a chopper. He did have a good sized lump on his forehead though."

"What about that Jill? Fordham's wife," said Hollis, "She was threatening to kill him when she found out about his 'Pole Cats' adventures and that Lady Captain, Jenny Milbank."

"Nah, it's not a woman. Not one her size anyway. Fordham is, was, a big bloke. She wouldn't have been able to handle him, not without an accomplice."

"Could the chef have been her accomplice? What were they arguing about, the chef and Fordham? Could it have been over her?"

"As I understand it, the dispute was to do with the food served up at last night's do. Anyway, I can't see Jill Fordham havin' it off with the chef."

"Milbank and Jones then," said Hedly. "Let's bring them in."

"Er, we haven't found Jones sir, as I just told you. He's scarpered."

"Get Milbank back in then."

"We're looking for him now. We'll bring him in when we locate him."

"Well get on with it and keep me informed," said Hedly. "I'm off to make out a report to Nelson before he gets to me."

"Don't forget sir. Mum's the word about the dope, eh?" said Annie.

While Annie and Al Hollis were going over their list of suspects, Jordan and Vaughan ascended the stairs to Snape's office. They knocked on the door and barged in carrying the three brief cases, full of money.

"Good morning gents," said Dave as he made a big show of opening the first case. "Where's that greedy bastard Fordham?"

"Dead." Said Snape.

"What? Dead? Why the fuck didn't you tell me when we were on the phone?"

"Because, I've just found out."

"Hell's bells," wailed Jerry, slumping into a chair. "Shitty cat! Shitty cat!! We're all done for." He started mumbling incoherently into his hands which now covered his face as well as the rest of his sobbing.

Snape and Blezzard looked at the hysterical Jerry and then at Dave.

"Cat?" said Snape. "Shitty?"

"He's a bit highly strung," said Dave looking at the ceiling, waiting for the stressed Jerry to pull himself together.

Arthur looked over at Charles who was now looking into the open briefcase, his eyes staring. Arthur followed his gaze and his own eyes grew wider. They both looked at Dave and then at Jerry, who was still sat slumped in his chair, head in hands.

"Take no notice of him; he'll be ok in a minute," said Dave. "What happened to Fordham?"

"They've just found him out on the course. Same place as they found Best, strangely enough. I can't think how someone managed to murder another one of our members and bury him in the same place as the first victim."

"It doesn't affect us, does it?" said Dave. "You said that you were going to be able to steer the investigators along a path that would not jeopardise our arrangement."

"We just have to keep our nerve," said Arthur, looking pointedly at Jerry. "There's no need for the police to look in our direction. They found a stash of cannabis in a large hidden shed next to the resting place of the unfortunate Best. They believe that he was in league with our missing green keeper, dealing drugs. They also think that Fordham was involved as he is very close to Best." He paused, "Closer now."

"Sounds good to me. Are you listening Jerry?"

Jerry looked up. "What?"

Arthur repeated the view of the way that he believed the investigation to be heading. Jerry tried to follow but found it difficult to concentrate.

"Ok, we'll leave these cases here and if I've not heard from you in one hour I'll assume that we're going ahead with our deal. The shares have been increased as we proposed and I'm happy for you to do what you will with Fordham's share.

It seems his greed has made you both even wealthier. We're getting out of here before the police are all over the place."

Dave grabbed Jerry by a limp arm and dragged him to his feet. "Let's go Jerry. We've got work to do."

The two developers left the office, closing the door behind them. Snape leapt for the door and locked it. Charles went to the open case and rifled through the top layer of notes. He had a faraway look in his eyes. Arthur opened one of the other cases to see a similar array of notes.

CHAPTER 16

- Call a spade a shovel -

"We're not getting very far with this lot, are we?" said Al.

"No. We're not. We're just going to have to try harder," said Annie. "Let's look at this lot again."

They went back to the board and looked again at their list.

"I know they are not in any particular order, but just so we can keep it simple, let's try and eliminate the weak prospects," said Annie. "Mark Norton may have had some dealings with the Chinaman and Best, but I can't see why either would murder him. And the Fordham murder doesn't add up in that scenario either. No connection."

"Unless he was in on it as well."

"Yeah ... But not likely. I think it's a weak one. Let's put them to the bottom of the list for now. We can get to them later if we're wrong."

"Right. What about the committee members he was arguing with. There's a bit of a connection there. Fordham was arguing with them as well, wasn't he?"

"OK, we'll have another go at them."

"Jordan and Vaughan as well?"

"Yep, we'll get at those two as well. They're definitely up to something."

"Chris Jones? What about him. He should be up the list, shouldn't he?"

"Agreed... even though there's no clear link with Fordham, the drugs could turn out to be the common denominator. Fordham was a pal of his and his wife said that he was coming into some money. A windfall that would get her a cruise, she said. I see the drugs being a better possibility than the hooky golf gear."

"You're right, that's typical drugs deal/bank robbery talk. A bloody cruise, eh? Probably loads of bling as well. Is that what you'd do with a windfall, a load of bling and a cruise?"

"Not without a receipt from Camelot." They both laughed. "They're the first one's we'd pull in, aren't they? Windfalls. Can't wait to spend it. Anyway, why would I do that when I've got such a good job in the force?" said Annie with a smile.

"Now, let's crack on. We're sounding like a right pair of blaggers." She put a ring around Jones's name. "We'll talk to him when we find him. In the meantime, let's get to a few more."

"What about the 'Pole Cats's mob?"

"I don't think so. It's just a knocking shop and unless they were in on some drugs deals the only connection is half the membership of the golf club."

"Probably half the constabulary as well," added Hollis with a smile. "If there is a drug connection, it's Jones that can join up the dots."

"Last, but definitely not least, Milbank. I know that the general consensus is that he hasn't got the bottle, but there are a lot of blokes in the nick right now that would be classed as 'not having the bottle'. Lifers that had never handled and axe or club up to the day they battered their cheating spouses to death."

"Or shovel."

"Shovel?"

"Wasn't that what was supposed to have killed our two?"

"Oh, yeah .... So Maxwell says. But they still haven't found the murder weapon. It just looks like a heavy, flatish plate with a sharp edge, like a shovel or a spade. Whoever it is, he seems to have taken great care in hiding the bloody thing. Anyway, let's find Milbank as well. I think it's one or the other."

"It's just a pity we didn't turn round last night when we saw him," said Hollis.

"We didn't know about Fordham then, did we?"

"Still a pity. If we had just stopped to give him a bollocking for shit driving, we might have saved Fordham."

"Yeah, whatever," said Annie. "You get on to that Blezzard later and see if there might be something in the club's affairs that might get them killed. I can't see it, but you never know. I'll do the same with Snape. If we do them separately they might just slip up. See if you can goad him into some reaction about his slapper of a wife. You never know, he might have been jealous."

"Ok," sighed Hollis. "Are you going to see Snape now?"

"No, I'm going to go out and have another look at the scene first. I think we're missing something."

"D'yer want me to come as well?"

"No, you go and find the pro', Mark Norton and see if you can find Tom Jackson as well. He may throw some more light on the Chinese gear. He must know somethin'. I'll see you back here in an hour."

"Blimey, are you lot here again?" said Jayne. "I'd have thought you would be keeping your heads down after the mess you made of the crime scene this morning."

"Here again?" said Mike. "We've not been away yet. You don't think we'd miss out on this lot do you. We've not had as much fun here since ...." He stopped, unable to recollect ever having any real fun at the club that involved death. "I suppose fun isn't the right term."

"Whatever we're having it's better than sittin' at home watchin' the telly, isn't it?" said Dermott.

"Who's the prime suspect then?" asked Jane.

"Suspects, you mean. There's loads of them," said Derek. He started running down the names that he had jotted down after sneaking into the, so called, incident room and copying Clowes's list.

"Hmmph," said Jayne. "All them? It's a wonder we're not on it. In fact, I'm a bit miffed they've missed me off."

"Why should you be on it?" asked Alan.

"Well, that dirty bastard Best tried it on with me a couple of time. I would have thought that deserved a mention."

"Jayne, you're just a potty doris," said Derek. "Just get us a round of drinks or I **will** go and add your name to the list. See if you like being locked up in the chokey while they check out your alibis."

Jayne laughed and said, "They're not rummaging in my alibis," as she started to put the order together.

"It is a fair list though," said Alan. "Look, Mark, Percy Milbank, Charles and Arthur. Bloody 'ell, Percy. He's just not got the bottle. Charles is a dick but murderer..?"

"None of them are, really. But someone's done it.... Or ... arranged to have it done," said Mike.

"Wait a mo'," said Dermot. "Chris Jones. What about him?"

"Chris? No. Not him," said Alan. "He's all right Chris."

"The cannabis, though," persisted Mike. "That might be a reason. If he's dealing with someone bad then maybe that someone bad is bad enough to do Best in."

"Yes, but why Fordham?"

"Well he's ..... He **was** Best's pal. He could have been having a slice of the cake. You heard what Jill said about him coming into some dosh. Drug money maybe."

"What about Winston?" said Dermot.

"What about him?" said Mike.

"Well he was always deep in conversation at the Stoat, wasn't he? He could have been at it as well. We know he likes a bit of a puff. And let's stay clear of the puff/pouf comments, eh?"

"You're right; he did seem to spend an unusual amount of time with Chris. We always assumed it he was the supplier of a few smokes but it was obviously the other way round. I'll bet he knows somethin'," said Alan.

"Well, don't look at me," said Jack. "I'm not asking him a question like that. 'Scuse me Winston old boy. Do you happen to be a drug dealer and while we're at it, did you do Besty and Fordy in?'"

"No Jack, you don't have to cross-examine Winston," laughed Mike, trying to picture the scene, and the possible consequences of such a question. "We'll pass the information to the boys in blue and let them handle it, eh?"

"Look who's on the list as well," said Derek. "Snape and Blezzard. What's that all about? And those new guys, Jordan and Vaughan."

"There is something going on there, y'know," said Jack. "I have been doing some background searches on those two. JD Developments are developers specialising in hotel and leisure projects."

"That's good, isn't it?" said Dermot. "Nowt wrong with members investing in the club."

"I'll bet it's not as simple as that though. I'd bet that they'd knock this down and build a hotel, gym and golf complex.

"A gym, that's good. We could do with some proper exercise, couldn't we?"

"Huh, we wouldn't be able to afford to be members here.

The fees would rocket so that they could keep riff raff like us out. We'd have to find a new place to do our moaning."

"No they won't," said Alan.

"Won't what?" said Jack.

"Knock it down."

"Why not?"

"'Cause it's listed."

"Listed, what's listed? Listed where?" said Mike.

"The lodge is a listed building and you can't knock a listed building down. That's what listing means, can't be demolished."

"I didn't know it was listed," said Jack. "It's not on the land registry. How do you know?"

"Some years ago I used to play golf with Tony Warburton, a big developer in Birmingham. He was interested in finding a place in the North West and I jokingly suggested here. He laughed and said 'No possible old chap. I've already had a look and it's listed'."

"Now that is interesting," mused Jack. "I think I'll pass that along the bus, just in case."

"What, you mean, in case they have any thoughts of doing a deal?"

"That's it," said Jack. "Right on the button. See you all later."

Charles was speechless, his eyes bulging as he stood staring at the cash. Arthur was just sat in his chair also staring at the stacked money, smiling faintly. The phone rang without either of them even looking at it. It carried on ringing and Charles suddenly pulled himself together, picking up the receiver with a trembling hand. A smile appeared before he said, "Hello, Charles Blezzard speaking."

The smile stayed for a while as he listened to the voice on the other end of the line. "Oh, hello Tony." The voice on the line continued its soft buzzing into Charles's ear. His smile began to fade and his face went white.

"Well why would that be important to us and why was it not on the land registry anyway?" The voice continued for a few minutes and Charles eventually said, "Well thanks for that. Very interesting. I'll pass it on to Arthur; he'll be back in a minute." He placed the receiver back in its holder and turned to Arthur. "We're goosed," he said. "The building is listed."

"We knew that, why should that be a problem?"

"We knew it but no one else did; Council, developers, no one. Now it's common knowledge. JD Developments can't knock it down so it's useless to their plans. The money will have to go back."

"No it bloody won't," growled Arthur. "I'm not giving up so close to the finish line."

He grabbed an open case and started counting out half the contents then laid it on top of the pile in the other open case. He snapped it shut, handed it over to Charles and said, "There's over two hundred thousand pounds in that case. Do you want to give that back?"

"There she is," said Derek, who had been peering out the window. "I'll go and grab her."

"I'd be careful about that grabbin' stuff," said Dermot. "They're not that keen on bein' grabbed these days. You have to buy 'em flowers an' then make a date, etcetera."

"Yeah, right," said Derek, ignoring the crack. He went to the front entrance as Annie was just approaching it, having looked further around the copse trying to understand how the perpetrator had got the bodies to their final resting place.

They exchanged greetings and Derek said, "I might have a bit more background for you."

"Oh yes? Such as?"

"It concerns the green keeper; I know you're looking for him."

"No comment," said Annie, cautiously.

"Look Annie, it'll be easier if we are frank with each other. I know you won't admit to the truth of everything I think I know but you'll have to give us a bit of credit. We're not dumb and we know about the cannabis."

Annie looked up sharply. "What do you know about the cannabis?"

"There's a shed full out there. Where the bodies were found. That's what is all over the club, common knowledge."

"Bloody hell. How did you find out about that?"

"It doesn't matter how we found out. I thought that you should know we have the name of someone you should have a word with."

"About what?"

"The cannabis. Look, if you don't want us interfering then I'll bugger off."

"No, I'm sorry Derek. It's just a shock to know that something we were holding back was common knowledge."

"It's like this, Annie. We're all retired old duffers who hang out here, moaning and gossiping. We hear things and are smart enough to put two and two together. We are also nosey bastards and, if you are good enough to write things on whiteboards in a strange building that we know our way around, someone might just take advantage and have a peep at said board."

"Why on earth would you bother?"

"'Cause we're nosey old bastards, like I jus' said. And, there are some considerable bragging rights to be gained when finding good gossip."

Annie smiled and said, "A bit like the force, I suppose. Coppers do the same thing; nosey bastards, always looking to get their gossip to the powers-that-be first. Bragging rights in the force means promotion, eh?"

It was Derek's turn to smile. "Winston D'Jemba, our 'social chairman'." He punctuated the title in the two fingered sign often used, generally in a sarcastic way.

"How is he connected?"

Derek outlined their theory about the way that the pot smoking Winston was seen in Jones's company off the club's premises and how there was no obvious reason why they should socialise, except for the exchange of drug supplies.

"Who is supplying who?"

"Well, we thought it was Winston doing the supplying 'til we heard about the shed; Jones's shed, we assume."

"Thanks for that Derek and I don't suppose you'd listen to my advice to steer clear of any more 'gossipin', would you." She copied Derek's two fingered speech mark sign.

They both laughed and went their separate ways, Derek back to the bar, Annie to look for Snape and/or Blezzard.

"Has anyone seen Percy Milbank today?" asked Jayne.

The assembled drinkers looked at her expectantly.

"Well? Anybody?"

"Body?" said Mike. "They're not looking for a body again, are they?"

"Oh grow up and give the smartarsery a rest will you. It's his wife on the phone. Has anyone seen him today?"

There was a chorus of negative grunts as the gang returned to their gossiping. Although the topics had changed from the murders, it was easy to get back on track. As Jayne's simple query had demonstrated. Such a query about the whereabouts of members was common, generally from wives, requiring jobs to be done. And, depending on who was being enquired after, the response would indicate whether the missing person was liked or disliked. Unpopular members would often spend some considerable time convincing their wives that they were innocent of whatever misdemeanour the mischievous members had concocted to pass on to enquirers.

Jayne went into the back and returned with furrowed brows. "Bloody hell, she's a nowty sod. Lady Captain my arse. She's no lady for a start."

"Why, what's up?" asked Alan.

"He's been out all night, said he wasn't home when she got in."

"She'd probably been out shaggin' as usual. Why's she bothering where he is?"

"She was kickin' off 'cause he was supposed to take her car for a service today."

"Out all night, eh? Hope he's not joined the other two, eh?" said Dermot. They all laughed; a bit nervously.

"Well, she wasn't that bothered," said Jayne. "She just said she'd get the lad from the garage to come and collect it and Percy can do his own tea, she was off golfing."

"Nothin' fresh there, then."

They returned to their conversation and picked up where they had left off.

"That bloody PM talks a load of bollocks. Gay marriage? What's all that about? Who the bloody hell is going to do the cookin' in that relationship?" said the chief homophobe, Alan.

"It's all a load of tosh," said Dermot. "The Prime Minister doesn't care about gays or immigrants. He's just after votes. The other lot are just as bad.

In fact the political parties are all the same now, just supermarkets with different names selling the same products in different packaging. Politicians are all tossers out for what they can get; some want power, some just want the money."

Jimmy walked in and, overhearing the last rant, said, "I've got a joke about them lot.

'There's a driver stuck in a traffic jam on the M25 round London. Nothing is moving and he is getting pissed off.

Suddenly a man knocks on the car window.

The driver rolls down the window and asks, 'What's going on?'

The man says, 'All the members of parliament have been kidnapped and the kidnappers are asking for £100 million pounds ransom. Otherwise they are going to douse them all in petrol and set them on fire. We are going from car to car collecting donations.'

'How much is everyone giving, on average?' asks the driver.

'Roughly, a gallon.'"

Jimmy walked away to the sound of laughing. He had learned not to hang around after he had told jokes to this lot. It saved the dissection and lectures that they persisted in indulging in.

"He's learning," said Dermot. "Scuttling off before we start takin' the Mickey."

"Yeah, but it's not the same though, is it?" said Mike. "It's like, only half a joke, not quite finished."

"Have we found out any more about our own 'politicians'?" asked Derek.

"John said he was goin' to do a bit of sniffing about," said Mike. "He seems to have some contact with Barns and Broxton, the last auditors."

"That should be interesting," said Alan. "He should be in soon. Get us up to speed."

"Did you manage to quiz the golf pro' and his assistant?" asked Annie.

"I did. Nothing new really. Norton admits to the golf gear but says it's not illegal. All he's doing is sourcing the kit at much better rates and it all adds up to benefiting the members."

"But they're forgeries."

"Ah, well that's where he's a crafty bastard, y'see. All his invoices, hand written, have the words Ping written clearly and the word Replica scribbled like R-squiggle. The squiggle looks more like a model number."

"Haven't the customers spotted it?"

"He says that the customers wouldn't know the difference between a Ping driver and a hockey stick. Model numbers are what they see in magazines and they are what they ask for. But when they actually have them in their hands, all they see is a nice shiny new club head and the promise of the three hundred yard drive that the advert claimed."

"What happens when they don't get the three hundred yards?"

"He convinces them that they just need a few lessons at thirty quid an hour and they'll soon master the club."

"What if they don't?"

"Well, that's when he up-sells them to the next model."

"That's downright cheating. He's cheating them."

"He says not. He said if he sold them the actual Ping, they'd still do the same thing, go through the same pain, buying yet another club. It would just be at twice the price. He's actually saving them money."

"Not good enough for a motive then? What did Jackson have to say?"

"Not much really. Just what he'd already told us. Except that he forgot about the argument that Norton had with Best in the car park the night before he was killed."

"Had a row with Norton as well, eh? I suppose that would have made a difference to our enquiries a couple of days ago. Then again, if we had known that we would probably have chased even more shadows."

"I did give him a bit of a bollockin'. He didn't know about the clubs though."

"Can't be much of a pro' then."

"He's not, according to some the more knowledgeable members. But he seems a nice lad that gets on with them all. How did you go on with Snape and Blezzard?"

"Nothing. They are cagey, though. They are nervous, especially Blezzard. Jumpy as a rabbit," said Annie. "I did get a bit of news off that ex-copper though."

"Oh, yes, and..?"

"It appears that our man Jones may have been doing a bit of business with one of the members, a Mr D'Jemba."

"What, dealing, y'mean?"

"Looks like it. We'll pull him in anyway and see where it leads. I think this must all hinge around the drugs and we're more likely to find our answers there."

"And Milbank?"

"Oh, we won't forget about him yet. Any sign of him?"

"Ghosh has just been round to his house and there was nobody home. Mind you, he wasn't too happy about going back there after last time. Both cars missing so we'll have to keep looking."

"He'll probably turn up here at some time. I've put an APB out for D'Jemba. Let's try and find him."

Just then her mobile rang. She pressed the appropriate button and listened. "Thanks. On way."

"Talk of the devil. D'Jemba's van's been spotted. Let's go."

"Phew, that was close," said Arthur with a big grin on his face. "Just got those cases stashed in time. Could have been awkward if she had walked in with them open, eh?"

Charles wasn't as happy as Arthur but he thought that getting the cases out of sight was definitely a good omen. He was getting a buzz now and had brightened up a bit.

"I've just had a thought about the listing on the building," he said. "I know someone in the planning department. Used to play squash with him years ago and we get in touch from time to time. I'm going to see if he fancies a meal at Romano's."

"Romano's? That's a bit out of your usual league isn't it?"

"It is, but I hear it's pretty impressive and our man might just fancy a back hander to get rid of that listing."

"Er, I think you had better tread carefully there, old chap. Bribery and corruption carries a heavy penalty, y'know."

"Bribery and corruption? What the fuck do you think we are doing? We've got over two hundred thousand quid in our cars from that very pastime. The only difference in this case is I will be the bribor, not the bribee."

"Is that a technical term, bribor?" laughed Arthur.

"We need to do something and at least I'm prepared to try to keep hold of my stash."

"Oh, calm down Charles. I have an idea as well and it may turn out to solve more than one problem."

"Oh, yes? Like what may I ask?"

"Those two bigheads don't know about the listing and when they find out the deal will be off, agreed?"

Charles nodded.

"So we need to get rid of the listed tag on the building, permanently. Yes?"

"Yes."

"We also could do with getting rid of the accounts while we're at it, couldn't we?"

"I thought they were cooked - and audited."

"They are, but I suspect if they were subjected to some real tight scrutiny, by a different, less friendly auditor .....," he left the rest unsaid.

"Stick 'em on a fire then," said Charles.

Arthur just looked at Charles and smiled. Charles's eyes widened. He shook his head slowly from side to side. "A fire? You're mad, a fire? No that's a plan too far."

"Listen Charles, if you think I'm going to jail for bribery and corruption you've another think coming. Burning this dump down would be easy. Even you could do it."

"Me?" wailed Charles. "I'm not doing it. No way. You can have the money back but I'm not doing it."

"Will you stop panicking? Every step of the way, the slightest thing goes wrong and you start wailing. We've got this far and there's no turning back, see. We can't. We've gone too far. You don't have to give the money back and you don't have to do the burning. Happy?"

Charles calmed down. "Who's going to do it then, you?"

"Sod off. I'll be in Leeds. As far away as possible and I suggest you do the same."

"What? Go to Leeds? I've never been to Leeds. I don't even know the way to Leeds."

"Not Leeds," said Arthur impatiently. "Just make yourself scarce, away from the area. An alibi, y'know, like in the movies."

"When?"

"Probably tonight. Just get yourself out of the way; dinner or a show, preferably far enough away to stay the night.

I'll let you know for certain before the afternoon is out. In the meantime, keep cool."

CHAPTER 17

- Calling Puck -

Paddy 'Puck' McDermott was on his fifth pint when he got the call. He was the product of a gullible mother and a recidivist father. A father who had told him many stories about the Irish troubles, riddled with tales of heroic battles with the bloody British and their Black and Tans. Tales of fighting in the bogs and ditches; of ambushes, robbery and arson.

Not that Donny McDermott ever featured in the annals of the Irish fight for freedom as he was far too often deprived of his own freedom in a number of different mainland prisons. Mainly just for the robbery and arson bit.

Young Paddy was a good as his father at starting fires and he was fondly named Puck by his mother after his third arson conviction, before he was fourteen. It was a barn at the back of the local spud farm where he was working the summer as a potato picker. He seemed to have a natural knack – for spud picking and arson.

"Hello Puck, It's me again," said a voice. "Are you ready for that bit of a job?"

"Are youse reddy wit' d'money?" said Puck.

"It's here in my hand now. A nice big envelope, as agreed."

"When?"

"Tonight."

"Oil be dere dis afternoon an' have a gander at d'layout,"

Annie and Al pulled into the car park of the Stoat and Ferret and stopped the car, just far enough away from the large white Audi that was parked in the far corner with the tailgate raised. The SUV was parked next to a white van, doors closed, rear end up against the pub wall. In the other corner of the car park, an old VW Passat appeared to be swallowing a couple of bodies, four legs still to be ingested. The unconcerned driver was talking on a mobile as she examined her nails.

The occupants of the SUV got out of the front seats and made their way to the back of the van, one being the dreadlocked Winston, the other being the larger figure of the shaven headed Garfield Bassong.

They started to unload sacks from the van, transferring them to the SUV. The driver of the Passat put her phone away and got out of the car as it suddenly regurgitated the two large bodies, simultaneously she nodding to Annie and Al.

They all ran to the SUV as one, the five cops were joined by three more who piled out of the pub. Winston and Garfield were quickly on the floor and handcuffed just as the paddy-wagon screeched to a halt in front of them. They were quickly loaded into the wagon and it screeched out of the car par.

"Now then, what have we got here?" said Annie to DI Malone, the drug squad officer, as they surveyed the sacks. "I do believe it's our bait."

"What bait?" asked Malone.

"It's a long story," replied Annie. "But we have been waiting for someone to claim this lot from our crime scene. It's linked to two murders."

"How come we weren't informed?"

"We didn't want it to leak to the murderer or murderers."

"Why would it leak?"

"Oh, stop being so territorial," smile Annie. "We did get you when the time was right, didn't we?"

"Yeah, I suppose so," said Malone reluctantly. "I just hope it doesn't happen too often. I was a bit suspicious though, when I heard that Hedly was in charge of your case."

Annie just smiled, happy that the missing cannabis now had a good reason to be missing. Hedly will have to explain why he didn't tell the chief. That was his problem but she knew that the jammy bastard would get away with it.

"We need to talk to D'Jemba now. He's a murder suspect," said Annie, both to Al and Malone. "And I suppose that the dealer, what's his name, will also be a suspect. Best and Fordham may have been the victims in some disagreement, eh?"

"Hang on," said Al. "Can we just step back a minute. Remember who we're dealing with here. Two Muppets from the golf club, getting mixed up with that quantity of drugs."

"Mmmm, I suppose you're right," agreed Annie. "But they might know something. We'll have a chat anyway." She turned to Malone. "Then they're all yours."

"Are you thinking of joining, then?" asked Jayne. She was chatting to a handsome, curly haired Irishman who had been signed in by Charles Blezzard. Charles had left him at the bar and said that he needed to get away as he was going out to dinner. "Oh," Jayne had said. "Where are you off to?" Charles had hesitated, "Erm, Chesterfield," he blurted out. "Chesterfield? That's miles away, isn't it?" she'd said, not really having a clue how far it was or what direction it was in. "Er, yes, erm.. We might have to stay the night."

She soon forgot about Charles and his dinner arrangements as she chatted away to the charmer at the bar.

"I'll be back in a mo'," she said. "I have to go and get a crate of Becks from the cellar."

"A crate," said Puck. "Sure dat'll be too heavy for a slip of a girrel loike yerself," he said. "C'mon, oil give youse a hand," he added, with a bit of a twinkle in his eye.

Jayne spotted the twinkle and grabbed the keys. They disappeared down the cellar.

"Did you see that?" said Alan.

"What?" replied Mike.

"Jayne. She just went down the cellar with that bloke."

"So?"

"I'll bet the dirty sod is after a bit of a grope, eh?"

"It'll be a change from the snooker room. I just hope Vinny doesn't find out, he can be a bit jealous."

"Will you two stop gossiping about the staff," said Jack. "We need to find out what's going on with the club's affairs."

"I would have thought that dead bodies were more important than affairs, club's or staff's. Murders and such should trump affairs, don't you?" said Derek. "Anyway, John's on his way. He said he's found out some more about the club's future and what may be planned for us suckers."

"Suckers?" said Dermot. "What's he mean, suckers? I'm not sure I like being called a sucker."

"That's what he said."

"Well, he can tell us himself. Here he comes now." Mike pointed out the window where they could see John striding down the path.

"Pils an' ice please," said John when he finally made his entrance. He followed his order by adding a list of drinks for those that wanted one.

All of the usual suspects wanted one, including one or two who were not in their company but hovered close by, hoping to be included in the round.

"Suckers, you said," said Derek. "One or two of us sort of took exception to that tag."

John looked up from his task, the careful pouring of his drink. He liked to see the amber nectar pouring over the clear cubes of ice, forming a nice clear head that rose slowly to the top of the glass. After taking a large swallow he said, "That's what that lot up there are taking us for, I'm afraid to say, suckers." He paused and took another swig of his beer. "A perfect word. It's a noun that defines a number of things; a thing that sucks for instance or, a young animal not yet weaned, amongst many other definitions. In this case, our case, the definition is, 'a person who is easily deceived or swindled'."

"Bloody 'ell, you're beginning to sound like Mike. Full of bullshit."

"Hang on a mo...," said Mike. "I have to confess to some bullshittery, it's in my genes, y'see. Full blooded Irish descent, y'see. But John sounds as though he is not trying to emulate my smartarsery. He sounds as though he's got proper information to divulge. He sounds serious. Let him speak."

"Thank you, old boy," smiled John. "It appears that the deal is almost done and it appears that our two new members, the JD pair, are in a consortium bent on knocking down the club and building a 'leisure based golf and country club'."

"Country Club? We're nearly in the middle of Manchester. How can it be a bloody country anythin'," said Alan. "An' what d'yer mean, leisure based."

"Gymnasium, saunas, steam rooms, beauty salons, etc., etc.," said John.

"You said knock it down?" said Alan. "They can't knock it down. I told you before, it's a listed building, remember."

"Yes, but as I already told you, it's not mentioned on the land registry yet so it looks like the solicitors handling this little coup haven't done their homework, eh?" said Jack.

"I doubt they'd be bothered about listing tags. They probably intend to just knock it down and say, oops," said Mike. "If it's not on the registry papers, they'll get away with it."

"Yes, well that's what I thought," said John. "So I made a couple of calls and I think that will be sorted out within a day or so. When the bad guys find out, the deal will be off."

"I still can't see why there was all the secrecy," said Jack. "If the club is in so much trouble, the members should know about every detail ...,"

"And whatever solution is being considered," interrupted Mike.

"I can't help thinking that someone is making an earn from this," said Derek.

"Other than the developers, you mean?" said Jack.

"Precisely. We were discussing the club's accounts the other day and something was said that started me thinking. The money that has come through here has been quite considerable and the annual results are very disappointing. On the surface they look ok and they have been audited but, then I thought, who by?"

"Who was it?" asked Alan.

"If you remember we changed our auditors last year. Did a thorough job too so we kept them again this year. However, it did occur to me as I was digging about that the potential profits in this proposed venture could be quite significant. There are quite sizeable payouts for a blinded eye in this age of the compensation culture."

"Zut alors! As Kermit would say. Could that be what Besty was up to?" said Mike.

"Zut? Alors? What the bloody ell's that?" said Alan.

"I think it means, 'crikey'," laughed Mike. "Or if you prefer stronger language, f...."

"No, crikey's fine," said Jack.

"Are we saying that Jonny Best was in on this buyout?" asked Alan.

"I doubt if he was in on it as a partner but he could have found out about it and tried to muscle in on the payout, eh?"

"And got rubbed out," breathed Derek.

"And Brian?"

"He was Besty's pal, wasn't he? Jonny might have got him involved, told him everything so he could get a piece of the action," said Derek. Then his eyes lit up. "That's it! That's what all the rowing was about. Fiddling books, accounts and stuff. The two bastards upstairs have been at it all along. Let's go and have a word now."

Just then, the curly haired stranger appeared behind the bar, carrying two crates of beer and a smug smile. He was followed by a blushing Jayne who was adjusting the belt on her skirt.

"Hello, Jayne," said John. "Who's your pal?"

"Oh, hi John, she replied, looking a bit flustered. "This is Paddy. He's thinkin' of coming here."

"He'd better get a cloth if he is," said Mike.

There was a burst if ribald laughter which included Paddy and the even more flustered Jayne.

"Are those two conniving bastards in their offices Jayne?"

"Nope, they both left early."

Derek took his phone out. "I'll phone that 'Any Clues' copper and give her a bit more background. I think them two bastards might have done our two bastards in."

The whisky drinking member, now quite a regular, headed off to make his own phone call.

"I've just had a call from our old fart, ex-cop, Derek," said Annie to Hollis, who was stirring one of two freshly made cups of tea. She had just joined him in the canteen where he was about to dig into his late lunch of burger and chips.

"Oh yes, and what did he want?" he replied just before he filled his mouth with three large chips that he had stabbed with his fork before generously covering them in ketchup.

"He's just given us a reason to get back to that club and question those two committee members who were keen to make us think we were dealing with the triads, peddling hooky golf gear. Y'know, Snape and Blezzard"

"Another motive? Blimey we'll have more motives than suspects the way things are panning out."

"It looks like the arguments they were having may be down to bribery and corruption and it may be wider than the golf club." Annie relayed Derek's account of the theory that had been expounded by the Grandad's Detective Bureau.

"What about Milbank? He's still our prime, isn't he?"

"Sure is, but he's still nowhere to be found. Strange, really," she added thoughtfully.

"Not at home when Ghosh called; not been seen at the club all morning," she added, picking one of the larger chips off Al's plate, dunking it in the heaped ketchup and popping it into her mouth.

"Where's Ghosh now?"

"He's gone to 'Pole Cats' just in case he's there, but it's a bit of a long shot."

"Sounds suspiciously like the same pattern as the other two. Missing and not following any of their usual behavioural habits."

"Doesn't it just. You'd better tell those two who are looking after the murder site to keep their eyes peeled. We don't want to find another one in that bloody hole."

"Shall we tell him?" said Al nodding towards Hedly's office.

"Yeah, we'd better. You phone Pinky and Perky and then go and get the car and I'll give him the heads up."

"What about me burger?" said Al with a pained look on his face.

"That'll take about a minute, the way you eat. Yer mother should have called you Dyson."

Ten minutes later they were in the pool car heading towards the golf club when Annie's phone rang. "Clowes," she said. The disembodied voice buzzed away for some minutes before Annie said, "You're sure?" Another interval. "Ok, thanks Ali, we'll see you later. You get back to HQ."

She put her phone away and said, "Looks like Milbank's off the list of suspects, then. He's got a perfect alibi."

"Not 'Pole Cats', surely?"

"Yep. Couldn't have done Fordham, anyway. Paid with Amex, even."

"Bugger," said Al. "I would have had a bet on it being him."

"You'd have lost then. Now, let's get those two at the golf club and then we'll find the two developers. They've got a few questions to answer as well, if not to us, to the fraud squad."

"They weren't very happy, were they," said John after the two detectives had stomped off down the path. "I'd say they were expecting you to have told them that the two suspects they wished to interview weren't here."

"Maybe they should be looking in the same place that Jones, Milbank and Kermit are hiding," said Mike. "They'll all be in it together, in that bit of a hole. Get Snotty on the case, he'll find 'em."

"Bloody hell, I told them our theory and gave them all the names involved," said Derek.

"What else do they want? They're the ones with all the contacts and staff. They're the ones who can issue All Points Bulletins, not us lot."

"Yes, I know. But a simple, 'they're not here at the moment' would have saved them a bit of a journey, wouldn't it?" said John. "They could have been APB-ing it from HQ, gettin' some other suckers to do the looking bit."

"Now that you mention the missing links," said Mike. "I wonder where Percy has got to. I believe Jenny was looking for him earlier as well. Somethin' about getting the car to the garage."

"And he's not been down here?" asked John.

"Don't think so," said Mike.

"He's not been here all day," interrupted Jayne from behind the bar.

"Oh you're back. Where's yer new boy friend, then?" said Dermot.

"Cheeky sod," she simpered. "He's not my boyfriend. He's a pal of Blezzard's apparently; he signed him in anyway then buggered off to somewhere called Chester's field or somethin'. Thinking of joining, it seems."

"Blezzard, joinin' where?" said Alan. "Chester's field, what's that when it's at home?"

She grabbed more bottles off the shelf at John's signal for 'the same again' and added, "No. Paddy's joinin' here. Anyway, that'd be good, gettin' some new, **younger, better lookin'** members in here." She pulled two pints of bitter. "And, as for Milbank, he's not been seen since last night."

"Oy, watch yer lip about younger, etcetera. That sort of talk could seriously affect your income," said Mike, who, like most of the old farts, thought he was still under forty and fit as a butcher's dog. A fine catch for any available crumpet.

"I don't suppose that Percy could be another victim of Mack the Shovel, could he?" said Alan.

"Could be, I suppose," said Derek. "We might just be looking at a serial killer who hates golf."

"Or golfers," said Jack, looking fearfully round the room. "Wait a minute, he added, suddenly brighter. "There is another common denominator."

"What? They all wear crappy sweaters?" said Mike.

"No. I'd go for naggin' wives," said Alan.

"More like shaggin' wives," said John. They all laughed at that one.

It went a bit quiet as they all got their refreshed drinks from the bar. There was a clinking of glasses and a chorus of 'Cheers' as they attacked yet another libation. It was quiet for another minute or two, no one sure what to say.

"Do you think they've tried the hole where the other two were found?" said Dermot.

"Knowing the way they've performed up to now, I wouldn't be surprised if Snotty carries on finding the lot of them in there. One by one, one a day. Any bets?" said Derek.

Larry came rushing in behind the bar and said to Jayne, "Have you heard the news?"

"Regarding?"

"We seem to have run out of bosses."

"What? What are you talking about?"

"Winston, the acting House Chairman, he's been arrested."

The old farts radar kicked in and all those with OFR receptors spun around ready to quiz the source of the signal. Larry saw that he had got the attention of the bar flies and he continued, "I just saw it on the five o'clock news. Winston. He was being bundled into the back of a paddy-wagon."

"Are you sure?" said Derek. "It can't have been on the telly that quick and how the hell did they get the film footage for the news that fast?"

"Are you kiddin', it'll be all over YouTube by now. Them scrotes around the Stoat are all kitted out with the best phones on the market and there are more pictures and videos generated up and down that road than security footage from the police cameras. As soon as the busies pounced, the local Tarantinos will have been out filming."

"Looks like our tip may have been a good one," said Derek quietly to John.

"Yes, and if they find out who tipped them off there'll be trouble. You'd better change your wheels for bricks, before they do."

"Keep mum, eh?" smiled Derek.

The bar began to fill up as more people came off the course and the old farts were now getting a bit rowdy. They had had a good session, being here for most of the day soaking up the gossip and expounding their now mixed up theories on the foul crimes that had been committed. They still had to bring their theory about the club's finances out into the open but they had thought it better not to as it was even a bit too tenuous for them.

CHAPTER 18

- Sambuca Special -

Puck had been a busy boy while he was flirting with the barmaid. He had managed to pocket the swipe card belonging to one of the old duffers at the bar. They all seemed quite content to leave them lying around so he helped himself. He had noticed Blezzard using the card to get access to the front door after he had been met by him in the rear car park, so he knew it would come in useful later.

He had pocketed the cellar key while he was helping her with the bottles of beer, just before rearranging her clothing a bit and then arranging to meet her the following night. However, that was another ruse. Although he was confident he could rearrange her clothing into a much more tidy pile, he had other plans for tomorrow. He needed to hurry to the locksmiths to get the key copied and returned, hopefully before they were needed again.

He had made a pretty good survey of the layout and the general condition of the target and he was pleased to note that it was a perfect site for even the most amateur arsonist. He rubbed his hands at the sight of the dry, open joists and the plethora of old, rubber clad, highly flammable cables hanging from between the beams. The plywood cladding that lined the walls and some of the beams, had added to his delight. The cladding had been an attempt to tidy up the slovenly work of the non-approved electricians and plumbers who had carried out their sloppy work.

"A piece o' praty-cake," he said to himself, already noting where to start the planned conflagration.

"Oh, hi," said Jayne as he re-entered the bar after his shopping spree. "Where did you get to? I thought you'd left without saying goodbye."

"Do oi look loik d' sort a' man who'd desert a lov'ly colleen loik yerself?" he said, eyes set in twinkle mode. "Sure, oi was jus' havin' a look around, a game o' snooker and a wee look at the course, o'course."

"Well, I'm glad you're back, I need some more crates from the cellar and I'm up to my neck here. Would you mind?" she smiled sweetly as she passed him the keys.

He almost jumped and clicked his heels with joy. "Easier an' easier." He headed to the cellar.

Curtice was feeling very low. He had done as Tom had said and, after he had gathered some kit and some cash that he was saving for a rainy day from under his bed, he had caught a train to Blackpool, leaving his Citroen hidden in a friend's garage. It was Blackpool where he had first settled on his arrival to the UK, tempted by the sights and bright lights he had seen on a promotional film over ten years previously. His ambition to be a chef had been sorely tested in the hotbed of the bistros in his home town of Paris. Well, it was the outskirts of Paris really; a rundown suburb, short on bistros and long on chefs.

The story that had caught his eye was in a film featuring the coastline towns of England and when he heard the term, 'The Jewel of the North' applied to the images of thousands of hotels and boarding houses in Blackpool, he was hooked.

"Bound to need loads of chefs there," he said to himself. "And we are the best in the world." failing to acknowledge that doing the tea for his mum didn't really count as cheffing. The famous illuminations, the well lit tower and the gaudy piers, bustling with happy holidaymakers, also played their part in his final decision to emigrate.

He sat on his bed contemplating his situation. He had heard some good news from Tom that morning, telling him about Fordham's murder.

"I'd say you're in the clear," said Tom. "The body was found in the same hole as Best's and I can vouch for your whereabouts at the time of the killing as can the members at thc mixed league dinner. So you can come back."

"Oui, mais, l'helico," wailed Curtice.

"What ?"

"I say, yes, but ze chophair. I heet 'eem wiz ze chophair,"

"No you didn't, you must have missed him because it was a shovel that killed him. Come on back here, you're in the clear."

He made his mind up. He packed his things, booked out of his boarding house and headed for the station. Mrs Pilkington, the landlady of the boarding house, breathed a sigh of relief as she waved him goodbye.

His offer to prepare the meal on the previous evening had culminated in the mass evacuation of the house due to the overpowering smell of garlic and the sight of trays filled with his favourite signature dishes, snails and frog's legs. The local chippy was the main benefactor, having to cope with forty hungry families from Accrington moaning about the foreign muck at the inappropriately named Seaview B&B.

"Have we employed a cellarman now?" said John, noticing the reappearance of the Irishman, carrying two crates.

"Well you lazy buggers wouldn't help me if I asked," said Jayne in a bit of a huff.

"We would if you'd let us rearrange your clothes like he seems to," said Mike.

Jayne blushed and started to stack the bottles in the cool cabinets. The lads, including Puck, all laughed and the old chaps turned back to their discussion. Puck said goodnight and reminded Jayne quietly about their date the following evening. He left the exit to the bar area and disappeared, turning swiftly down the hall to the cellar stairs, having left its door unlocked. After relocking the door behind him he went down the steps to the back of the room where he had found the perfect place to hide and settled down to wait.

"I'm a bit peckish," said Dermot. "Is there any grub on?"

"Don't think so, Kermit seems to have disappeared since he walloped Fordham," said Mike.

"I'm not surprised. Fordham would have sacked him and anyway, after the discovery of the body, he became a suspect for his murder," said Derek.

"Nah, Tom said he was in the clear; he could vouch for him," said Mike. "Anyway I saw Tom before and he said he had word Kermit's on his way back."

"Not soon enough to do me a butty, though," muttered Dermot.

"Oh stop moaning. Ask Jayne if she can get that new girl to do us some butties," said John. "We can't go yet. Or failing that, we could get a Chinese delivered. If the club can't provide us with grub, we'll get our own, eh?"

There was a chorus of agreement and Jan, the new girl, was duly dispatched to the kitchen to rustle up some sandwiches. She returned and informed the hungry golfers that there was no bread and the bacon looked a bit suspicious.

"Cor, you'd better call the cops," said John. "They're looking for suspicious stuff, what with all these murders and drug running and such."

"Right, give me a pen and a bit of paper," said Dermot. "We'll have a Chinky."

Dermot took the orders from the hungrier members; the less adventurous abstained, willing to rely on crisps and nuts to sustain them for the rest of this rapidly growing session.

The place was getting busier, news of Fordham's murder attracting the more curious elements of the club's membership. The delivery of the food soon added to the excitement, its aromas attracting attention, some disapproving mostly envious. There soon followed a flurry of calls to the Chinese takeaway for more food. The gathering had now become an event.

As the night progressed, the bar got rowdier, and voices had to be raised to be heard. Glasses clinked and jokes were swapped. All kinds of discussions were in session, differences of opinion ignored by all but the one with the current opinion.

Gareth Jarvis, recently returned from his motoring holiday, was boasting loudly about his 'soirée on the Amalfi Coast' where the flowers were more flowery, the sea was bluer, wine was more winey and, it was the best holiday he had ever been on. He began to bore all who were near him with accounts of his exotic meals, scuba diving with the sharks, speeding down the twisting roads in his convertible with the wind in his hair, etcetera.

It was at this juncture that Mike was reminded of his favourite holiday story, probably by the boasting of the posturing Jarvis.

He told his pals, in a louder voice than usual, about a tourist, a pretentious Brit, who had been drinking in a Spanish bar. The bar was pretty full and there was a fair collection of tourists drinking and having a good time.

The subject of preferences for various brands of liquor came up and when Sambuca, an Italian liqueur, was mentioned, nobody had heard of it.

Our intrepid know-all Brit had recently come across this

particular libation at his local Italian restaurant, where they had produced sherry glasses filled with a clear liqueur, to which the waiter ceremoniously added a couple of coffee beans before touching it with a lit taper, creating a neat, blue tinged flame. At the time, this after dinner ritual had become very popular in the more chavvy restaurants and our hero became a bit of a devotee of the daft fad. Now, when the know-all Brit saw he was the only person to have 'the knowledge', he ordered a round.

"Camarero, four Sambucas, por favor," he yelled at the barman.

"Que?" said the barman.

After asking four more times, each time in a louder voice, the waiter finally recognised the poor pronunciation of the Italian drink and arrived with four wide brimmed martini glasses and poured the white liquid, not quite filling the glass.

"C'mon," said our man. "Fill 'em up."

More sign language followed and the barman duly filled them up. He began to walk away from the drinks and the witless Brit, beginning to get a bit impatient, shouted after him, "What about lighting them?"

When the barman replied, "Que?" the now grumpy Brit took out his lighter and lit the first one. "Like that," he said triumphantly, at exactly the same time as the 'whooomphh' that the ignited alcohol made. The adjacent glasses, almost touching each other, followed suit and chorused their own 'whooomphhs'.

The stunned Brit, seeing his error, tried to blow out the nearest inferno, succeeding only in blowing the burning liquid over the side of the glass where it immediately carried the enthusiastic flames along the bar until they reached the tastefully arranged drapes that hung down the wall at the end of the room. Needless to say, the flimsy artificial silk fabric acted like a very short fuse carrying the flames to the overhanging netting that had been designed to give the fast disappearing bar some atmosphere. All this happened in five seconds. By the time the first shout of 'fire' was screamed, the whole of the bar was in flames.

The barman had made it worse by thrashing at the flames with what he thought was a wet towel. This only served to knock over the remaining three glasses whose trail of flames was happy to find new avenues of destruction.

In addition, the barman's towel was now adding to the chaos.

When he saw the fire licking round his wrist he had hurled the flaming rag away from himself to the back of the bar, knocking over a lone bottle of brandy, the cap of which was lying beside it.

It was a blessing that this bar was at ground level with plenty of escape doors and windows.

When the flames were finally extinguished there was even more access available.

As the story unfolded to gales of laughter Gareth Jarvis sat sullenly on his bar stool, face like thunder. He was furious that his holiday stories had been trumped by this old reprobate's shaggy dog tale.

"Bollocks," he said as the laughter had subsided. "That's just an urban myth. It never happened. There's nobody that stupid. And anyway, it'll still blow out no matter what size the glass is."

"Oh yes?" said Mike. "You think so, do you?"

"Yes, I do smartarse."

"Mike, will you stop winding him up and get the beer in," said Derek.

Mike turned back to his pals. "Yer right. What's the shout?"

The bar started buzzing again and left Gareth staring at his drink, brooding about the put-down he had just been subjected to.

Puck McDermott stretched out his aching limbs and looked at his watch.

"Time to get busy," he thought, without a trace of an Irish accent. He dragged his bag from behind the crates, which he had hidden earlier, and zipped it open. He surveyed the wires, cords and switches that lay on top of various bottles and blocks of sinister looking substances and selected the bits he felt he would need for this particular job.

He moved over to the malevolent looking boiler that seemed to be glaring at him and assessed the best place to attach his fire raising paraphernalia. Opening the front panel he looked at the perforated gas bars that would be ignited when the thermostats and time switch made their demand for heat.

He draped some of the knotted cords from the front of the opened hatch and closed the panel loosely trapping the cord. The cord was then attached to one of the rubber clad cable looms and wrapped around one of the blocks of flammable glycerine compound, made from a recipe passed down from his dear old dad. He secured everything with a tape that would disappear in the heat of the intended conflagration and waited for the right time to add the accelerant to the cords and move their ends closer to the gas bars.

Puck returned to his hiding place to wait for the right time to act.

Chris Jones had made a number of attempts to contact Winston D'Jemba, not knowing that his erstwhile partner had been locked in the slammer, occupying the next cell to Garfield Bassong. He was anxious to know whether the stash had been discovered, as he was sure it had, or whether the cops had spotted it. There was no mention of the drugs in the newspaper coverage and he was beginning to hope for the impossible.

After reading the last report in the Sun he was even more optimistic that the shed had remained secure so he decided he would get on the ferry and see for himself. He had shaved of his beard, donned a respectable suit and a pair of horn-rimmed spectacles. He disembarked at Hull in a Dutch registered BMW and had driven to Manchester to have a nosey around.

He drove around the back of the club and parked his car in the rear car park. He made his way to the back of the clubhouse, hoping to see Curtice in the kitchen. Looking through the window he saw a girl he didn't recognise, rooting around the kitchen looking for something, opening drawers, cupboards and fridges before leaving empty handed.

He was about to go down to the shed when he spotted a red glow in the trees. He pushed himself further into the shadows and watched the trees carefully. There was some more movement and then he saw a small red light arcing out of the trees into the pond nearby.

"Cops" he thought. "They're watching the place, I'd better bugger off."

He went back to his car ready to leave when he saw another car arrive and park up facing out to the copse. It flashed its lights and waited. A few minutes later a uniformed officer appeared in the headlights which were then switched off.

The officer bent by an open window and spoke to the occupant of the car for a few minutes before taking, what looked like, a flask and a package. He then turned and made his way back to the copse.

"Looks like he's there for the night," thought the disappointed Jones.

He watched the car and decided he would bugger off when that car did. It was obviously an unmarked cop car and he didn't want his Dutch registration plates being noticed.

He settled down to wait the cops out.

"D'yer see dat glash dere?" said an inebriated Gareth, addressing the new girl.

"What glass?" she replied, looking nervously at a row of approximately forty glasses; beer, wine, spirits and some other nondescript shapes.

"Whash'yer name, deeer?" he slurred.

"Jan," she replied, looking around nervously. It was her first night and she was a bit surprised at the number of people that were there. She had been told at the interview that the place was full of golfers who didn't drink a lot and the ones that did were old men that sat in the corner gassing. They were the ones to look after as they were the best tippers.

She had been rushed off her feet for the last two hours, groped three times, twice by the old farts who were supposed to be harmless and then had to wash up after what appeared to be a Chinese banquet. She was ready for quitting and the final straw was closer than she thought.

"Well, Jan, shee that martini-ni glash? Pash it 'ere."

She did as she was bid.

John spotted the glass moving from its place on the shelf and nudged Mike. "Look, he's taken the bait," he said. "Don't look yet but pass it on, I think he's going to have a go at the Sambuca."

The nudges were passed from rib to rib and the occupants at one end of the bar observed Gareth from the corners of their eyes as he stared at the glass.

"Get me d' Sandbuca-ca boddel," he tried to say.

"Sambuca, you mean?"

"That'sh wod I shed."

Jan passed him the bottle.

He pulled the cap and started to pour the clear liquid into the martini glass. His hand was unsteady and there was some spillage. Of those members who would normally have had the sense to stop Gareth, only one was close enough. The problem was that he was asleep, gently snoring, his lush, dark haired head resting on the bar next to his whisky.

Gareth had filled the glass to the brim and had replaced the bottle on the bar. He looked around him, unsteadily, and spotted what he was searching for. A lighter.

Now Gareth wasn't really trying to disprove Mike's story at this time, he was genuinely curious. After giving it some thought he concluded that he was still right, since he had been known to blow out the brandy flames on his flambé dishes when trying to prove he was an accomplished chef to his posh dinner guests.

The 'whooommph bit was true enough and its sudden appearance was greeted with a cheer from the now fully attentive watchers, all drunk enough to disregard the danger that the whole place was now in. The cheer was accompanied by the screams of the bar staff, all of who **had** spotted that danger immediately. However, not one of them was fast enough to stop Gareth's next experiment. When he huffed his best huff, the flames, as Mike described in his earlier story, followed the fluid that overflowed onto the bar, joining the generous spillage accumulated from his attempt at pouring the drink with his unsteady hand.

Jan had not actually heard Mike's tale and so she didn't know what would happen when she tried to beat out the flames with her towel. It was almost like an action replay but without any goals. Open bottles, burning towel, some party decorations that festooned the bar; couldn't be better for a disaster. Doors were flung open and screaming members spilled out onto the patio and practice putting green, one, now fully awake, with his hair on fire.

Chris Jones was close to nodding off when he suddenly came awake to the sound of the screams. The kitchen door had burst open and people were streaming out, coughing and spluttering. The car that he was watching disgorged the two detectives; one, a woman, with a phone to her ear, the other, a man racing into the building.

As he watched, two uniformed shapes rushed out of the darkness, from the direction of the copse, where his shed was.

He got out of the car and made his way in the opposite direction, out into the darkness, towards his shed. He wanted to make sure of the fate of his tenderly nurtured crop.

The chaos at the club receded into the background as he carefully made his way through the trees, towards the clearing. He reached the shed and his heart sank as he noticed the padlock was no longer on the door. Deciding he had to make sure, he made his way to the shed, almost falling into an open hole, and pushed the door open. Once inside he switched on his torch.

"Bollocks," he muttered. "It's gone. All gone. All that work. Gone."

He swung his torch back and forth only to see some sacks and cardboard boxes that had been left stacked against the wall. He ran towards them, and, in a fierce rage, he lashed out a kick at the first box he came to, sending it spinning into the centre of the room. He lashed at another and another, cursing and swearing as he did. He stopped suddenly, realising that the racket he was making may be heard and he tried to pull himself together.

As he gathered his wits he played the beam of his torch around the boxes, breathing heavily. Just as he was about to go he saw a white shape at the bottom of the pile of sacks.

It looked like a face, staring at him.

"Oh no! They've left another guard," was his first thought. But, when there was no, "'Ello, 'ello, what's all this, then?" he looked closer.

"Bloody hell! It's Percy Milbank," he breathed.

Puck had just completed the final touches to his handiwork when the screams started. He didn't know what to make of it as Jayne had told him the place would be locked up by ten o'clock; eleven at the latest. He had intended to leave at midnight so that even the car park would be empty and the staff would be in bed, heating off, not due to be switched on again until eight in the morning when he should be just about ready to be heading out of Holyhead on the early ferry to Dublin.

He began to panic when he smelled the smoke and, fearing he would be trapped by a fire set by some competitor, he decided to make a run for it. His fire had been set to go off in the morning, and it would.

If that cheating bastard Snape thought he would get away without paying him he would regret it; especially when he woke up in the ashes of his own house.

He made the top of the stairs, unlocked the door and slowly opened it. He slipped out into the corridor and shut the door behind him without relocking it. He felt the heat from the flames and, being a professional, he headed in the opposite direction, through the kitchen and out into the rear car park.

"Paddy," shouted Jayne seeing him dash out. "I thought you had gone ages ago," she sobbed as she fell into his arms.

"Sure oi was after passin' an' didn't oi see da lights on," lied Puck. "I taught yez moight a late shnifter an' when oi got here, didn't oi see da pandemonium." He looked into her eyes and added, "Oi went in dere t' make sure yez were safe," said the smooth tongued bastard.

The sirens could be heard approaching from the nearby main road and everyone gathered in groups, nowhere near the designated fire assembly points as designated by the local fire officer when granting the club's fire certificate. As they swept into the car park the engines were met by an unruly drunken collection of panicking survivors, all trying to direct the fire-fighters to different locations.

By the time the firemen had assembled their equipment, connected their hoses and started to head for the fire, a smoke stained DC Al Hollis emerged from the front entrance carrying two fire extinguishers, one under each arm.

"It's out," said Hollis to the first pair of fire-fighters he met. "It's made a bit of a mess and there's a lot of smoke, but I think its out."

"Well done, mate," said the leading officer. "We'll need to go in and douse it all down though. There may be some glowing stuff that can start up again." Pairs of fire-fighters entered the club with hoses and proceeded to soak the site.

"That's your fault," said John, looking at Mike, a wicked grin on his face.

"True," said Mike. I deliberately set fire to the club with the aid of a witless wanker. Well known arsonist's tool, a witless wanker."

"That tale," said Dermot. "Was it true or was it an urban myth, like Gareth said?"

"True, mate," said Mike. "I was there, y'see."

"There?"

"Yep. In fact, I was the witless wanker in the tale," said Mike with a big grin. "It takes one to know one," he added. "It happened on our trip to Benidorm. Y'know, the one with the lorry an' the boat."

Jayne wandered over to the laughing group, looking around her as if searching for something or someone. "Have you seen Paddy," she asked.

"Not since he was carrying up the crates from the cellar," said Dermot. "I thought you said he had gone home."

"Yes, he had. But he came back. Said he saw the lights on from the main road and decided to come back to take me for a drink," she said. "Went into the flames to make sure I was safe," she added with a faraway look in her eyes.

"Saw the lights on from the main road?" said Alan. "As he was passing? Passing where exactly?"

"What do you mean?" said Jayne.

"You can't see the club from the main road, there's a motorway in the way."

"Oh he must have meant the motorway," she said, dismissively.

"If he did, he'd have to do ten miles to the next junction and then come back another ten miles. Must be well smitten with you, eh?" said Derek. "Went into the flames, did he?"

"Yes, he did," said Jayne, a defiant look in her eyes.

"He wouldn't know there were flames. Not from the outside," said John. "Just as he couldn't have seen the lights from the main road, or the motorway. Not with those bloody heavy duty drapes the ladies committee decided to spend a soddin' fortune on."

"You don't want to be believin' us feckin smooth talkin' Irishmen, Jayne. He's up to somethin'," said Dermot.

"Oh he's just tryin' to get into her knickers," said Mike. "Best of luck to him, I say."

Jayne turned away in a huff and continued looking for the elusive Puck, who had made a fast exit when he saw the fire engines and the police uniforms.

Chris Jones was desperate. When he saw the body he almost fainted with the shock. He looked around the shed and tried to think.

What does all this lot look like? What if it was Winston or Garfield who had cleared the cannabis?

The fact that there was no news about the discovery of any drugs reinforced his theory that his partners had moved the stuff. And how come the police hadn't found the body? The drugs gang must have done him in. It would hardly be Winston though; he was a nice guy, always happy and friendly, wouldn't hurt a fly. But that Garfield; he was a nasty piece of work and so were his pals. He had a sudden vision of the reaction of the cops when they found Milbank. His shed – his body.

"I'm goin' to get the blame, I know it," he said to himself.

He made a decision. A dumb one, but then he was dumb. He moved the boxes out of the way and looked down at the corpse. There was a dark stain in the middle of Milbank's chest that surrounded, what looked like, the handle of a screwdriver.

"Right Chris," he said through clenched teeth, "let's get this thing moved."

He moved the body onto a large sack and dragged it outside, heading for that handy hole that had already been dug at the side of the clearing. He cursed mightily when he'd almost fallen into it on his way to the shed but he was now thankful he wouldn't have to dig one himself.

"Oh, that's handy. It's just the right size as well," he thought as he slotted Percy into place. He went back into the shed, over to the corner where he kept his spade well hidden in the rafters.

He didn't notice the bloodstains on it in the fading torchlight, the batteries running a bit low.

CHAPTER 19

- Riot or Earthquake? -

There were no fire engines in sight; they had left some two hours earlier and the car park was empty save for those cars left by the more inebriated participants of the previous night's excitement. They would be collected as the day wore on. There were members arriving for their Saturday competition unaware of the fact that their club had nearly burned to the ground or that it had been saved by the heroism of a single police officer. Mark and Tom had both stuck their heads in the clubhouse to look at the damage and, having seen them, Annie instructed them to stay close for further questioning on the murders.

Annie and Al had met the fire investigation officer, Tony Johnson, in the clubhouse. He was now trying to construct his report along with the two detectives and the Health and Safety Officer, Bert Callard.

"Sambuca?" he had retorted, when Jayne had given her account of the incident earlier.

He repeated the weary barmaid's account to the detectives and the H&S representative, trying to keep a straight face.

"I'll bet you thought that golf clubs were populated with intelligent people, captains of industry, lawyers, judges and the like," said Annie. "Well, I can tell you that you couldn't be further than the truth."

"Yes, but.... Sambuca. How the hell do I write that up? Aren't there some H&S issues here," said Johnson, looking hopefully at Callard.

"Health and safety?" said Callard through gritted teeth. "Some dickhead blows burning alcohol all over the club bar like some demented fire eater, aided and abetted by an hysterical barmaid throwing burning fireballs at the curtains and you're looking for some breach of the H&S rules? You couldn't make rules for that."

"Calm down," said Annie. "I think he was just joking."

"Joking? Someone could have been killed," said a slightly quieter Callard.

"It would have just added to a growing body count," thought Annie. "This is nearly as bad as a Midsomer Murders script."

"As it is, the club will be sued by half the members for post traumatic stress as well, as the burns," continued Callard.

"Don't forget the hysterical barmaid; she must have a claim under breach of her working conditions."

"And that poor bugger asleep on the bar with the wrecked toupee," said Al. "That was an expensive rug and, up to last night, it had been undetectable. Nobody knew he had one and he is absolutely gutted, mortified. And he was scalped as well, come to think of it. Hedly will put him down as another victim of those red Indians he was going on about earlier." He was finding it very hard not to crack up and daren't look at Annie. He had to get out of there. "I'd like to be a fly on the wall when they put their insurance claim in as well," he added. "Mind you, it could have been worse. If those extinguishers weren't handy...."

"All right. Sounds to me like the bloody hero wants a pat on the back," laughed Annie. "An award, maybe."

"There's no real structural damage actually," said Johnson. "All bar fittings and furniture really."

"Jammy bastards," said Al. "I should get free membership for that."

Below them the boiler kicked into life.

"Well," said Annie. "We've got some murders to get on with; you sort out the damage to the furniture."

"Oh, I won't be long now. That's the job of the loss adjustor, the damage. I'm just here to find the cause and make sure it's out."

Curtice chose this moment to return to the club. He walked into the lounge and his jaw dropped. He looked around open mouthed, taking in the blackened wreckage surrounding him. He then caught sight of the two police officers.

"Hello Curtice, where have you been?" said Annie, before he could disappear again. "We've been looking for you."

"C'mon Curtice," said Hollis. "Let's go and get the kettle on and then we'll have a little chat."

Puck was sat at a window seat of the Holyhead to Dun Laoghaire ferry with a pint of Guinness in front of him. He looked at his watch and noted the time, eight fifteen.

"Dublin for lunch," he thought, in a perfect English accent. "The place should be burnt to the ground by then."

The previous night after he had escaped the clutches of the besotted Jayne, Puck had phoned Snape who had assumed the fire he had been informed about had been Puck's work. On hearing the events of the night before and the exaggerated account of the damage, he quickly arranged a meeting for him to collect the second part of his fee. He was told to meet Blezzard and collect his cash under the clock on the Roman Wall in Chester. Charles had decided, at Snape's suggestion, that Chester was a better location for his alibi than Chesterfield; easier to explain being a popular, more convenient place for South Manchester people to visit.

Puck had waited patiently under the clock until he finally saw Blezzard emerge from the Grosvenor Hotel, looking furtively in both directions before spotting the fire starter leaning against the ancient Roman wall.

"Good grief, Paddy, couldn't we have made it a bit less obvious?"

Puck had looked up and down the street and, failing to see a single person, said, "Sure dere's only d' two of us in sight. Dere's not anudder soul t' be seen, t' be sure."

"There could be police looking out of every window," said the nervous Charles, "with cameras filming every action."

"Jus' gimme d' cash an' oil be outa focus, wot wid me bein' so fast, y'see," said the smiling Puck.

Charles had reached into his coat and pulled out a fat manila envelope, handing it to the happy Irishman.

"Tanks a bundle for d' bundle," he said, turned away and strode off down the street where he had parked his car.

Charles went back to his hotel and returned to his room, where Janice was still fast asleep. They had pushed the boat out last night, champagne, oysters, lobster thermidor, more champagne and finally liqueurs.

Janice had been over the moon. She had never seen Charles like this. It was such a change in his stingy lifestyle that it made her a bit suspicious about the reason for his newfound generosity. She'd decided to push her curiosity to the back of her mind until he stopped the spending spree. Little did she know how soon it would end.

"Now then Curtice," said Annie. "Tell me all about it.

They were sat in the dining room, Annie Curtice and Al, all clutching the freshly brewed cup of tea.

"I heet meestair Forhham wiz ze chopphair, an' I sink I keel heem," he said, blinking as he spoke, concentrating on his English pronunciation. A bit like his cooking, he had a long way to go.

"No, you didn't kill him, but that does explain the bump on his head," said Annie.

"Hang on," said Hollis. "If I can make out what he is saying, he hit him with a bloody cleaver. That has been known to be a bit fatal, hasn't it?"

"It was a shovel that killed Best and Fordham, not a finely honed meat cleaver," said Annie. She looked up from her notebook, sniffed and then looked toward the kitchen door. "Have you got something on the stove in there?" she said to Curtice. Before he could answer, Larry walked in and said, "The lights seem to have fused. We'll have to call Sparky and get him to sort it out." He sniffed the air. "What's that smell?"

"I've just asked that," said Annie. "Are you boiling some socks?"

"Yeah, smells a bit ripe alright," said Larry. He walked into the kitchen and reappeared some minutes later. "Nothin' burning in there, on the stove or in the oven."

"Has that fire inspector gone?" asked Annie. "There might be something still alight."

Al walked out of the dining room and went into the ravaged lounge. Callard and Johnson were looking closely at the bar where Gareth had been sitting.

"Can't you smell that burning?" said Al.

"It all smells of burning in here, mate," said Johnson, sweeping an arm round in a semicircle, intending to convey all the damage and the inference that any fool smelling it should know where it came from. "Detectives, eh?" he said to Callard, who tutted his agreement.

"No, smartarse," growled the detective. "It's not like this smell. It's 'orrible. Come in the Dining room and see if you can smell it." Al turned and left the lounge, the other two following him.

As they entered the dining room, Larry was just ending his phone call.

"He's on his way but he thinks it is just a fuse, although he did say that the fire may have caused some damage. He said to look at the circuit breaker at the bottom of the cellar stairs. I'll get the keys and have a look, eh?"

Larry headed for the stairs and went up to get the keys; the two inspectors went to inspect the kitchen.

Annie turned to Curtice. "Right Curtice, where were we up to?"

"He hit Fordham with his chopper," laughed Al. "That must have been some sight," he added.

"Must 'ave been some chopper as well," said Annie with a smile.

"Don't let Hedly hear you talk like that," said Al, lips pursed. "Not with the way you take the piss out of his inappropriate comments."

They heard Larry come down the stairs and turn towards the cellar, keys jangling. The door rattled and then there followed an almighty roar from Larry, **"Fiiiiire, fiiirre,"** he screamed, the scream was accompanied by a different roaring that didn't sound good. Then, even before anyone had actually reacted to the shout, there was a ground shaking explosion that made them all dart for the nearest exit. As they burst out into the sunlight they saw Larry tumbling out of the fire escape at the side of the building. He was smouldering slightly and coughing. "Hack, hack, harrrkk, hack," he hacked.

"What happened," said Johnson, phone already in his hand.

"Haaarrkk, hach, hakkity, hahack , haaaaaaark, ptooey," hacked Larry, a bit rudely, thought Johnson.

"Bloody hell, look at that!" shouted Callard.

They all span round to follow Bert's pointed finger. Flames were gushing up from a grid that covered the cellar window, licking close to Larry's car.

The coughing bar manager dashed to his car searching his pockets for the keys. Finding them, he scrabbled at the lock, scratching the bodywork as he tried to locate the keyhole, made more complicated by his violent spluttering. He finally managed to wrench open the door, start the car and reverse it away from the searching flames.

"The fire trucks are on their way," shouted Johnson.

"They had only just finished sorting the gear out from last night's fiasco and they wouldn't have taken it too seriously if I hadn't been the one that rang it in."

"Why not? It's a bloody fire isn't it?" said Annie.

"Sambuca, that's why," said Johnson. "The story is all over the force, probably on Twitter and Facebook as well."

There was another explosion, shaking the ground.

"What the hell is that?" said Hollis. "Sounds like gas bottles blowing up."

"It is," said Johnson. "The gas in the bottles and barrels of beer will be getting heated up to a fair old temperature. I suspect they're blowing up. All that beer sloshin' about in there might even keep the fire down a bit. Hopefully one will blow out the gas pipe to the boiler. It's probably blowing like a blowtorch now."

Larry had parked his car and returned to the firewatchers as they waited for the engines to appear. They watched in awe as the flames gathered strength and broke through on to the first floor. Windows began to blow out and more bright orange fingers greedily drank in the extra oxygen.

"My shit!" moaned Larry. "All my shit's in there. All gone... All gone." He stared at the smoke and the flames billowing out from every opening, more being added as the windows began to blow out, one by one.

As the sirens wail grew in volume, the ground floor collapsed into the cellar.

Chris watched the two detectives dashing out of the back of the clubhouse, accompanied by Curtice and two others, one in uniform which he assumed was a copper. He recognised the detective from the fire the night before and, seeing them, he cursed his stupidity in returning to make sure he had made no mistakes in the darkness while putting Milbank in that convenient hole.

His anger at his bad judgement call paled into insignificance as he observed the destruction of the clubhouse, despite the efforts of the fire brigade, now pumping gallons of water into the angry conflagration that wouldn't be quelled.

Even though there was a great deal of distracting activity that may have taken the attention of the police that were now all over the place, he decided that a single car trying to leave would be certain to draw attention, especially foreign plates, so he sat tight, slumping lower in the seat in an attempt to be even less noticeable. He hadn't accounted for the sudden appearance of Keith Smithson and his nosey dog. He was always very friendly towards Snotty and Keith, who often stopped for a chat when he was having his break out on the course. Chris would feed scraps to the friendly little mutt, a kindness which was now just about to haunt him.

The dog was sniffing around the car and started barking before Chris had even noticed him there. Keith shouted his usual ineffective call to try to get the dog from doing whatever he was doing and Snotty, as usual, ignored him, meaning that Keith would have to go and put his lead on.

Chris was trying to get even lower in his seat but the fact that the steering wheel was on the wrong side of the car attracted Keith's attention, making him look a little closer. At the same time, Hollis's attention was drawn to the dog's insistent yapping, annoying even over the noise of the current bedlam.

"Chris," shouted Keith over the din. "Chris Jones. Where the bloody hell had you disappeared to, and where's yer beard?"

Chris was now beginning to panic. "Piss off," he mimed frantically at Keith, waving his hands in a dismissive, 'go away' gesture.

The puzzled Keith just went closer and approached the driver's door, pulling it open in order to make sure he could hear what the distressed looking green keeper was trying to say. The happy dog jumped up, into the car and bounced about, yapping loudly, happy to see his old pal and hoping for a biscuit. Hollis was watching this strange scene and he also noticed that the car had a Dutch registration plate. It was only when he saw the howling Snotty go flying through the air that he really took notice. Grabbing Annie by the arm, he dragged her towards the BMW and the now angry Keith. He was waving his fist and shouting expletives at the car's door, which had been slammed shut after the small dog had taken its short flight.

The car's engine burst into life and moved off sharply, scattering the approaching detectives, Keith and the still barking Snotty. He careered round fire trucks, police cars and various golf trolleys that had been abandoned in the panic, only just managing to avoid everyone, and anything, in his path.

Annie was already on the phone as Chris was clearing the gate, narrowly missing DI Hedly's unmarked Ford Mondeo.

The first report about the previous night's fire had reached Arthur Snape in the early hours and, as he had assumed that Puck McDermott had completed the job, he instructed Charles to settle up with the fleeing arsonist. When he finally found out the actual cause of the first inferno and the real extent of the damage, it was too late to stop the transaction.

"Sambuca?" he barked down the phone, pretending to be enraged since he still thought that the place had been destroyed. "What the fuck do you mean, Sambuca? How can a glass of Sambuca destroy a golf club?" Inwardly he was marvelling at McDermott's skill as an arsonist, being able to bring down a building like the clubhouse with a glass of Sambuca.

His mood changed though, as he listened to the reply and the fact that the club was only superficially damaged and his feigned rage turned into the real thing.

"Superficial," he spluttered. "It sounds more than superficial to me. Hasn't it damaged the structure?"

He listened to some more information from Larry before adding, "You mean that the structure won't need to be pulled down?" There followed more information over the phone before he realised he had sounded disappointed that the club wasn't razed to the ground and tried to cover his dismay. "No, of course I'm happy that the place is still sound," he said. "But I am disappointed that our members could create such damage by getting so pissed and out of control. We'll have to revise our rules on the subject of behaviour at the bar. I'm leaving shortly and I'll come straight there as soon as I get back to Manchester."

He finished his call and immediately dialled Charles's number.

"Have you paid that bloody Irishman?" he yelled down the phone.

"Yes," said Charles, putting the phone back to his almost deafened ear. "You told me to. You said that the job was done, the clubhouse destroyed."

"Yes, well I was wrong," growled Arthur. "That first call I'd had was from that dope of a manager, Larry. He said that the place had almost burned to the ground.

His second call, which I have just received, was to tell me that the fire officer has been round and has told him that the damage s only to the fixtures and fittings."

"And what about the structure?"

"Sound, not touched. New bar fridges, optics, carpets, curtains, furniture and decorating and the place will be as good as it was. Still sodding listed. It seems that the fire was caused by a burning Sambuca being spilled over the bar. It spread and the whole bar went up in flames."

"What the bloody hell was that crap fire raiser doing?" said Charles. "Did he just set a liqueur on fire and expect it to burn the place down?"

"He wasn't mentioned, come to think of it, but we will find him and when we do, we'll see if he fits in that hole that Best and Fordham were found in. They must have finished with it by now."

"I suppose we better get back there and see the damage for ourselves. I'll see you back there. I should be there in about an hour, after I've dropped Janice off home."

Arthur ended the call and began to pack his things into his case, shouting to his wife through the bathroom door, "Get a move on in there. We have to get back to Manchester as soon as possible. The club's burned down and I need to be there."

He didn't hear his wife's response, which was just as well. "Bloody good, that's saved us all a job. It's about time that dump was demolished," she muttered as she combed her hair, slowly."

Snape arrived at the club and pulled into the car park after convincing the constable at the gate that he was an important officer of the committee. He was met with the sight of total destruction, smoke still pouring from what appeared to be the empty shell of the old lodge. The front entrance had collapsed, as had much of the left hand corner of the building, along with a large section of the eaves and part of the roof. Although he had wanted to burn the place down to enable him to significantly line his pockets, he couldn't help feeling a pang of regret to see the old place destroyed in such a way.

He saw Larry with the fire officer and the police, all enthralled at the sight of the final throes if the destruction of the clubhouse.

"Larry!" he shouted as he approached the silent group. "Is this what you call 'superficial damage'?"

Larry turned in surprise. "Mr. Snape!"

Before he could say any more the Treasurer continued, "Are you telling me that all this was caused by a drink?" He could hardly contain his glee. "Has the insurance seen it yet? he said, pretending to care. "I suppose they won't agree to pay out for Sambuca damage?"

"I tried to phone you but couldn't get you," said Larry. "The fire started up again. Seems that this lot didn't put it out properly," said Larry, nodding towards the fire officer.

"Hang on," said Johnson, bristling at the accusation. "We don't know that yet. Not until I've had a chance to investigate."

"Rubbish," said Larry. "Your lot had a quick shufti after this hero had saved the day and buggered off laughing when they found out what had caused it. Couldn't wait to get to their Facebooks. I mean, there's already footage of the after effects on YouTube, titled 'Sambuca - Burns all the way down'."

"I think you'll find that the TV cameras will be here any minute as well," said Annie with a grin.

DI Hedly interrupted. "I think we'll have to leave the fire to these boys now. We still have a murderer to catch."

"Right sir," said Annie as she moved her colleagues away from the club officials. "We seem to have a lead on the green keeper who was identified earlier. It appears he may have been hiding abroad, in Holland."

"That's good," said Hedly. "Have we told Interpol?"

"No need, he's back in the UK now."

"In the UK? Where?"

"Ah, well," said Annie hesitantly, "he's just driven out of here actually, in a black Beemer with Dutch plates."

"That wouldn't be the one that nearly ran into me, would it by any chance?"

"Yep, that'd be the very one," said Annie.

"And you missed him?" Hedly's tone was critical and seemed to be aimed directly at Annie.

"Look guv," she bristled at the implied criticism, "there was a fair bit going on, y'know. Lots of panic and distraction. If it hadn't been for our favourite body finder, we wouldn't have seen him."

"Body finder?"

"Snotty, the dog."

"What, y'mean Snotty recognized him and pointed him out. 'Look officer, there goes our prime suspect'."

"Sir, that sarcastic streak will get you in to trouble one day," said Annie, now reverting to the usual patient, patronising demeanour she adopted when having gained the moral high ground with her boss. "No, Snotty recognized his scent," she continued, "even while he was sat in the car. The barking alerted Keith, his owner, who recognized Jones even without his beard. When he shouted out his name it alerted us. We tried to stop him but he roared off. Hard to stop, them Beemers, when they get going. Anyway, I've got an APB out for him."

"Good," said the chastened DI. "It shouldn't be too hard to spot a Dutch registered Beemer, should it? What was he after, I wonder?"

"We didn't mention the drugs in the press and if he was in Holland he wouldn't hear about D'Jemba and Bassong's arrest. He probably thought that the stuff was still there."

"Maybe he'll try again, so keep those two constables on high alert, just in case."

"High alert?" thought Hollis. "That's a laugh with those two. Alert is difficult enough, high alert though, not too sure about that." He kept his misgivings to himself.

"Oh, and Curtice, the chef, has turned up. Seems he was in Blackpool all the time. He thought he might have killed Fordham, but he only clipped him. Tom said he had seen Fordham rubbing his head moaning about a stroppy chef. He told Curtice to bugger off home and let Fordham cool down."

"Where is Curtice now?"

"He's gone round the back. The last time I saw him he was just staring at the fire. The poor bugger's out of a job now."

Charles arrived and had to park his car two hundred yards from the club, unable to get past the growing crowd. He managed to talk his way into the car park when one of the constables recognized him from the day before. He joined Arthur who was finishing his call to Jordan.

"I've just told Jordan about the fire," said Snape. "He was a bit miffed, to say the least."

"Miffed? It solves all his problems."

"Yeah, true. But he wasn't aware that the listed building tag was a problem, was he?"

"Did you fill him in?"

"Not on the phone, no. I said we would meet him later and give him some good news and not to worry about what he thinks is bad news."

"Are you going to tell him about the firebug?"

"'Course I am. He has to know the risks we have taken for this deal. We have to show him we're not just sat on our arses, collecting the money, haven't we?"

They both stood and looked at the smouldering ruins, each lost in their own thoughts. They ignored the noise of gathering crowds, the shouts of the reporters and flashes from the cameras as they each watched the memories of over forty years drifting away before their eyes.

"It's a bit sad to see it go, isn't it?" said Charles.

"It is, but the three hundred grand compensation sweetens the bitter pill, eh?"

"Mmm. Not sure that it does really. I had a good day with Janice yesterday. Just like old times and she was great fun," he said wistfully. "I'm not too sure about Thailand now."

Snape looked at Blezzard, eyes widening. "Thailand? You were going to go to Thailand?"

Charles looked up at his partner in crime, "Well, I was only thinking about it," he said defensively, immediately regretting his slip. He should never have let that out, especially to someone like Snape.

Snape started to laugh. "Thailand, what a knob you are," he said between guffaws.

"Hello you two," said Annie Clowes, who had approached the conniving pair from the rear. "Are we finding all this a bit funny?"

The two committee men spun round in surprise, Snape immediately stopping his chortles. They were met with the stern faces of the three frowning detectives.

"We were looking to interview you two yesterday but they said you had both left early. Why was that?" asked Annie.

"We are free to leave here any time we like, young lady," snarled a huffy Snape. "It's not a paid job we do, y'know. Hon. Secretary and Hon Treasurer, the Hon bit stands for honorary; means unpaid, d'yer see?"

Annie looked at Hedly and said, "Blimey guv, he's as good as you at that sarcastic stuff. Can get a soul into trouble that sarcasm," she added, now looking at Snape. "Can we start again? I'm aware that we can't do this in your office," she said, pointing at the clubhouse, "but if we can move over here away from that lot," she indicated the baying reporters, "we would like to ask you both a few questions and it would save us taking you down to the station, y'see."

"Look," said Snape, calming down. "I'm sorry I was a bit sharp, but we have had a bit of a shock and it will take some sorting out, insurance and things. The members will still want to play their golf. We'll need to organise some Portacabins to carry on our golfing activities and ..."

"Yes, yes, I'm sure you have a lot to do sir, but we still have two murders to solve. So, do you mind answering my questions?"

"Ok, in answer to your question about leaving early," said Snape, "I had a dinner to attend in Leeds and I went there with my wife. There were over two hundred people there and I was on a table for ten."

"And I was in Chester," said Blezzard, nervously.

"Chester?" said Annie, eyebrows raised. "Why were you there sir? Were you at a golf dinner as well?"

"No, I was there with my wife. It was a treat for her, shopping, dinner, a few drinks and a nice room in a nice hotel. Our breakfast, however, was curtailed with the news about the fire. We had to rush back here."

"What hotel would that be, sir?"

"The Grosvenor. Y'know, that one next to the clock."

"Next to the clock, you say? Nope, can't say I know Chester, but I'm sure we'll find it when we check it. Thanks for that gentlemen. Now, I believe you might have something to tell me about your dealings with JD Developments."

"JD Developments?" said Blezzard, a bit too quickly in Annie's view. "Who are they?"

Snape was quick to take up on the hint that the police had something, although he knew it could only be gossip. He said, "Dave Jordan and Jerry Vaughan, Charles. Y'know, the two new members, just joined, remember?"

"Oh yes, JDD," said Charles relieved that Arthur was taking up the sticky stick.

"Well, I tried to get them to use my services, accountancy y'know," continued Snape, "but they were well covered in that field. Pity, I could have saved them a few bob as their accountant."

"So they're not involved in any dealings regarding the sale of the club?"

"Well if they had any notion of buying this place, they'll not be wanting it now, will they?" he said, looking at the ruins.

"That depends on why they wished to buy, surely" said Annie.

"Well you'd need to ask them that question, wouldn't you?"

"Oh, we will." She paused, looking in her notebook. "So there's nothing in the rumour that your books aren't quite accurate?"

"Perfectly ok, audited and signed off as they should be," said Snape firmly.

Annie looked at him and held his stare for some seconds before saying, "Good, we'll be able to have a look at them, then, won't we?"

Snape turned round and looked again at the remains of the clubhouse and said, "Well, best of luck, m'dear. They're in that lot. Just had them returned to us last week."

"That's a shame, eh?" said Charles, "It would have cleared us of any accusations of scurrilous fiddling of the club's accounts. The very idea is preposterous."

"Ok, that'll be all for now. Don't be too far away; we'll need to speak again."

The three detectives walked away leaving Snape and Blezzard alone.

"They're on to us," said Charles as soon as they were out of earshot.

"No they're not. Someone has fed them a bit of gossip about the rows we had with the two victims the other day, probably that Larry, and they are guessing adding two and two and making five.

Keep your head Charles, or you won't be able to keep your money."

He paused and then added, with a wicked grin, "Then how are you going to get to Thailand, eh?"

The five members, recently dubbed 'Grandad's Detective Bureau' were making their way up the third fairway, determined not to be left out of the excitement. Having been refused entry at the gate after fighting their way through the crowd, they had decided on this alternative route. They had made their way around the back of the course and climbed over the fence that surrounded its extremities. They had managed to get over the outer fence with a great deal of grunting and cursing and also succeeded in defeating the attempts of a very prickly privet hedge to repel them. The sharp edges of the privet hedges had torn at their clothes and scratched their leathery skins, drawing blood from the bleeders and yelps of pain from bleeder and non-bleeder alike. They were now nearing the thicket of trees that had been the cause of the excitement up to now, heading for the latest episode in their now active life. They could see the column of smoke spiralling up into the sky and the swirling debris it carried in its thermal draught, breaking away and cascading back to earth, staining the grass even as far as the copse, some two hundred yards from the clubhouse. They trudged on in silence, passing Partington and O'Hara hiding in the bushes, waving to them as they continued to the car park.

Tom appeared in one of the golf buggies, a set of clubs mounted in the carrier at the rear.

"Hello Tom, where are you off to?" asked Alan.

"I'm trying to get a bit of practice in."

"What, with all that goin' on?" said Mike. "That's dedication isn't it? I didn't know you had a lot of that dedication stuff."

"Cheeky sod, I practice loads of times. Usually before you lazy buggers get here."

"Here, that's no way to address us members, young man," said Jack. "Show some respect."

Dermot looks around and after surveying the terrain, he said, "This isn't a very good spot for practice, is it? No room, what with all this water and the trees over there. And don't forget Pinky and Perky in there. They'll be waiting to take the piss at any bad shots."

"Who?"

"The two cops in the bushes, guarding the 'murder scene'."

Tom looked over at the copse. "Oh those two," he scoffed, "they're too busy getting bacon and sausage butties to be any good at guarding anything. No, I just managed to rescue the two buggies parked beside the kitchen before they went up with the rest of the club. Now the path down to the practice ground is blocked with fire engines, so I'm going round this way."

"Good lad, you keep it up. See you later," said Jack as they continued their trudge to the clubhouse, what was left of it.

"Jesus," said Alan, as the burning building came into sight. "Look at that."

"Those dozy buggers with the hoses must have missed a bit last night, eh?"

"The Trumpton Fire Brigade would have beaten them lot," said Mike.

"Trumpton?" said the puffing Dermot. "Where the 'ell is that?"

"Trumpton? Y'mean yer don't know where Trumpton is? It's famous. It's in Trumptonshire, just north of Northamptonshire." Jack and Derek started laughing.

Mike carried on, "It's got a fire station whose commander is Captain Flack."

"How the hell do you know the name of any bloody fire station commander?" asked Dermot, English geography not being his strong point, being Irish; nor was kid's TV programmes.

"Not only that," continued Mike, warming to his task, "I know the names of all the firemen. There were the twins, Pugh and Pugh, let me see now, then there was Barney McGrew, er, then Cuthbert, Dibble and Grub."

"Will you stop it," said Derek. "You must have watched more telly than the kids to remember all that."

"You bet I did. They used to ask me questions about it, every bloody night. They wouldn't go to bed 'til I explained the entire story to them. They can't remember Trumpton but its well and truly stuck in my head."

"A kids TV program, y'bum," said Dermot. "Y'bugger, you got me goin' there."

"Bloody hell, look at that," said Jack as they reached the car park and got a clear view of the decimated building, smoke still billowing from every window.

They advanced a bit closer and were met by the recently airborne Snotty, now back on terra firma.

Snotty greeted them with a couple of yaps and a lot of wagging tail.

"Go find some more bodies," said Mike as he petted the little dog's head. He saw Keith stood with Curtice and shouted to them. Keith waved and came over to join them.

"I've just seen Chris," he said. "The bastard threw poor old Snotty right over the car park."

"What? Have we missed the dog chucking competition?" said Dermot. "I told you we were late," he said to Mike.

"You're just trying to get yer own back, aren't you?" said Mike. "What's happened Keith?"

Keith recounted his story, unhappy that this sad tale wouldn't earn him the copious amounts of brandy that his dog's previous escapades had.

"He's one of the chief suspects," said Derek. "They'll be hot-footin' it after him now. It'll be a national manhunt."

"Don't be daft," said Dermot. "There's no point in it bein' national. He's here in Manchester. What'd be the point in hunting nationally?"

"What?" said Derek, not quite understanding the Irishman's logic.

"Well it'd be a waste of time sendin' coppers door to door askin' about him in London, or Southampton wouldn't it?"

"Or Trumpton," said Alan, straight faced.

"'Cause he's here in Manchester, isn't he Keith?" continued Dermot.

The daft conversation was interrupted when they saw the three detectives coming round from the front of the clubhouse, heading straight for them.

"The bloody clubhouse has burned down," said Dave gleefully as Jerry walked into his office. "Razed to the ground apparently."

"Why is that good?" asked the puzzled Jerry.

"Well, we were looking to build a health and fitness complex alongside the golf activities, weren't we? How do you think we could accomplish that with that old crappy clubhouse in the way?"

"We would have to demolish it," said Jerry, the advantage slowly dawning on him. "That would be expensive, both time and money expensive."

"Good," said Dave, genuinely surprised that his naive partner had grasped even a tiny portion of his plans. "You're getting the picture. That's good. We now need to close the deal fast before members see that the insurance payout will solve their problems. We're meeting Snape and the club trustees later. We'll finalise the details of the buyout and close it up tomorrow. Done and dusted."

Hedly was the first to reach the small group of members, noticing the dog eyeing him up with his tail wagging and his head tilted to one side. "You lot again," he said. "How the hell did you get in here?"

"We're members," said Alan. "How did you get in? You're supposed to be signed in y'know and there's cops all over the place. We could lose our licence if you don't sign in."

All the lads started to chortle at Alan's sharp quip and Annie and Al joined in, the dog accompanied the laughter with his yapping version of a chortle. Hedly blushed and Annie stepped forward to head off any embarrassing response from her inspector.

"Ok, that's enough of that. Members or not, you're not supposed to be so close to the fire, health and safety, y'know. Let's move away, we wanted to see you anyway. A few more questions need to be answered and we appear to have lost our incident room."

They moved to the far side of the car park and Annie faced them, like a schoolmarm.

"Right," she said, "you told me that there may be an illegal connection between your committee officers and JD Developments."

"That's right," said Mike, "That JD crew have definitely made an offer and plans have been submitted for a substantial redevelopment. There is also some suspicion that the accounts don't add up and there have been two or three arguments recently, apparently about skulduggery in accounting procedures. Jonny and Brian were involved in those arguments and they were seen having a tete a tete around that time that looked a bit odd, y'know, not like just two pals having a chat. They were planning something, something serious. Two and two... etcetera."

"If what you're saying is true, that would give either party a motive for getting rid of them," said Hedly, anxious not to let Annie have all the say in the enquiries. "You know them. Are they capable of murder?"

"Who Snape and Blezzard?" said Derek. "Not in a million years. They are both clerks, reached quite high in clerkery, admitted, but clerks for all that. Devious, but not murderous."

"What about organising someone else to do it?" asked Annie.

"I doubt it. They aren't the type and they wouldn't know how to recruit someone that would kill for money."

"Have you seen any strange happenings, or even strangers, around the club over the last week or so?" asked Hedly, fighting to keep at the forefront of the interview.

"Strange or strangers. There is a difference you see. Fifty percent of the golfers here are strange and do strange things. However, there's not many strangers here, except the organised golf societies."

"That's right, there's no public bar, y'see. You need to be signed in, and even when a stranger is signed in he would usually be sat or stood in the company of whoever ... Wait a minute, what about that Irish bloke who was trying to get into Jayne's knickers yesterday. He wasn't with anyone was he, stood chattin' to Jayne most of the afternoon."

"And who signed him in?" asked Annie, taking a keen interest.

"Charles Blezzard," said Dermot. "Remember, Jayne said Blezzard signed him in and then left early to go to Chesterfield."

"Chester, or Chesterfield?"

"He said Chesterfield."

"What was his name, this Irishman?" asked Annie.

"Paddy Mc somethin'," said Derek.

"Dermot," said Mike.

"What?" said Dermot.

"No, the Irishman," said Mike, now grinning.

"Yes I know I'm Irish, me mam told me, years ago."

"No, the Irishman's name, Dermot."

"No it wasn't, it was Paddy," said Derek.

The three detectives looked at the old duffers as they started up another inane discourse.

Annie was gettin used to them now and waited until they stopped buggering about. She knew they were doing it on purpose; pretending to be senile seemed to amuse them.

Hedly just looked from one to the other wondering whether they should really be in a home.

"Have we finished?" she finally said.

"Paddy McDermott was his name," said Mike smiling at the performance. "It stuck for obvious reasons."

An exchange of glances between the detectives told Derek that they recognised the name. "You know him, don't you," he said.

"Oh, yes, we know Paddy 'Puck' McDermott all right. I'm surprised that he gave his real name though. He must have been sure that all evidence of his signature modus operandi and prints would be wiped out in the flames, eh?"

"Puck?" said Derek, "That's a strange name for an Irishman. Does he like matches?"

"Got it in one," said Annie. "I'll have to have a word with the fire inspector. He'll know what to look for. It seems that this lot wasn't caused by your Sambuca after all."

"What about the murders? Did he do them as well?"

"I doubt it. He's a firebug and his record is only classed as good 'cause he has managed to cause more than twenty million pounds worth of damage without actually killing anybody."

"In that case, you'll need to have a go at that JD mob. Maybe they are 'the mob'," said Alan.

Hedly's phone rang. He answered it and listened for a few minutes.

"Puck McDermott," he said.

He listened again. "We're already onto him. He's probably on the ferry as we speak. The Garda will send him back as soon as he docks." He listened again. "He was, was he? Pity he didn't collaborate with us, eh? It might have saved his barnet." Hedly closed his phone.

"Seems we had a Commander Pond of MI5 watching our friend Puck and also Mark Norton. He's in hospital with second degree burns to his head."

"That guy in the corner, always drinking whiskey," said Annie. "We never actually got round to him, he always seemed to be at the other end of the bar from us.

"Well Puck is down as an IRA terrorist and when Pond spotted him he reported in and was told to wait and see if he tried to make contact with Jimmy Wu."

"Not as good as they think they are, eh?" said Annie.

Hedly fixed a glare at Curtice, who had stood by quietly, hoping not to be noticed.

"What about him?" said Hedly, indicating the chef.

"Don't think so guv, we have already had a go at him and, apart from having a barney with Fordham he wasn't away from witnesses long enough to have carted the body out and bury it."

"Just make sure you don't go skipping off to Blackpool again, we've still got a few more questions that we need to clear up."

"Are you goin' to keep after our club fiddlers? Snape and Blezzard?" asked Mike.

"I'll pass that to the fraud squad, they'll be able to sort that lot out. JD Developments and any involvement they've had with your council officers won't be hidden for long. We'll have a go at them for a better account of their time and we'll get their phone records."

The detectives walked away looking for the fire inspector. They then needed to find Chris Jones.

He was still their prime suspect as the killings looked more likely   to   be   drug   related.

"It appears that our three o'clock meeting has been cancelled Jerry," said Dave.

"Oh, why's that then?"

"It seems they may have been arrested," said Dave, staring out of his window overlooking the canal. It was a cool location in the prestigious Hart Building, a high rise block in the redeveloped Ship Canal dock area. The move had impressed the clients he wanted to get at, clients who were corruptible. They knew that he must have handed out some incentives to get into a block like this and he had. It looks like he might have to call in a few favours.

"Arrested? What for? They can't have found out what we're up to can they?" said Jerry, a look of fear crossed his face.

"Oh I doubt that. We've covered our tracks pretty well and whatever they have done is their problem. I'll get in touch with the trustees tomorrow and we'll go ahead without them. It'll save us some cash if their locked up anyway."

"What about the cash we've already given them?"

"We'll have to put that down to expenses. Anyway, they did the job. Got us the deal and demolished the building. Result. That saved us the aggravation of saying 'oops' when we knocked down the listed building."

"Listed, they didn't say it was listed. We couldn't have knocked down a listed building."

"Oh don't panic. The powers that be had forgotten to add the fact to the land registry. How would we know it was listed? Not that they could have done anything about it, anyway. When it's down, it's down."

"Arrested though, I'm not sure I like that. It's a bad omen and, what if they spill the peas?"

"Stop worrying, any peas they spill can't get back to us. We're pea proof." He laughed; a bit nervously, Jerry thought. "I can see shitty cats in bags, ready to get out," he said to himself.

"Now then Kermit," said Mike, "what did they have to say to you?"

"Nozzink. Zey jus' assed me kwestions 'bout meestair Fordham an' wat appen' weez ze argument I 'ave weez 'eem."

"And you told them?"

"I say to zem wat I say to zem before. Zat meestar Fordham, ee call my cookeen ees sheet, so I eet eem wiz ze chophair, on ze 'ed," he pointed to his forehead, illustrating where he had hit Fordham in case there was some difficulty with the audience understanding the whereabouts of 'ze ed'.

"And then what happened?" persisted Mike.

"I sought I 'ad keeled eem, so I run out an' I run eento Tom. I tol' eem wat I deed an' ee say not to worry, go an' clear ze tables an' ee weel 'ave a shat weez eem an' calem eem down."

"Yes, well that's when Tom came running in to us, remember, said he couldn't find him," said Dermot.

"Mmm." Derek thought for a minute. "How long were you clearing the tables, Curt?"

"Eet was habout feefteen meenutes een ze dineen room cleareen ze cornair tables an' zen I clear deeshes an' seengs eento ze keetchen, maybe all togezzer, sirtee meenutes."

"And no sign of Fordham?" said Derek.

"No."

"He must have scarpered, in fear of gettin' a proper choppin' up, eh?" said Alan. "And he must have run into Mack the Shovel."

"Something's wrong here," said Derek. "He can't have just disappeared under all our noses. Someone must have seen him. And where did his car go?"

"They never found it did they?" said Alan.

"So you went home then, did you?" Derek asked Curtice.

"Oui, Tom say I betair go een case ee come back an' geev me ze sack. We bose go 'ome een my car. I take Tom 'ome, zen I go 'ome, I seenk zat eef I go away for a few days, eet weel be ovair an' I go back to ze work."

"Curiouser and curiouser," said Derek, shaking his head.

The fire engines had gone and, after the reporters had interviewed the members milling about the front entrance, they began to drift away. Other members came in their turn to see what damage had been done to their clubhouse and to see what they were doing about their course and competitions. Mark and Tom were on hand to reassure the members that, as far as all the professional staff was concerned, it was business as usual. Competitions would be organised and the shop would be open so that golfing life would not miss a beat. Curtice was also making arrangements to organise facilities to provide tea, coffee, hot dogs and bacon butties.

The boys were joined by John in the Stoat and Ferret whose landlord was delighted by the club's mishap.

"O'course yer welcome in 'ere," he said, planning to hike the prices as soon as the poncy golfers had spread the word about the cheap beer prices. "It won't be cheap for long," he thought. "As soon as they've got all their mates in here, I'll up the prices and blame the brewery.

"Looks like I missed all the fun," said John. "I've just been down to the club to have a look. It's a proper job, isn't it? Surprising what a bit of alcohol adds to a party."

"You've not heard, have you?" said Mike. "It wasn't the Sambuca that finished the club off. It was Jayne's boyfriend, and his nickname is Puck."

"What, like the matches?"

"Spot on, Sherlock."

"He's not my boyfriend," said a familiar voice.

"Bloody 'ell, it's our Jayne," said John. "What are you doin' behind that bar?"

Jayne was smiling broadly, happy she had taken John's advice. He had suggested that she should toddle over to the Stoat and tell them to expect an increase in their clientele numbers and being as how she knew all of the additional customers; it might be a good idea to add her to the staff rota.

"A good idea that, John; thanks for that." She turned to Mike and added, "And he's not my boyfriend."

"Who, John?" laughed Alan. "You'd better watch out claiming a married man as yer boyfriend. His Anne'll give you a clout if she gets to hear of it."

"No, I mean that Paddy. He's a lying sod, pretending to go into the flames to rescue me, an' all. He also promised to take me out tonight."

"You should look out for them smooth-talking Irish lads," said Dermot. "They're good at the ol' knicker-adjusting talk."

"Don't worry Dermot, you're the only Irishman I'm going to trust in the future," replied Jayne as she moved to the other end of the bar to serve one of the regulars.

Annie and Al were back at headquarters, transferring their notebook entries onto their computers in order to prepare their individual reports. Hedly was in his office waiting to collect their reports so that he could compile the final state of the case, which he would pass to Nelson, his immediate boss.

Annie's phone rang out and she picked it up, "Hello," she said a bit sharply, still concentrating on her report. Hedly was already pushing for its completion.

She listened, her concentration suddenly broken. "And why would we do that, O'Hara?" More information followed. "Now listen very carefully, O'Hara. You and Partington stay exactly where you are, do not and I stress not, touch anything. We're on our way. Oh, and do not, under any circumstances, let that dog, his owner or any of the old farts that keep destroying crime scenes, anywhere near that site. I mean anywhere."

She paused and listened. "I mean five hundred yards worth of anywhere; and if they try to get closer, shoot 'em."

She listened again. "Yes O'Hara, I know you haven't got a gun. I was jus... Just arrest them," she said, giving up.

She slammed the phone down, looked over at Hollis and said, "Get yer coat, we're off to that club again."

"I'd say that isn't an invite to the Stork for a night of winin', dinin' and dancin', when you say 'we're off to the club'," he said, grabbing his jacket.

"Correct, I'll shout Hedly; tell him his report will have to wait." She knocked on Hedly's door.

Hedly looked up and beckoned her to enter.

"Just had a call from the golf club. It seems that someone has filled in the hole," she said.

"Filled the hole in?"

"That's right. Don't know who or why or how."

"Well I think we'd better concentrate on the how first," growled Hedly, standing up slowly. "I thought that the bloody place was on twenty four hour guard."

"It is guv, but we've had some distractions to contend with, remember."

"Distractions? We're supposed to deal with distractions. That's our job, our speciality. Our superiors aren't going accept 'distractions' as an excuse for the violation of a crime scene are they?"

"I know guv," said Annie, trying once more to calm down this highly strung man who was getting stressed again. "Bur two murders and two fires, plus drug dealing and missing suspects, all in the space of a few days, sir," she pleaded. "We arc a bit understaffed as well."

"Right," he had taken a deep breath, knowing that Annie was right. "You and Hollis get down there and I'll report as much as I can to Nelson. Where's Ghosh?"

"I sent him to Chester sir, to check out Blezzard's story."

"Ok, I'll send him down to you when he gets back."

"I think we need SOCO down there as well as this is the freshest scene we will get," said Annie. "I think we might find our last missing suspect in that hole."

"Coroner's Office?" asked Hedly.

"Not yet, we don't want any more piss takin' if we can help it. Let's try and get this one right."

Hedly sat down and returned to his report and Annie headed for the car followed by Hollis, phone clamped to his ear.

Chris Jones sat on the bed of his motel room, watching the TV, trying to sort out his very confused brain. He was feeling very negative about his recent decision making skills, or lack of them. His return to the UK was looking to have been the start of a string of bad moves. Going back to the hut was pretty bad one as well, but he was beginning to think that the burying of the body was the baddest. The news about the destruction of the clubhouse had made the national news and when they announced that they were looking for the arsonist and linked the whole thing to the murder of two members, he took a much keener interest in the bulletin.

"The police are interested to interview two men in connection with the crimes, one being an employee of the club, Mr Chris Jones and the other a known arsonist, Patrick McDermott."

He went cold. He couldn't contact his partner, Winston, and as he feared that it was Bassong who murdered Best and Fordham, he daren't try to contact him.

When the police find him, the discovery of the Lady Captain's husband will be the last straw and he, by his decision to bury the body, has left himself in a vulnerable position.

Up to that moment, all they could do was accuse him of allowing cannabis to be grown in his shed and maybe a bit of smoking and dealing, but murder!!

Now another decision was brewing.

He grabbed his coat and picked up his case, before heading out the door.

The two sheepish constables stood like statues, their eyes peeled for any one of the names that the angry sergeant had listed. The sight of the little white dog appearing at the edge of the course, just close to where the five old codgers had climbed the fence earlier in the day, made their blood run cold.

"Go and tell him to bugger off, quick," said O'Hara to his pal.

"You go an' tell 'im. I'm not good with dogs," replied Trev Partington.

"Dog? He's no bigger than a decent sized cat," said O'Hara. "Don't tell me yer scared of him."

"Not scared exactly. It's jus' that they don't take kindly to me. They growl an' bark an' stuff."

"Who are you more scared of, the midget dog or Annie?" said O'Hara, seeing that the dog was getting close to the five hundred yard barrier that Annie had stipulated.

Partington saw Keith come into view and, feeling safer seeing the owner, he reluctantly agreed to warn them off. O'Hara watched as Partington walked towards the dog and his master. Snotty, being a generally friendly mutt, ran towards the constable, yapping his doggy greeting as he trotted forward. Keith called Snotty back as he was aware that the short sighted dog could, on occasion, be confused by uniforms and he could, and often did, attack any uniform that looked like a postman.

It was unfortunate that the old style helmet had been replaced by the less ridiculous peaked cap as Snotty always recognised the old style bobby, being a traditional sort of dog. Ignoring Keith's calls he trotted on towards the shape he saw approaching him and as he got closer his trot slowed and his eyes squinted in order to focus properly. The yapping ceased and the teeth bared in that smile that signalled, to those that recognised the signs, that an attack was imminent.

The nervous Trev didn't recognise the signs and, trying to ingratiate himself with the little terrier, he got down on his haunches and smiled broadly, clicking his fingers and saying, "Here boy, come on," and stuff that usually gets dogs to run towards the caller, in the hope of a biscuit.

He didn't realise that his smile and his large white teeth was a direct challenge to the feisty terrier who was frightened by nothing, especially not a poncy postman. Snotty darted forward, growling in a tone that belied his size, almost loosening Trev's bowels. Trev tried to stand up, hoping that the owner would get there before the dog tore him to bits. However, his heel had caught in the handcuffs dangling from his belt and, in attempting sudden rise from his crouch; he lost his balance and tumbled over. As he fell he saw the teeth approaching and, in the distance, the sight of the owner, huffing and puffing without a hope of getting there in time to save him.

O'Hara, having watched Trev's nervous approach to the dog, couldn't believe his eyes and, seeing that Keith hadn't got a hope of reaching Partington in time to save him from a mauling, immediately sprinted forward in order to save his mate.

Keith and O'Hara arrived at the same time and saw Trev rolling about with one foot caught in the handcuffs and the other caught by the trouser leg, which was in the dogs jaws. He had managed to grab Snotty's collar, preventing him from progressing to the actual meat of the leg, much to the dog's annoyance. Trev couldn't escape, he was trapped. The result of the scuffle was - Snotty, one fall, Trev, nil.

It was pure bad luck that Annie and Al had chosen that very moment to make their way into the clearing, puzzled by the absence of the guards.

They became aware of the barking dog, accompanied by Trev's shouts for help and Keith's attempts to call his dog to heel, but they couldn't locate where the noise was coming from.

"They're priceless them two," said Al.

"Aren't they just," agreed Annie. "Sounds as though they're managing to keep that bloody dog away though. Be thankful for small mercies."

They proceeded into the clearing and saw that the hole had, in fact, been filled in. A spade was lying neatly beside the freshly dug soil. The two cops looked at each other.

"What have we here?" said Annie.

"Looks like a spade to me," said Al.

"Shovel," said Annie. "Remember, spade, not a good word."

"Oh, yes. The seminar on race relations. How could I forget?"

"We'll get Forensic to have a look at that, might be a print or two on it," she said as she heard cars arriving in the car park.

Half an hour later in the gathering gloom, they observed the face of Percy Milbank slowly appearing, framed by the soil that was being carefully removed by the forensic officers.

"Right," said Annie, "Call Maxwell. We need to get back to HQ and push the search for Jones."

The boys were still holding court in the Stoat where more members had drifted in, hearing that it wasn't as bad a pub as they had been led to believe.

The regulars couldn't believe how their normally quiet 'early doors' had been disturbed by a whole new demographic wearing strange kit.

Not a shell suit between them. However, once they were seen to be a harmless addition, making for a better atmosphere, the pub settled down into a happy buzz.

There were things to be discussed regarding the future of the golf club and the subject of finance came up. Jack had just arrived with the astounding news that Snape and Blezzard were at police headquarters answering questions relating to the club accounts. "Fraud Squad have got them, I believe,"

"Yeah, but they've still got to explain their connection to Jayne's boyfriend, the firebug," said Mike. "If they're connected, they'll be up for firebuggin' as well."

"Bloody hell," said Jack, "Charles and Arthur, arsonists. It doesn't bear thinking about."

"More to the point, there's murder to consider," said Derek. "If they can burn down the club.... I mean it was their life. I just can't believe it."

"And if they're guilty of something you can't believe they was capable of, why not murder. They could have killed someone with that fire."

"I think that the cops' prime suspect is still attached to the drug element," said Derek. "Chris, Winston and that Wythenshawe dealer."

Annie and Al got back to HQ and swiped their ID cards at the desk reader. As they went towards their office, the desk sergeant called them over. "Someone waiting to see you," he said.

"Not now, we've got a suspect to chase," said Al. "They'll have to wait."

"Well, he's already been waiting over an hour. He came in just after you rushed out."

"What's his name?" asked Annie, ready to go to the lift.

"Jones, Chris Jones," said the desk sergeant.

Annie and Al looked at each other. "Where?"

"Interview room three."

"I'll go and introduce myself," said Annie. "You go and tell Hedly then get back down here."

Al headed for the lift and Annie made her way to Room three.

Tom Jackson and Curtice came into the Stoat and, seeing the group of golfers at the end of the bar, they headed over to join them.

Curtice spotted Jayne as he got to the bar. "Jayne, 'ow are you? I see zat you 'ave ze new job already."

"Hi Curt, yeah, John suggested it. Listen, they don't do any food here, do you want me to put a word in?"

"Oui, certainement," said Curt.

"Look Kermit," said Mike. "I think you should be aware that the regulars in here will be quick to call you a frog and Kermit more than we do. Are you happy with that?"

"Weel I 'ave to fight wiz zem."

"Not if you take no notice. They won't mean it; it's just a gentle Mickey take. These lot aren't as politically correct as golf club members. They don't have to follow the same rules, but they are all the same as us."

"Hokay, Kermeet ees no so bad a name," said Curtice slowly, realising a job's a job. "Zat's good zen. Put een zat word, eh?"

Chris was sitting in the interview room, his elbows on the table in front of him and his head in his hands. He was almost asleep, having been driving or just sitting in his car for over twenty four hours. The only time he was vertical was when he left the car to find the shed empty except for the extremely dead body. The burying of the body merely added to his level of exhaustion and the trauma of doing so prevented his taking advantage of his brief rest in the motel room at the back of the Blue Parrot in nearby Altrincham. The sudden opening of the door made him start and one of his elbows slipped off the desk, exaggerating the lurch forward normally associated with a drunk snoozing at the bar.

"Well, well," said Annie. "At last. We've been looking all over for you. Didn't think you were an international criminal."

Annie was followed in by Hollis, who had brought their file in with him. They both sat down and Annie began to put tapes into the recording equipment. All the time talking to Jones.

"You're not actually under arrest at this stage, but if you refuse to answer our questions then I will formally arrest you."

Chris wasn't aware that she was just adding time to his incarceration since once he was under arrest they only had forty eight hours in which to gather sufficient evidence on which to actually charge him.

"I came in voluntarily," protested Chris. "I'll come clean to growin' a bit of grass, well that's my job, y'see," he tried to smile, but his heart wasn't in it. "Well, anyway, I did grow a bit of stuff, just for me mates, y'know. Anyway, when I came down to the shed that mornin' and saw Best lyin' there in that hole, I bloody shit myself."

He looked at the two detectives and, when he got no response, he continued. "Well what would you do? I could see it in a flash. My shed, cannabis, what would you think." He paused, still no response. "Well, what did you think? I know what you thought; you thought that I had done it. Anyway, I wasn't goin' to be blamed for murder."

Another pause, eyes darting between the stone faced cops. "I remembered the night before, the argument I had with 'im, an' threatenin' him. I knew you'd think it was me."

Finally Annie spoke, "You're right, we did think, and do think that you are one of our prime suspects. Not just Best but also Fordham, who we believe was in your little gang as well. He was found in the same hole. And guess what, we have just found another stiff, Percy Milbank, buried in the same hole. This time the grave was finished properly, the shovel lying tidily by the grave."

"Spade," said Chris absentmindedly.

"Spade?"

"Yes, spade. It's a spade, not a shovel."

"Spade then," said Annie, bowing to the professional. "Whatever you call it, there is blood and fingerprints on the handle. Yours I'd guess."

"Look, I don't deny that I put him in the hole," said Chris, his voice sounding panicky. "But I didn't kill him. I thought that it was that bastard Bassong and his thugs that did for Fordham, and the other two. But he was in my shed. Another one in my shed, and I thought if I could hide him, I could get back to Volendam. You'd have had a job findin' me there."

"The shovel, I mean spade," said Al, "Where did you hide it?"

"I didn't hide it. I forgot to hide it, that's why I came back. I left it on the bloody floor." He ran his fingers through his hair, tugging it hard in frustration. "I should have wiped it and put it back under the beam, where I always hide it."

"Hide it? Why would you hide it?" asked Annie.

"'Cause the other lad's keep nickin' it and it's me best spade. Had it for years and those other buggers would leave it lyin' around. It was bound to be lost or nicked. So I found a perfect hidin' place for it."

"Anyone else know where you kept it?"

Chris shook his head slowly. "I know, that looks even worse doesn't it? I don't think anyone else knew." His shoulders slumped and his head returned to his hands.

"Ok, Chris, that's all for now, but we're going to have to keep you in custody, what with your ability to skip off abroad."

"Do what you want, I just want a sleep. A cell can't be as bad as the bed I just tried to rent earlier today."

Annie switched off the tapes after adding the required information, time, persons present, etc. And Al called a constable to process the exhausted Jones and find him a cell.

CHAPTER 20

- Club meetings at the Stoat & Ferret -

Sunday morning brings out the social golfers, teams of four who play a more aggressive version of the game. Readers may be confused by the contradiction in terms; 'social' and 'aggressive', but the best of friendships are often tested on a Sunday morning, the day that the Lord designated as a day of rest, reserved for peaceful pastimes, golf probably featuring high in the His list. (That would have been before the advent of the Sunday morning fourball format.)

Golf is a strange sport, normally played on an individual basis, each player trying to best the course by completing his game in as low a number of strokes as possible. It is even quite normal to play the game on one's own, attempting to beat the standard number of strokes that each hole demanded, depending on the playing distance of each hole.

Without trying to explain the intricate rules of the game, it is incumbent on each player to follow those rules with a degree of honesty not equalled in any other sport. That some cheat is the nature of the human race, however, in golf, the percentage of cheats compared to the total number of participants is extremely low.

Now Sunday golf brings a different ethic to the game. Players, who are normally fanatically honest in their application of the rules, gentlemanly in their conduct and respectful to their opponents, seem to morph into a different species altogether when playing a Sunday morning four-ball.

The format of a 'fourball' comprises two players on each side who contest each hole by trying to take the least strokes, the best score of either partner being counted as 'the score'. The team that wins the hole takes one point, which is called 'a hole'. Then there is another important ingredient to the game, 'the handicap', which is better left unexplained, as it often confuses the issue and usually is the cause of the greatest number of arguments and fights on the first tee.

Many players wager various sums of money on the outcome of the game and there are a number of variations on the construction of these wagers.

It would be easy to blame the arguments, and the breakdown in good will, on the inclusion of the wagers but the magnitude of the bet doesn't seem to dilute the ferocity of the disagreements generated during, or at the end of a game.

Gamesmanship is varied and can be very imaginative, coughing and the movement of clubs or feet during a chap's backswing being the most common. This is an additional ingredient in both the financial outcome of the game and the future relationship of the players.

As the 'Grandad's Detective Bureau' were warming up for their usual Sunday battle they had a brief board meeting on the latest progress of their current cases.

"Just had word from Bollington & Hearst," said Jack. "Remember, they're the auditors that Tony and old Partridge came up with. It was a good move getting the books and accounts over to them when we did, otherwise that fire would have got them, eh? Anyway, they've just confirmed it. You were right all along Mike; those two conniving bastards fiddled the books."

"Yer jokin'" said Mike. "Blimey, that's a first; one of my hunches paying off. I was the one that said Man United wouldn't win a tap last year, and they won the double."

"Well you were right on this one, chum."

"How much?"

"Three hundred K."

They all went quiet. Derek was the first to speak. "That's a lot of motive," he said. "People have been killed for less than that."

"I don't want to speak ill of the dead," said Alan, "but I'd have done 'em in for much less than that. Why didn't anyone ask me?"

It was time to tee off so the group began the ritual of selecting their fourball sets and tossing up for partners. As the ritual proceeded, Derek's mobile trilled out its musical ringtone. He answered it with an apologetic look on his face, acknowledging the demonstration of bad form, having his mobile switched on.

"Well that's good news," he said, interrupting the group's attempts to organise themselves. "That was Tony Drummond. He says that the insurance payout will more than cover the rebuilding of a new clubhouse. It was valued at one point eight million quid and, with the club's readjusted books showing a healthy balance, we can start the project immediately."

"Oh goody, that means we will have a new clubhouse."

"Yeah, but with this lot," said Alan, "it'll take them five years to get the bloody foundations down."

They all started laughing and the first fourball drove their balls off and set off down the fairway to look for them, all now full of good spirits, laughing and joking as they strode down the path.

That wouldn't last for long.

"Hackett's just phoned," said Hollis.

"Who?"

"Y'know, the Fraud Squad inspector we called in. He asked for Hedly," said Al, "but I said he was out."

"Good lad," said Annie, glancing over at Hedly's office, where he was deep in conversation on the phone. "What'd he have to say?"

"Snape and Blezzard have coughed. Apparently the books had been taken over to another auditor last week and they've found a massive discrepancy, three hundred grand. When faced with the facts, Blezzard gave them everything."

"Jesus, how the hell did they hide that?" said Annie.

"With a great deal of imagination apparently. It seems that they had a number of complicated deals with the rail people and they were able to confuse the accounts with the value of some of the land value write offs and actual cash compensation. As I said, imaginative. They got a suitcase full of cash as well."

"Well if they had already swindled the club," mused Annie, "why did they need to get involved with JD Developments, I wonder."

"The hard cash was one hundred and fifty grand and that was the first instalment; the same on completion."

"Jesus, that's some deal. Well we'd better get over there and ask them a few more questions about the murders," said Annie, getting her handbag. "And we need to get at the two from JD Developments as well. I'm now thinking that one of those four organised the killings, no matter what our retired sergeant thinks. Have they found the cash yet?"

"I've sent Ghosh and a team to follow up on the search warrants. He's gone to Snape's house first.

He said something about making a better job on her than he did with   Mrs   Milburn,   whatever   that   means."

"Bad news Jerry," said Dave as he replaced the receiver. His face was serious, white with a definite green tinge round the gills.

"Bad as in shitty cat bad?" asked Jerry.

"You saw it all along, didn't you?" said Dave, his face changing and his gills reddening. "In fact, you're the one that put the mockers on it, it's your fault. You're such a negative bastard that it spread all over the whole deal." He was getting angry at the very thought that Jerry had somehow caused the downfall of his master plan.

"That call was from the trustees of the club. It appears that they have found their missing funds and Snape is under arrest with his pet dickhead, Blezzard. Snape had pleaded innocent, saying it was Blezzard who signed all the papers and signed in the firebug. They've even got CCTV footage of him paying the arsonist. It looks like Snape will get away with it, unlike you."

"Me?" said Jerry rising from his chair, face contorted in an angry grimace. "Me? How the hell can I be blamed? All I did was follow every bent move you made. I always have." He walked over to the window, looking out at the spectacular view. "You're right. I have been a proper dickhead, haven't I?" he said, more to himself than for Dave's ears.

Dave was stunned by Jerry's outburst, falling back into his expansive executive chair. He pulled himself together and, overhearing Jerry's quiet remark, he said, "Jerry, you've always been a dickhead. That's why I chose you."

Jerry turned around, fixing Dave with an angry glare. "Is that right? Well I'll show you who the dickhead is. I'm going to the police and I'm going to tell them everything, see. I'm going to cook your chicken good."

"Cook my chicken, eh?" Dave was smiling, an evil smile. "How are you going to achieve that?"

"You're as crooked as a....." He searched for a crooked example, "a, um, a spring, that's it a twisty spring."

"That's a helix."

"What?"

"A spring; it's a helix. Y'see, you can't even get similes right. And you must remember that you are the FD of this company.

Your signature is on all the papers that are on file, including the money we drew from our slush fund to pay your brother dickheads at the golf club. In fact, I was about to call in the police to report my Financial Director for embezzlement."

Jerry looked at the smug face of his boss and something inside snapped. He looked around the office, his eyes falling on the heavy waste paper bin next to Dave's desk. He grabbed it and slowly moved over to Dave, whose face was turning grey, with gills more green than red.

The players all trouped into their alternative clubhouse bar, the Stoat, either still bickering about the tactics of their opposition or, in the case of the victors, gloating about their success. Winners collected their winnings and losers paid out their losings. Demonstrating how little the magnitude of the bet played in the resulting rows, the five pounds worth of winnings were the first coins to disappear over the bar.

"Hey," said Derek. "I've just been speaking to that Clowes doris and she says that Snape and Blezzard have confessed."

"What to, murder?" asked Mike.

"No, the fiddling and the arson; well, the organising of the arson. They've implicated JD Developments as well."

"Not the murders then," said Jack. "Well who else is in the frame?"

"Chris and Winston seem to be doubtful now as well," said Derek. "Some of their alibis check out, neither one could have done all the killings; but I suppose they could have alternated."

"Or organised it," said Dermot. "Like Snape organised the arson."

"Yeah, well what about that Irishman?" said John with a smile. He was one of the winners and was in a chirpy mood. "He could have done it. They're all trained for that blowin' up stuff an' murder, aren't they?" He looked at Dermot.

"You're looking for a dunt in the mouth," said Dermot. "I'll take that kind of talk from no man." He was looking for an excuse to give someone a clout as he was one of the losers.

"Calm down Dermot," Mike quickly cut in. "He's only jokin'." He paused before adding, "An' it was only a fiver."

"Look, the only murder that should easily have been spotted was Brian's," said Derek. "We were all here, along with a roomful of diners and members there at the bar. What did we all miss?"

"Let's go over it again," said John, face now serious, not wanting the smack in the mouth that Dermot wanted to sell.

"Wait a minute, let's get a beer first," said Alan. "Jayne, c'mon, let's have a bit of service over here," he shouted.

Jayne began pulling the beers as Derek went over the facts.

"Right," he said, "Kermit goes into the kitchen and Brian follows him. They have a row and Kermit tries to decapitate Brian, misses and donks him on the head."

"Then he does a runner," said Mike.

"Bumping into Tom," continued Derek. "He tells Tom he's hit Brian with his chopper. And before you say it, don't. This is serious." He glared at Mike who was looking innocently skywards. "Tom tells Kermit to calm down and he'll go and try to calm Brian down."

"Why would he think he could calm down someone who had just been clobbered with a hatchet, especially Brian?" said Alan. "Do you honestly think that Tom would be the man who could calm you down if you had been clobbered with a hatchet?"

"Whatever," said Derek. "Tom sends Kermit to the dining room to clear up and goes into the kitchen to speak to Brian. The kitchen's empty so he has to start looking for him. That's when he saw us in the bar."

"How could he disappear in that time," said Dermot. "It can only have been two or three minutes from Kermit clouting Brian and Tom finding the kitchen empty; five minutes at the most."

"No," said Jayne, placing three pints on the bar. "It was at least fifteen minutes."

All attention turned to Jayne.

"What do you mean?" said Derek.

"I've already told the other two coppers that Brian followed Curtice into the kitchen and Curtice came back into the dining room about five minutes later, clearing up the dishing-out area, then starting on the tables. I helped him for part of the time, maybe four or five minutes."

Mike said, "That's what we just said."

"I know, but I was in the bar for at least another ten, maybe fifteen, minutes before Tom came into the lounge looking for Brian. That makes at least fifteen or twenty minutes, so he must have spent some time looking for Brian before he came in to you lot for help."

"That's it! That's the gap we have missed," said Derek. "Twenty minutes is all you'd need to do him in and stick him in his car; moving it out of sight in the thicket at the end of the car park."

"Tom!" said an awestruck Jack. "You mean Tom Jackson, don't you?"

Silence reigned for a couple of minutes before Derek dug his mobile from his pocket.

Annie was just finishing Jerry Vaughan's grilling and, after he had broken down completely, he finally pleaded manslaughter on the grounds of temporary diminished responsibility under extreme provocation.

"Jerry, he's not actually dead," she said. "He has to be dead for it to be manslaughter."

"Not dead?" Jerry looked up, his face twisted into a mad grimace. "You mean I didn't finish the bastard?" He looked down at his hands again. "That's an ill wind, sick of blowing."

Hedly looked at Annie, mouthed, "What?"

Annie shook her head and shrugged, trying not to smile.

"What about the three bodies at the golf club? Was that extreme provocation?" said Hedly.

"Golf club bodies? Nothing to do with us. I just wish the place had burned down before we had ever heard of it."

"You didn't want to kill them when they wanted to be cut in on the deal?" persisted Hedly.

"He probably did, that devious bastard Jordan, but he finally agreed to pay up. Bloody hell, when they started being bumped off, he even agreed to pay their share to Snape and Blezzard."

"Well, when he finally comes out of his coma, we'll ask him that, eh?" said Annie.

"Out of his coma?" said Jerry. "Can't I have another go at him?" he added, a hopeful look on his face.

"Stop that Jerry," said Annie sharply. "That's not going to help your defence of 'temporary' diminished responsibility, is it?"

Annie and Hedly looked at each other, both shaking their heads and finished the interview, sending Jerry back to his cell.

"He's still denying the murders and we can't actually tie either of them in with anything to do with the victims; only embezzlement, bribery and corruption, plus arson in the committee men's case," said Annie to Hollis later. "We've recovered Snape's share and, guess what, Jordan's fingerprints were all over the case and the money. That gets both the JD fellers in the bag; well one in the bag, the other in intensive care. What about that, eh? Mild mannered Vaughan battering him with his own waste bin; left him for dead and gave himself up. It looks like we're stuck with Jones, D'Jemba or Bassong as murder suspects."

"We'll need to do a bit more work; try to break down their alibis, 'cause they're not that good for our case; unless they did them in relays or organised them."

Just then, Annie's phone rang. She answered it and, after taking down the information, she thanked the caller and waited for Hollis to finish his own call.

"Guess what?" she said.

"Hedly has solved the three murders and he's been promoted to Chief Constable," said Al with a broad grin.

"Annie looked at him coldly. "You're getting as bad as him with that sarcasm, y'know. Mind you, that could even get you promotion if he's any guide."

"Sorry," said Al. "I couldn't possibly guess. What's up?"

"The fingerprints on the spade," she said. "Only two fresh sets, Jones and that young professional."

"Tom Jackson?"

"The very man. I wonder how his prints got on the secret spade."

Her mobile rang. "Yes," she said. After a few minutes she said, "Thanks for that Derek." She paused before continuing. "Y'know, I think that you lads have solved our case, well done. Thanks again." She rang off and looked over at Hollis.

"Well?" he enquired.

Annie passed on Derek's information and sat back in her chair, arms folded.

"Bloody hell, that's it, isn't it?" he said. "But why did you tell that old duffer that he had solved the case?"

"What would you rather have, him taking the credit and getting even further up the ladder," she said, nodding towards Hedly's office, "or the lads at the club being credited as the true 'Grandad's Detective Bureau'. The press will love it and he will hate it, so will whoever promoted him."

Hollis smiled, "You're a crafty sod, you are. You will go far in the force if there's any justice."

"I'll go and tell him that we think we might have our man," she said, looking over at Hedly's office, "you go and pull Jackson in."

Annie fed the tapes into the recorder, switched it on and gave her name and rank before adding the names of the other occupants of the room, Hedly, Tom Jackson and the duty solicitor Jason Horrocks. She opened her case file and cleared her throat. Looking up at Tom, she began the interview by reminding Tom of his rights.

She then began the serious business, "Tom we know you did it but why?"

Tom looked at Horrocks and seeing no help forthcoming he looked back at Annie and said, Which one?" he said simply.

"Let's start at the beginning, eh."

Tom paused, rubbing his face as though he was washing it furiously. He stopped the rubbing abruptly and said, "'Cause they were all twats. They were all trying to harm me or my friends, so I stopped them."

Annie shook her head slowly, "Ok Tom. One at a time, eh? The first one was Jonny Best, how exactly was he harming you?"

"He was trying to blackmail Mark into taking counterfeit Chinese golf gear. He threatened to report Mark to the club, and the police. That'd mean I'd be out of a job. I couldn't have that. I saw him come to the course and when he said he wanted some lessons, I said I'd meet him on the third. I was a bit late and he had already teed off, putting his ball into the copse. He was already walking in to the trees when I actually got there so I followed him in. When I saw he had found the hut with the cannabis in it I knew I had to do him in."

"You knew about the cannabis?" asked Hedly, needing to be seen to be in charge.

"Oh yes, I helped Chris sometimes, I needed the money. Anyway, while he was inspecting the stuff, I sneaked in and crept over to where Chris had hidden his shovel."

"Spade," corrected Annie.

Shovel," said Hedly, "you've seen the directive on that word."

"The correct word for that implement is a spade, sir. And if the defence were to cross examine us on our knowledge of the murder weapon, how will it look if he gets acquitted 'cause we called a spade a shovel?"

Hedly went quiet.

"Carry on Tom. You found the spade," said Annie. "How did you know where it was?"

"Chris told me, I needed to use it sometimes with the fertilisers. I was the only other person to know where he hid it. Anyway, I went up behind him and gave him a good wallop with it. I then went outside and dug a hole as quick as I could. I wanted to bury him deeper but I knew that I needed to get back quickly and establish where I was. I saw Curtice and made a big show about a bacon butty so he'd remember me. I intended to get back to finish the burial properly but that bloody dog got to him before I could get back."

"What about Fordham? Why kill him?"

"He was going to call the police and get my pal Curtice sent to jail. He'd called Curt's food shit and poor old Curt had retaliated a bit too strongly. I tried to calm him down but he wouldn't listen so I knocked him out with a chopping block and got his keys out of his pocket and stuck him in his own boot. That's when that stupid prick Milbank decided to slap me on the back. He thought it was Fordham until I stuck that screwdriver in his chest. It was quite handy the way he fell on the buggy cover I had just used to drag Fordham to his car."

"Why a screwdriver?"

"Lucky really. I had just been sorting out a dickey connection on the battery charger of one of the buggies before I had gone to see Curtice. It could easily have been stuck in Fordham but the wooden block seemed a better idea."

"Go on."

"I quickly wrapped him in the buggy cover, shoved him in the back seat and drove the car into that deep thicket at the end of the car park. I then legged it into the clubhouse shouting about his disappearance.

It was all confused then with the old farts running about and his wife creating a fuss. I got Curt out of the way so the timing couldn't be ironed out. I had hoped that it wouldn't be clearly remembered by the time he got back, if he ever came back."

"It was those old farts that remembered the timings and got you fingered for that murder," said Annie. "The rest was supposition. You said that you hit Fordham with a chopping board, he died of a spade wound."

"Ah yes, well I had thought the chopping board had done the job and I wasn't sure what to do with the bodies so when Curt dropped me off home, I went back to the club on my bike. I had intended to drive somewhere else to bury the bodies when I saw the two cops who were guarding the shed called up to join in the hunt for Fordham. 'That's handy,' I thought, 'there's a hole down there already, just the right fit.' I used one of the buggies to ferry the bodies down to the shed and I was dropping Fordham into the old hole which I'd made a bit deeper, when he suddenly woke up. The spade came in really handy there. I clouted him before he had time to fully recover. I didn't think I had enough time to bury the other one so I hid him under some rubbish in the corner. I was just in time 'cause that Winston appeared just as I'd got the buggy back. He was dressed in black, with a black balaclava and I wouldn't have seen him if he hadn't smiled at something. His teeth were gleaming in the moonlight, like as though they were on their own, like a Cheshire cat. Anyway I followed him and saw him loading the cannabis into some sacks. There was loads of it and when I saw it would have taken him all night to shift it, I thought that the two Bobbies would get back and catch him in the act. That'd let me off the hook, him being caught in the act."

"What did you do with the car?" said Annie.

"Ship canal," he said brightly. "Bike in car, car to canal, bike out of car, car in canal, bike home. I wish I'd thought of that in the first place, you'd never have found the last two. I thought that I'd got away with it. That bloody dog."

Hedly and Annie cleared up a few more points, ended the taping session and removed the tapes for processing. Tom was then led off to a cell.

EPILOGUE

"Y'know lads, I think I prefer it in here," said Alan.

"We should write to Blezzard and thank him for burning the clubhouse down," said Derek.

"It wasn't him," said Alan. "He just signed the firebug in. Crafty bugger that Snape, he organised Puck, what a name, eh? Anyway, Snape organised him and that silly bugger Gareth Jarvis almost did the job for him."

"Nearly did for him, y'mean," said Dermot. "If it wasn't for that detective, the Sambuca story would have been the talk of the north."

"The last time it happened, said Mike, "It was the 'talk of the Costa Brava'. Burned down a knockin' shop."

"Don't tell Tarquin that," said Alan. "He'll have the customers payin' extra for insurance."

"Er, just a minute, how do you know Tarquin?" said Mike. "You've been samplin' the goods haven't you?"

"No I haven't smartarse. Kermit's been tellin' me all about the place. He knows 'em all. Dancers, Tarquin and even got a list of his best customers."

"How would Kermit know all that?" said Mike.

"You won't believe it, but he's convinced Tarquin that they should put food on. Make it compulsory to have food as well as drink. He did as well, convince him I mean. He's already started. I think that pouf bouncer fancies a bit of frog's leg and Kermit had better watch it, otherwise he'll find his sausage roll in trouble."

"He's not doing bad is he, our little Froggy mate?" said John. "What with bar snacks here at the Stoat during the day and Pole Snacks at the Pole Cats at night."

"Bacon butties in the morning, for the early start golfers as well, don't forget that," said Dermot.

"Well, getting back to the embezzlement," said Jack. "They've tied Jordan and his mate into the affair. Snape had one hundred and fifty thousand pounds in a case in his study, Jordan's prints all over it."

"I heard Jordan's in a coma in Wythenshawe Hospital."

"I think there's a few who'd like to see Snape and Blezzard beside him," said Jack.

"They've still not got Blezzard's share of the graft money though, have they?" said Jack. "It seems to have vanished without trace."

"So has Janice," laughed Alan. "Probably found out that her daft hubby was set for Thailand and decided to hop it somewhere similar. After the cops had taken that house apart, looking for the money, she tarted it up, sold it and then just disappeared."

"She'll be back, pretending she's made a stack wherever she's been and settle down just in time to join our new club," said Dermot.

"Still no foundations, what did I tell you." Alan piped up.

"Who needs it, I think I'll carry on comin' in here, even when it's finally built," said Mike.

"What makes you so sure you'll still be here when it's finished?"

"What, me move house, at my age?" laughed Mike, deliberately ignoring Alan's implication.

"Those boys in the nick won't see it finished, though," said Jack. "Arson's a bit serious, they could have killed someone."

"I think there were enough bodies lyin' around the course without addin' more to the list," said Alan. "The body count was already referred to as a 'Massacre at the Golf Club' in the Mail."

"I like the one in the Sun better," said Mike. "The editor must be a golfer. 'In a bit of a hole' sounds just right."

"I don't think Tom will ever get out," said Jack. "I'm afraid he's unlikely to even get out of the high security wing of Broadmoor."

"He was a spooky sod," said Mike. "Hard to believe really. He seemed a bit quiet, but harmless enough. It's a good job none of you lot excited him otherwise you'd have been stacked in that 'bit of a hole' near the hut."

"I know," said Dermot. "Doesn't bear thinkin' about. There's a couple of times I've thought of clippin' his ear'ole, just to gee him up, y'know. He could be a bit dozy."

"Good job you didn't eh?"

"Stranger still though, is how he got the job," said Jack." Have you read his background; it was in the Mail on Sunday last week."

"We don't get posh papers like you Jack," said Alan with a smirk.

"It's not posh," replied Jack, "It's just not got any tits in it, that's why you don't like it."

All the boys were now more interested in the relative merits of the red top publications and their willingness to dish the dirt on the plethora of so called celebrities, footballers and their wives and especially, politicians; and of course, the tits.

When that discussion started to falter Derek remembered what had started it and said, "You were talking about Tom's background Jack. What about it?"

"Well, it appears he was a strange child and worried his father until he found the perfect pastime for Tom's insular demeanour; golf. Before he took up golf Tom had been in various scrapes which were brushed under the carpet. Any kid who had crossed his path, either by bullying him or by preventing him from getting his own way, were often the victims of strange mishaps; even pets who had transgressed often disappeared.

The golf allowed him to stay out of trouble, mainly because he was able to practice for hours on his own. His ability at golf wasn't remarkable, but was of a sufficient standard to get him to a level that enabled him to try to obtain his assistant's card.

Mark had upped his grades in the practical side of his apprenticeship; though the article didn't say why he would do that, but he did. I think Mark knew more about Tom than he'd let on and he was a wee bit scared of him. Mark also managed to help Tom through some of his exams.

It also seems that his handicap was helped a bit by other means. They say his prowess at the actual game needed some help from his feet, no doubt taking lessons from Partridge."

That brought a large guffaw from the golfers.

Those of the regulars who were now friendly with the golfers had to be familiarised with the connection, which brought more laughter.

"Carry on Jack," said Tommy Parker, a local butcher.

Jack picked up the story, "Well, after he'd got his card, time passed and more rumours began to circulate about his football skills. He was being watched more carefully and time was running out for him, since his scores were getting higher, more like an amateur's equivalent handicap of seven or eight. He was now in danger of losing his card because he was at the stage where Mark couldn't keep covering for him.

His frustration was probably beginning to make him look more closely at what, or who, he thought was to blame for his shortcomings."

"He was just a crap golfer, why didn't he just go and get another job?" asked Tommy.

"Don't know, but he wasn't interested in anything else. Anyway, it appears that there was a bubbling volcano under that golf hat, just waiting to erupt," said Jack.

"Bubbling volcano? Bollocks," said Alan. "He drank orange juice and sat in the corner; never really joined in with anyone, even when he sat with us. We tried our best with him but he never responded."

"They're like that, those volcanoes," said Mike, feeling a bout of smartarsery coming on. "People have lived under volcanoes for years, even when they knew they were bubbling away, still do."

"Surely not, dear boy," said John, spotting the opening that Mike had left. "Under a volcano is a heaving mass of bubbling white hot magma and gasses, waiting to burst out into the atmosphere, which would surely prevent anyone building a house underneath it?"

""When I say under, I didn't mean 'under' as in 'under'. I meant 'under'." Mike smiled, relishing John's challenge.

"Oh, sorry, I thought you meant, 'under'."

The very puzzled Tommy was trying to follow the train of this burst of geological nonsense and Alan had to break it up. "Stop it you two. Come on Jack, finish this before our beer gets flat. Why did he suddenly pick on those three in particular? There were much better candidates for popping into Besty's Copse."

"Well in Jonny's case Tom had found out about the Chinese scam and had not been happy with Best's threat to expose Mark if he didn't take the container of hooky gear that was on the way. Mark had said that it could mean the sack for him and Tom would be implicated, the shop shut and, end of job.

Tom liked Mark and felt he owed him for all the help he'd given him and, he didn't fancy losing this job. The final straw was finding out about Best and Jenny Milbank. Tom was giving Jenny lessons and she did a lot of flirting to get them for nothing."

"So at the first opportunity, Jonny was toast, eh?" said Dermot. He added, "Brian Fordham, what did he do?"

"Fordham?" continued Jack. "Well Fordham was giving Kermit a hard time, according to the paranoid chef. Fordham's crap French and Kermit's insecurities left them both with entirely the wrong impression about their relationship.

Kermy hated Fordham because of the things he said but Fordham actually liked Kermy because he was a good chef and gave him the opportunity to show off his crap French to those that knew no better. Fordham's was an impulse killing, not planned, but Brian was just standing next to the wrong volcano at the wrong time."

""Not under," said John, grinning. Derek shot him a warning glance. "Oops, sorry," he added.

"And Milbank?" said Alan.

"Tom disliked Milbank because his wife did. During Jennie's lessons she constantly moaned about him and his cheating ways. Her dalliances with the odd member were attempts to make her pig of a husband jealous. Annie told Derek what Tom had said when he saw the final position of the screwdriver and the owner of the chest it protruded from. He said to himself, 'Now that's a lucky break; saves me a job later on'."

"Some piece of work, that boy," said Tommy Parker. "He would have been a good butcher's apprentice. Gets rid of all that magma stuff, choppin' up a dead cow."

The large group that the story had attracted all burst out laughing and Jayne was called into action.

"Definitely a good spot for us old reprobates, eh?" said Mike to Alan.

THE END

ABOUT THE AUTHOR

Mike had taken up the pen some twenty years ago and decided he would only write for fun; just about things that made him laugh. The plots that emerged were born from real events and then sort of twisted into storylines that were farcical and farfetched but just about possible.

He used characters based on friends and family and, in some cases, even got their permission to use real names for their avatars. This was writing for pleasure and he had loads of fun whilst constructing them.

So if you like a laugh and it's light relief you want, have a look at his second book, a farcical murder mystery set in a golf club.

It has little to do with the actual game of golf but takes liberties with the type of people who frequent the clubs. However, as cruelly as some of the characters are actually portrayed, there are some who can be recognized as typical.

If you favour suspense then the other one is a change in genre, a murder mystery set in postwar Berlin and Manchester.

See over for short synopses of both.

You can find more about the author on his website
http://www.mikesleater.co.uk

ON THE ROAD WITH DORIS

An intrepid bunch of reluctant sailors are press-ganged into the journey of a lifetime. It was a trip beyond their known geographical boundaries that would test their nerve. Much the same as the legends of the past. They are tasked with the project of transporting a cabin cruiser from Manchester to Benidorm, strapped to the back of a lorry.

Their difficult journey is complicated by the skullduggery of smugglers, intent on using the naive Mancunians as couriers for mysterious contraband. The five travelers are not aware of the consignment of forged banknotes that have been stowed aboard, or their stowaway. Their progress is further hampered by their ignorance of the documents needed for the movement of their lorry and themselves. Passports being the simplest of their worries seemed insurmountable. What chance had they got of getting the rest right?

The encounter with deadly terrorists and the attention of incompetent north African robbers who are well past their worst only adds to the confusion.

Buy it now on Amazon.co.uk

A PACKAGE FROM BERLIN

A murder mystery set in wartime Berlin and post war Britain.

A young boy finds a wartime diary in the early sixties which tells the story of a mysterious package that had belonged to Heinrich Himmler. The package, which was reputed to hold a priceless and powerful secret, had found its way to an army clearing hospital in 1945.

A ruthless Nazi group has followed the trail of the package to Manchester, getting ever closer to their quarry.

A wounded soldier, who appears to know the secret location of the package, disappears with the nurse he has fallen in love with. The police are baffled, finding themselves involved in a plot that gets more complicated as the years pass.

Two decades later the boy's school essay sees the hunters and the police in a frantic race to locate the package.

Wherever it is hidden, the diary holds the key.

Buy it now on Amazon.co.uk

Printed in Great Britain
by Amazon